The Vampyre of Moura
and
Return to Moura

Virginia Coffman was born in San Francisco and worked in the Hollywood studios during the Golden and Silver years. She has worked on many TV scripts as well as acting.

She began writing in 1959 and since then has had over ninety titles published. She now lives in Nevada, where she continues to write enthusiastically, although ancestral ties with France and Britain frequently bring her to Europe.

The Vampyre of Moura

and

Return to Moura

Virginia Coffman

Pan Books

The Vampyre of Moura first published 1997 by Severn House Publishers Ltd
Return to Moura first published 1999 by Severn House Publishers Ltd

This omnibus edition published 2002 by Pan Books
an imprint of Pan Macmillan Ltd
Pan Macmillan, 20 New Wharf Road, London N1 9RR
Basingstoke and Oxford
Associated companies throughout the world
www.panmacmillan.com

ISBN 1 405 00440 1

1 3 5 7 9 8 6 4 2

A CIP catalogue record for this book is available from
the British Library.

Printed and bound in Great Britain by
Mackays of Chatham plc, Chatham, Kent

The Vampyre of Moura

For Donnie Coffman Micciche,
without whom nothing would be possible,
and with whom all things are better.

To Valerie

I

A GRIM, wild countryside it was, and had always been. From the coach window the Moura Woods, whose ancient chateau was my husband's French birthplace and, in many ways, his tragedy, looked much as they had looked on my departure three years before. No doubt my Irish imagination joined with painful memories on this day of my return to show me the Moura Lands in their most forbidding lack of color: the snow-piled heath, the steely sky, the stark, blackened woods devoid of all life except the lank, hungry wolves which I could occasionally see foraging among the denuded trees.

The three years of my widowhood had been busy, filled with welcome hard work since that dreadful October day in 1818 when I was officially informed that Edmond Moura had been shot as a Bonapartist, his estates confiscated to the French Crown. In any case, Moura was a coffin to me without its master, and before the night was out, I had packed my old portmanteau to leave, as I thought, forever the place where I had known both my greatest joy and the sudden anguish of his loss.

The creaking old Diligence had once rattled on its way through a countryside parched and desolate in the aftermath of the Imperial defeat, carrying me, a girl of eighteen, to an unknown Moura. Now, at twenty-four, having been in the interval married, widowed and returned to my original occupation as a housekeeper, I expected Anne Wicklow Moura should be a great deal less influenced by the frozen Moura Woods, the wretched starving wolves, the general atmosphere of decay. It was not so, however.

Though the crimson cushion "squabs" of the coach were new, I suspected its springs were those of the weekly Diligence which first brought me to Moura, and in spite of all my efforts, I once more rattled around on the cushion like a pea in a loose pod. This time I was not alone, as I had been on my first ride six years ago. My fellow passenger, a tall, red-haired man with military side-whiskers, a three-caped greatcoat and boots of an English cut, was obviously well-traveled; for he had leaped into the coach at Vichy, flicked an indifferent glance at me, then propped his boots up on the cushion opposite, folded his arms, and fallen asleep instantly. But the cushion did not wholly accommodate his considerable length of limb. Every ten minutes he crossed or uncrossed his legs, jarring me in the process, and all this without so much as blinking his eyes.

I wondered what business this stranger could have in such a remote area. He appeared to be somewhere in his late thirties, and if he was English or Scottish as he looked, his age would have made him a military enemy of France during most of his life. Perhaps he was merely a traveler after all, but this seemed a curious province for the usual luxury-loving British subjects making the Grand Tour.

I lowered the coach window and received a biting view of the snow-shrouded Moura Woods at dusk. Nevertheless, I very nearly decided to shorten my journey by an hour or two. It would be so easy to descend from the coach at the Moura porter's lodge and walk half a league through the woods to the chateau. I might possibly reach the place at nightfall—much simpler than riding into the village to meet my informant, Kate Moura, then retracing my steps with her by pony cart to the porter's lodge and up the long, icy estate road to Moura Chateau after dark. But my time had been bespoken by my husband's cousin Kate, through a letter in the post to me. I was to arrive at Moura as a newly hired housekeeper of Kate's choosing.

If good-natured Kate believed there was something strange and "unholy," as she called it, taking place among the French government's new tenants at the chateau, it was wiser to approach the mystery in her way; though I confess there were moments on my journey when I began to suspect Kate had read too many of Mrs. Radcliffe's ghostly romances. She would next be seeing deadly monks, fatally fair females and bloodstained shrouds in the legendary chateau.

My fellow passenger, the red-haired man, startled me suddenly by speaking in French as bad as my own, while his eyes played over me with an almost insolent survey, and then glanced out the window.

"Damme, but this is gloomy country! Or am I being tactless? I hope you don't live hereabouts, Miss—er—Mademoiselle."

In ordinary circumstances I should have made a brief response, but this fellow seemed so much the superior British traveler, absurdly out of place, that all my Irish volubility came to the fore.

I started to answer him in French but something about the behavior of his eyebrows suggested that neither his knowledge nor his temper extended so far, and I changed to English, agreeing that the Moura Woods were indeed gloomy at the moment but they would show in better colors by spring.

"Thank God I shan't be here to see it." A bit more graciously, he added, "Don't tell me a bonny lass like you finds herself at home among the Frenchies!"

"Well then, I'll not be telling you," I agreed, much entertained by his unusual manner which had about it such an insulting directness that one need not mince words with him. But I had been less than candid; since Moura was my rightful home, and the home of Edmond's other surviving relations.

Our delapidated coach had made rattling good time thus far, and it began to seem possible that we should reach the village of Moura within the hour. I confess that even after three years, I had no wish to be arriving at the chateau itself during the hours of darkness, but this seemed unavoidable in any case, thanks to the erratic schedule of the local Diligence. Now, as I was congratulating myself upon meeting the ever-cheerful Kate sooner than I had hoped, what should we hear but the coachman's call to halt his team! Previous experience with the Diligence should have warned me it was to be expected.

"What now?" asked my haughty neighbor.

I looked out, getting a slap of chill air on my face and was thankful I had put stiff new ribbons on my bonnet; for the wide green watered silk bow served not only to refurbish the well-worn millinery but kept my throat from freezing. I did not above half like what I saw. The wagon-rutted High Road was only wide enough for our coach and we had, in every sense, reached an impasse. The nervous team was nostril to nostril with a pair of ancient nags bearing a tumbrel whose right front wheel spun in an icy rut.

"I very much fear we've an accident ahead of us," I said, and was not surprised at his reaction:

"Good God! I might have expected it in this benighted land."

He unfolded his legs and begging pardon brusquely, stepped over me to open the door.

If he doesn't straighten matters, he will make such a rackety noise as will force us through, I thought with amusement as I watched the proceedings from the open door of the coach. My supercilious fellow passenger strode along the icy rut at the roadside, very close to the hovering presence of the Moura Woods. While I would have been the last to wish he might take a tumble on that slippery surface, I couldn't but be tantalized by the possibility.

The driver of the tumbrel, an ancient, heavily bundled fellow who looked as decrepit as his horses, appeared deaf to boot, and a shouting match began between him and our own impatient coachman. My red-haired acquaintance could not make himself understood by either side and I foresaw a long, fruitless time of waiting in this bitter cold air. Since the tumbrel could not be raised because the wheel would not get purchase in its slippery rut, our own coach was unable to pass. In the meanwhile, with the watery winter sun gone down an hour before, we were in a fair way to freeze.

When more debate threatened to lead to blows, I thought it time someone used a dram of common sense which seemed extraordinarily lacking. I glanced down at my good Morocco walking slippers whose flat heels would offer little protection against dirty snowbanks or mud and slush. However . . .

Since the steps had not been let down, there was a very long drop to the ground which jarred my whole frame but I shook out the wrinkled skirts of my traveling coat and retied my bonnet ribbons, while I got my equilibrium back. I nearly trod on the tassels of the old reticule Edmond had given me on my twenty-first birthday, the last of his many gifts to me, and I picked it up and touched it to my cheek, dirt stains and all. It made me painfully aware of my surroundings, and I peered into the gray recesses of the Moura Woods which, in Edmond's day, had never seemed quite so gloomy. Then I made my way with care along the parts of the road which appeared to be frozen.

The loudly shouting men appeared stupefied by my arrival in their midst. Our stout, red-faced coachman complained to me in the rapid local patois that the Diligence had the right of way since time out of mind and this *Species of Cochon* from the Robber Castle was well aware that he should remove his cart with its unspeakable burden to a wider place in the road where the Diligence might pass in safety. I was aware of the local aversion to Moura Chateau and its nickname but I saw my traveling companion raise an eyebrow at the mention of the "Robber Castle"; so he, at least, understood that much French.

"That's as may be. Now, let us set about solving it," I said quickly to forestall more chatter and turned to the bundled old man from Moura. He had removed one mitten and was trying to calm the fretted nags, who clearly were so terrified that even his touch produced more nervous fretting. Neither this act nor his stooped posture was in any way peculiar, but as he mumbled in confusion that it was impossible to back up his tumbrel because of the spinning of the big wheel, the pale flesh of his hand gleamed in the cold, misty light that was reflected from the snow. The fingers were long and very lean, with sharply tapered nails, extraordinary prehensile hands for an unlettered peasant of this countryside. Curious now, I glanced at what I could make out of the old man's closely bundled face, but saw nothing significant: a pallid cheek, gray witchlocks of hair curling down over what appeared to be a domed forehead of surprising proportions. The eyelids were lowered respectfully and I was intrigued by this shielding of his eyes from our sight.

The Englishman was looking from me to the two Frenchmen with considerable astonishment and also, I think, disapproval.

"Pardon me, Ma'am, but do you think you really belong here? I mean, it's obviously no place for a gentlewoman."

"Obviously not, Sir," I told him, attempting to soften what sounded like a rude setdown with a smile. "But then, as you'll be observing, I am not a gentlewoman."

That completely overthrew him. "What the devil can you mean?" He looked me up and down in what remained of the dim light. "You are certainly not a Fancy Piece. Or even—" He looked just a trifle more pleasant, though still perplexed. "Nor even a Bit-of-Muslin."

I laughed at that. How surprised the gentry invariably are to discover that one need not be a gentlewoman in order to dress in reasonably good taste! "I am a housekeeper by profession," I added and wondered if I had lowered myself in his esteem. It was hard to tell. He always looked so satirical, as if the whole world were a joke in amusing but unmistakably bad taste.

"Naturally then," he remarked, "as a housekeeper, you are familiar with cart-wheels and other roadside calamities."

I caught the jibe in that and said sweetly, "At any rate, I know them well enough to place some brush before the wheel to keep it from spinning."

The gentleman sighed. "Just what I have been attempting to tell them in their heathen language."

When I repeated my suggestion in French, both the coachman and the muffled old man exclaimed at once in great enthusiasm, and shuffled over to the edge of the road to gather up snow-covered branches from the floor of the woods. My companion ruffled his hair with one hand and stared at me.

"I say, Ma'am—whoever you are, that was capital! I begin to suspect you may be anything you make claim to be. You produced our rescue with the devil's own ease."

"Not at all," I reminded him politely. "The devil is reputed to be red-haired."

This time I actually achieved a grin from him. He offered his hand to me and I bobbed a respectful curtsey, luckily skimming my skirts over frozen ground.

"Anne Wicklow, Sir." I was careful, as always, not to give my married name.

"Captain Edward Surtees, Madam, of the Wellesley Brigade. At your service."

"How odd! My—I knew someone who fought against your brigade at Waterloo." I must be on guard against gratuitous chattering like this. As Edmond's widow, I might still be regarded as an enemy of the present Royalist government. But I was pleased that in spite of my disclaimer, he continued to treat me with as much politeness as he probably showed to anyone.

We watched our stout coachman, who had heard a suspicious rattling in the woods just beyond the light, as he scampered out to the road where he dropped a bundle of sticks and dead brush in front of the wheel of the tumbrel. His obvious haste and fear attracted the attention of Captain Surtees, who glanced at me questioningly.

"Wolves," I explained. "They are starving this time of year."

"What a pity! I confess I share our coachman's notion. I prefer to reach Moura Village in a condition to eat my own dinner. Not to provide these unfortunate creatures with theirs."

I laughed but was distracted by the arrival and sudden attention of the stooped old man from Moura. Doubtlessly being used to the wolves, he paid the unseen creatures no heed, nor did they harass him as he threw down his own branches under the wheel, but I was keenly aware that his carefully lowered gaze managed all the same to expend itself upon me. The Captain started to walk back to the coach, holding out a hand to me politely. Out of the corner of my eye I saw his gesture but I was fascinated by the behavior of the old man.

As I turned to follow Captain Surtees, I caught a brief glimpse of the old man's eyes. While obviously past middle age, they looked far from weak. The power of those pale, gleaming eyes with their reddened rims stayed with me long after I was lifted back into the coach by the Captain.

In a few minutes we were rumbling on our way through the Moura Woods, past the tumbrel and its exceedingly odd driver, who perched high on the board seat, turning his head and watching us as we rattled and swayed along. Although Captain Surtees' manner did not encourage conversation—he had crossed his arms and was thoughtfully studying the opposite cushions—I said hurriedly:

"I beg pardon, Sir, but did you take note of the old man who drove the tumbrel?"

"Not particularly. I was more interested in his cargo which gave our fearless coachman such a start."

I had noticed nothing within the high sides of the wagon. "His cargo?"

"A freshly pegged box of considerable length. I am reasonably certain it was a coffin."

"The Saints preserve us! A dead body?"

"I devoutly hope so; since it was clearly on its way to burial."

"But so furtive, so heathen!"

"Precisely my view of these people." He shrugged. "But after all, it is invariably done."

"What!"

"You will allow that even in civilized countries the dead are buried, sooner or later. On the whole, I prefer that it be sooner. But it's a matter of taste."

I rolled my eyes in disgust and looked out the window again, but the tumbrel had now fallen behind us and I could scarcely see it. The Captain's casual analysis of the box and its contents put it in quite a different light. There was no reason that I could think of why the dead of Moura should not be decently buried. Still, there was the old man himself, furtive, apparently humble, but disquieting, all the same. And beyond this encounter which might be common enough in other circumstances, there was the prickling memory of Kate Moura's summons to me.

II

I UNFOLDED the letter from my reticule. The small, flickering light in my corner of the carriage was a poor thing by which to read, but a blind man could hardly have trouble with Kate's huge scrawl which was as lavish as her own character. It also had some hint of her preoccupation with anything in pantaloons.

> Anne, Dear Cousin:
>
> Our last bit of chatter by the post was far too short. How good it would be to see your face again, though I shall be in jealous fits at that Irish complexion. Confess! Do you use Hungary Water on your skin to attract those delicious men who always take a fancy to you? I have begun to polish my teeth with a dreadfully old Tincture by Greenough. Are you acquainted with it?

My dear, you really must come to Moura. Come as Anne Wicklow, the new housekeeper. I shall meet you at the Duplessis Arms Inn in the village. There are unholy doings at the chateau. It was ever an amazingly disagreeable dungeon, to be sure, but this is the outside of enough.

The tenants have set up an Academy for Young Females of Quality, and thus far, I would not entrust my favorite enemy to their care, much less a delicately nurtured young idiot of a female.

Please do come. You will know what to do to avoid disaster. You always have, and you will render more easy your favorite cousin,

Kate Moura.

My reply had given her the probable date of my arrival which was confirmed in day and hour upon my boarding the Paris Diligence to Vichy where I would, I hoped, find this rattling old coach that passed through the Moura Country.

"Is it a lover who causes you to knit your brow?" the Captain asked suddenly, implying that he had been watching me more than I suspected.

"I am a widow," I told him with what I hoped was an expressionless voice as I folded and replaced the letter.

He crossed his long legs and encouraged me airily, "Well, don't despair. You may capture another. It is invariably done, I believe."

He really was beyond anything! But I knew he was trying to tease me, and with great difficulty I stifled a laugh. My reaction appeared to surprise him, which gave me a very poor opinion of the females he had known.

Shortly after, we came to the great stone archway which marked the Moura estate road. Beside the road was the little two-story stone porter's lodge which had been Kate Moura's home as long as I had known her. Kate spent, or misspent, her youth as a member of several theatrical troupes in various capitals of the Napoleonic World, including a prolonged visit to Britain by way of a smuggling felucca.

There were no lights at the windows of the lodge which, I hoped, was an indication that Kate was waiting for me according to plan, at the inn in the village. Whatever her tale about the strange doings at Moura, I was more inclined to believe her, after having encountered the tumbrel and its driver. I half expected the coachman to slow his team at the junction of the Moura estate road, but to my surprise, he whipped up the horses and made even greater speed until neither the estate road nor the lodge remained in sight. It was clear that the reputation of the chateau had not been raised in the years since Edmond's death.

"Gad's my life! What next?" the Captain demanded, having been thrown against me abruptly as we thundered around a curve onto the old Roman Bridge which left the Moura Woods behind and brought us rattling and jingling over a deep, primeval valley.

I explained, "We are nearing Moura Village."

He sat up and looked out. "Not very promising."

I smiled to myself at his impossible notions. What could he possibly have expected here in the very heart of one of France's most ancient provinces? It was not Paris, after all. As I was buttoning the tight bodice of my coat, preparatory to descending from the coach into the icy night, he startled me by the sudden annoyance in his voice:

"You find me ridiculous; don't you, Ma'am? I should very much like to know why."

I went on buttoning. There were seventeen buttons, an absurd fashion altogether. "You are mistaken, Sir. I do not find you anything at all."

He bit down so hard on his lip that I winced for him, but I was relieved when he managed a wry smile.

"Quite true, Ma'am. Your shafts hit home. If you had been at *Quatre Bras*, Old Boney might yet be in the Tuileries."

For all of our truce, however, neither of us had a word more to say to each other. The coach pulled up before the ill-lighted innyard shortly after, and his journey and mine had come to an end, for the moment.

Although it was no concern of mine, I could not but wonder what a man of the Captain's sophistication found to occupy him in a town as small as our village. As the single ostler employed here was caring for the coach team, the coachman demonstrated one reason for his cherry red nose and stoutness by downing an enormous meal of roast hare, a fat capon, and a bottle of the local *vin ordinaire* which had quite evidently been awaiting his arrival in the Common Room.

I was about to ask the sullen, dark-eyed barmaid in the taproom where I might find Mademoiselle Kate Moura when Captain Surtees leaned over the taprail and demanded in his abrupt way, "Are you acquainted with a female named Tyra Stavko in this town?"

The barmaid's sullen mouth had softened amazingly under the Captain's eyes as he began to speak, and she said with an eager effort to please him, "You refer to the so-lovely lady Tyra Stavko. She is the mistress of the *École des Jeunes Filles*."

"Then you know her."

"But yes. One naturally admires such beauty when the lady is generous as well. A foreign lady; is she not?"

"I believe so. The name would indicate as much. And where will I find her?"

"But at the chateau, Monsieur!"

He brushed this aside, and then smiled unexpectedly. "No. No. In the town. I've no wish to have that father of hers witness the first tender moments of our meeting."

"How true!" the girl agreed with a little shiver that intrigued me because I guessed they were discussing the new tenants of Moura, and these comments bore out Kate's warning. There was something wrong, or at the least, unpleasant about the Master of Moura's *École des Jeunes Filles*.

I turned away to look for Kate, who must have heard the usual noises attendant upon the passage of the Diligence, but she was not in sight. Knowing her habits, I wondered if she had found an attractive male and was closeted with him in one of the rooms of the inn. Heaven help the Captain if

Kate caught sight of him! She had a marvelous eye for externals in her choice of men, and I myself was not blind to Captain Surtees' outward attractions. The innkeeper stopped me. He was a new man since my days at Moura, a small, dark gnome. He rubbed his hands together on his leather apron, inquiring enthusiastically how he might oblige me. I asked which parlor he had given to Mademoiselle Kate Moura. He was surprised.

"Not so, Mademoiselle. I regret. If the charming Mademoiselle Kate were here in one of my humble rooms, I should certainly know it. You are perhaps not aware that Mademoiselle now resides at the chateau. I believe she teaches the young ladies the language of the English." He lowered his voice with a slight tilt of the head to indicate Captain Surtees. "Though one wonders why it is thought necessary for pretty children to learn the language of those barbarians."

Much amused, I tried to avoid the Captain's eyes; for he had clearly heard the innkeeper's comment and was staring at me with such deliberation I finally gave in and looked his way. He was laughing. He could be extraordinarily winning when he set himself to it.

"We both seem to be forsaken, Ma'am. Shall we dine together and show our fickle friends how little we need them?"

Tempting as the offer was, I thought it wise to make my excuses; since he seemed closely involved with the very people I had come here to deceive and to investigate. I was considering what would be the most plausible excuse, when the dirt-stained young ostler came rattling into the taproom in his noisy wooden sabots.

"The cart has arrived from the Maître Stavko. Is there a Mademoiselle Wicklow here? She is to be taken up for the ride to the chateau."

"*Mademoiselle?*" Captain Surtees repeated, looking at me oddly.

I raised my gloved hand, said to the ostler, "I am Mademoiselle Wicklow," and dipping a curtsey to the Captain, smiled and thanked him for his offer. "But," I added, "it might have proved awkward later, should you dine at Moura and have your bed and plate supervised by a recent dinner companion."

"What pride the girl has!" he remarked wryly, but surprised me by taking my arm, and escorting me through the Common Room in which several men were huddled by the fireplace and one traveler was eating at the long table opposite our recent coachman. The Captain's good manners were gratifying; for, as a solitary woman, my presence aroused a deal of attention of the wrong sort among these men. We stepped into the rocky little yard where fresh coach horses were being led out, and the Captain, studying me attentively, said after a silence:

"I wish you were not going, you know."

I shivered at the sudden cold of the air and turned up the high collar of my traveling coat. "It is cold. But I daresay there will be something to eat and a warm fire at the chateau."

"I did not refer to the weather. I meant—" He looked around, frowned and shrugged. "I'm damned if I know what I meant. Nothing on this journey has been as I imagined it would be. It is a strange countryside. A strange, unnatural feeling in the air. I don't like it. Especially for a pretty creature of my own nationality to be left to her poor devices. It is sheer desertion."

"You are being much too kind," I began but was a trifle shaken when he took up right hand and without a by-your-leave, removed my glove and touched my palm to his lips. If I did not bear in mind that he was here solely for a bit of dalliance with Lady Tyra Stavko, I should have been in a fair way to lose my head, if not my heart, over him. Fortunately, the reminder came in time. I was able to retain an appearance of calm friendliness.

"Well then, up you go." He lifted me with admirable ease, petticoats, skirts and all, up onto the seat of the pony cart, and I was just about to remind him that I should not be pitied, since the chateau and my friend had been good enough to send the cart for me, when something in the Captain's stare made me look at the driver beside me. It was the bundled old man who had driven the tumbrel with its strange cargo an hour since. This was disquieting. I began to share the Captain's uneasiness about being ushered to Moura in my present company. The coachman seemed to exude an odor of foulness and death. But, of course, that was merely my imagination again. I was connecting the weird being beside me with the digging of a grave. . . . And if Captain Surtees had been right, and the box in the tumbrel was a coffin, who then was dead?

I said quickly to the old man, "Is Mademoiselle Kate all right? Nothing has happened to her?"

"Nothing, Mademoiselle. She will see you in your apartments."

That was a relief. For an instant, remembering the past, appalling history of Moura, I had wondered if horror would repeat itself.

"All right, Miss Wicklow?" the Captain asked me.

I said it was and then reached out my hand to him. "But I'll be thanking you for your concern, all the same. You have been kinder than I deserve."

"Probably," he agreed with a charming grin as he shook my hand and checked to see that my portmanteau and my bandbox were safe under our feet.

The old man gave the sturdy pony the office to start and I said to the Englishman, "Good-bye, Sir."

"Not good-bye," he called as we passed him. "Perhaps we'll meet at the chateau. Mind now! You must have my sheets well aired. I detest damp sheets. And I shall expect a delicious ragout set before me. Nothing less, nor more. My tastes are simple but firm. I shall expect to be treated with special consideration, however, since I am on intimate terms with the family housekeeper."

I laughed and the pony trotted out of the innyard onto the main street of the village. When I looked around and could no longer see the Captain, I felt a depression descend over me. He might be here for a romantic assignation with the woman who conducted the Girls' School, but there had been enough gallantry about him so that I felt safer for knowing he was nearby, and it was a poor trade, entirely, to see him gone and the strange, muffled man now so close beside me.

"Have you been employed long at the chateau?" I asked presently as we left the village and headed once more over the Roman Bridge to the Moura Woods and Estate on the far side.

A man of few words evidently, he shrugged, making me aware by his reticence of how dimly I could really see this person who was seated next to me, yet his size and appearance were only known to me in the most vague way. Because it annoyed me that he behaved in so secretive a fashion—a purposeless masquerade, surely!—I decided to try and entrap him. If he lied about his past, I might then have a genuine basis for my lack of trust.

"Were you at the chateau during the lifetime of Monsieur Edmond Moura?"

Somehow, I had reached him. He raised his head out of the cumbersome shawl he wore around his neck and the lower half of his face. Once more, as in that minute by the tumbrel when he chilled me with his glance, those icy, terrible eyes flashed upon me.

"You mean to make a joke, do you not?"

"A joke? Why should I do that?"

"But who should know better than you, the names of the employees of Monsieur Edmond?"

There was nothing very ambiguous about that. Kate Moura may have been my friend, but she was also an incurable rattle. She must have hinted something of my identity to this fellow, or worse, to the entire staff. If so, it would be impossible for me to carry out our plan to investigate the conditions, since those odd masters of the *École des Jeunes Filles* would not be complete fools. And what, in point of fact, were the Captain's beautiful Madame Stavko and her father doing at Moura, aside from teaching the young ladies how to appear to advantage at the shabby court of Louis XVIII?

It occurred to me rather belatedly that this area was an odd place in which to set up a school at all, so far from the sophistications of the more modern provinces. One would think these Stavkos preferred the medieval desolation of Moura! Absurd idea. It must be the first question I asked of Kate.

There was little more to be gained from this creature. I was of two minds whether he was dangerous in himself. If it was true that Kate had confided my identity to his employers and perhaps my mission as well, then I could do very little at the chateau except act in my obvious capacity as housekeeper, and brazen the thing through. As I realized the probable uselessness of my long trip to Moura, a trip that might even be politically dangerous if my identity as Edmond's widow became known to the government, I could, with great gusto, have shaken that good-humored chatterbox until her teeth rattled.

It was a silent ride along the High Road walled in on both sides by the woods, a silence punctuated by the even strike of the pony's hooves upon the hard ground, and the occasional, startling flutter of a bird sweeping low across our path as if to peer into our faces as we passed. It was too cold and the wrong season for bats, but one of the ugly little creatures darted out of a dark copse, so close to me I was nearly blinded by its strong, steely wings. Throwing my hand up to ward it off, I cried out. My companion scoffed at my fears in his strange, faintly accented voice:

"They will do you no harm," and he added the disquieting rider, "not while you are with me."

"They could do me a deal of harm if they become caught in my hair," I reminded him, setting my tousled bonnet more neatly in place.

We reached the great stone arch over the Estate Road almost before I was prepared. It annoyed me furiously that I should be terrified to enter my husband's home, and I sat up straighter, stiffening my back with pride, if not with courage. During the last three years since the announcement of Edmond's death and my own departure, the letters of M-O-U-R-A, deeply carved in the apex of the archway, had once more become filled with lichen and the dust of time. I stared up at it, and remembered many things, saddened and depressed, but then, I had expected the reaction when I made plans for my return.

To change the direction of my thoughts, I looked over at the stone building heavily coated with vines, which had been Kate's home in France. Expecting to find it dark as it had been several hours ago, for Kate was presumably staying at the chateau, I was surprised to note the flickering glow of candles behind the portieres of a bedchamber upstairs. Gradually, as we rode past, I noted a faint light on the ground floor as well. Forgetting my recent pique with my grim companion, I exclaimed, "That is odd. Has Mademoiselle Kate returned to the lodge this evening?"

He did not so much as glance at the ancient stone walls. "Not so. When one of the demoiselles is ill, of an illness that may carry contagion, she is placed there. And a recent coachman who died of a fall. He was laid out there."

"But who cares for them?"

He shrugged. "Lady Stavko's maid. Or the lady herself. She is widely acquainted with drugs, herbs, the treatment of the Putrid or Bilious Fevers." It was the longest speech he had yet made to me, and put me again in mind of the accent with which he spoke. Like his hands, the accent did not match his personality, or the personality he had assumed; for the language itself was a gentleman's language, impossible for the uneducated peasant that his task and clothing proclaimed him to be.

"Are the young ladies often ill at your school?" I asked, unable to conceal the irony in my own voice.

"It is not a healthy place, this Moura. Nor ever was," he reminded me, proving once more that his knowledge of Moura's past was very thorough.

III

THE PONY began to behave with less self-control after we entered the Estate Road. He moved erratically from side to side, cutting across the wagon ruts of the narrow road that was scarcely more than a footpath. The strong hands of the driver, now mittened again, managed to bring the pony back to an even keel but it told me much about the atmosphere at Moura when even the livestock was troubled by it. Perhaps, though, the pony had sensed the presence of wolves in the depths on either side of us. I had now become convinced of the evil here and the really puzzling aspect of it was not the guilt or innocence of the Stavkos, but Kate Moura's curious about-face.

A light snow was falling by the time we reached the bridge over the moat that now appeared to be gently coated in white, where once, in my first memory of it, there had been a sluggish little channel of water full of overgrown vegetation. Beyond the plank bridge with its conspicuous lack of any guardrail or handhold, was Moura itself, built as a robber fortress in the Ninth Century, and little better during the first half a millennium afterward.

The low, heavy front of the building concealed the courtyard around whose chilly depths the rest of the chateau formed a rectangle. The four towers not quite at cardinal points had long since fallen into disuse and, except for the haunting and ubiquitous presence of the East Tower, were very little more than crumbling heaps of stone. The pony cart stopped before the low iron-bound door which served now instead of the ancient drawbridge entrance.

I saw there would be no gallantry here. I swung myself

to the ground and brushed off the snow from my bonnet and my shoulders while the surly driver threw down my faded portmanteau and my bandbox, whose gay lilac ribbons were slightly the worse for their recent out-of-doors ride on top of the Diligence.

Left to my own devices while he led the pony and cart around to the stables, I reached for the door knocker whose wolf's head, long a symbol of the ancient Moura family, now had been freshened to such a gleaming polish I scarcely recognized it. The sound of my knock reverberated through the silent, snowy air. I glanced over my shoulder, more or less from habit.

The woods encroached upon the road beyond the bridge and, despite the protective lacing of tree branches overhead, the summer's underbrush was buried in snow. Standing out in grim contrast to that snow were two gray wolves, silent and watchful, their yellowed canines flashing white in the gleam from the storm lantern over the door. I wondered at their courage. Hunger made them desperate, probably, but they had not been used to approach so near the house in our day.

I stooped to throw a stone at them. That would send them scuttling, since there appeared to be only two of them. A school for young ladies was the last place in the world where I would have expected to find hungry wolves prowling the premises. Then I thought better of frightening the animals. It occurred to me that the less the Moura household knew of my previous experience with the creatures, the better. Though I had grown used to them during my life at Moura, and even felt a little perverse sympathy when Edmond and the gamekeeper shot them, I remembered that the year before I came to Moura, packs of these starving wolves had killed several of the local peasants poaching in the Moura Woods.

Perhaps the wolves recognized in me a reluctant sympathizer, or more likely, they attacked only when they sufficiently outnumbered their prey. I raised my hand to the brass knocker again, with a crawling sensation at the back of my neck which warned me that my two gray watchers had dog-trotted a few steps closer.

Under my hand the door creaked open just as it used to do. Instead of one of the familiar servants, or another like them, however, I was surprised to see a languid-looking young lady of fifteen or so with dazzling red-gold hair worn in the newest Paris fashion—all curls and snarls, while at the same time, she was unmistakably dressed for bed in her long, trailing nightgown.

"Oh!" said the girl faintly, looking me up and down and speaking in English. "You must be Miss Kate's housekeeper. You may as well come in. Unless you want to be eaten by those horrid creatures out there." Her manner suggested that it wouldn't much matter to her what my fate was.

I agreed that I was Anne Wicklow and she stepped aside, almost as if she feared my contamination. I wondered at her night clothing so early in the evening, but perhaps the school had Spartan hours.

"May I see Miss Kate as soon as possible?"

The girl ran a smooth, work-free hand through her curls and she yawned. "I suppose so. It's not my concern. We don't wander around this wretched tomb after dark. Jailer's orders, you know. What with the sickness, and all."

With my portmanteau in one hand and the bandbox in the other, I stepped directly into the great hall and looked around. The hall was refurbished here and there. Many portieres and wall hangings of green velvet gave the room a spurious look of richness, but the high rafters, the vaulted ceilings seemed scarcely to have been dusted, nor the cobwebs removed in the past three years, and the huge fireplace was like a blackened mouth with its starvation diet of sticks and faintly burning brush. I stood before what remained of the fire, and removing my gloves, held my hands out to the heat.

I was depressed by my reception, or lack of it, and wondered what efforts it would take to get even the most miserly supper tray served to me. In any case, that was secondary to my meeting with Kate. I still had a lingering fear that at the last minute I would find her dead or disappeared or impossible to meet for some other ghastly reason. This seemed even more likely when my indifferent young Committee of Reception admired her red-gold curls at the old unsilvered mirror on the wall and immediately after, vanished down the dark passage.

A heavy door slammed somewhere, and I jumped nervously at the sound. I was beginning to expect something sinister, dangerous. You may conceive my delight when Kate Moura came rustling into the hall from the direction of the broken North Parapet. And looking superbly well it seemed at this distance! All my premonitions could not have been further from the mark.

Kate always appeared big, buxom, jovial. She was generous and selfish at the same time, conscious above all of her bodily pleasures. So long as neither Edmond nor I had ever interfered with these pleasures, and so long as Edmond had supplied her with an allowance of two thousand livres per year, Kate was excessively pleasant. The years since had not seemed to change her, as she came striding through the long room toward me. She wore a full-skirted sumptuous gown of yellow taffeta and a black velvet spencer fitting tightly over her well-endowed bosom. Against the thickness of her brown hair which had begun to gray becomingly, the result was stunning. I wondered at this richness in clothing and even in jewels. But perhaps she had found a rich protector. I wished her well.

"My dear Anne!" She took my two hands in hers and I was surprised at the slenderness of her fingers. They had formerly been plump, like her face, whose broad cheeks and jawline had narrowed becomingly. . . . *Surprisingly,* I added to myself though I did not say it aloud.

"How good it is to see you, Kate! You will never know," I said in all honesty. "I began to be afraid—"

"Afraid of what? For me? What could happen to me? Only good things, I do assure you! Anne, come along to your room. We've set you apart from the children. Such chatterboxes! Babble, babble all day. Not by night, though, happy to say. The Maître sees to that. Come along."

"My boxes?" I reminded her and reached for them, seeing that nothing had happened since I removed them from the cart and set them beside the fireplace.

"Leave them, Anne. You may become the faithful retainer tomorrow. Tonight you are to be indulged." She put an arm around me and more or less ushered me to the hall door. For an embarrassing second or two I had started toward the North Tower which led to the master bedchamber on the floor above. She may have understood but wisely did not mention it.

The passage was dark as always. Even in my day we had not been able to keep these long, rambling passages adequately lighted. No matter how often we set carefully shielded lamps about, sooner or later the drafts sweeping through the old rambling pile snuffed each and every candle. Kate took up a spill burning on the hearth of the little receiving room across the passage and lighted a branch of candles, each flame of which had a metal hood.

"Same old trouble with the drafts?" I asked in an undervoice, remembering that I was to be a stranger in this household.

"Yes, but this should do. So tiresome, Chérie! I am persuaded it is the sole cause of our losing all our servants constantly."

"You have an extraordinary coachman," I admitted.

She raised the candles to study my face. "How so? The other fellow broke his neck, falling down the East Tower steps not two days since, and what with the problem of servants, God knows Lady Tyra and the Master must have dragged in one of the local peasants to fetch you to Moura." The candle flames were so close I blinked, wondering at her curiosity about my face. "What did you mean? How was he extraordinary?"

"Merely in—" It was remarkably difficult to explain without giving offense to this unexpectedly pricklish Kate. The old Kate would have laughed or jeered at such matters, but this one seemed to feel that any criticism of the staff was a direct hit at her friends, the Stavkos. How could one say that the bundled old man with the strange eyes was alarming for no better reason than his appearance of someone hiding his real self from view? We seemed entirely alone, preceding our attentuated shadows up the narrow south staircase to a series of rooms I had nearly forgotten above the medieval dining hall. I took this moment of what I hoped was our privacy to ask Kate directly, "Have you told anyone who I am?"

"You are Anne Wicklow, a competent housekeeper. I once knew you in my travels. You were employed in the household of a Venetian family." She smiled. "All perfectly true, you will allow."

"And yet," I suggested, "the man who drove me here to Moura knows I have been here before."

This stopped her momentarily as we reached the upper passage and I looked around into the chilly darkness, feeling furtive, wondering if I had been mistaken in my suspicions. Still and all, the driver said some very odd things. He must have known my identity in one way or another.

"You are quite certain you told them nothing of—of my husband?" I asked.

Kate hesitated, then waved the branch of candles so airily in punctuating her denial that we were nearly thrown into darkness. Whether she was telling me the truth or ashamed of her lie and childishly covering it, I could not tell. I was not encouraged to believe her, however. I said no more until we had stepped into the chamber assigned to me. But when I was inside the room with its pleasant candlelight, its warm, even oppressive red damask hangings, I knew suddenly why I was oppressed.

Kate looked around proudly. "Well then, it's quite the thing; don't you agree? Far enough from those silly young girls across the courtyard, and yet cozy. There is a small fire laid in the grate. You see? It is actually a bed-sitting room . . . Chérie, why do you look like that?"

She was quite right. It was not an unattractive room,

and in view of the drafts, the creakings, and the scampering of rats in the walls, this place was far superior to some of the lodgings provided for housekeepers. I shook off my forebodings, the shadow of the past; for in this room I had once seen a young girl laid out in death, laid out on this bed, with candles at head and foot, and in that moment I had known my real haunting fear of Moura.

"It is charming, Kate. Thank you. I was only remembering something that happened many years ago, the night I first came to Moura."

"Well, then! Make yourself at ease. Be comfortable. You see? Your boxes are here."

I looked where she pointed, in the corner beside the huge, dark armoire with its aging mirror, and was astonished to see my bandbox and portmanteau sitting there, though I had neither seen nor heard another living soul in the great house since Kate appeared to greet me. Indeed, had it not been for my brief encounter with the languid young lady in curls, I should have been in a fair way to wonder if we actually were the only human beings in the chateau. The unseen arrival of my luggage disproved my ridiculous imaginings. "Shall I meet my employers tonight?" I asked as I opened my portmanteau and began to hang articles on the pegs in the armoire.

She laughed. "You are free until tomorrow. With any discretion, you'll have a post here as long as you like."

"Kate!" Her air of mischief was all very amusing, but it did not serve to cover my real concern. Kate understood my tone well enough.

"Tomorrow, Chérie. Tonight we must eat and be warm and think only of pleasant nothings."

"Kate, why did you send for me? What was the unholy thing at Moura?"

She looked as though she might coyly avoid my questions but when I reached for the door, to stop her, she shrugged in the old, careless way, and stepped back inside. In the brief silence between us that followed, I clearly heard the sway of her taffeta skirts. She noticed the crisp sound, too, looked down and then admitted, "Since Cousin Edmond's been gone, I haven't worn Paris gowns, you would say."

"I'd not be knowing. I'm nobody's moral guardian."

"But my dear girl, it's precisely the morals of the affair that I knew you'd dislike. You and that Irish Damnation business. And they've—the Maître's been excessively kind. . . . This gown. A dozen others made to my order in Paris." She held out her hand which winked like a golden eye. "Topaz, my dear. Not as elegant as it might be, but behold the diamonds that frame it. One can even see it flash in the darkest, deepest hour of the night."

"Name of God, Kate! I've no interest in all this—if it makes you happy. It is nothing to do with the matter." I lowered my voice. It had gotten quite out of hand, but she really was impossible. More quietly, I added, "Was it all a lie then? The unholy people, their criminal past? Villainy afoot . . . All lies?"

She held her hand out before her, that unfamiliar, thin white hand, turning it this way and that in order to catch the light on her new ring. "All lies," she echoed, smiling. "I merely wanted to oblige the Maître. He needed a housekeeper. And I knew you wouldn't leave your post but for a good cause."

But the lie was now, tonight, not in that letter a month ago. I, at least, knew Kate Moura that well.

"He must be very attractive," I suggested and went on hanging up my three gowns, a pelisse, my good spencer, the coat I had worn.

She laughed abruptly, a curious sputter of laughter. Almost, I would have thought, an effort to convince herself. "Hardly attractive as we used to think of men. But quite unlike anyone we've ever known. He has great—" She stopped, stared at me, wordless.

"Charm?" I guessed, amused in spite of everything.

"Hardly! Power, Anne. That's precisely what the Master has. Power! Over all of us. I've seen it demonstrated among the students. Even when they fear him."

I wished she would not call this new lover of hers the *Master.* It had been the servants' name and mine, for my husband before our marriage. I wondered why she denied the word *charm,* or *attractive* for her lover. It was not really like Kate. She was fond of very attractive things and people. Power had never before interested her.

"Look, Chérie, shall I have a supper sent up to you? Then you can rest early. Tomorrow will probably be busy. There will be the Master to meet, and the students and the staff. You might say he rules the day and Lady Tyra rules the night. They manage this huge old dungeon very well, very systematic."

It is a strange thing, altogether, I thought. . . . *But Kate wishes to avoid me. . . .*

There were times tonight when I suspected that she actively disliked me. Still, as she held out her jeweled hand and clasped mine, saying she was "off to the kitchen" I knew I must have imagined these qualities in Kate which were so unlike the woman I had known years ago. I thanked her and she left me.

What an extraordinary silence everywhere overlaid the ancient walls! Even the rats had stopped scrabbling. Perhaps all this might be explained by the evening's snowfall. I went to the window and drew aside one of the heavy crimson portieres to get my bearings on the location of the room. The rectangular courtyard was carpeted in snow. There was not a track on it. If I looked slightly to my right I was prevented by the curving wall of the East Tower from seeing the master bedchamber and others in that passage which paralleled the heavy front of Moura.

No lights appeared on the courtyard side of that passage, but then, it would not be possible to see the lights in the master bedroom. What was the new Master like, this elderly fellow who was neither attractive nor charming, yet possessed what Kate called power? I was becoming a cynic. *Money is the key to the winning of Cousin Kate,* I told myself.

I was about to drop the portiere into place when I noticed the several lighted rooms along the far side of the courtyard opposite my own quarter of the chateau. These, according to Kate, would be the bedchambers of the young ladies, and I wondered briefly at the languid English girl's remarks about "the sickness and all." There could not be many students who made up the school or I should certainly have had some signs of them before this. Particularly sounds. I had not spent the formative years of my life at work in an English Girls' Academy without learning something of the noisy ways of young ladies.

Apparently not all of the household was determined to hide itself away tonight. As I watched, most of the candles in a chamber at one end of the corridor were snuffed out and I was interested to see a single light appear shortly after on the ground floor where a door was opened into the courtyard and the light abruptly streamed across the snow.

Greatly intrigued, I wondered who could be walking out in the frozen night at this hour when it was so much pleasanter—or perhaps merely simpler—to cross the building indoors. This must be one of the young ladies, and I could only suspect by the furtive air about the business, that she was conducting some forbidden enterprise. A moment or two later I saw the girl as she was partially illuminated by the hooded candle she carried.

An unusual girl, indeed! She appeared preternaturally tall, wore a long garment, probably a travel cape of some light color that looked like white wool, whose deep sleeves, I trusted, kept her arms warm; for she stepped out across the courtyard toward the East Wing which housed the Master's quarters. As I made out her features more clearly, I noted the length of her black hair against the stark absence of color in her cloak. The woman—for she was no schoolgirl—seemed entirely unaware of the elements about her, the snow underfoot, the icy, stagnant air of the courtyard.

She passed into the building and beyond my sight. I realized suddenly that this unusual woman might well be one of my employers, Lady Tyra Stavko. I was less willing than ever to believe that Kate, with her topaz-aura, was telling me the real reason for her excited summons to me.

Shortly afterward, a light appeared at one of the apertures on the great staircase leading to the master suite in the East Wing. If I remembered correctly, that passage, by twists and turns, eventually wound its way through the East Tower to the passage outside my door. I felt a sudden, surprising revulsion against meeting the strange woman tonight.

IV

I WAS so engrossed in spying on my prospective employer, as I supposed her to be, that I did not hear the clatter of sabots in the passage outside my door. The knocking suddenly disturbed me, making me start with unaccustomed dread. I closed the portieres, still wondering about the strange woman I had seen, and went to admit a skinny little urchin with my supper tray. Nothing on the tray steamed or smoked, and I was not surprised to discover that the plates were scarcely lukewarm. Instead of a refreshing and welcome pot of strong tea, I found a little straw-covered bottle of the local red wine.

The child stared at me eagerly out of enormous dark eyes, pointing to the tray. "How . . . is, Mademoiselle? How . . . is?"

Moved by his desperate fear, I assured him it was what I liked and he had done well. His smile was worth my small lie. There were ugly, livid scars on his body, visible above the open throat of his worn and food-stained shirt. I wondered momentarily if he was mistreated here at Moura, but however frightened he might be, the scars were not fresh, probably not as recent as the time the Stavkos leased the chateau and its grounds from the French government.

"Have you served the Maître Stavko for long, boy?" I asked him as I sat down at the square gaming table that was to serve me for my meals.

He shook his head and watched me begin the rapidly cooling *cassoulet* which tasted far better than it looked. The boy's hair was tousled, unwashed. I began to think he himself had never been bathed. But this was not an unheard-of condition in the less advanced provinces and certainly wasn't the boy's fault.

"Draja. *Moi-meme.*"

His French was limited or he was shy. I could not guess the nationality of the Stavkos except that their name suggested Eastern Europe, either the Austrian or more probably the huge Ottoman Empire. I had seen many Turkish traders in Venice and they had the same curious colored flesh as this boy, a rich, almost copper-green look that was unexpectedly handsome. His presence suggested more than ever that his master and mistress were oddly out of their usual element here deep in the almost unknown interior of France. They must have a really vital interest in the education and polish of young ladies, both French and foreign.

"Boy," I said suddenly, pointing to the earthen dish before me that contained beans, slices of sausage and greasy but not unflavorful pork bits. "Are you hungry?"

His big-eyed gaze slipped away from me and even from the earthen dish. I suspected his problem while he was furtively seeking an answer and when he looked up again, I made a point of smiling so that he would feel he could trust me. Fortunately, he did so. His dirty young face broke into a spectacle of sunny humor.

"Non, Madame." He made motions of eating and rubbing his stomach. From these eloquent gestures I realized he had already had his fill of the *cassoulet* on his way to my room, doubtless grubbing into the food with those unwashed hands of his. I grimaced at the picture it conjured up but refused to let the idea repulse me, at least against the boy, Draja.

"Well, then! After tonight, you'll be eating as much as

you can hold, but it must be in the servants' dining hall. . . ." He was trying hard to understand and I added firmly, "Or in the kitchen. Ah! You like that. You shall eat in the kitchen." I thought of suggesting that he bathe meanwhile, but this seemed too much to expect of either my French or his; so I sent him on his way, explaining where I would place my tray in the passage beside my door and that he must return within the hour and return it to the kitchen.

He understood, doubtless from my language of gestures, and nodding vigorously, went off down the passage at a tearing run, not the least impeded by his heavy sabots. I marveled at his ability to make his way through those dark, gloomy halls, but I supposed he must have had a deal of practice during past months. Still . . . What occupants had there been in this sector of the chateau since the Stavkos came? Other housekeepers, perhaps? Some of the young ladies?

I doubted that. These fastidious products of the aristocracy would never suffer the ill-lighted, ill-kept halls and chambers here about. As an experiment, I passed my hand over the wall of the passage beside my door. When I examined my palm inside the room, there could be no doubt. My palm was blackened with what was very likely three years' accumulation of dust and grime. I bolted the door of the chamber, thankful for the bolt at least. That too, was of interest; since it was a new bolt which glistened in the warm light of this crimson room. Was it coincidental that the room assigned to me should suddenly be provided with this protection? I was of two minds whether to thank Kate, or to ask the reason for all this care of me.

By the time my attention returned to more immediate concerns, everything on the tray was cold except the fat-bellied little bottle of wine which remained, obstinately, too warm. I nibbled the crusty bread that was baked slightly sour, but no less delicious. Then I ate a kind of pudding of heavy, soggy objects which I guessed were bits of the same bread. I had eaten worse meals in my life, and it was infinitely better than no meal at all. Being thirsty, I poured and drank a mug of the wine. It did not greatly satisfy my thirst, but it did imbue me with a certain degree of courage and good cheer. I felt much better afterward, when I set the tray out in the passage beside my door.

An hour later, however, after having emptied my boxes, hung the proper clothing on the wall pegs, and put the rest away in the old spice-scented chest at the foot of the curtained bed, I was not in the least ready to sleep. I looked around my little room, drew a breath, felt the tight, close pressure of the walls, and wished I might, as in the old days, set out on my rounds through the inhabitated sector of the building. I was not an Irishwoman for nothing. Many is the day I had walked to Moura Village and back, and while I dared not reveal my knowledge of the chateau by "making my rounds" tonight, I knew I would not sleep easily having had so little exercise during the day. I too could not walk the way I longed to go, toward the front wing of the house; for that would be an intrusion upon the privacy of the present Master of Moura and his daughter. Since the pupils were hustled off to bed shortly after dark, I had a pretty fair notion the Stavkos would not wish me prowling about either. Lord knows I had served my apprenticeship in more than one great house that confined its secret, or its disgrace in some forgotten closet. Few households in my experience were without their secrets and unless called upon to deal with them, I took care to look the other way.

I wrapped myself in my old green cashmere shawl and threw open the window. The silence of deep night seemed to enshroud our world, though it was scarcely past nine. The early evening's snow had long since stopped falling, but the footprints of the lady I saw crossing the courtyard half an hour previous were completely obliterated. It was as if they had never existed. . . . The curious thought fluttered through my mind, and I tried to be amused at my own too fluent imagination. I was ever a person more alarmed by ghostly visitations than by the manifold real dangers of the world in which I often found myself.

After a time, all the lights in the young ladies' bedchambers along the far side of the courtyard were snuffed except three at strategic points, which I assumed were the upper corridor, the staircase and the courtyard entrance.

Sleepless or not, I knew it was time I was making ready for bed as well. Tomorrow would be exceedingly busy, and there was the business of meeting my new employers. Always uncomfortable, it was doubly so in this case when my suspicions had been roused against them long before our first meeting. I was beginning to wish very heartily that I had never received Kate's silly note with its sillier ramblings about unholy doings. One might have guessed, knowing Kate, what that warning would have come to. A few trinkets, some not unattractive garments, and Kate's prejudices, her hatreds and fears were salved.

I poured water into the cracked china basin and washed. Then I brushed out my hair to its proper length and prepared for bed. As I tied the neck ribbons of my bedgown and stood for a few minutes before the embers of the fire, warming my hands, I felt quite comfortable. It was nct until I put out my hand to snuff the bedcandle that I suddenly saw, in my memory, that other sight upon the bed, the body of a girl scarcely out of childhood. My hand trembled and almost withdrew. The bed, its worn crimson hangings, even the coverlet, filled me with remembered horror. Then, angry at the tricks of my own mind, I pinched the candle briskly and climbed the two little steps to the bed. Like Captain Surtees, I too preferred my bed linen aired and not damp. Fortunately, in this case, someone had been so obliging as to clean, dust and change the linen in this room. I could have found myself in much worse case elsewhere.

Getting to sleep was another matter entirely. I thought about the young girl I had found in this room years ago, and this led me to even more painful memories. By some effort, I turned my thoughts to the present, wondering about the pair who had established an Academy For Young Ladies in such an unlikely place. Still and all, though they remained unseen, they had gone to some little trouble to make me comfortable here. It was hardly a fault of theirs that what appeared very like a murder had once occurred in this room. Probably the Stavkos had never heard of that former tragedy.

During the half hour since I snuffed the bed candle, the wind had risen, carrying with it remnants of that snowfall which blanketed our world earlier in the evening. Every gust brought whistles and moans as it assaulted the ancient house and all its endless drafty corners. Now, indeed, I was sleepless and wondered what else might disturb my first night in Moura after three long years. My window was pelted with flying snow in fits and starts, but my room was perched too high in the chateau for me to worry about the origin of those pinpricks against the glass. I did rather wish I had closed the shutters as well as the portieres, but that would have made the room appear very much a coffin, in some respects.

Presently, as I might have expected, a shutter somewhere else in this wing of the great house came loose from its moorings and began, first to squeak and then to bang back and forth. What with my not having my accustomed exercise that day, and my sleeplessness, the uncomfortable memories of this place, and especially this room, I was in a fair way to developing a headache. And now the rhythmic banging of a shutter! So rhythmic I could anticipate the seconds between the reverberating noise whose echo was beginning to throb behind my temples. What a maddening thing, just as I hoped to get to sleep!

I raised up on my elbows, listened attentively, wondering where, precisely, that accursed shutter might be, and then plumped up my pillows and tried to muffle the noise with them. All to no purpose. Since the shutter was quite evidently banging against the wall behind the bed, my act of muffling the sound in my pillows only succeeded in drawing the persistent blows to me through bed and tester and all.

I got up a few minutes later, found my slippers and drew on my lilac robe, tying the sash securely around my waist to keep it from blowing in any drafty halls I might be forced to navigate. I opened the portieres a little way and pushed the casement window outward, remembering to keep a tight grip on the window; for a stiff gust might have torn the frame from my hands and set it banging before it was torn off its hinges and broken.

I had to lean far out to get a clear view of the annoying loose shutter. It was on the floor below and several windows to the west of my own. There were no lights anywhere on this face of the building; so I must be in the South Wing alone. I could not count on anyone else to fasten that shutter. Then, getting an unexpected mouthful of snow and with my hair whipping around me like Medusa's snake locks, I drew my head in, and closed the window. Being used to the dark by this time, I found I had some added help from the smoldering coals in the little grate. I felt for the soft, much-laundered towel by the basin, dried my face, and then gave my tangled hair a few long swipes with my brush.

As I had not the least notion of hurrying through this deserted wing in darkness that was as thick as peat, I lighted the bedcandle from a coal in the fireplace and managed to put a chimney upon it from the branch of candles on the exquisite chequered gaming table. Then, to be equipped for all emergencies, I reached my portmanteau and from the concealed pocket under the bottom layer of stiffened cloth, took out the half dozen keys I had formerly used at Moura.

At least, I thought, as I unbolted the door and peered out into the passage, *I shall have the exercise I longed for,* though in a far more annoying way than I had hoped.

When I unbolted the door and looked out, I would have given much to take the easterly direction toward that part of the house I had come to know so well, but I could picture in my mind's eye the displeasure of Monsieur Stavko or his daughter if they came out into the passage and saw their new housekeeper prowling about, talking of loose shutters, for all the world like a footpad captured in the night. In any case my direction was through the westerly corridor if I wished to attend to the accursed shutter.

I started out along the passage, interested in the fact that when I lived here I had known so little about this section of the house beyond the room to which I had been assigned upon my present journey. I was grateful for the silence of my slippers as I felt my way past various unused rooms with their doors ajar. Those rooms could hold anything but they seemed to be filled only with unused and even ancient furnishings. There was a storm lantern hung over the lintel of a door on the left of the passage—a curious, secondary corridor, and one I could not remember having noticed in the old days. It had been there, of course, but probably for many good reasons had been unused. I guessed now that it led toward a subsidiary staircase into the huge medieval dining hall below these rooms. I had already walked several minutes and finding my robe scarcely a warm enough shield in these damp and infernally drafty walls, I hurried my steps, grateful to reach the flight of stairs that wound its way down to the floor below and, if my memory served me well, to that section of the courtyard rooms where I would find the loose shutter.

Although the staircase looked forgotten, as much of this wing was uninhabited, when I reached the lower floor corridor, I noticed that new equipment had replaced the old in surprising places. The big, iron-bound door that opened on the courtyard in my husband's day was now fitted with heavy new hasps and bolts—and it was bolted or locked from the courtyard side, of all things! Without the keys in the pocket of my robe, I would not be able to reach the courtyard from this end of the wing.

I had no wish to venture out in the blowing snow at this hour, in any case, but upon looking to the right, I found what I was searching for, the first floor passage, only half a story above the courtyard and directly below my own floor. The shutter certainly belonged to one of the rooms along this passage. As usual, in this house of intricate additions built onto the original edifice every century or so, I soon found my way barred by a door. The door, as I vaguely recalled, had always been here but never before was it closed or locked until now; for it simply cut off the passages from two directions and had been totally unnecessary. I rattled the latch, tried it several times, but it was unmistakably locked.

I held up the light and examined my keys. Very likely, the battered, darkened old key which unlocked most of the other unwanted doors chopping up the South Wing would work here. I tried it and though rust on the key itself made difficulties with the freshly polished lock, when I applied pressure, the key turned and the door opened with surprisingly little noise. The hinges had been oiled in the recent past.

The passage continued here, much as it had done on the floor above. I went into each of the first two empty rooms to examine the shutters, but everything was in order. The third and fourth rooms were locked so I tried the key which had formerly served for the bedchambers. It opened the third door and revealed to me a room partially furnished, with piles of linen on the floor and a denuded four-poster bed. I soon saw why the former occupant had deserted the otherwise comfortable room. The curtains at the window had been badly burned and a good section of the carpet blackened as well. The acrid odor of burnt cloth still lingered in the air.

Feeling devilishly uncomfortable, I quickly went to the window, thrust aside what remained of the drapes and looked out. Both shutters were open and fastened back upon the wall of the building. The window itself could only be opened against iron grillwork very like the bars imprisoning females in the Spanish-speaking kingdoms. The grillwork on the ground floor of this wing had been added since our day. At one angle of the window I could just barely see and hear the loose shutter I had been seeking. It belonged to the next room, which was locked, as this had been.

I moved along the corridor to the next door, which yielded as readily as its neighbor to my key. That is to say, there was a certain amount of pressure needed, thanks to the rust on my keys. I pushed the door open, and holding my candle high, looked for a place near the window where I could set the candle while I tried to secure the shutter. The noise of its banging reverberated through the little room which was very like its neighbor. This, one however, was completely furnished, including a four-poster bed with heavy green hangings. The bed, shrouded and muffled in that heavy tester and curtains, depressed me. I was grateful the Stavkos had not assigned me to this room.

There was no table by the window; so I set the candlestick on the top step beside the big, shrouded bed, and opened the window curtains. As I had seen from the room next door, there were the neat, romantic grillwork bars before the window. When I opened the window, I found it impossible to reach that infernal flapping shutter. I tried vainly, several times, to extend my arm between the iron bars but because the window itself could only be opened about a third of the way, I was unable to reach around it to do more than touch the swinging shutter with my fingertips. I stopped, took a deep breath and tightened my muscles to reach out again.

It was at this moment that I felt the faint breath of fear on the back of my neck. In that short time I knew, though I had heard no sound, that I was not alone in this room; that, in fact, I had not been alone since I turned the lock and entered. As I turned around, the light from my candle on the bed-step was shifted slightly and then, its upward sweeping motion nearly blinded me.

V

APPARENTLY, THE WATCHER had been concealed in the deep shadow cast by the bed and its hangings. When my candlestick was raised so unceremoniously in another's hand, its light flared up to cast in weird highlight and darkness the woman I had seen crossing the courtyard not an hour earlier. I am considered a tall woman, but she was taller than I, and though my hair tumbled about my shoulders now in the most untended way, that extraordinary mane of hers, blacker than the shadows that engulfed the courtyard beyond the window, fell sleek and straight nearly to her hips. Her dark, deep-set eyes had an oblique, almond shape which would doubtless captivate the male sex but could hardly entice me; for they put me suddenly in mind of a devil's eyes. Her moist red lips were parted in a smile as she watched my reaction. I am persuaded she knew to an exact degree the rapid beat of my heart, the prickling cold of my fingertips. Slender as she appeared, the woman was far too corporeal, too evidently of the flesh, for me to suspect she was a ghostly visitant; yet very briefly, in that room, and seen so unexpectedly, she put me in mind of the supernatural. And if not a ghost, what could she be?

She was the Lady Tyra Stavko, of course, and one of my employers. I managed to conquer my shameful paralysis of fear to curtsey and make a fumbling explanation.

"Pardon, Madame. The shutter made such a racketing noise I came down to refasten it, but I can't reach it in the wind. . . ."

"The shutter. But it is quite still now." No puzzled frown crossed that pale, broad, unwrinkled brow of hers when she contradicted me, an indication that she knew perfectly well the noise would stop, and for that reason, I suspected that someone must be outside the window at this moment, holding or fastening the shutter. Either that, or this strange creature held power over the elements. Certainly the world of the night—at least our little world at Moura—was strangely silent now. The gusty wind had died abruptly. The only sound I could make out with absolute certainty was my quick, nervous breathing. It was a humiliating thought.

"Mademoiselle Wicklow, curious names, these—Irish! You are the female recommended by Kate Moura, are you not?"

"I am Anne Wicklow, the new housekeeper. That is," I quickly added before those over-ripe lips of hers could do so, "—if my references are satisfactory, Lady Tyra."

She did not deny the identity I gave her. Her tongue flicked over her lips so quickly it put me in mind of a viper's agile tongue, and she smiled. The candle light gleamed briefly on her strong teeth.

"Most satisfactory, I am told by—someone who described you at great length. I now understand why."

The intimation was that a man had described me; but I was not yet acquainted with a male member of the household. Young Draja who brought my supper would hardly qualify. It aroused in me a greater uneasiness than ever. It was as if every move of mine, every breath, even in my room, were known, watched, reported. I made as if to pass her, wondering all the while how I should make my way back to my chamber without the candlestick she had taken up.

"You have not yet answered me, Mademoiselle," said the lady, looking hard at me out of those oblique eyes with their secret depths.

"I beg pardon?"

"I know the cause that you say brought you to this room—"

"The cause that *did* bring me, my lady," I corrected her.

"Yes. Well then!" For a relieved few seconds I thought I was free to go. She must have known and played upon my hope, because, moving a trifle to bar my way, she added belatedly, "How did you get here, Mademoiselle?"

Nothing could be easier than the simple, honest reply to that: "I came through the upper passage, down a flight of stairs to the courtyard door and turned . . ." Too late, I began to see the trap. There was only one way to handle it. I must brazen out my lie which followed hard on the truth.

"Yes?" the lady urged ever so gently.

"I turned to the right along this corridor and entered to this bedchamber. There was a key in this door."

She reached into her garments, obviously to check upon the situation with her keys. Meanwhile, I surrendered the single key to the door of this room. Better this surrender than the entire set of my keys.

"Amazing," remarked Tyra Stavko, accepting the key with

a light amusement that did not fool me. She was certainly playing cat and mouse with me. "You have a rare talent, Mademoiselle. You walk through bolted doors, into and out of locked corridors, and all with that so enviable calm."

No answer presented itself except the continuation of the lie which I now counted upon to serve me.

"I do not understand you, my lady. There was but one bolted door beside this one, the door which opened on the courtyard. Had I been able to open that door, I should have tried to fasten the shutter from the outside and not chance disturbing anyone who might be in these rooms."

This time the pretenses were gone, the veil of amusement brushed from her face. Unwilling, unthinking, I looked into her eyes, the candle flame between us, and discovered the disquieting power of those eyes which robbed the observer of all volition, rather as a serpent mesmerizes its prey before devouring it. It was with a genuine effort that I broke this hold upon my senses by looking away, stepping around her tall, white-robed form and made my way across the room. I had my hand upon the latch of the door, angry at my weakness—for my fingers were shaking—when she called to me:

"Anne Wicklow!"

"Yes, my lady."

"I am expecting a—neighbor at the westerly postern gate for a late supper. You will oblige me by lighting him to this corridor . . . if you please."

I reached for the candle, then, remembering, glanced down at the robe and nightgown I wore. Clearly not a costume in which to receive a gentleman, even at my employer's instruction.

"Do not mind. My friend will give it no thought," she said with a tiny edge to the words, and I realized that for the first time during our odd meeting, I had somehow agitated her, as she had so recently agitated me. And I did not know why. I wondered at her clandestine meeting with a neighbor, as she put it, in her own household, but assumed as she instructed me that it was her father whose knowledge of the meeting she feared.

Poor Captain Surtees! I thought with wry amusement. If my suspicions were correct, he had a rival near the chateau itself. I wondered if he knew or guessed that the lady's romantic habits were nearly as free as his own. Always assuming, of course, that it was a lover I must lead to her here in the usually locked and bolted South Wing. I began to understand the reason for the locks if she feared discovery of her rendezvous.

"I am afraid I must fetch down a cloak of some sort," I insisted as politely as possible, and when she started to object, I explained in my broadest dialect, "Sure now, my lady, I am that chilled I could freeze the very fingers of me!"

I supposed she understood at last that I was not being merely troublesome. I wasn't very surprised when she sighed and moved away from me and, a moment later, pulled a dusty pink cashmere shawl out of the coffin-like old armoire in a far corner of the room. "This will do. It looks to have been here an eon, but a bit of shaking will set it to rights. Now, will you go?"

Fortunately, I took these seconds, when I shook out the shawl before throwing it around my shoulders, to give thought to Lady Tyra's command. I therefore had enough sense at the last second or two to ask, "Which is the way to the postern gate, my lady?"

She gave me a sharp, cutting look which plainly directed me westward. After a pretense of confusion, I understood the location of the postern gate, nodded my assent, and left her in the room. I had known from long experience the location of the West Wing of Moura, but the postern gate was not an area which should be known to a newcomer like myself. For this reason, I had asked the Lady Tyra how to reach it most rapidly. As I hurried on my way, tightly wrapped in the old pink shawl, I hoped that my manner sufficiently fooled the lady and her father about my knowledge of the labyrinthine ways of Moura Chateau. The longer I remained at Moura, the more keenly I felt that Kate's first fears of "unholy doings" here were justified.

Once I was out of sight of the Lady Tyra, I cut through several short corridors and a flight of steps not generally known to newcomers at the chateau, with my elongated shadow for company and no weapon but the candle and its hood. I could thus reach the postern gate more rapidly, without freezing to death in the drafty halls. I confess I was most curious to see my strange employer's "neighbor" whom I supposed to be a lover. When I threw back the bolt of the little iron-bound door, clutching my shawl to avoid the blast of winter air, you may conceive my surprise, and none too pleasant a surprise, when I beheld Captain Edward Surtees, stamping his boots up and down on the frozen ground, and beating his forearms vigorously to ward off the cold.

"Good evening, Captain," I said in English, with my face composed and my manner as nearly as possible that of the Imperturbable Housekeeper. "You are a trifle late. Was there a bit of a dustup making your way here?"

He grinned at my pretense of expecting him and stepped inside, slamming the little door shut on what my suddenly flaring candle revealed of a wintry forest, a few snowdrifts, and a single pair of almost transparent, glowing eyes which I correctly guessed were those of a Moura wolf. The Captain had seen those glowing eyes too, and gave an elaborate shudder.

"Do you know, that damned dog has tracked me for the last hour! I am beginning to think no rendezvous is worth all this secrecy. Though I have worked up an appetite for what supper I've been promised."

I smiled at that and did not add to his discomfort by telling him his "damned dog" was a hungry wolf who had been scouting him. Then I was momentarily discomfited by the attention he gave me, looking me up and down and remarking with a matter-of-factness that relieved his observation of any offense, "Why the devil did Tyra send you to fetch me up? You look half-frozen." As I wrapped the shawl more closely around me, trying not to be conscious of his attention, he added so brusquely I was forced to laugh, "Don't think I am making objections on my own behalf. I assure you, a vision like yourself is rare upon any occasion."

"A vision, indeed!" I scoffed as he took the candle and hurried me along with a hand under my elbow. "In dusty, borrowed plumage."

"Very fetching, all the same." He had caught his fingers in the lacy weave of the shawl and in extricating himself, stopped abruptly, holding the candlestick closer with his free hand, the better to illuminate the threads. "See here, Miss Wicklow! Have you hurt yourself tonight, perhaps in the scutffle to unpack your boxes?"

"No, Sir. Why?"

"Because these stains look uncommonly like blood. Not yours, I trust."

I gazed at the spots which were like faded chocolate stains and I ran my fingers over them, agreeing privately that he was right. But this was hardly a conclusive sign. I reminded him, "There are many stains of this color. This is, after all, a school, and in schools, young ladies very properly are served a pot of chocolate on their breakfast trays."

"Doubtless." He grinned and slapped my shawl-covered hand briskly. "In any case, take care."

I agreed that from this moment I should take care to refuse all garments that showed stains of bloodthirsty crimes.

"You may jest, my dear girl," the Captain assured me, "but I haven't forgotten the coffin we saw being transported along the High Road."

I reminded him, "And yet you visit this place in deep night. Are you aware that few of the locals dare to cross the Moura Woods by daylight? You, on the other hand, stroll through the woods at midnight, pursued by prowling wolves. . . . Mind the step, Sir."

"Good God! You mean that poor starving canine was a wolf? I must make it quite plain to Tyra that any further rendezvous should be made in Paris."

It was, to be sure, no concern of mine; yet I confess, I

felt a strange sensation akin to jealousy at the image of the red-lipped, pale-fleshed Lady Tyra Stavko meeting Captain Surtees with the object of romance. He was so very healthy, so humorous and charmingly human. She, on the other hand was . . . I had almost said she was inhuman. Whatever she was, I feared her influence over the volatile Captain.

We came into that part of the house dominated by the great dining hall and I was shocked to find myself trembling in the most cowardly way, as I expected any minute to meet Lady Tyra. I concealed this as best I could, but not soon enough. The Captain had reached around me to push the door open into the passage in which I had left my female employer. The gesture brought us close and he murmured, suddenly concerned, "You really are frightened, aren't you?"

"Absurd! What should I be frightened of, indeed?"

He pushed the door open with an impatient shove . . . anxious to meet his lovely hostess, no doubt. But he did favor me with the crooked, quizzical smile I had already learned to watch for with pleasure.

"Not of me, certainly."

I laughed and agreed. Then this small gaiety died abruptly. Tyra Stavko had appeared out of the distant darkness in the passage and was moving toward us.

"I will leave you now," I said, stopping with what must have been an almost insulting haste and turning back. Even in these rather obvious circumstances, with the lady who was undoubtedly his paramour approaching him, I was foolish enough to hope he would express a word of regret at my departure. I was properly paid out for my foolishness. He gave me an absent "good night" and I had only one rather petty revenge. I took the candlestick, leaving him to the dubious if lush pleasures of Lady Tyra in the darkness.

As I went up to my quarters again, I became suddenly aware of one accomplishment. The shutter had definitely ceased to bang. Tyra Stavko's doing, no doubt. The woman had many unsuspected talents. I wondered at Kate's curious reversal, since it was almost inevitable that Kate and Lady Tyra should come to blows over the first available male. I only regretted that Captain Surtees appeared to be the first.

In my present mood I was not in the least surprised upon entering my bedchamber to see a sleek, dark little creature scurry across the floor, startled by the light of my candle. Rodents were common enough in my early memories of Moura. But this one put me in mind of the ugly little bat who had investigated us on the High Road.

Now, what'll I be thinking of? I asked myself angrily. *I'll never get to sleep if I let my nerves be played upon in this ridiculous way!*

I bolted my door and threw off the shawl and was about to remove my robe at the foot of the crimson damask hangings of the bed when I saw again in my mind's eye, the body of that child I had once known, laid out in the funereal light of four candles on this bed. Instead of removing my robe, I kept it on and crawled into bed. But even with this warmth, I found myself unable to snuff the candle, so I put it on the candlestand, closed the bed curtains and tried to sleep.

Presently a door slammed somewhere in the South Wing and seemed to echo through the courtyard. I guessed it was the door I had heretofore found locked and bolted. I thought this over, relieved that I had not confided to Tyra Stavko the existence of the extra set of keys which I possessed. At the same time I knew a wholly unaccustomed pleasure in the thought that the slamming of the courtyard door might indicate an end to the supper rendezvous between Captain Surtees and my eerie employer. If a supper was ever intended!

After that, my mind was full of thoughts, on less pleasant, though no less puzzling elements than the Englishman. If Tyra Stavko was so strange and so dedicated to the hours of night for her entertainment and her social engagements, what must her father, the Maître Stavko, be like? I shivered a little at the thought, and sank down further under the coverlet, into the warming, protective confines of my bed, falling asleep afterward by this aid.

It was an hour or so before dawn, during a deep but

dream-filled sleep, that my dreams began to impinge upon reality. While still in my sleep, I was conscious of the latch on my door being tried so lightly that I could not at once distinguish it from other vague noises, such as the scrabbling of the local rat population.

We really must introduce some enterprising cats at Moura, I remember thinking.

The sound when repeated, was quite distinct, however, and at last, I knew. I must have heard the slight push, as if an extra pressure had been exerted, even before I opened my eyes. When I did so, I saw the old-fashioned metal latch move up and down, as if of its own volition. It stopped shortly after, but it had not been a sight to make me sleep well and securely the rest of the night.

VI

THERE ARE few things more depressing to the new day than the first light of a sunny morning seen through the stale, guttering flame of a night candle. I snuffed what remained of the candle and opened the shutters.

Over the low battlements and crenellations of the ancient house I could see a cold, clear, blue sky which heightened the stark treetops and gaunt limbs of the encroaching Moura Woods. There had been no snowfall since early evening and I could still see in the snow the imprint of boots across a corner of the courtyard. I supposed these were Captain Surtees' footsteps upon his departure last night. Eliminating the intricate corridors, he had cut directly across the courtyard.

His footsteps are as direct as he is, I thought, smiling a little, but upon further thought, I was not at all sure

Edward Surtees was a straightforward, honest man. For one thing, he might have told me he was coming out of the village to Moura last evening, instead of letting me take the pony cart in the dubious company of the Moura coachman. And an unlikely coachman the fellow was, when all is said!

Perhaps, though, Captain Surtees, a gentleman born, did not like to share his rendezvous with a prospective servant of his mistress. His conduct in regard to Lady Tyra Stavko was very odd, all the same. He had certainly not appeared to be overcome by an uncontrollable passion for the lady, unless one counted that last minute of absentmindedness when he saw her moving—I had almost said *floating*—along the passage toward us.

I looked down to see the lady's footprints across the courtyard. There were none. She must have taken the long way through the two great wings of the house to reach her own apartments, unless she slept in the South Wing. I rather hoped not!

Meanwhile, as I daydreamed, I found myself shaken by what clearly was a vigorous kicking upon the door. It was the charming little urchin, Draja, who stood in the passage holding my breakfast tray of hot tea, a basin of thick porridge and bread. Small wonder that with his hands full, he had resorted to his feet to rouse me. I asked if he had eaten his breakfast and after a scowl and a smile of belated understanding, the boy agreed in his own strange language that he had eaten.

I asked him when I might see my other employer, the Maître Stavko, and the boy recognized the name. He babbled at great length, pointing across the courtyard toward the students' quarter and grabbing at his head, and groaning. From all this I assumed Stavko was having difficulties with his pupils, a not uncommon event in the best regulated academies, even less surprising if he possessed any of those eerie qualities I had noted in his daughter. I let the boy go on his way and he skipped off down the corridor. I envied him his high spirits on this of all mornings; for I found myself somewhat agitated by the prospect of my first encounter with Kate's "Maître."

But a cup of the strong tea, together with the porridge the boy had brought, was satisfying after last night's meager supper, and I was soon my old, enthusiastic self. That is to say, I became anxious to set about my work at Moura, whether this might be my familiar post as housekeeper or the more complex role Kate Moura, ever the actress, had assigned to me. Besides, the more rapidly I began to work, the less time I would have for pining over the happy past or the dubious future.

I chose my gown carefully—a deep blue wool that was laced over the bosom and around the neck in brighter blue velvet ribbon, a gown to which no one could take exception for its daring, nor could my appearance be faulted as too drab for the authority of my office. I wore my second-best day slippers laced over the ankles. After surveying my appearance from foot to head, I bundled my hair on the nape of my neck, skewering it in place with hair bodkins, and brushed out a few unruly locks around my face so as not to suggest a severity that might put off the house servants who would be under my jurisdiction. And precious few there were of those, according to my observations of the last twelve hours!

It seemed to me that I took an unconscionable time in dressing and making myself presentable. But then, my post here, and at this time, was so very irregular! For all I could be certain, I might be on my way back to Italy or England by noon, depending entirely upon the mood and whim of the school's master. It would be exactly like Kate, under sufficient persuasion, to have betrayed my secret purpose to the very people she herself had accused. For many reasons, it seemed to me that already Lady Tyra would be happy to have seen the last of me. It was a feeling that I confess was reciprocated. Even after several hours' sleep and the addition of daylight as well as common sense, I could not acquit her of being an unusual and uncomfortable creature to be near.

As I had not yet been summoned to attend upon my new employers, I assumed that I had better report to the kitchen and stillrooms where my first order of business, as in most households of my experience, would be to make my peace with the cook. Until I showed a disposition to be friendly and companionable, the cooks invariably held me in strongest dislike, expecting my interference or a false sense of superiority. As I had begun my life in service as a scullery maid, my knowledge of cooks and their temperament was thorough.

I made my way along the passage, cutting across one sector of the great East Tower to reach the main living area of the chateau, its east front. Here I glimpsed the master suite far down a corridor to my left and, avoiding it with an effort, went down the staircase to the ground floor. I was headed toward the kitchen and stillrooms when I heard running footsteps across the melting snow of the courtyard, accompanied by much girlish chatter and at least one voice raised in strong hysterics.

"They did it deliberately, just to scare me, just to be horrid!"

I wondered what dreadful girlish crime had brought upon this blanket accusation, and in a couple of minutes found myself plunged into the midst of the melee as several young ladies, who appeared to range from thirteen to seventeen or so, poured into the wide passage between the great hall and the kitchen quarters. They were a bright flutter of gowns, sashes and complicated arrangements of curls and furbelows. I felt pleasantly at home with them and their ways, remembering my years as housekeeper at Miss Nutting's Academy for Select Young Females.

"Oh, Mademoiselle!" the leader cried, pinching at the sleeve of my gown. "Have you seen that disgusting girl? Where is she hiding? The Master is out-of-reason cross with us because Effie says the blame is ours. And we did nothing." She shook me in her excitement. "Nothing! Do you comprehend me?"

"I comprehend you perfectly, young miss," I said. "Let

me go, if you please. You are making my teeth chatter." I smiled at her, however, as the pretty redhead, looking only momentarily abashed, let me go and turned around rapidly to catch sight of the elusive Effie.

One of the other girls mourned with the self-concern of youth, "Mon Dieu! That Elfreda! If she goes and does something outrageously silly, like throwing herself off the battlements, the Master won't let us go into the village at the next carnival. It's grossly unfair!"

"Why will she do something silly like kill herself?" I asked in English with an irony I do not believe the girls recognized.

The red-haired miss seemed vastly relieved that I spoke her native tongue and she burst forth into an explanation of one Elfreda Swiversedge's behavior in which there were startling hints of rats, mice, mysterious "other rodents" and an assortment of complaints about Elfreda's total absence of humor. The English girl's tangled tale was elaborated by other students whose varied remarks I untangled with the help of my long experience early in life. While they spoke, a part of my brain concentrated on various hiding places nearby in the old chateau. A fruitful subject.

Suddenly, another sound cut through the shrill, girlish voices and I lost the trend of the vivacious argument. I guessed at once that the interruption was the doing of Istvan Stavko, the Master of the School, and was surprised at my own uneasiness at the prospect of my belated meeting with the father of the mysterious Lady Tyra. The fact that this man, with the vibrant, cutting accent of Middle Europe, was both Kate's ogre and her new hero did not commend him to me in a light any warmer or less forbidding. The order was punctuated by the sharp little "whirr" of a stick snapped through the air.

"Ladies! Ladies, if you please! Back to your studies. This will mean longer hours at your lesson in Court Behavior."

I wondered what Istvan Stavko could teach these addlepated, though charming young ladies about decorum in the new British Court of George the Fourth, who was hardly more kingly than the stout, tired old Bourbon who had climbed up to the French throne after a lifetime of machinations.

There were whispers and a few nervous giggles among the girls. They parted in a kaleidoscope of colors and ribbons, and I saw the Maître approaching me, stepping from the sunny courtyard into the half-light of the wide passage. A tall, austere man, with the frigid, unbending grace I had observed in members of Middle-European aristocracy. Gray hair and a cool, penetrating gaze were suited to his acquiline nose, and the only resemblance I could see between Istvan Stavko and his daughter was about the mouth. Stavko's lips were sensuous and well-shaped, the only slash of color in his face.

He stopped abruptly upon seeing me, and I sank into a deep, respectful curtsey, while I studied him without seeming to do so. With a thin, flexible willow wand bent in an arc between his long fingers, he looked the perfect "Maître" and I was not surprised either at the abrupt, uneasy silence of the girls, or at Kate's description of the man's "power." I too might have trembled under his gaze, but for the fact that I refused to reveal what I was persuaded he expected of me. I would not fall under the spell of either that dubious power or the sensual mouth. If I were to judge from Kate's experience, both could be deadly.

"So? This will be our Mademoiselle Wicklow. . . ."

Maître Stavko put out the willow wand and gave me a smart little tap on the shoulder which made all the girls giggle in amusement. It turned my face red with embarrassment and unexploded anger. I arose quickly, admitted I was "their Mademoiselle" and then, to regain some dignity, I suggested, "The young ladies seem to have mislaid a Miss Swiversedge. Perhaps, Monsieur, I may begin my duties by locating her while the students go about their classes. Afterward, I am most anxious to receive my orders for the day, if it please you."

"It does," he said with what I suspected was the slight inflection of mockery. "By all means. Go back to the small salon, young ladies, and apologize to Madame Kate for this delay. I will assist Mademoiselle in the search for that elusive child."

I was not at all desirous of sharing the search with Maître Stavko. I felt that his eyes saw far too much and might, conceivably, see, all too fast, that I had been in the chateau before. I knew this was our first encounter; for he was not a man easily forgotten; yet every time I caught his glance, I had the distinct sensation that I had seen those eyes before. It was particularly alarming because I knew we were strangers.

The students began to trail out of the passage and into the courtyard, chattering among themselves and looking over their shoulders at us, or maybe the invisible Elfreda, in secretive ways that did not reassure me. Obviously, the girls' attitude did not disturb Stavko. He struck the willow wand briskly against his other hand.

"Which way do you suggest, Mademoiselle? It is of considerable importance that we find the Swiversedge, of all the young ladies."

"I should hope so, Sir." I started across the passage in the direction of the long, medieval dining hall, then paused and could not resist the question, "Why Miss Swiversedge so particularly, Sir?"

"Because no one stands in greater need of lessons in Court Decorum."

That made me smile, and though Stavko did not join me in my amusement, his lips curved in what I supposed must be his own form of smile. He walked beside me and it was at least a minute or two before I realized how much I was betraying in this swift, knowing approach to the dining hall.

"Why do you stop?"

"I'm sorry," I said. "But I assumed the young lady had gone through the corridor into the South Wing."

"It is not a corridor, Mademoiselle. You are walking into the dining hall." He pushed open the two great doors with a great sweep of his hands and without dropping the little willow wand.

"Am I?" I asked hurriedly. "How silly! Of course, the child could hardly hide in a place like this. Why, it's quite barren!"

He studied the huge, shadowed room with its beamed roof where once the Moura banners and ancient pennons had hung. "Do you find it barren? Strange. I often walk through the room and seem to feel the primordial past close about me. It was one of the inducements to the leasing of the estate." He looked at me too steadily for my comfort. "Have you never known that sensation?"

"I'm not precisely sure I understand you, Sir."

"I mean, the peculiar sensation that past and present are one. That the dead of centuries are still here with us, perhaps among us at this moment in time."

"No," I said. "I never felt that. Nor should I wish to. They have had their time, and we have ours in which to live." Suspecting he deliberately talked this way either to test my knowledge of Moura's history, or to disconcert and frighten me, I went on a bit tartly, "I shall not intrude upon the dead of times past, and I'll be thanking them to show me the same courtesy."

Whatever his intent, I did not let him know he had in any way succeeded. When there was no reply to my words, I looked hard at him. He seemed thoughtful, gazing at the high beams as if he fancied, in his mind's eye, all the banners of Moura crusaders and other Moura knights that had hung here in my husband's day. Then he lowered that large, keenly intelligent head and smiled at me. I was oddly, and annoyingly, relieved at this sign of his returning good humor.

"Very true, Mademoiselle. And very discreet. One hopes the Swiversedge child is as discreet. These old houses produce curious phenomena. Not surprisingly, the young ladies play truant now and again. But they always regret it. Imagination at their age is very keen."

I could only suppose these remarks were in the nature of a joke. In any case, I pretended to accept this view.

"Monsieur, I hardly think an Academy for Young Ladies

will provide any terrors greater than those of the imagination. That would hardly recommend Moura to the parents of your young ladies."

"Ah, but you see, our young ladies have no parents."

We were walking back across the passage. The gaunt shadow of the East Tower cut across the courtyard entrance to the main apartments. I was thinking of that ancient vantage point with its view of the entire countryside, and for a few seconds after he had spoken, his words seemed to linger on the bright, sparkling winter air. I was startled when I really understood his remark.

"No parents! But surely you cannot be serious, Monsieur."

For the first time, I felt I could not be mistaken. This aloof aristocrat, with his definite, though not unattractive accents of another and unknown land, was teasing me.

"All heiresses . . . All orphans. Am I sunk deep in your suspicions, Anne Wicklow?"

I was uncomfortably aware of being laughed at, though I could not even make out a smile upon his severe face, and I stammered, "N-no. It is certainly not my place to—"

"To suspect we murder our orphans after first forcing them to make over their estates to us? Well then, you are in the right. We do not. In any case," he added with a wry grimace, "we could not. They all have guardians, and these guardians, let me assure you, are far more solicitous of their wards' fortune and properties than the usual parent who, in my experience, is too concerned with making a place for himself—and more probably herself—at court."

I laughed. "You relieve me. I shall promise not to suspect such gothic doings here. But in my own experience of young ladies, they will find themselves deep in the literary crimes of *The Monk* and Mrs. Radcliffe upon any excuse."

"Good. So long as they remain confined to *The Mysteries of Udolpho* we are agreed that the students here may imagine what they like, and you will not credit half the fantastic tales they *do* imagine about such an ancient estate as this. . . . Where, meanwhile, would you suggest we search next for Miss Swiversedge?"

But I was not to be entrapped so easily. "I cannot guess, Monsieur. What areas do these imaginative young ladies frequent at this corner of the building? I have not seen the entire chateau yet; so naturally, I could not be in the happy position of knowing."

"Naturally, you could not."

I wondered if I, like his pupils, had an over-active imagination, or did he mock me again in that last remark of his? I was still naggingly aware of the odd sensation that I had met him before, which was stuff and nonsense. Perhaps it was only a resemblance to his daughter that I felt, but that seemed unlikely. Whatever my suspicions, I found the daughter repulsive despite her not inconsiderable beauty, while the father was both alarming and fascinating, like a book whose finale one dreads even while plunging on toward that very end.

Once more, I broached the subject of the vanished Elfreda. "Shall you take the courtyard hereabouts, Monsieur, and I will go the other way to the stillrooms?"

He gave his palm several punctuating taps with the willow wand, shrugged and agreed. I waited until he had turned his back and I could be sure he was not spying upon me in some odious way. Then I went to the kitchen and put my head in, not liking to seem too familiar until the cook and I were friendly.

After three years, during which the chateau was locked and bolted by the Royalist government, and access to it forbidden by a completely unknowing, uncaring King's Prosecutor in Lyons, it had never occurred to me that the same cook who had ruled my husband's kitchen with a hard, red hand should still be here. But so it was. I found myself apprehensive as I had been six years ago when I once more caught my first glimpse of Matilde, a powerful, solidly built peasant whose hard face was framed by a halo of uncombed, flaming hair. Women very like her, I always thought, had sat beneath the guillotine in Paris, knitting as the heads rolled. Surely, Kate had not known of Matilde's presence when she first sent for me! Of all the women I worked with in the precarious relation of housekeeper and cook, I suspected Matilde had liked me least, though she and I lived in a state of armistice for my husband's sake.

Matilde, checking supplies brought out of the stillroom, grunted at the sight of me and I, who had managed to stand reasonably firm against the strangeness and mesmerizing quality of the two Stavkos, felt my knees weaken a bit in the presence of the Terrible Matilde. I spoke quickly, seeing the tousled, slatternly girl I supposed to be the scullery maid come bouncing in to dump cabbages out of her apron onto the table before Matilde.

"I am Mademoiselle Wicklow, the housekeeper. I am told you have all meals and menus in your charge."

"Ay." She did not curtsey. She had once told me, quite unnecessarily, that though born in 1770, she considered herself a product of the Revolution. "You be the *Citoyenne* Wicklow. I understand." From the way she looked at me, challenging, unblinking, I had a sudden notion that she was saying more than she appeared to. "I understand," she repeated sharply, and I nodded. This time, I too understood.

"Well then, I am looking for one of the students who may have come through here. A young lady named Elfreda Swiversedge."

The scullery maid sputtered laughter and Matilde made a threatening gesture, wielding a cabbage in her big, powerful hand. The girl ducked, then leaped out of her reach, still giggling but with dirty fingers over her mouth. Matilde looked as disdainfully at me as at the girl.

"That Elfreda—the stout one with the so-hideous name, she is often in my kitchen. Sometimes, she sits there by the fireplace, very nearly in the gate, and talks of food. But she is not here this morning, as you may see."

I glanced at the huge, blackened hearth with its many hooks and hanging kettles, its several grates and broiling areas that had prepared food for Moura during the last five centuries with few repairs and even fewer modern amenities. It was a filthy, sooty place but not an uncomfortable corner on a windy night. If the Swiversedge girl was unhappy, fond of food in the bargain, she might very likely choose this old kitchen for her refuge. Though I had no knowledge of the girl beyond a few superficial facts, my sympathies were gradually being aroused so that it seemed more and more important, as the minutes went by, that she should be found, and rapidly.

"Can you suggest where else I might look?" I asked Matilde, with a quick glance in the direction of the scullery maid. Perhaps the girl would have some idea. She did not appear to, however, or if she did, she did not immediately confide in us.

Matilde said in her sharp way, "The old carriage-house? The storage chambers in the West Wing? Who knows?"

"Or the ancient cellars and the horrid dungeons under the castle," put in the scullery maid surprisingly.

Matilde and I looked at each other. The cook asked, "Isabeau! How do you know about those places? They are not in use since the Mouras lived here."

Isabeau wrinkled her nose and made ready to scramble out of the cook's long reach. "I looked into the passage once, when you sent me for the pickled turnips. That heathen Borgos has been all through the cellars. He says they come out through a well in the south fields."

"Very true," I agreed amiably, before Matilde could put the girl against us. "But Mademoiselle Kate says the doors are gone and all the skulls and bloodstains carefully removed."

The girl stared at me and then, as if pleased at my tone, laughed. "All the same," she persisted, "it is enough to send one of those high and mighty schoolgirls off into the vapors."

"This fat one," said Matilde, "this Effie person, she would come this way to take the cellar steps. We use them to reach the wines and the pickling cellar. There is no other entrance to the wines. It is impossible. So, you see—she is elsewhere." She shrugged, and waved me away.

I recognized the truth of this; for in my day, the only other door had been sealed after a maid broke her leg in an unfortunate tumble down the steep, ill-lighted stairs. I thought a minute, then looked up. I was remembering the entrance to the East Tower which opened upon the courtyard and whose spiral steps might prove inviting to an adventurous girl trying to evade her friends and threaten a spectacular suicide. Matilde followed my every move. She understood more quickly than I credited to her.

"Likely it is the tower. Have you tried there, M'amselle?"

"Thank you. I will try," and left her. At least, I had advanced from the brusque "Citoyenne" to "M'amselle," a very large step for Matilde! She was surprisingly knowing. I had wished her to suggest the tower so that I might search there and afterward report with perfect honesty that I received the suggestion from the cook, with the scullery maid for witness, should that girl prove to be a spy for the Stavkos. I was forever in fear that one of my employers would discover my true identity.

Out in the sunny courtyard, I took care to look around and consider other possibilities before I stepped across the now slushy cobblestones to the tower entrance. It seemed to me that I had caught a glimpse of something, undoubtedly *someone*, high up in the turret embrasure of the tower. If the child had climbed that high in her anger and fear, she must be exceedingly angry now. Or exceedingly desperate. Probably the latter.

I picked up my skirts and with a sigh, started to climb, round and round, several times passing open embrasures which gave clear views of the snow-covered countryside, sparkling under the sunlight. But I was too concerned with the problem of the elusive Effie Swiversedge to enjoy the well-remembered view.

The echo of my slippers upon the worn stones seemed to carry throughout the old tower. It distracted me and I stopped now to look back, around the spiral steps as far as I could see. Not more than a few steps. And for the first time, I wondered if I had been followed up the tower, toward the turret. I did not like it. I knew it was mad to think of harm coming to me here in the morning light, amost within sight of the entire household, but it did occur to me that once I reached the turret, there would only be one way in which to retreat: down by this means, past anyone who chose to lie in wait for me.

Angered at the absurdity of my own imagination—surely as bad as Stavko's pupils!—I took another and more determined step upward. Again, the echo seemed unnaturally loud, the grating of shoes heavier than my thin-soled slippers upon a dusty step. I paused, glanced upward, straining to see if, by happy chance, the sound came from above. It would be an excellent turn of events if the young Elfreda should decide to return by her own volition.

The interior of the tower, and the distance between each open embrasure, was always shrouded in a moldy, gray dark. Even on the warmest summer day I had touched the wall and found my hand loathsome with slime and the soft, colorless growth that moved gently under my fingers, seeking once more its ancient home. But where there was an opening upon the strange, almost primeval world of Moura, sunlight cut across the gloom of the steps in a welcome path of warmth.

I made my way to the next embrasure, stood momentarily in that sunlight, getting a clear, northerly view of the broken North Tower, the woods beyond, and distantly, the High Road where it curved out into the open to cross the Roman Bridge. Nothing seemed to move in all that space; yet I knew there was a life of sorts beneath the stark tree limbs, and under the melting carpet of snow.

Just as I knew, when I turned to listen again, that Elfreda, or something else animate, shared the tower with me at this minute. I preferred to believe it was the girl herself.

VII

I LEANED OUT of the embrasure, looking upward, and was barely able to see one side of the more lengthy opening in the turret. A bright pink satin ribbon fluttered where it had been caught on the dangerous and heady little shooting platform just below the turret embrasure. From this platform, the plunge to the stones of the courtyard far below was a hideous one and, in its day, had been used for a number of suicides, as well as at least one murder. It made me dizzy to look down and contemplate such things. I hurried upward.

A piercing brightness ahead told me when I neared the little turret chamber, open to the world on two sides, one of which, above the shooting platform, was as tall as a man. I ran up the last few steps and into the turret so rapidly my coming must have sent the poor child huddling there into a spasm of terror. I stopped abruptly at the sight of her.

The round room itself gained its light mostly from the large opening that faced an easterly direction, and slightly to the north. This opening in the stonework had long since lost its single protective row of roughly hewn stones so that one backward step too far would send the unwary explorer hurtling out into space. Possibly the body would lodge on the projection of the shooting platform which was no wider than the length of an archer's boot; for it had been here, in unlamented days gone by, that men had stood to drop boiling pitch upon hapless enemies in the courtyard far below. But, from experience, it was known that anyone falling out of the turret would, in three cases out of four, plunge past the platform and not stop until the body smashed upon the ancient cobblestones of the courtyard.

Here, then, so close to that crumbling edge of eternity, I saw the kneeling, huddled form of a girl about fourteen, the unbecoming puce-colored silk skirts of her dress flying out over space, her plump, round face raised to me in puppy-like terror, her complexion mottled with dried tears.

I tried very hard to make my smile reassuring as I moved toward her, with infinite care not to further alarm her.

"Oh," I said calmly, "I am ever so glad to see you, Miss Elfreda! How brave of you to climb all this way up here! I wanted to come here from the moment I arrived last evening. Exploring, you know . . . But it was dark and I was so terrified of the place, you'd scarcely credit how my knees shook. . . . Then, when you came up, I made up my mind if a small person like you could brave those steps, then a woman as tall as me could make the effort."

I was vastly relieved to see the terror gradually drain from her face so that her round eyes and two hesitant dimples beside her mouth made a charming appearance.

"Were—were you really afraid?" she asked me in a breathless, little girl voice.

"With that slime upon the walls, and me venturing my fingers upon things that had legs and moved in the dark? Mother of Heaven!"

Elfreda, seeing the little chain and crucifix at my neckline, regarded me as one does a wild beast that is safely caged. "You're a Papist! They said I should meet them if I was sent to school in France. But most of the girls are Church of England. And the Maître— Well . . ."

"You'll not be telling me he is Church of England!" I exclaimed, amused at the notion. "I assure you," I added, trying to be as sober on the matter as she was, "I shall not try to convert you to the Faith of Rome. Nor do I bake little children into Communion Loaves, as I'm sure you've been told."

This made her giggle. She would soon be in highfeather,

and I rejoiced to see it. I liked that honest, round countenance. Being now more confident, she became also, and disastrously, aware of her looks, of the full skirts blowing out over the edge of the turret embrasure. In a fussy, anxious gesture, she reached out behind her and tried to smooth the flaring skirts.

"No, Miss Elfreda," I said, far more calmly than I felt, as I stepped toward her, trying not to excite or make her move suddenly. "You look charming there. But you know, I think you would look quite the thing in a buttercup yellow gown." I was within reach of her now, after what seemed an age of maneuvering. "Or . . . yes. A green barred silk. You have hazel eyes, haven't you? They are very unusual, you know."

"Are they?" Thank heaven she had stopped teetering on the edge of danger. She gazed up at me, still on her knees, and blinked and then smiled. In praising the child I had not lied, I thought, as I held out one hand negligently to help her up so that she would not panic over her danger.

"Hazel eyes are most unusual," I reminded her, partly as a healing draft administered to make her respond a bit faster. Her prolonged hesitation made me progressively more anxious. "When you come down, Miss Effie, we will see how much the new barred silk becomes you."

"No. It won't. I'm too fat." She wanted pitifully to believe me. She began to brace her muscles to get up off her knees, a precarious business. If she showed any weakness, she would fall backward, out into space.

"Of course it will. You'll be all the crack. Wait and see." I chose this second when she half-believed me, to take a secure grip on her wrist. Even so, she was an unexpectedly heavy weight when she swayed, losing her balance, and it took every ounce of my strength to pull her into the center of the turret where we tumbled in a heap.

"Ouch! My elbow!" Elfreda cried, rubbing it and grimacing.

I was so relieved, and so cross with her at the same time that I said severely, "You are fortunate it is only your elbow.

It might have been your head!" But then the ridiculousness of our positions, both of us sprawled on the stone floor, made me laugh, and after peeping at me cautiously a couple of times, she grinned too. But as we sat there recovering our breath and our equilibrium, her smile faded. She complained,

"At first, I only wanted to scare them. They hate me. All the girls hate me and put mice in my bed and bite me in the dark and do horrid things like that, just to scare me."

I got to my feet, aware of a few bruises, a long tear in the sleeve of my gown, and several dusty spots across the skirt. I was sorry about the tear. My wardrobe was not extensive, and my present post with the Stavkos was by no means certain. However, the main problem of the moment was in a fair way to being solved: I had begun, I hoped, to win over the unhappy Miss Swiversedge.

It was not until the girl was on her feet as well, and brushing herself off, that I remembered another troublesome detail. I saw her stop in the act of shaking out her skirts and stare, in great agitation, at the turret entrance to the steps which lay in darkness beyond.

"What is it? What did you see?" I demanded too sharply, whirling around to stare in that direction. I saw nothing but what I might have expected, the half-dark of the tower steps.

The girl whispered, "I didn't precisely see anything. I heard it. A grating noise. They are forever watching us. If it isn't the Master or the Lady, it is someone else."

"What do you mean? Who?"

"Like the Master's Familiar."

"His Familiar!" It began to sound as though Stavko had been correct in his belief that these girls were creating an imaginary situation involving witchcraft.

"His Familiar is that wicked Miss Kate."

Poor Kate! Never had I thought to see the pleasure-loving Kate Moura condemned as a kind of subordinate witch. I wondered if she had heard the suspicions about her. Knowing Kate to be no more a devil's familiar than I was, I began to have certain doubts about the rest of my suspicions. Was it possible that the children themselves were responsible for the chilling sense of the netherworld that pervaded Moura?

"Come along," I said, hearing a more severe note in my voice. "If we spend any more time here, the other young ladies will be far more proficient in Court Decorum."

"Much I care!" But she came with me all the same. We walked rapidly down the first of the spiral steps, Miss Elfreda keeping close by my rustling skirts, peering ahead every few seconds, with the understandable desire to see around each turn. But by this time, having neither seen nor heard anyone spying upon us since my early scare, I was half of a mind to dismiss all my first suspicions and substitute for them a common sense but careful investigation of these students.

"Tell me—that is, if you've no objection, Miss Elfreda, why did you climb all the way up these steps, and what did you really have in mind to do in the turret?"

She exclaimed dramatically, "Kill myself! That would show them all they can't put rats in my bed and call me a 'plumper' and bite me and play their tricks on me in those horrid, vile corridors."

"But, Miss, if you jumped out of the turret, you would be in sad case to enjoy their discomfiture when they found you," I pointed out practically.

She sighed and admitted that she had not intended anything in the nature of a permanent death. "But I'm so unhappy, you've no notion! I wanted to hide, and the girls were forever talking of the turret, what it must be like, and how they didn't dare to go into the tower. But then I began to hear someone coming up the steps behind me. I got so scared, when I reached the turret, there was no place to go. And afterward, you came. Weren't you afraid?"

Although I was very much aware of the slimy darkness around us, I had long since stopped hearing strange sounds on the steps below. The natural, childish fright of Miss Elfreda seemed to make nonsense of my own weird fancies. Nonetheless, when we had passed the second embrasure and were making our way through the intervening darkness halfway down, I did hear the odd, scraping noise repeated, apparently below us.

I hoped my companion would not notice this, and we took several more steps, with Miss Elfreda close behind me, holding onto the sash of my gown before she whispered, "Do you hear?"

Her round hazel eyes were like saucers, almost lighting the dark. I put my finger to my lips and she understood; she waited until we were at the next embrasure, with its welcome bar of sunlight, before she murmured, "Who do you think it is?"

I had no more idea than she, but I was determined not to let whoever spied upon us know that I was on the watch. I preferred that these trickster schoolgirls, if they were responsible, or the Stavkos, should think me foolish, blind and unsuspicious.

"Hush," I said, and added with a gesture toward the steps below, "We will soon be out of here." I added in an undervoice that I felt could not be heard beyond us, "You were angry with the other young ladies because they frightened you with mice? They could do you little harm. I once had mice as companions when I was a little girl and scrubbed the church steps in County Wicklow."

"Not mice!" she whispered shrilly, with a quick glance over her shoulder. "A dead rat in my bed. They said it was a live mouse, but I saw a big one, a rat. And when I ran out in the passage, to pummel Jessie Tynford, I fell over a bed-stool. And something bit me. I think I fainted. . . ." I caught my breath, but she hurried on with a recital of the wrongs done to her. "Rosemary Tynford—she said she met you last night in the great hall—anyway, she found me, and she and Marie-Monique got me to bed."

"Then why did you run away today?"

"Because," she said patiently, "they laughed at me and said I'd imagined the whole of it, that no rat bit me and they'd only put a tiny, live mouse in my bed. And they showed him to me. But they lied. The thing that bit me—

I felt its teeth! I knew they did it all on purpose because I'm so f-fat!"

"You are a trifle plump. That is all. So you mustn't think such things. Your eyes are much prettier than Miss Rosemary's, and when you are not weeping and angry, your mouth is prettier too."

"Prettier than Rosemary's?"

I thought of the girl, who admitted me last night. Though pretty in a light, rather flyaway fashion, she had, it seemed to me, a petulant mouth and an indifference to all but her own comfort that detracted from the admiration she might otherwise deserve. Of the two girls, Effie Swiversedge could well blossom into the lovelier woman. But not while her complexion was mottled by tear stains of self-pity. I hoped someone would eventually "take her in hand" in the *cant* phrase of the day.

One thing Miss Elfreda must definitely forego: those fanciful tales of being bitten by great rats. Or was she hinting that the bites were part of the girls' persecution?

I deliberately changed the subject as we resumed our winding journey, "Who chooses your gowns, Miss Elfreda?"

"Call me Effie. . . . My guardian is Mr. Gunderson of the London and Leeds Bank. His wife selects my patterns and has them sewn by a seamstress in Leeds." Then she looked up at me, puzzled, wondering, I suppose, if I changed the subject in order to allay her fears, but I was actually curious to know whether these girls at Moura were under any other adult supervision beside that of a pair of strangers like the Stavkos. If not, then the unsupervised girls might either be guilty of petty mischief such as had been going on here, or they might be mistreated in any way—even murdered—with very little response from their guardians to whom their estates would be an added source of revenue. And this despite the statements of the Maître Stavko about the great interest of the guardians!

Effie stopped again and listened, but when I did not do likewise, she came on, holding so tight to my sash that she pulled it all askew. Our eavesdropper could no longer be heard, and, in fact, might prove to have been a figment of our combined imagination, but I resolved after this experience that at no time while I remained at Moura, would I hold secret conversation with anyone until I had proved to my own satisfaction that there was no possible hiding place for an eavesdropper.

"Well now, Miss Effie," I said briskly, as though nothing more serious was upon my mind, "we should make a beginning by putting you into quite a different wardrobe. And perhaps when you see how you are all the crack with the other young ladies, you will have no necessity to nibble so many sweets, or to run away, and threaten suicide, which is a sin and very wicked."

Even in the dark I could see her eyes sparkle at the prospect of new clothes, if not of suicide, and I was much relieved. Meanwhile, we came to the bottom of the tower, and stepped out into the chill sunlight of the courtyard where we nearly trod upon Kate Moura, who had stooped on a little snowpack to retie the lace-strings of her fashionable sandals.

At the sight of her, Effie gave me a triumphant "I told you as much" look which was not reassuring to me when I recalled my belief that Kate, of all people, could not be involved in the mischief by or against these girls.

"Ah! There you are!" said Kate, dropping crimson taffeta skirts over a much-admired ankle. "Anne . . ." I glanced at her quickly and she amended, "Anne Wicklow, I am to show you about the estate for your future plans."

"Very good," I said, "but first, I must make repairs to this gown."

With just a trace of impudence, Elfreda asked, "Why aren't you up in the Red Salon teaching decorum, Miss Kate?"

Kate's dark eyebrows raised. She said flatly, "Class is out, Miss Effie. Disruptions may be annoying but they are not fatal. Hadn't you better run along to your china painting class? The Master may not remain in his present good mood."

Elfreda blushed and began to look hunted. I was annoyed

with both of them, Kate for having crushed the girl again, and Elfreda for being cowed at the first sign of a reversal. When the girl gazed at me nervously, I tried to encourage her: "Show them all, Miss Effie. Remember that you have had an experience. They will envy you."

Her small, round chin went up and she managed to say in a firm voice, "I shall be mysterious. I shall just hint at my adventure."

"And smile," I reminded her.

She answered me with a big smile and went clattering across the cobblestones toward the students' wing while Kate remarked in a loud voice, "Gad's life! What a flat! One would think such creatures would learn after being thrown in among fashionable young females for days on end." As Kate herself was looking unusually pale in the gaudy light of day, I thought she laid herself open to reprisals for that remark.

"You find her unattractive? I thought her quite charming," I said, trying to disagree with Kate only pacifically. I did not wish to argue the matter when so many important things about Kate and about Moura were still unanswered.

Kate took my arm, leading me off toward the South Wing of the house. "My dear Anne," she said with one of her hoarse, breathy laughs, "how should you know what attractions a fashionable female should possess? You've been a dowd all your life." When I looked amused at the standards by which she rated a woman's attraction, she squeezed me affectionately. "A beautiful Irish dowd! And we all love you just as you are. But, Chérie, you cannot seriously set up for a lady of fashion while you wear a gown of that deep, violent blue in a season when pale cyclamen and amber are the thing. Or to wear a narrow sash when wide ones are invariably worn."

A trifle self-consciously, I began to retie the sash while Kate, with a helpful air, criticized my neckline, the way I wore my hair, its excessive length, and the tightness of my sleeves. I paid little attention to what she said because I began to notice that Kate was breathing heavily and had one hand pressed to her left side, exactly as if she had been hurrying up and down several flights of stairs. Was it remotely possible that the Stavkos had sent her to spy upon the students, and me? If so, she was indeed far from the friend I had once trusted.

"Kate," I broke in finally, "I may be a dowd, but you are certainly a rattle. Now, be serious a moment. What was your meaning when you sent me that letter about unholy doings at the chateau?"

"Oh . . . that!" She shrugged. "I think you must have seen a bit of the cause this morning. Those infernal brats! They are forever throwing difficulties in the way of the Master's plans."

"What are the Master's plans?" I asked, less ironic than curious. Certainly, after my experience with Effie, I was more inclined now to suspect the girls of troublemaking. Effie's tearful and indignant description of bitings by rats, as well as other mischief promoted by her companions, had somewhat revised my suspicions of the Stavkos.

"If he succeeds here as he has in Varna and Budapest and St. Petersburg, it's my hope he will go on to Paris, and even London, establishing these academies. He doesn't like the cities, though; so I expect he will set up his schools in remote places, but within a few days' travel of the capitals. However, no matter where he goes, girls like these silly creatures will invariably throw difficulties in his way with their tricks."

"You mean he and his daughter have had trouble like this before?"

"Invariably. Of course, Lady Tyra is not well, and the Master has to oversee everything."

Considering Tyra Stavko, I had seldom seen a woman who looked so very full of the blood of life—far more so than Kate here—but she seemed unaware of this. We had stepped into the dim, depressing corridor which led to the staircase near my bedchamber and I could not resist the obvious remark, "Then why does Maître Stavko persevere in a profession so unsuited to his . . . family situation?"

Somewhere above us a door slammed and the sound must have aroused Kate to anger. She turned on me passionately, making me take a step backward in haste to avoid her overpowering physical defense of Istvan Stavko. "It is not his fault. It is entirely the fault of that daughter of his." I could not disagree on that score; since I held no brief for Tyra Stavko. "Lady Tyra!" she exclaimed with loathing. "I would not put anything beyond her. And those wretched schoolgirls. All of them, making trouble for him at every turn."

In fairness, I reminded her, "Everyone in the province seems determined on setting difficulties in the way of Master Stavko. He does not look to be a man so easily mistreated, bullied and cowed by a parcel of females."

Jumping to his defense again she began awkwardly, "I do not mean to say he is mistreated by them, precisely. He is too strong for that, too dominating. I meant only—" She breathed a relieved sigh. "We are here," and flung open the door of my room. As she was before me, I did not precisely see what she referred to when she remarked with a laugh, "You have developed some new habits, Cousin. You did not used to be so careless."

Careless was not the word I should have chosen. The room was in a state of disorder bordering on chaos. Some of my clothing removed from the wall pegs and cast upon the floor, the mattresses and coverlet on the bed overturned. Signs everywhere, to me, at least, that there had been vandals here, someone with a childish notion of mischief, or—something more serious. Kate looked at my face and then back to the room. She stooped and picked up my good green spencer with the shoulder epaulette, while I gathered my tasseled reticule and my only pair of *glacé* gloves. As we worked, Kate said, "Just the sort of thing one might expect when you befriended that fat, unattractive child."

"I don't think so," I said; for I was giving this shambles some serious thought, and recalling the slam of the door we had heard. "I believe we interrupted a search of my room."

She stared at me. "Whatever for?"

I was sure I knew the object of the search and I felt for the Moura keys I wore pinned in the folds just below the waistband of my petticoat, but I shrugged.

"I cannot imagine!" I lied. Three years ago I would never have lied to Kate.

VIII

"I AM CONVINCED it was one of those ghastly young females," Kate said positively. "It is exactly the sort of thing they would do!"

I tried to control my annoyance at her effort to ignore the person I really suspected. "In heaven's name, why should the students do this to me? They don't even know me."

We came together as we folded a crumpled sheet, and for a second or two stared into each other's eyes. It was painful to me that there should be such mistrust between us, but I stood my ground, with the conviction that it was she and not I who behaved oddly, unlike herself. Kate spoke suddenly.

"If they did not do it, then who is responsible?"

"Why can't it be Lady Tyra? The boy, Draja, told me she has apartments in this wing." What a fluent liar I was becoming!

Bewildered, Kate backed hard against one of the bed posts while I finished folding the sheet. "Impossible, Anne. Quite impossible!"

"How so?"

"Because she—she sleeps late. Tyra Stavko is never seen out and around before n—" She swallowed and added abruptly, "N-noon."

I had the extraordinary notion that she was about to pronounce some other word and caught herself, but the whole affair was unlikely to be resolved as long as she was bound to the Stavkos; so I gave her up. A pity, I thought, that I had been so stupid as to blurt out my suspicion, but at least I had the dubious satisfaction of discovering that Kate had become a part of whatever evil was here at Moura. Small wonder that she had failed to meet me in the village. She probably wished me at Jericho! And here I was, asking questions, suspecting her precious Stavkos, and perhaps approaching too closely to whatever evil was being perpetrated.

I made a quick, if belated retreat. "I believe you may be right. The students probably saw me with that little Swiversedge girl, and if they really are annoyed at her, playing their tricks with rats and other unappetizing nonsense, this would be exactly their idea of a capital joke."

"Very likely." But Kate was unnerved. I was not mistaken. The minute I mentioned Tyra Stavko she had been alarmed, whether for my safety or, more probably, the Lady Tyra's possible bad health, I could not be certain. I was now satisfied that I would be unable to confide in Kate, even to protect my life. It was a sad, disillusioning business entirely.

I said, with a casual gesture toward the room, "I'll attend to everything here and meet you within the hour, shall I?"

"As you say. In the main hall." She picked up the old rose-flowered cashmere shawl by the door and was preparing to toss it to me when something about it caught her attention. "Is this yours, Chérie?"

I told her Tyra Stavko had loaned it to me last night—forgetting that I had not previously told her of our meeting—and Kate began to examine the dusty, well-worn shawl with extraordinary interest. Then she shook her head.

"It is rather like one belonging to a former pupil here. Girl named Cléa Raines. Funny. We looked everywhere. She wanted it so badly when they took her away."

I was feeling ill-tempered and disappointed as I straightened the room so that I paid less attention than I might have to her chatter. "Well then, we will find the girl's address and see if the post will carry it to her. Where does she live?"

"The Channel Islands. I think Guernsey was her home." She sighed. "Poor creature."

I looked up. "What do you mean—poor creature?"

She caressed the shawl between her fingers, then abruptly tossed it to me, so quickly I was unprepared and almost dropped it. Kate said, "She took a sickness. Just seemed to waste away. Her old nurse and a governess came to fetch her away. Someone wrote the Maître several weeks ago from her home, to report her death. A pity. But then, she never was strong." Kate shrugged and went out into the passage, leaving me with the dusty shawl and a horrid consciousness of death all around me. I handled the shawl with more care now, almost tenderly, as if this care could somehow ease the tragedy of the girl's untimely death.

I did wonder as I remade the bed, whether the mischief at Moura during the present might be caused by the young ladies in revenge for the illness and death of their fellow student. It was a mere vagrant thought. I banished all notions of that sort while I restored the room to some semblance of order. At the same time I was more or less consciously aware that in my refurbishing of the room, I removed some of its chief sources of trouble to me. The bed hangings came down because someone had ripped the hems. Even the candleholders which had once heralded the wake of a young girl in Moura's old days now were tossed away. Someone had examined the bases though I could scarcely have concealed my keys there.

In the end I felt more comfortable with the new room which, in my view, held none of the ominous feeling of its predecessor. When the chamber with its now Spartan severity was at least clean and neat, I changed to one of my two workaday gowns, a lilac wool with Venetian lace collar and cuffs, and went out of my room to the staircase where I paused. According to my agreement with Kate, I should now take this staircase to the courtyard, cross to the East Front of the building and the main hall. But I remembered all too clearly the events of last night as well as my first suspicions of Tyra Stavko today when I saw the results of the search.

From curiosity and certain deep-lying desires to see Lady Tyra's receiving apartment by day, I changed my mind and went hurrying along the corridor as quietly as possible. I followed the same route I had taken last night, lighted by occasional windows facing on the courtyard and set at the end of narrow passages. I passed the steps to the little still-room beside the dining hall and went down the northerly staircase, as far as the courtyard door that had been locked and bolted the first time I saw it last night. It was locked again and I listened briefly, half-fearing that a sudden, silent, gliding Lady Tyra would mysteriously appear out of darkness, as she had to Captain Surtees and me.

I stepped into the corridor where I had originally found several chambers locked. Then, returning with the Captain, I had found our passage made easy, in order to bring him to his mistress. It made me wince even now to admit that relationship. Now the corridor was sealed off again by the locked door. Very much, I thought with a grim smile, like the Perrault Fairy Tales. I touched the keys in the folds of my petticoat, but decided I would not venture to use them at this time. I wanted to preserve as long as possible the secret of their possession. It was bad enough that Lady Tyra, and doubtless her father, should guess I had the keys, but they could not be entirely sure until—and if—they found them or caught me using them.

I turned and started back to the stairs, wondering all the while if Tyra Stavko was asleep in a room off that locked corridor, waiting to awaken at . . . was it to be noon? Or some later hour?

I was relieved to hear the sound of perfectly normal footsteps in the upper corridor. It seemed unlikely that these heralded the furtive, silent movements of Lady Tyra. Whoever it was, the person had just passed my room. A servant at Moura would be doubly welcome to me now. Curiously enough, the only ones I had seen were highly specialized: Draja, the boy, and Matilde, the cook, with her mischievous assistant, Isabeau. Hardly the normal complement of a house with so many members. Still more proof to me, with my preconceived suspicion, that for many reasons, the Stavkos could not keep a respectable staff of servants at Moura.

The light from a narrow window beyond the courtyard door behind me illuminated the staircase while placing me in shadow. I was still on the lowest stairs when a man came around the corner of the corridor above and started down. I had the satisfying experience of catching Istvan Stavko off guard. My own step had apparently been as stealthy as his daughter's; for at sight of me, a shadowed, silent figure in silhouette, he hesitated on the stair. I said nothing, prompted by a mischief I was ashamed of, but his expression in the gray light filtered up from the courtyard window was so very odd, I could not resist the impulse to test his reaction. He, the Master of Moura, whose cold, pale eyes could cut one to pieces with a glance, was suddenly alert, and so tense there was contagion about it. His voice shocked me by its frigid, restrained anger.

"Are you mad? What are you thinking of?" And then followed a burst of condemnation in a language unfamiliar to me, but the emotion was recognizable, despite the incomprehensible words. I suspected, of course, that he believed me to be his daughter. His eyes flashed in that frightening and strangely familiar way, and still I could not imagine where I had seen him before.

I stood my ground, though my knees played me false by their weakness. Istvan Stavko's anger was impressive. I do not know the exact second when he discovered his mistake; for he was skilled enough to recover almost before I took another step upward and into his clearer line of vision.

"Pardon, Monsieur," I said. "I am afraid I don't understand you. Have I displeased you in some way? I know I should be out upon rounds with Miss Kate, but you see, there was a—an accident to my room, and we—"

"Please, Mademoiselle, explanations are not necessary."

He had changed to English, and so quickly, so easily I might almost have imagined the previous violent minute or two. He smiled. I became aware of his mouth, almost, one might say, consciously exciting, and I looked away. He came on down the stairs until he was just above me and I was forced to beg him again to excuse me, this time in order to pass him.

"But why, Miss Anne? I cannot permit you to believe I habitually use such tones to the ladies at Moura. Let me serve in Miss Kate's place and show you our Academy for Select Young Females."

My knees were now firm but I could not seem to recover from that horrid time when he must have taken me for his daughter. What, in such a case, would his attitude be toward anyone who was not so closely related? I shuddered to think of it.

"No," I said. "If you will excuse me. You see, I've forgotten my–" He looked down at me with just the degree of surprise and indifference that reassured me. "As you say, Miss Anne. I suggest you will eventually begin your survey of the household across the court, in the young ladies' wing." He inclined his head slightly. I curtseyed and he would have gone on. But I considered the ridiculousness of my excuse, and turned back.

"Actually, it was only a matter of changing my slippers. But I am at your service if you like, Sir."

"Thank you." He smiled pleasantly, impersonally. I wondered if he had known all along that I would come with him. He made no effort to take my arm, although his good manners were unfailing, once he had discovered I was not the first unfortunate object of all that wrath, his daughter, Tyra.

At the bottom of the stairs as he was reaching into his pocket for a chain of keys, I carefully avoided looking in the direction of the corridor which lay at my back, and cut off, halfway down its length, by that other locked door. Nonetheless, the Maître glanced at me from under his brows, and beyond me to that corridor and the closed door in the distance.

"Have you examined the lower half of the South Wing yet, Miss Anne? Something might be done to refurbish it. It might even be made to serve some useful purpose. But after you have seen it, you will know better than I."

There'll be the devil to pay, I thought, *if he catches me up in a flat out lie. Far better to tell as much of the truth as is necessary. . . .*

"It is very dark, I believe, Sir. I was aroused last night by the banging of a loose shutter and I traced it to a window opening upon the courtyard, off that corridor. Of course, it was not locked last night."

He looked at me as if trying to read into my soul. Indeed, he may have had that capacity. I rejoiced at having told him a reasonable amount of the truth.

"And did you find those rooms very promising?"

"Promising?" I was all innocence. "How? In what way?"

"Did you find the broken shutter?"

"Oh, no! Your daughter attended to that."

"So you met Tyra?" He knew perfectly well I had met his daughter! I was convinced of it now.

"In one of those rooms. Yes. But there was nothing to be done about the shutter, so I left. As I say, the corridor was not locked last night."

"Did you speak with her for very long? Did she point out your duties, that sort of thing, Miss Anne?" There were still slight traces of that Central European accent, but I guessed he hoped to get a fuller explanation—or perhaps entrapment—from me in my own language. It may be, too, that he knew the attraction and power of that accent upon the feminine ear.

"She asked me to carry out a commission for her. But she must tell you that, Sir. It is not my place to do so."

When he smiled and that dangerous, watchful light in his eyes was subdued by a pleasant humor again, I felt I had gone far enough with the truth, while leaving the story of Tyra's rendezvous with Captain Surtees to be handled with the woman's own discretion. At the same time I was not at all sure that the Maître did not know all about the rendezvous. At least, I hadn't committed the serious error of lying about it.

"Well, well," he said as, with a gracious gesture, he ushered me out into the courtyard. "We will see which shutter gave the trouble last night."

I was nearly blinded by the bright midday sunlight, gleaming on the melting patches of snow and I had to blink a couple of times before I could make out the windows of that locked corridor. But the shutter must have been mended during the morning. I was not surprised. The Stavkos thought of everything. I wondered if the Maître believed my story since it was no longer susceptible to proof. I pointed to what I supposed must be the room where I had met the Lady Tyra.

"I believe it must have been that window. The drapes are open, and the shutters are fastened back. She had them repaired, no doubt."

"No doubt," he agreed briefly, and began to cross the courtyard toward the students' wing. I could see some of the gay young faces pressed to the windows, noses flattened, in their curiosity to observe either the school's Master or me, their heretofore unknown housekeeper. I wondered what they thought of me, what portrait Effie Swiversedge had painted of a new housekeeper whose capabilities, or lack of them, would have a deep influence upon the everyday lives and comforts of the young ladies.

"May I ask, Sir, what is the size of the staff at Moura?"

"It varies, but is never large. At the time your predecessor left us some five weeks ago, there were twelve, including the housekeeper herself, and two gardeners, who will not be recalled until a thaw sets in. The cook, two housemaids, a kitchen boy, Old Chamfers, the fellow for odd carpentry. This also includes my own man, Borgos, who acts as my valet, and his wife, Tzigana, something more than my daughter's maid. She has reared Tyra, as she reared Tyra's mother and helps the young ladies in many ways, as well."

"Lady Tyra's mother is dead?"

"These many years." He clipped that off sharply and I

could only suppose it was still a painful subject, though his tone had almost suggested a different emotion. Whatever it was, he obviously had no desire to speak of it; so I tried to clear his dead wife from the subject at hand.

"What maids serve the young ladies?"

"Aside from Tzigana there is a girl named Lotte. She speaks little French and less English, which keeps the chattering to a minimum."

I should think it well might, but I did not say so. Curious, how many of the servants were foreign. As though a deliberate attempt had been made to sever all communication between the students and the Stavko household.

"I count but ten, Sir."

"A maid was dismissed a fortnight ago, and the coachman died the day before your arrival. He broke his neck on one of those steep flights of cellar steps hereabouts. The chateau was not built for comfort."

"The Moura steward was not kept on, then?"

He made way for me to enter the courtyard door of the students' wing by which, early last evening, I had first seen Lady Tyra glide out upon the snowy courtyard. I was so engrossed in these and other puzzling thoughts about the Stavko family that it startled me when, once we were inside the building again, he remarked unexpectedly, "I am surprised that you should know of the Moura steward, Miss Anne."

I lied promptly. "Miss Kate happened to mention him."

"Ah . . . that would explain."

He had almost trapped me, whether accidentally or on purpose, I could not say, but I meant to give him back his own payment in kind.

"Since your coachman is dead, Sir, I assume it was Old Chamfers, as you call him, who carried me to Moura in the pony cart."

He avoided committing himself on Old Chamfers, which was a surprising fact in itself. "What was your opinion of the man who brought you here?"

I shivered. "An odious, frightening creature. He seemed almost capable of—of anything."

This time I could not mistake the faint amusement in his eyes as he agreed, "Very likely," and by taking my hand, indicated that our way was to the right and not the left. Here some improvements had been made since my day. The staircase was carpeted, with candle sconces at every turn, until we reached a gallery which, I confess, had been an empty, unused, and ostensibly haunted passage when my husband first came back from the Wars to refurbish his ancestral home. Between us, we had not had the time or money to restore the North Wing before our life together was at an end. For a brief moment I resented the changes made under the direction of the Stavkos, but I was quickly impressed by the effect upon the students of the Maître's arrival in their midst.

He had just turned to me, looking warmly, and unexpectedly charming, to explain the wainscoting and the newly painted ceilings, when several young ladies almost tumbled out of their rooms into his arms in a spurt of requests, demands and giggles.

"Oh, Maître! Sally says—" "Marie-Monique wants—" "That silly Elfreda insists—"

I did not look at him directly, but as I freed myself from his grasp, went over and curtseyed to Effie Swiversedge, I managed to glimpse the expression on the Master's austere, intellectual face. I did not believe he was pleased at the interruption. I even fancied that in those austere lines of his face was a suggestion of cruelty and dislike for these eager young chatterboxes. Then, as he replied to each quizzing girl with polished good manners, I chided myself for what had been a disquieting conceit on my part. It was hardly likely that a man of his maturity would prefer the company of a widow of twenty-four to these fresh young creatures of fifteen.

Miss Effie flushed at my curtsey and put her hands out, as if she would help me to my feet, but I had already straightened and was looking her over, pleased by her good spirits after the Covent Garden tragedy she had enacted this morning in the turret. She stood on tiptoe and whispered shrilly in my ear, "They're so impressed, you've no notion! Don't tell them I was frightened when you came."

"Certainly, Miss," I agreed promptly, raising my voice. "And an exciting adventure it was!" I could hear the small talk between Maître Stavko and the young ladies, something about a Waltzing Ball they were desirous of holding here at Moura. I could not imagine his consenting. The intimate dance from the Austrian Empire was considered most improper by parents and schoolmistresses of my acquaintance, but meanwhile, Miss Effie had taken me aside to tell me in conspiratorial tones:

"You remember about the rat-bites . . . when I fainted in the night?"

"I remember very well. Are you feeling more the thing now?" I studied her face, her hands, and that portion of her throat bared above the neck frill of her gown, but saw no signs of the rat-bites she had mentioned.

"Well then, Miss Anne . . ." She began to whisper again, which made our actions look inordinately suspicious to anyone who might be watching us. It was a possibility I wanted to avoid at almost any cost. No suspicion must be attached to the girl for the reason that she might fall into danger if it was believed that she saw too much of what was happening, nor could I afford to be too much observed. Then I would not be permitted to move freely about the chateau and find out what crimes—if any—were being enacted here. I was far from believing in Kate's belated disclaimers. The Kate of that early letter posted to me was much more the true, observant Kate of my acquaintance.

"We had a girl here that was taken sick and when they brought her home to Guernsey it was too late and she died."

"Yes. I know. Miss Cléa Raines."

Effie took a big breath and finished in triumph, "I'm not imagining the rats. Cléa complained of the same thing, and Hedi von Preysing, the girl who shared her room, didn't believe it. But now, Hedi shares a bedchamber with me and when the other girls said I was a liar, Hedi believed me."

"Where is she? I would like to speak with her." I looked around for the perceptive Hedi but Elfreda shook her head. "She won't admit it to anyone else. She's afraid. Because of what happened to Cléa Raines."

I could not lay any blame to the girl for that. It was all excessively odd and whether the Stavkos, or the children themselves, were responsible, something serious had certainly occurred here and was continuing to occur. Fearful that my conversation with Elfreda, and especially its air of secrecy, would be noted by the Master, I smiled pleasantly at the girl and patted her on the shoulder.

"You are locking in excellent spirits, Miss Effie, I am happy to say." This was more loudly spoken, for the benefit of any undesired listeners. I said then in lower tones, while pretending to alter the collar of her gown, "What was Miss Cléa's feeling? Whom did she hold responsible for her illness?"

Effie shrugged. "She thought it was one of us, playing tricks. She said her family would—would avenge her."

"Avenge!"

"Not to me, you understand. She said it to Hedi. No one else knew." Her round face puckered up in thought. "Maybe she is avenging herself now. From the grave!"

With difficulty, I prevented myself from feeling a chilly prickle at this remark. But I did look over my shoulder, thinking that the gesture of doing so was the height of absurdity. I saw and heard so much activity between the Master, the chattering girls and a stocky, bovine maidservant whom I took to be Lotte, that I could hardly have expected to see the ghost of the dead Cléa Raines hovering over us.

"Which of the young ladies is Miss von Preysing?" I asked Elfreda.

"She isn't there. She is in our chamber, laid upon her bed with the headache."

It seemed to me that I was under the scrutiny of Maître Stavko, but I could not be sure. He turned from me at just that moment in order to discuss the plea of the languid, tousled beauty who opened the door to me when I arrived at Moura. Nevertheless, I considered his observance of me a warning.

IX

I BEGAN to arrange the new, ugly, puce-colored ribbon with which Effie Swiversedge now bound up her curls.

"Do you have other colors?" I asked, with a frown that I hoped would warn her.

She was gratifyingly quick to understand. "Yes. In my room. I haven't as many pretty ones as Hedi does. But come along, do." She took me by the hand and led me along the hall which was painted a cream color, the paneling with a narrow, gold-leaf scroll, and was altogether a cheerful place, lighted and warmed by sunlight from the open doors of the young ladies' chambers. Before we reached the room Effie shared with Hedi von Preysing, she said casually, "Tzigana is with her now, feeding her a beef jelly—ugh!—but it should serve very well if we can be rid of the gypsy. . . . Hedi speaks that awful language the Maître and Lady Tyra speak in private sometimes; so Tzigana likes Hedi better than us, I think. Not that I care!"

For an instant I could not place the gypsy name, but then I recalled that she and her husband, Borgos, were personal servants to the two Stavkos. In the present circumstances at Moura, I pictured in my mind's eye this gypsy woman, rough, dark, violent, with a power of the evil eye. It was, therefore, a pleasant surprise to see the elegant, almost dainty woman with a halo of fine-spun white hair that shone in the sunlight with an occasional thread of its original red-gold color. She was sitting on the side of a four-postered white bed that had no tester or curtains, and she looked up and rose as we entered. Her eyes were brightly, eerily blue. Even as I admired the lovely gentlewoman—and she appeared all of that—I was aware of the mesmeric power of her eyes as their gaze flicked over me. I smiled at her, acknowledging with an inclination of the head her curtsey to me. I would be, technically, her immediate employer in the household.

"How is your patient?" I asked as Miss Effie and I crossed the room to the bedside of the dark, thin Austrian girl who pushed away the spoon and the bowl of jelly which Tzigana had been persuading her to eat.

The girl's voice was querulous as she cut in, before Tzigana could answer me, "Dreadful! Ghastly! I am forever having headaches. All my life. I must be calm—left alone—until they go away. Everyone knows that except this hateful old witch."

Tzigana gave me a helpless look and shrugged as she retrieved the bowl and spoon before they could be overturned.

"Poor child!" she explained to me while Effie went over to talk to her roommate. "I have known these cases many times. A migraine, you understand. I am afraid, without her cooperation, nothing can be done." She spoke remarkably well, with only a trace of accent, and I wondered that this woman, so well-mannered, so lovely, with both compassion and dignity, could have reared that sinister and cold beauty, Lady Tyra Stavko.

"I wonder if I may speak to the young lady," I suggested and before I could go on, I was interrupted by the rudeness of Effie, who cut in abruptly:

"The Maître wants you, Tzigana. We'll take care of Hedi."

The old woman looked as perplexed at Effie's behavior as I did. She started for the open doorway, hesitated, then said to me apologetically, "I wonder if it might wait until later. The child badly needs calm and sleep."

"Yes, of course. I'm sorry." I felt that I had pressed too hard, been too anxious, thus giving the very weight to my request which I hadn't wanted anyone but Effie herself to suspect. For this reason, I now made a strategic retreat, pretending the matter was of little importance.

In the end it was Effie and I who left the room. When we looked back, Tzigana had put a cold compress to the sick girl's head, and was saying in her pleasant, low voice: "Sleep, my dear. . . . Think pleasant thoughts and sleep."

Effie closed the door, then whispered fiercely to me with clenched teeth: "I hate her! I do hate that old witch!"

I was so astonished that I found myself at a complete loss and could only stare at the girl's violent, contorted little face.

"Nonsense!" I said sternly after recovering from this totally unwarranted violence. "She is a very ladylike and genteel woman. Nothing of the gypsy camp about her. She wore a shawl and gown such as your own grandmother might have worn. And her manners were far better than yours, Miss Effie."

"Much you know!" the girl muttered.

I determined to ignore these bad manners but it was difficult to ignore young Effie. When I went to ask the Master's permission to join Kate, Effie came pattering after me with the reminder, "When will you see to my wardrobe, Miss Anne? Can we send to a mercer's shop for lengths of new muslin, and silk, and ribbons, and bonnets . . . ?"

"Yes, yes. But later." I wanted to ask her to find out what she could about Hedi von Preysing's knowledge of the doings at Moura, but there was too great a danger of being overheard, so I put this off to a later time, when I might combine it with the ostensible subject of refurbishing Effie's wardrobe. I said, "I must get permission from the Master, perhaps from your guardians as well."

"Oh, fusty business! Do you promise?"

"I promise."

She retreated then, looking excited at her future prospects, and as Stavko joined me, glancing after her stocky little figure, he asked me, "What witchcraft have you performed? The child looks very nearly pretty."

My thoughts were upon her briefly as I replied without considering what I said, "It is having someone care about her. I told her no more than her companions here, that her garments, their style and color, were not becoming. But I gave her hope for improvement. Hope is the most precious of all gifts, to my notion."

His smile at this was strangely warm in the frigid arrogance of his face. It nearly warmed me with the feeling that one has when an awesome stranger may yet become a friend. Like Effie Swiversedge, I too needed reassurance. Was it thus, I asked myself in a realistic vein, that he had completely dominated my old friend and confidante, Kate Moura?

"Just so, Miss Anne," and taking my arm, he began to continue our tour of the complex old chateau until we approached Kate herself in the gallery joining the students' wing with the main hall of Moura. The gallery had been painted, repaneled and in many cases, was much lighter where full-length window portieres replaced warped shutters, but all this almost excessive window-space gave the long gallery a gray look, reflecting the wide sky which had begun to cloud over and promised more snow by nightfall.

My first sight was of Kate, in a gown of black velvet—surely an odd choice by day!—but a flattering one at any hour, setting off what had always been her rich, voluptuous beauty. It served as a background to a dark jewel on her capacious bosom. The jewel flashed, now wine red, now glowing like a blackened coal, and Kate fingered it self-consciously. I had never seen her wear it in the old days. Either the shade of the gown or the colorless daylight pressing in at the windows gave Kate the same unnatural pallor I had noticed before. It was still disquieting in the healthy, almost muscular woman I thought I knew so well.

She was obviously waiting to catch Monsieur Stavko and I only hoped she did not think I had deliberately maneuvered to get the Master to myself. She came forward and took Stavko's other arm. I, of course, freed myself from his loose hold upon me the instant I saw her, but she may have seen the gesture despite my effort. I bobbed a slight curtsey to her, for the benefit of the watching Stavko, but I was made aware at once that she wanted to be rid of me.

"May I be excused?" I suggested, with the logical explanation, "I should like to speak with Cook about the various meals ahead, the obtaining of food . . . That sort of thing."

The Maître glanced from Kate to me and I had the unpleasant sensation that he was about to throw difficulties in the way of my peacekeeping efforts, but he changed his mind, agreed courteously, "By all means, Miss Anne. I will speak with you later in the day. About the—ah—studies of the young ladies. I should like them to be conversant with duties in a great English household so that they may know the staff problems."

I curtseyed. "As you wish, Sir," and walked away along the gallery. The accoustics were such, however, that I could still hear Kate's conversation with him, even as I was at the far end of the lengthy gallery:

"The fellow has come. A tutor in history, he says. But mark me, Istvan, he has an easy eye for a female. There is liable to be trouble. Someone is sure to find out about the crime. If the girl had been of good family, he would not be walking free with blood on his hands."

"Don't dramatize," said the Master icily, but he went to a window high over the courtyard and looked out. Kate stood close to him, likewise staring at the courtyard below.

Meanwhile, I was very much in the position of an eavesdropper. I hurriedly left the gallery and found myself in an upper hall of the East Front, where my husband and I had made our home. I tried to keep my duties in mind; yet I could not but wonder at the employment of a man "with blood on his hands" as Kate expressed it. I thought it must be a typical exaggeration on Kate's part, and if so, she had likely exaggerated when she wrote summoning me.

On the other hand, if Kate had come under some sinister and bloodthirsty influence of the Stavkos, why would she still be concerned for whatever evil things were happening here? In any case, from what I had just overheard, such matters as a man's "bloody hands" in no way disturbed the Maître Stavko. Of the developments at Moura thus far, I must remember the Master's reaction above all. I must remember this every time I was tempted by the Master's occasional smile or his fascinating accent to soften my suspicions of him.

I passed the broken North Parapet and noted that someone had placed a barrier of low stones across the outer and unprotected edge, one story above the entrance drive. I was amused at my own momentary annoyance to find this change. I had made so many mental criticisms of the rest of Moura under the Stavkos that I was beginning to resent even the improvements.

I walked over to the edge and looked down at the bare, stone front of Moura. Beyond the narrow, pebbled driveway was the moat, sluggish as ever, but at the moment faintly veiled by snow, which improved its appearance. The boy, Draja, was down on the little moat bridge about to exercise a very creditable-looking mare which I supposed must have brought the bloody-handed history tutor to Moura. At least, the fellow had made Draja happy. He was very good with the sleek, black mare, gentle, but with a firm hand. I hoped he would know what to do if the mare caught a whiff of one of the wolves foraging through the woods. From Draja's attitude, I thought he knew his problem better than I did.

I went back into the corridor past the master apartments I once shared with my husband. More or less by accident, I had already played the eavesdropper today and I felt it would be an ignominious thing, surely, to be caught peering into Istvan Stavko's bed chamber; yet I was delighted to discover that someone had thoughtfully, in my opinion, left the door open almost my arm's length. The curiosity was uncontrollable. I stopped and, without leaving the passage, gazed at the room I had known so long and so intimately.

The great bed-hangings were incredibly enough, the same as those we had known, deep and heavy crimson. The room's masculine furnishings were Moura-owned, all as my husband had left them. The portieres, the carpet, the armoire, the little table by the door . . . all as they had been. All but the dust, the look of disuse. It was as if no human being had entered this room since my own departure three years ago. Greatly tempted, I ran my forefinger over the familiar little table beside the door.

Emphatically, this household had a pressing need for a housekeeper! When I examined my fingertip, it was quite black with dust. Perhaps the room really was not occupied by Stavko. There was a cloak hung on a peg near the armoire, and the cloak looked new, clean, very much in the present style, with its many capes and its length. And certainly, the shooting jacket I had seen the Master wearing earlier today, and which he had changed when I met him a second time, was now carelessly thrown over the Milord chair across the room. So I must assume Istvan Stavko did occupy this chamber. An extraordinary business it was!

I went on to the stairs, more and more perplexed. I was aware of endless possibilities, one of which was that Stavko used the chamber as a tiring room and actually slept elsewhere. However, there was so much which aroused my curiosity, even my fear, that this latest puzzlement was all of a piece with the rest.

Meanwhile, though, there was my own work to be done. I had accomplished very little to this moment and until I found proof of any crime committed here, any unholy doings, I must, at the very least, fulfill the tasks for which I was hired. I owed that to my own sense of honor, as well as to my employer. On my way to the kitchen, I walked the length of the great, brooding main hall, remembering the students' request that a Waltzing Ball be held. I thought how odd this room would look with a dozen young females whirling along under its sooty rafters, and the room full of girlish laughter, perhaps for the first time in its nine hundred year history.

Matilde was busy giving orders for the young ladies' luncheon when I arrived. When the girls and Draja finally set off to serve in the small drawing room which, I gathered, was now the students' dining hall, I discussed the menus for the week with Matilde and asked her opinion of the previous housekeeper, since there seemed a deal of unfinished business in that department.

"Ay, that one. Hopeless, I swear, Madame."

"Mademoiselle," I reminded her, after a glance around.

"Well, then. Worse even than yourself when you first came to Moura. Yes. Worse even than that."

I had to laugh at her ingenious way of insulting me over the shoulder of the departed housekeeper, but I reminded her, "You have not told me in what way she was impossible."

"High spirits," she grumbled.

"High spirits? But I don't understand. Why—"

"Strong spirits," she corrected herself. "That ancient harridan is into the bottles forever. And drunk before those young females."

"Then there was nothing—strange. Nothing mysterious about her dismissal by Monsieur Stavko?"

"Ah, that, now! The only strangeness is that she was not earlier dismissed." Then Matilde turned and looked me full in the face. She could be impressive at such moments. "You need look no further in that direction for mysteries, believe me. What happens at Moura is of much more strangeness."

"In what way?"

She shrugged. "Me, I work. I cook and see to the home gardens, the wine cellars, the so-special foods for so-special persons. These are what I do. The strangeness, the diet of starvation for the Lady Tyra, the dainty jellies for the silly, giggling young things . . . they are for you to say. Once, I told M'amselle Kate of this. She said it is a place for you."

"Matilde! You talked to Mademoiselle Kate about suspicious things here?"

"And she tells me later—to forget it. She tells me we were wrong, she and I. So?"

This only bore out my own conclusions that Kate had come under someone's spell. The evidence indicated that it was the Stavkos rather than some mischievous girls. I asked, "Was anything else attempted? Was any magistrate informed?"

Matilde banged pots and pans together before throwing them into a wooden tub to clean. "But, of course. After the young miss was sent home to the Channel Islands, the *Procureur du Roi,* the King's Prosecutor, you know, sent a man here. All was as it should be and he went away, but it is said at Moura that the family of this Raines female sent the man."

So there had been investigations that came to nothing! This would mean either that the doings at Moura were innocent, or that the guilty parties were thoroughly prepared for investigations. I would have given a good deal to know the history of the Stavkos at their previous Academies for Young Females, but at present there seemed to be no way in which such information might be obtained by me. I had neither money nor influence, and could not rely upon the post for delivery of letters to places like St. Petersburg and Varna—wherever that might be.

When Matilde and I had made plans for a more varied diet involving frequent use of vegetables preserved in the cellars through the barren winter, and less use of Matilde's great all-purpose food, lumpy porridge, we made certain changes in the duties of the maids and the kitchen boy wherein the hearth of a small parlor adjoining the students' dining salon should be used to heat and often to prepare meals for the young ladies. In this way, everything ought to be served freshly cooked, or at least warm.

By the time I myself sat down to delicious new-baked bread, a small variety of preserved vegetables from the cellars, and a glass of the sour local wine, I felt that a considerable amount had been accomplished in my capacity as housekeeper. There would be much that needed doing about the laundry and such day-maids as were hired during the weekly housecleaning or upon special occasions, but the linens, I discovered, were all cleaned by two widowed sisters who were estate tenants and came to the postern gate weekly, riding a tumbrel drawn by a tired old mare.

Everywhere I turned, I found barriers between the inhabitants of Moura and any outside knowledge of them. I suspected that for the weeks immediately before I came, the gracious and dignified Tzigana had handled my post, and I was pleasantly surprised that the gypsy appeared to bear me no malice.

"How curious!" I remarked to Matilde late in the day as a complaining Isabeau and I came back to recover the food-stained kitchen linen for our bundles to be deposited at the postern door. I had just encountered Tzigana briefly while the woman arranged a dainty tea-tray to entice Hedi von Preysing to eat. "Have you ever known a gypsy with blue eyes and fine hair like that?"

Matilde grunted. "That one!" She took a cloth and reached into the great fireplace to draw the blackened kettle toward her on its hook. She stirred the staff's dinner of stew with lamb and kid and vegetables bubbling in a savory liquid, but as Isabeau's uncombed head raised and the girl started to say something about my comment, she caught the quick look from Matilde's stern, dark eyes and subsided.

I was annoyed by all this secrecy and burst out impatiently, "Will you be telling me now, what it is you know of her? She has been very respectful to me, and helpful to the students. She is most efficient, and seems good tempered." My fingers itched to box the ears of the saucy Isabeau, who giggled and then rolled her eyes knowingly.

"Out!" Matilde commanded the girl, with a gesture of one red elbow that even intimidated me. The girl made a flippant *moue* with her sultry lips and retreated, but I noticed that she remained in the stillroom doorway, listening. Matilde gave a heavy sigh, hit the stew kettle, and as the deep metallic ring died away, she asked the abrupt question, "You do not fear the evil eye?"

This had very little to do with the genteel old lady I had seen and I was puzzled. "Are we speaking of Tzigana, Lady Tyra's maid? I believe she is more than a maid. I saw her attending Mademoiselle Hedi this morning with an almost motherly affection. She seems amazingly efficient."

Matilde came away from the fireplace and studied me with the dripping wooden spoon still between her fingers.

"You think the devil's eye is black? But no, silly one! Always, so long as they tell tales of witches and their Familiars, and Vampyres and the Vorlog of the forests—so long it is known that blue is the evil eye, and red is the hair."

"B-but the woman's hair is—"

"It is white now. But once, many years gone by, when the world was younger, her hair was red. I can tell."

I had long been told that the devil had red hair; yet this . . . I stood staring at her a few seconds before the incredible absurdity of it washed over me and I began to laugh. "That would make an Evil One out of every person with blue eyes and red hair. Matilde, you have been listening to too many ghost tales."

She was a woman of uncertain temper and my laughter seriously ruffled her; so I left the kitchen and went my way, completing my rounds of the open wings in the chateau; for I wished to know also if we had forgotten the linen anywhere, and what areas should be refurbished or opened to use, and what should be closed. These were my superficial reasons. Beneath all this deliberate physical exertion, however, I was aware of dreadful, gnawing worries about the people here at Moura, about their health, their danger, and the possible guilt of some among them. I knew that a cautious, discreet woman would turn her back upon this place with its memories, its corruption and a possibly monstrous secret. But I needed the urgency of this, the necessity to keep myself constantly busy. Even the terror was a spur to my thoughts. It kept them from dwelling on the dead past.

Late afternoon, tired and dusty after my trek through endless chambers, salons and galleries, I walked the length of the main hall. I was on my way to the kitchen quarters across the passage when a movement outside the long east windows attracted my attention. To my astonishment, when I went to the window and looked out, I saw Captain Surtees on the further edge of the moat bridge, looking every bit the dashing rogue.

This time the Captain was out of uniform and I thought his fashionable fawn-colored pantaloons and the many-caped greatcoat did his tall, trim figure no disservice. The boots too, with their reversible tops . . . In short, I was sorry, indeed, that his sole purpose in visiting Moura was a rendezvous with Lady Tyra!

Bars of sunlight, shooting downward through a heavily clouded sunset, managed to make the Captain's breeze-blown ruddy hair look all ablaze, and I smiled, recalling my conversation with Matilde about Evil Ones and red hair. The Captain had a walking stick which he used much as the Maître Stavko had wielded his willow wand, pointing it at various aspects of the building's facade. I couldn't imagine what he was about, and when he suddenly saw me and waved the walking stick in salutation, I found myself waving back. He made gestures of talking and pointing again at the front of Moura. I did not understand him, even when he motioned toward the edge of the woods and two of the young school girls came out, giggling, of course.

One of the girls, tightly buttoned into a spencer too small for her, was my friend, Miss Effie Swiversedge. Her companion was the languid, pretty girl, Rosemary Tynford, who had met me at the door when I arrived yesterday.

Had it only been yesterday? It seemed to me that I had been here for an eternity, plucking away at endlessly renewed spider webs.

"Come out!" Miss Effie beckoned to me unmistakably, but I shook my head.

. . . What under heaven is Captain Surtees up to with those girls?

He joined Miss Effie in vigorously beckoning to me, and after a struggle with myself, I obeyed. The only explanation that occurred to me was that the Captain had found these girls out walking and befriended them in order to get inside Moura for his rendezvous. He must certainly have a great attachment for Tyra Stavko. Not that I should be surprised,

I told myself, admitting finally that Tyra's beauty was exceptional.

I went out on the moat bridge, shivering in the wind but undeniably warmed by the toothy smiles that greeted me. Even young Rosemary deigned to show some enthusiasm. While the Captain kissed my hand, with absurdly elaborate politeness, Effie burst out, "The most famous thing, Miss Anne! We've an officer from the Wellesley Brigade to tutor us in history."

I stared at the Captain, who looked at me as innocently as that highly sophisticated face could look.

"You are to be their tutor at Moura?" I asked.

He pretended to be hurt but I knew he was amused. "My lovely colleen doesn't seem at all pleased. May one ask why?"

That I could not bring myself to tell him. I was still stunned by the discovery that Edward Surtees was the man Kate shrank from. Even Kate, who was under the spell of the mysterious Stavkos, could not bring herself to accept this "bloody-handed" tutor, Captain Surtees!

X

"It comes to me as something of a surprise, Captain," I said and tried to make my smile appear natural. "I had no notion you were versed in history, of all things."

"Of all things," he mimicked, grinning at me over the heads of his young pupils, "it seemed the least likely to trip me up."

I mouthed the word "fraud" to him, trying to avoid the girls' inquisitive eyes, but Effie caught our expressions, first his and then mine, as he murmured with a mock-plaintive air, "A touch, a touch. Your point, Anne—my girl."

"You call her Anne?" Effie wanted to know, staring at him wide-eyed. "She's not precisely a servant, you know. So you can't call her *my girl* either."

"You've made her blush, in any case," remarked the detestably observant Rosemary.

"So I see. Delightful, isn't it?" and with that, much to my relief, the Captain began to point at the bleak, stone front of the chateau with his walking stick, explaining in the most educated way, the ages of the various additions. As this was far beyond my own education, I started to retreat, but the Captain was unexpectedly knowledgeable and, reaching out with his free hand, caught my skirts. Effie giggled at my attempts to extricate myself without embarrassment. What a rogue the fellow was!

Rosemary, for her own reasons, was disgusted at these goings-on, and cut rudely into the Captain's lesson in architecture.

"You had best attend to your history, Sir, because the Master says one cannot do two things successfully at once."

The Captain looked at me and laughed, but without letting me go, he favored me the severe criticism, "You hear, Miss Anne? Why do you dally? Miss Rosemary does not wish you to reach her high level of education."

"I dislike it excessively," said the young lady, who saw no humor in his remark. "She is only a housekeeper, after all, and education should be reserved for those who may profit by it. In my view—"

Effie interrupted to call her a "fusty, pompous little silly!" and they appeared about to come to blows when I tried to calm them. But here I found it necessary to defend myself mentally as well as physically from the Captain's amused command in an undervoice, "Let them quarrel. It will give me more time to discuss the history of architecture with you."

I found it difficult to remember that this devilishly charming man had a past even more unsavory than my suspicion of the Stavkos. However, from past experience I had learned it was vital to my status at Moura that I should not receive a setdown in the presence of the students.

I made no more moves to free myself. Though my back was to the chateau, I made up the most logical excuse that might serve. "I suggest, Sir, that you may be under observation from friends a trifle more mature than these young ladies. I am persuaded you will not wish to begin your work at Moura in their bad graces."

The Captain chided me, "What pompous remarks from those romantic lips!" A remark that I ignored as mere buttering of the compliments he uttered so lavishly, but then, as he glanced over my head at the battlements of Moura, I saw his features change. The girls had both gasped, and I swung around uneasily. At first, I noted only the time-blackened stone facade, but as my gaze traveled upward against the fiery aftermath of sunset, I saw the Lady Tyra Stavko standing on the battlements, her pristine white wool cloak rustling around her like the wings of a bird of prey in the evening breeze. She was looking down at us and though I could not see her eyes in the silhouette she made against the sky, I could well imagine their cold, metallic gleam fastened upon us.

The Captain stared at his inamorata with a puzzled frown. Then he looked at me, returning to his teasing, sardonic air. "Remarkable! Truly remarkable! I'd no notion you could see through the back of that Irish head of yours. . . . Well, young ladies—" This to the gaping girls. "Our Miss Anne has unsuspected talents. And now, we would do well to get indoors before some of Miss Anne's wolfish friends come stalking after us."

The girls exchanged uneasy glances, but an instant later they were clattering across the moat bridge without even looking over their shoulders. Captain Surtees and I followed at a pace an observer might call leisurely but not, I hoped, quite deliberate enough to anger the woman on the battlements. I confess that even after my short acquaintance with her, I was by no means courageous enough to desire her enmity.

The white-haired Tzigana met us in the passage outside the great hall and Rosemary ran to her with obvious pleasure. Just as obviously, Effie stopped at sight of the pleasantly smiling woman and with a sly look at me wrinkled her nose in distaste. I tried to conceal her aversion by speaking quickly to Tzigana.

"The young ladies have been taking lessons from Monsieur Surtees on the history of the chateau's architecture. I hope they understood the subject better than I."

Tzigana agreed with me in her dignified way that was like her smile, deliberate and warm. She spoke to me in her excellent English with its soft hint of accent. "I quite agree, Miss Anne. I too find other subjects more—shall we say—more sympathetic to my interests. The past, when it deals with humanity, however, is a different thing. I feel that it is a part of me. As I am a part of the past." She made a little graceful gesture, adding politely, "But then, I am much older than you, child."

Miss Rosemary complained she was hungry, and with a flippant wave at me, she took Tzigana's hand and I thought they would have walked away, but Effie held back. Both the gypsy woman and I looked at the girl, I with a feeling of responsibility for her that I had felt since our encounter in the East Tower, and Tzigana in a perplexed way. It was she who said whimsically, "The dinner should be very special, very superior tonight, Miss Elfreda. It was chosen by Miss Anne."

"Oh? That's different!" Effie's head went up. It was at once embarrassing and gratifying. She gave me a big grin. "Did you truly plan the dinner, Miss Anne?"

"Only in part. Matilde planned the whole."

"Then, at least, we shan't be poisoned," Effie remarked with a dogged raising of her chin. While Tzigana murmured something wearily to me about children, Rosemary pulled on Effie's arm.

"Oh, Effie! Don't be so everlastingly tiresome. Do come along."

To my great relief, they went off toward the courtyard and the students' wing, followed at a more sedate pace by Tzigana. It was only then that I allowed myself to look around, mentally making up some excuse to the Captain for Miss Effie's behavior, and saw that he was gone. How quickly he must have hurried to Lady Tyra's side! It was a very lowering reflection.

In some secret agitation I ate my dinner with the staff in their dining parlor. At least, this served two purposes. I had the company of lively Draja, the chattering gossip Isabeau, and the others, including Old Chamfers, whose age and half-blind eyes showed me at once that he had not been the malign and knowing coachman who drove me to Moura. The other purpose served was that their company kept me from reflecting upon the real character of the dashing Captain Edward Surtees.

I learned nothing useful to my secret investigation at dinner, but I did manage to accomplish that object exceedingly important to any housekeeper. I became better acquainted with my staff and hoped I had persuaded them that I could be trusted, both as their taskmaster and their friend. It took some doing with the dull, lethargic Lotte, but eventually she smiled when I was able to persuade Matilde to give her an extra jam-tart for dessert. We parted on these excellent terms.

The evening was to be devoted to mending linen and trimming and replacing the lamps in the several leagues of corridors that made up the ancient house. I had scarcely completed my first round through the corridors on the East Front and was about to begin upon the South by crossing one side of the medieval dining hall, when I realized that the enormous room was occupied. At the far end of the hall the head of the table was brightly lighted by several branches of candles. Faces stared at me and because of the distance as well as the lights and shadows between us, I could not at once identify them, but I began to retreat, aware that I had blundered upon my employers, dining in regal style in a hall that would have accommodated fifty in comfort or a hundred with a trifle less elbow-room.

I had already been seen, however, and with my hand

upon the high, heavy latch of the nearest door, I was summoned back by the authoritative voice of Istvan Stavko.

"Stay, Miss Anne." As I hesitated, he added belatedly, "If you please." I remained in my place, not certain what to expect, rather hoping I had done nothing amiss. I should have very much preferred not to be in Master Stavko's bad graces. He looked to be a man who had strong views about failure or work done carelessly.

Like a deep, metal chime came Lady Tyra's voice. "Father, you frighten the child. Come nearer, Anne. Let us see if it is really you or a wraith who prowls these corridors so silently."

I resented her description of me as "prowling" but to add the plaint that I was stealthily silent was merely to describe herself and I had a strong desire to tell her so. I kept my Irish temper in check, though. Long experience in such posts had inured me to accusations of various sorts. As I advanced down the room I did think it more than a trifle strange that she should think of me as "child." She had not appeared to be above thirty at the outside, and I was twenty-four. Perhaps, though, like her father and her maid, Tzigana, she felt herself a part of history, even a part of the past.

As I came into the circle of brightness that surrounded them at the far end of the heavy baronial table, I saw four people, dressed for dinner, with an elegance surprising in an area so far from the fashionable town houses of France. Stavko and his daughter shared the head of the table, with Kate Moura at one side, on the Master's right, and Captain Surtees across from her, to the left of Lady Tyra. I curtseyed deeply, while I tried to determine the precise feelings of Kate and the Captain. The latter, looking handsome in his regimentals, gave me a pleasant greeting which I considered odiously familiar.

"My compliments, Anne. You remembered that I dislike damp sheets and prefer my bechambers well aired. Thank you."

Lady Tyra's dark brows were raised as she gazed from

him to me, and while she hardly looked pleased, this was more than made up for by Kate's friendliness. I was not so stupid as to imagine that it was the old, dear friend who gave me a "Good evening, Chérie. Gad's life but you are looking well after such a strenuous day!" Kate was being her charming self for the same reason that Lady Tyra disliked me. Both of them suspected there was some prior liaison between the Captain and me, a notion that Kate must relish if she imagined I might otherwise have designs on Istvan Stavko. Such a double misapprehension was quite enough to set my teeth on edge.

The last of the four to address me after that moment of my entrance into the medieval dining hall was the person whose reaction I awaited now with an additional irritation of the nerves. The Maître Stavko had been watching me closely, almost suspiciously, to my heightened imagination. I was forever sensible of a guilty conscience; since I really had come to Moura under false pretenses. The cold, ageless, icy look in his eyes perceptibly softened as I looked at him, straight and direct, for the first time, and I was conscious of a kind of inner weakness. Not quite the tingle of physical warmth a man like Captain Surtees could arouse in a female, but a strange, mesmeric quality which made it difficult for me to look away from him. Absurdly enough, the effect of all this was to make me drowsy. Hardly a romantic symptom, or flattering to Stavko.

When he spoke it was sensibly, in a businesslike way that knocked all such silly notions completely out of my head. "You are precisely the person I wish to see, Miss Anne, once dinner is completed. I would appreciate having your opinion upon some papers my pupils have prepared on the subject of overseeing a large household, and more especially, a large staff. Most of our young ladies will be marrying such problems. We desire in particular to prepare those who come into the peerage through the wedding band."

"Very sensible, I am sure, Sir," I said in equally businesslike tones.

"Excellent. I will expect you in an hour, shall we say?

In what I believe"—he looked inquiringly at Kate—"is called the green parlor."

"The green velvet room," she corrected him and then, noting how my body stiffened, for I was standing nearest her chair, she looked up at me, and in her handsome dark eyes was the familiar, warm look of the old, lovable Kate. "Anne, you will find the green velvet room very easily." She glanced at the others, explaining, "It has a history in this household."

I knew quite well about the green velvet withdrawing room which was an attractive little salon down the corridor from the great hall and formerly used by the Moura ladies, during the gentlemen's session with their after-dinner wines. The chamber's importance otherwise was as a haunted room, and for that problem, I had no remedy. I did not believe in ghosts, but neither did I believe my eyes deceived me when they made out strange doings in the room.

"Yes, Miss Kate. I will find the room. I thank you." But I did not like it, and Kate knew it. She had once shared my disagreeable feelings about the place.

While I made my brief curtsey, I managed a brief glimpse of the eating habits of the four. In regard to Kate and the Captain, nothing could have been more natural. They both were finishing a second course, consisting of a succulent roast of lamb with vegetables, a sauce redolent of herbs and the juice of the meat, and were about to embark upon the sweets. They had completed a first course of a local carp unusually but successfully poached, with fresh greens from the forcing house of the home garden.

Istvan Stavko and his daughter were quite another, and far more curious matter. Their pewter plates looked as pristine and gray for the second course as, I began to feel, they had looked after the first course. They obviously had different dining hours and merely made a pretense of eating with Kate and Captain Surtees. Maître Stavko was sipping a local red wine, Lady Tyra, on the other hand, drank nothing but water.

I left them all to their odd diet and went on my way.

Before meeting Master Stavko, I stopped by the students' wing and found most of the young ladies in their parlor, chattering while one or two worked at some rather appalling china painting. The pretty Tynford sisters were telling fortunes with a pack of cards that I recognized as the gypsy Tarot, and I supposed they came from Tzigana, who was not in the little salon.

As the room shared by Effie and Hedi von Preysing was close by, I went on and rapped at the door. Effie herself came to meet me with her finger to her lips.

"Hush! She's finally gotten to sleep. What a time she's had! Poor Hedi!"

"Is there anything I may do? Anything to bring?" I asked but Effie said there was not. She looked up and down the hall furtively, then motioned me closer. I should have been prepared. Her eyes were dramatically narrowed.

"Miss Anne . . . It's small wonder Hedi is sleeping. You know what that dreadful old crone did?"

I sighed. She must be referring to the dignified and gentle old lady who had impressed me with her excellent sense. "What did she do, Miss Effie? What wicked thing?"

"She fed her a drug. Hedi wanted to see you. I know she did. And Tzigana fed her laudanum drops. Isn't that horrid?"

I said practically, "It depends entirely upon the purpose of the drops, I should think."

This did not satisfy Effie, who reminded me tragically, "If I am fed laudanum drops, I hope you will know it was—it was unwillingly."

I wanted to smile at the tragic grandeur of her attitude, which was so very like what she was, an imaginative little girl, that I found it difficult to take her seriously, so I replied to her half-plea, half threat, with the assurance that if she was given laudanum for a severe case of migraine, I would have something to say about it. At the same time, I looked around her at the dark-haired girl on the pale bed and wondered when I would be able to speak with her.

"Let me know at once when she is able to talk to me," I said. "You know where to find my bedchamber?"

"Yes." Then she grew suddenly exuberant. "Or in Matilde's kitchen. When I find life insupportable, I go there. The old witch of a cook is dreadful, but I like the warm room and the smell of all those good things cooking."

I smiled ruefully at the realization that any woman older than Effie must, of necessity, be referred to as an old witch, but I reminded her that if she was to have a fine, handsome figure like the prettiest of the other students, she must think less of the kitchen and more of restraining her extravagant diet. She pouted but promised, and as I was leaving her, I nearly trod upon the toes of Tzigana, who was close behind me when I turned around.

"Has the Master finished dinner?" I asked the woman. "Then I must go."

"Yes. The Master believes in punctuality." She smiled. "It is absurd, for he has all the time in the world. . . . But so it is."

Upon the spur of the moment I lied fluently. "Miss Hedi is unhappy with the condition of her mattress and bedstead. I shall be in to see her later this evening. Or perhaps in the morning." I said this to test her, but the woman nodded agreement in her quiet way.

"Tonight would be best, if you are not otherwise engaged, Miss Anne. If her sleeping conditions are not their best, she will hardly be restored to good health. The girl has taken a few drops of laudanum but that will have worn away shortly. The migraine, you know."

There had been no attempt to keep me from seeing Hedi later in the evening. If the woman had been the poisoning witch Elfreda made her out to be, she would scarcely have suggested I return the same evening. There would have been talk of postponing my interview, of seeing her tomorrow or another time. Nothing could have been more honest, pleasant and straightforward than Tzigana's attitude.

I looked at the belligerent Effie, trying, with a smile and a significant nod, to indicate that she had been rather beforehand in her accusations, but the girl slammed the door shut in Tzigana's face and mine. It was simply no use trying to break down that curious fixation of Effie's. I tried to think of something to bridge the awkwardness as I left, but the gypsy shrugged. She seemed used to these bad manners, though I thought a little color appeared on her high cheekbones.

A few minutes later I had banished the girls from my mind briefly while I girded myself to enter that nasty, unhealthy green velvet room and spend several evening hours in the company of Istvan Stavko, an ideal companion in such a place. Strange, though, what an effect he gained when he wished to be conciliating. I must watch that as I must guard myself even more in Captain Surtees' company. That man whose bloody past was demonstrably true or false, was very likely the more dangerous of the two men.

I walked through the long gallery on my way to the front of the building, and wished someone had given orders to close the drapes of those many long windows that gave the dark, starless night so many eyes to peer in at a solitary walker like myself. The shaded candle I carried gave off a strong, steady little flame, undisturbed by the beginnings of the night breeze outside, but that light itself made me a target for the eyes I could fancy watching me through those floor-length windows. The feeling grew so that when I heard a tapping, scratching sound I had an awful fear it was something trying to get in at me through those windows high above the cobblestones of the courtyard and the moat outside the north walls. In the most cowardly way I hurried my last steps that brought me out of the gallery into the dank, dusty regions of the corridors in the East Front of Moura.

I paused there and looked back, holding my light high. Effie had been right about one thing. Some excessively large rats resided at Moura. The one who darted across the floor of the gallery now might have inflicted a very ugly bite upon Effie or the young lady who went home to die. This rat, caught briefly in my light, had little eyes that glistened like rubies to my powerful imagination.

At least, the creature served to hurry me along on my way. But I promised the intruder, "a trap will be mending your nightly habits, my friend," and then I was amused at the contradiction in terms. Perhaps we human beings and not the rats were the intruders here. Tomorrow too, I would set up systematic daily dusting throughout the occupied quarters. Corners like the Master's bedchamber and the long gallery, as well as the dank corridor I walked through now, were apparently dusted seldom, if at all. That custom, or lack of it, must be mended.

Unexpectedly, I came upon Kate near the broken parapet of the North Tower as I crossed to take the stairs down to the ground floor and the green velvet room which was nearby. Kate seemed to be on the way to her room and yet, by her lingering so near the velvet room door she made it clear to me that she wanted to delay me. When I came off the staircase into the hall, she put one hand out in an effort to stop me.

"Not yet, Chérie. The Maître is speaking with the new history tutor."

I stopped and she motioned for us both to move closer to the door but to remain silent. I understood why at once; for we could hear the conversation within through the door which was ajar. Stavko was asking the Captain questions about his past and I could imagine the Master utilizing all of that Grand Inquistor's look which came naturally to him. Certainly, his voice, though polite, gave evidence of that cool, contemptuous superiority I had guessed at, though he was heretofore both polite and kind to me.

"Since you seem aware of the services required of you here, Captain, there should have been little need of this conversation."

"No need at all, I assure you, Stavko," came Captain Surtees' voice with a light, almost insolent undercurrent. "Upon my word! I'd no notion it was so late. I am promised to the young ladies for a lesson in the waltz . . . if you will excuse me." He seemed very near to the door now and Kate and I moved away in haste. But he was stopped by the Master's sharp command.

"One moment more of your so-valuable time, please. I am fully aware of that business at Marseille, and so is Mademoiselle Kate Moura; since it occurred while my daughter was visiting in that city, she saw fit to confide in me. I have been persauded to give you this chance. But any attempt at a similar . . . violence here will mean dismissal and worse. I shall not hesitate to have you turned over to the office of the *Procureur du Roi.* You escaped with your neck intact the first time—"

"An accident, Sir," the Captain put in defensively. "The girl was attempting suicide. Silly little fool would not believe the—ah—relationship had ended. We struggled over my letter opener and she was stabbed."

Kate and I stiffened. Then she put her finger to her mouth again and I was silent as the Master said in a horrid kind of irony, "Very true. An accident. The second such *accident,* and in my house, would certainly bring you to the guillotine. You understand, my friend?"

This clearly agitated Surtees, who must have swallowed hard or rubbed his throat as he replied in a choked voice, "Perfectly. You might have spared yourself and me this distasteful business of a reminder. It was only my cursed temper. It is unlikely it would happen again."

This ghastly confession seemed to negate his claim that the girl had committed suicide.

Stavko said, "Very unlikely, I hope."

After that, the Captain slammed out of the room and almost into Kate and me. He paused just long enough to remark to us sardonically, "No wonder he is so well informed. I see he has his spies everywhere." He strode away rapidly.

That left me, at least, both shocked and ashamed. His accusation had been very nearly true, but what I had learned of him was quite as terrible as Kate's first hints indicated.

XI

I WOULD HAVE preferred to meet Master Stavko at almost any other time; for his mood after that interview must be crabbed, at best. Kate guessed my reaction and overcoming what I suspected were her baser instincts, she tried to cheer me.

"Don't question him, and don't be too inquisitive. Be your own charmingly efficient self and you'll bring him to a pleasant mood without half trying."

I whispered "Thank you" and rapped on the door which the Captain had left as he found it, still ajar. But I confess a sense of depression had settled over me, induced by Surtees' bland boast that the remarks about his crime had a basis in fact. It was also beginning to nag at me that the Stavkos showed a curious taste in the hiring of tutors. If Surtees actually was involved in the knife death of a young woman, why would the master of a school for young women be at the expense of employing him in a situation so pregnant with danger to the students? Perhaps Stavko got the Captain cheaply. More likely, though, he had simply allowed himself to be over-persuaded by his daughter's taste for Edward Surtees.

But the voice which told me, "Enter, Miss Anne," had all the persuasive power and the mere shadow of an accent that I associated with Istvan Stavko when in a good humor. I stepped inside and would have left the door open —the atmosphere in the little velvet room had always been oppressive—but the Maître called to me, "Close the door, please. I detest the habit of servants to eavesdrop."

I did as he asked; it had been more in the nature of a

polite command, and I crossed the room slowly, my steps soundless upon the deep-piled green carpet. The tall, spare figure of the Maître was at one of the long courtyard windows. He seemed to be framed by the splendid old green velvet portieres which he had pushed aside in order to stare up at the East Tower. I said nothing as I stood by the little tea table, waiting for my instructions. But as always, I found the room's air heavy and I was forced to take deeper breaths, and to steel myself against the impulse to look around me, into the velvet-soft corners of the room.

So intent was I upon the alien atmosphere in this small and quite unspectacular room that I must have been under the close scrutiny of Stavko for a full minute before I was aware of it. The experience was less flattering than unnerving. He did not smile when I caught him staring at me. His full lower lips twisted, and he said coldly:

"Sit down, Miss Anne."

In the most gingerly way, I sank onto the edge of a stiff little Louis Fifteenth chair, beginning to suspect that despite that first pleasant tone as I entered, he intended to give me a cutting scold about my work. To my great relief, he took a sheaf of elegant pressed and scented letter paper from the slender tea kettle stand nearby and laid them upon the table beside me. I did not know how agitated I was until I saw my fingers shake as I lifted the students' writings and began to leaf through them.

While I was doing so, Stavko watched for my reaction, explaining, "It is my—our hope, that these young people may be prepared, in some slight way, for their social life when they have been presented at Court. As you British say, they are not 'out' yet. When they have gone from here, and are presented to London or Paris society, they will inevitably be married and find themselves the chatelaines of great houses. These presentations and the responsibilities of correct marriages . . . these are our responsibilities. And you will oblige me, Miss Anne, by giving advice to our young ladies. You may be called upon frequently in this capacity."

"I understand, Sir." I began to smile as I read on, finding

an occasional absurd line in these statements of the students' own thoughts on the subject of the management of a great estate. The Master's tight-fleshed face softened a trifle, while he followed my reactions to the girls' unconscious humor.

"They are singularly innocent of the practical aspects of life," I remarked presently, hoping thus to deflect that cold-eyed interest in me.

"Precisely. Their need of a little common sense, among other qualities, is quite evident."

For a few seconds I thought I had never heard such contempt, such lack of real, heartfelt interest in his students. But when I slowly raised my head, looking up at him with what must have been a baffled expression, he smiled, his well-shaped full lips gleaming faintly in the candlelight. I found myself avoiding his face, especially his mouth. I was torn both by revulsion I could not explain, and a curious and frightening attraction to those lips.

"They are amusing, the young ladies," I began apologetically. "But very sincere. That is to say, Miss Elfreda and—and others . . . They will make good wives, good chatelaines of great houses. It is merely a matter of training and perhaps too, of confidence in themselves, their ability to issue orders." As he continued to smile, making me more and more uncomfortable, I went on, hoping to provoke some other response. "You must know, Sir, it is as great a talent to issue orders correctly as to receive and carry them out. You do understand this about the young ladies?"

"Oh yes," he agreed, with that dreadful and incomprehensible amusement. "I understand a great deal about young ladies. You forget, I think, that I have had intimately to do with them for many . . . many years."

I could not control the swift, ironic comment, "Intimately, Sir?"

"As their schoolmaster, their preceptor and tutor." His tone hardened. "How else did you suppose I meant, Miss Anne?"

"I don't know. I don't quite know what I did think." I shivered and began to get up, avoiding his eyes as before.

He put out one lean hand, the long, shapely fingers cutting painfully into the flesh of my lower arm. "I have not done with you, Miss Anne."

"I beg pardon, Sir." I found myself slowly sitting down again, wondering if I was about to see the dangerous side of Istvan Stavko. In any case it would serve no purpose if I screamed. It was highly unlikely that I had a friend at Moura to answer my call for help.

I do not know what I might have expected if there had not been an interruption at this time, though hardly one that I would have prayed for. Across the room behind us, the passage door opened. I looked around hopefully, only to see the Lady Tyra moving over the carpet toward us, with her serpent's grace. Prompted by this interruption, Stavko's attention was taken from me and I seized the chance to wrest my hand free of his painful grasp.

No one spoke until the woman was close to us and I saw, to my discomfort, that Lady Tyra's eyes glowed with that cold fire which was so unnerving in the Maître.

Her metallic voice broke the silence. "Father, have you gotten the truth from her?"

I felt the palms of my hands damp with cold sweat. Could the creature have guessed my real purpose here at Moura? If Kate were sufficiently pressed, sufficiently persuaded or enticed, she might very well betray me. At such a moment, trapped as I was between the gaunt, elongated shadows of the two Stavkos, I found the possibility of their knowledge horrifying. Even as Stavko answered his daughter, I was darting glances around the velvet-hung room, wondering if I would be better served by physical or mental agility.

"You interrupt us, I think, Tyra," he said in a cutting voice. "However . . ." As he paused, I looked up quickly. I could not be certain but I sensed rather than saw in his face that my immediate danger was over.

Clearing my throat, I ventured hurriedly, "If there is anything I may tell you, I'll be that pleased to oblige, Sir."

Lady Tyra did not speak. There was always about her the quality of a sleepwalker and I noticed that in most of her dealings with the inhabitants of Moura, she acted through another person. If she had been a dead woman, she could not have seemed less human, less a part of our world of reality. She gestured with her hand and Stavko spoke for her.

"My daughter spent a few nights in Marseille some weeks ago. She met Captain Surtees at a posting house in that city."

Lady Tyra cut in angrily, "Of what concern is this? Ask her, Father."

"Very true. Miss Anne, where have you known Captain Surtees before?"

I was inexpressibly relieved at this climax to my fears. "Where? But on the coach, of course! The Diligence between Vichy and Le Puy. There he came, the long-legged boastfulness of him, thinking to conquer the world with his soldier's ways."

Very rudely, Lady Tyra remarked, "She is lying. He has known her before. He could not have such an interest in her merely from a coach ride. I have seen how he looks at—" She broke off.

I looked my scorn at this but when I saw that Maître Stavko was eyeing me rather intently, I protested, "All the same, it is true, Sir."

Stavko fingered the papers I still held in my hands. Lady Tyra and I watched him, I with fresh anxiety. It was hard to know what she thought, but whatever it was, it did not promise well for me. On the other hand, when Stavko raised his head he was smiling, a peculiar, knowing smile that puzzled me excessively.

"No, Tyra," he said, surprising both of us. "Our Miss Anne may well be telling us the truth, in every detail. I have reason to believe they shared the Diligence, but as strangers."

While his daughter was doubtless considering fresh objections to me, I took the papers out from under his hand and stood up again, slowly this time. I didn't want to repeat the difficulty I had when I tried to leave some minutes before.

"If I may, Sir, I'll be making my rounds now. I promised one of the young ladies I would see to a mattress that is more comfortable. You understand, it is sometimes wise to provide these children with all the comforts during their sleeping hours. They will be healthier by day. Don't you agree?"

Lady Tyra said something to him rapidly in their strange and, to my ears, sinister language and he laughed.

"You are in the right again, Miss Anne. The health of our students must be our primary concern. Go about your work, and then"—I looked back at him—"why, then, you must go to bed as well. Your health, too, is our primary concern."

"Thank you. You are too kind." I made my curtsey to them both, half-expecting one of them to put out a hand to stop me. When I turned my back upon them and walked to the door, I would not have been the least surprised to have one of them somehow reach the door before me and bar my way. It was with a silent prayer and profound gratitude that I reached the gloomy passage, closing the door of the velvet room upon the two Stavkos. I had not taken my candle, and the walk back to the students' wing was one nervous scurry from bracket lamp to embrasure-candle, with the Moura dark far too prevalent between.

Beyond the long gallery was the students' wing, and there I would take up a light from the small salon, but meanwhile, pursued as I was by phantom steps and the ruthless, reaching hand of Istvan Stavko, it gave me an uneasy jolt to see someone standing at the far end of the gallery, where the students' corridor began. From the faint light of the starless sky, I could make out the white hair and dignified figure of Tzigana. I was immensely relieved to see her. She was the one person belonging to the present control of Moura whom I trusted. She spoke gently now.

"Do not be alarmed, Miss Anne. I am awaiting my husband. The silly creature has gone into the village, and I make no doubt he will return in sad condition."

I had many problems, many fears upon my mind and I repeated, puzzled, "In sad condition? How so?"

"Wine," she explained succinctly. "The blood of the grape, as he calls it."

Such knowledge boded no good for Moura. It needed but this drunken servant at a School for Select Young Females to double our problems with the girls' health and moral atmosphere. I sighed and I am afraid my response was caustic.

"I trust you will prevent him from being seen by the students."

"Be certain of that, Miss Anne. Borgos knows his place. He will not be permitted to frighten the young ladies." She added with the first grim note I had heard her use, "He would do well to obey me. He knows what will become of him if he oversteps his place here."

This was an unexpected revelation to me. Even with the housekeeper's ubiquitous position in a household, one seldom hears so blatant a boast of wifely influence upon her husband. But I thanked the woman and would have passed her to enter the students' wing when she suggested gently, "If the Fraulein von Preysing is still asleep, and it is urgent that you speak to her at once, please inform me. There are medications we may use to arouse her."

"I hardly think it will be necessary to go to that length," I said, "but I thank you for your assistance. I feel certain the young ladies value you greatly. You must stand in place of a parent to many of them."

"Not all, I fear." Her smile was a little sad, a little wry. "For you will have noticed I do not stand high in the graces of Miss Elfreda."

I turned back upon impulse and asked her, "Have you any notion why this is so?"

She shrugged. "It is, I believe, a small jealousy. Fraulein von Preysing speaks to me on occasion in her native tongue. She is Austrian, as perhaps you are aware. The language is not comprehended by Miss Elfreda. So simple, our prejudices!"

"Yes, but this dislike seems to have begun before the two girls were placed in the same room. Were you equally well acquainted with Miss Cléa Raines, who became ill at Moura?"

The woman looked at me quickly, her face illuminated by the flare of a distant light beyond the east end of the gallery and moving erratically toward us.

"Was something said, Miss Anne? Is there gossip that I do not know of? Miss Cléa was ill, a fragile child, at best. Her blood was of a thinness inconceivable. We formed the habit of preparing meats for her that were scarcely more than charred. Meat juices are efficacious at such times."

I had little experience with these matters and could only accept her authority. In order to explain away my own folly in bringing up a subject on which I would have been wiser to pretend ignorance, I agreed in a noncommittal way. "Quite true. I believe any dislike of you must be born of jealousy over the attentions you have shown to Miss von Preysing. The girl's complaints grow tiresome and it's my opinion no one pays any heed to her." I hoped, with this lie, to avert any possible danger from young Effie's head, but Tzigana was quicker-witted than I had supposed.

"Yet she seems not to have proved tiresome to you with her—as you call them—her complaints."

I yawned, covering a moment of confusion. "Perhaps. Perhaps. To confess the truth, my interest in that little chatterbox is a very strong desire to change her style of dress and her diet of sweets. Any other complaints she must take to you. Or to someone else."

Was I mistaken, or did she breathe more easily, and appear less tense, less guarded? I could not tell because the light which had been approaching us from the East Front suddenly flared up at the opposite end of the long gallery. It was a storm lantern in the unsteady hand of a bull-necked man with massive shoulders and a stocky frame to match. I did not need Tzigana's exasperated intake of breath to tell me this beetle-browed drunk, lurching through the gallery to us, was her husband, Borgos. I regretted now that I had remained long enough to witness what promised to be an awkward and very private moment between husband and wife.

As surreptitiously as possible, I moved backward. Another step or two and I would be in the students' corridor. Tzigana's back was to me. She let her husband come toward her and when she spoke, I was surprised at the menacing power in that slim, elderly female with her halo of white hair. Her spate of recriminations sounded even more chilling because the language was unknown to me. The fellow lurched into Tzigana, obviously making excuses in the same tongue. With unsuspected strength, she reached out to prevent his fall, and the storm lantern rolled onto the floor.

Fortunately, the lantern did not break, and though there was a brief flareup of light, I put the student papers in my left hand and managed to rescue the lantern in my right. I was hanging the lantern from my wrist by the looped leather thong when Borgos, in an effort to avoid his wife's surprisingly strong hands, flung himself upon me, exhaling powerful alcoholic fumes. His weight dragged me back and back, cracking my skull hard against the corridor wall.

I remember showering the floor with papers, groping with one hand to hold the lantern while the other thrust angrily, uselessly at the great clumsy weight of him. Surely, his wife would help me! It would be a matter of seconds . . .

It seemed forever that I struggled to evade the drunken dead-weight of Borgos without the slightest assistance from the gypsy woman. In the flickering light from the lantern now on the floor again, I caught brief glimpses of her. She had raised to her full height and was looking at me, her face wiped blank of all expression. A dull, numbing ache at the back of my skull grew steadily worse. I made another enormous effort to throw off the weight of the now-comatose drunkard but nausea and then darkness washed over me. In the delirium of those few seconds, I even fancied the quiet face of Tzigana had broken into gleaming, dreadful pleasure.

XII

My head ached so abominably it was impossible to remain unconscious for long, I thought. I discovered that I was being shaken until my teeth chattered, which in no way restored my head to its normal equilibrium and I murmured plaintively, "If you'll give me peace, I'll be that grateful!" A half dozen young, high-pitched voices talked at once, asking where I hurt, arguing the best treatment, with frequent accusatory remarks directed at Tzigana, whose quiet, yet concerned face was the first I saw when I opened my eyes. I tried to withdraw from her touch, but was chided by the bright, irritating voice of Jessie Tynford, who said, "You mustn't shrink away like that, Miss Anne. Tzigana practically saved your life. She knew exactly what to do when you. fell. And but for her and the Captain, who was on his way to his quarters, you'd still be unconscious, no doubt."

With an effort that made me wince and grit my teeth, I raised my head until I saw Captain Surtees. He was standing behind several of the girls who were in various stages of night clothing. The Captain looked down at me with what I could only consider an interested curiosity. The least he might have done, I thought resentfully, was to make a pretense of sympathy. I ignored the bright interest in his eyes and demanded flatly of Tzigana:

"What have you done with your husband?"

She held out a wine mug to me, saying in her calm way. "Be assured, Miss Anne, Borgos is locked away. You are quite safe. As to Borgos, his headache tomorrow will far exceed your own."

I tried to smile but it was a painful effort. The girls all

chattered with great gusto about the drunken Borgos, by which I gathered that they had seen him behave in this fashion upon previous occasions. A charming atmosphere for young ladies their age, upon my soul! Later, of course, in rationalizing the matter of Borgos, I decided that the handling of a man in that condition might come into the field of necessary knowledge, just as the girls must learn the duties and instruction of their household staffs. But the handling of a heavy, powerful drunkard would never have been considered suitable to a girl's eyes in the school of my old mentor, Miss Nutting.

Some good angel warned me to make no more protests and objections else, in my present condition, I should reveal something of my real purpose in returning to Moura. The girls were still chattering when Captain Surtees rested one hand hard on Jessie Tynford's shoulder, which set her to giggling, and he leaned over her dark-gold head to suggest:

"Shall I take you across to your chamber, Anne, my girl? I have a deal to say to you, in any case." That did not sound in the least promising.

More juvenile giggling followed this, and all the off-key little sounds, like tinkling bells, only increased my headache. I sat up. Of all the indignities! I was still on the floor of the gallery, leaning back against the corridor wall. I might have been drunk myself, for all the look I must present to these many, and useless, viewers. One of the girls, Effie Swiversedge, was kneeling beside me on the floor, and she offered her hand to help me to my feet, just as the Captain, with very little ceremony, jerked me up between two of the students and hard against him. I think I had not yet recovered my balance, but I made an elaborate pretense; for I was now afraid that either the Captain or Tzigana would play upon any weakness they suspected in me. Next time, without the presence of the students to witness my rescue, I might not survive the "accident."

"Come along," the Captain ordered me in a slightly bored

but determined voice . . . as one who would do his duty by me though he died for it.

"If you please . . . my head!"

The gypsy Tzigana raised her hands. An instant before she touched my brow with a wet cloth pleasantly perfume-scented, I felt of the tousled hair above my forehead. It was still damp from the woman's previous ministrations. I began to wonder belatedly if I had imagined that nasty, gloating expression on her face just before I fainted.

"Thank you," I said, severely polite and waving away the scented cloth. "It is entirely unnecessary. I am well now." She withdrew a few steps and the girls began to break up into pairs, buzzing privately about me and, I daresay, about the whole undignified and ridiculous business. To think that I should be struck down, not by a worthy opponent but by a drunkard who accomplished the business while totally unconscious himself!

Captain Surtees shook me, a trifle less painfully this time. "You are the most annoyingly pricklish creature! You can scarcely stand, so don't shrink from me. One would think I were your friend Borgos."

I almost wished he were. At least, Borgos was a simple, uncomplicated villain, too full of wine—"the blood of the grape" his wife called it—to be much more than a dead weight. Villains like Edward Surtees, being so complex, were far more difficult to resist. . . . That is, to fight, I added, after a little thought.

Tzigana asked quietly, "Will you assist Miss Anne across the courtyard to her chambers, Captain?"

But I had many duties before the evening was done. "Nonsense! I must see to Miss Hedi, and replace the lamps in the West Wing, and go to—"

The Captain began to hustle me along rudely. "You are going to your bed, my fair colleen! And be cosseted yourself, as a change."

My dogged struggles provoked a stifled giggle from one of the crowd of girls in the corridor and I yielded, partly in desperation, partly because I was in no case to do otherwise. We were scarcely beyond the girls' hearing, across the gallery, when the Captain remarked:

"You look devilish bad, Anne. Shall I carry you?"

I felt too sick to reply, or even to take offense; so I simply shook my head and stumbled along, setting one foot before the other, with considerable help from him. It seemed incredible to me that a mere rap on the back of the skull could possibly make me so weak even my limbs almost failed me. Going down the staircase past the broken North Parapet, I grew dizzy and thought I should further disgrace myself by being physically ill before the eyes of the satirical Captain, but we were spared that, at least.

In the dank chill of the courtyard I recovered a little. "I cannot think how I came to be so foolish," I said after several long breaths of the winter air that cut so much my throat ached. "And now, to be going to my room with dinner scarcely past— It is beyond my understanding."

He looked at me oddly. "Dinner scarcely passed? In God's name, what time do you think it is?"

I felt a new uneasiness before I asked, "Well—what is the hour then?"

"Very near to midnight, my dear girl. Time and more for you to be resting."

"I'll thank you not to joke about the time after what I've seen, this night," was all I could think of to depress his absurd tendency to joke. What a time for humor!

He made no effort to prove his silly claim and said nothing for a minute. The night wind, whipping around the rectangular courtyard, seemed to claw up the ice off the thin carpet of remaining snow, and the Captain, with his arm a band of warmth around me, rushed me to the courtyard door which, for reasons known to the Stavkos, was kept locked.

I protested, "Oh, no! You've got it all wrong. Not this door. They keep it locked."

"A guinea to ha-penny says you're wrong. See?" He pushed the door open and I was too glad to be within the drafty hall away from the wintry blasts to do more than mumble a "thank you."

The truth is, it was only later when both my head and I felt more the thing that I realized the Captain would naturally have the *entrée* to his paramour's sleeping quarters. I looked along the ground floor passage where I had seen the Captain meet Lady Tyra the previous night, but there was no indication of life there.

We went up the stairs, I, at least, relieved that I had already provided lamps or candles for these once sinister, dark passages. Even so, it was a long way between two lighted niches and when we reached my own little bedchamber I was tired enough to lean against the door as I made a respectful good night to my escort and remarked acidly, "I trust you will find your way back to—to where you are spending the next few hours." He would scarcely have far to go, merely along the passage and down the stairs, then a few doors to his right on the ground floor.

He removed my hand from the latch with very little courtesy, and opening the door, looked around my room. I thought *What curiosity!* and resented it with a vehemence borrowed from my resentment at a skull that still ached slightly. He satisfied himself, for whatever purpose, about my room and took my hand as if I were a child. With my surprisingly weak hand in his, he led me across the carpet to the one chair the room afforded and seated me.

"What *are* you about?" I demanded crossly.

For answer, he took up my bedcandle and held it so close to my cheek that I tilted my head and strained to avoid it. Dumbfounded at his behavior, I stared up at him. He was scowling.

"Good God! What did that fall do to you? You're as pale as a ghost. Where are those bonny pink cheeks, and that Irish sparkle of yours? Where is the saucy impudence of you?"

Tired as I was, I knew I was being insulted in a most ungentlemanly way and I rose to the bait, trying at the same time physically to rise, but he pushed me down as though I were a tavern wench he'd bought for the evening.

"I'll thank you to be leaving, Captain—Sir! If you've nothing better to do than take me to task for my ugliness—well, all I'll be saying is— You're quite the cruelest man in nature!"

"Now—now—now . . . Tears are going to blur those clear Irish eyes. And that'll be the finish of you."

"Holy Saints preserve me from—from—!" I felt so angry I forgot entirely about my tears of weakness and self-pity and raised a hand to slap him hard. But he took that hand and held it down and to my unspeakable astonishment kissed me in a playful way on the cheek and then the lips. Very practiced. Very charming. Then he backed off slightly and smiled.

"Yes. You're not feeling yourself at all. Else you'd have given me another flash of that temper of yours."

"Go away," I said. "I'm so tired I couldn't raise another hand if my life depended—"

He put his forefinger over my lips. "Don't say it, Anne, my girl. Get yourself into your little trundle bed and lock and bolt your door and don't open it until morning, not if the devil himself should knock!"

I looked up at him, blinking with the effort to keep awake and alert.

"What do you mean? I'm not likely to open my door at night."

"Good child." He turned away, glanced around my bedchamber and walked to the window. He pushed the portieres aside and as I watched, puzzled by his actions, he tried the window latch. It seemed to satisfy him and he pulled the portieres closed and still without so much as a by-your-leave, he went to the door and examined the bolt.

"Now what?" I asked.

"When I leave, lock this."

I yawned and said I would.

"Anne—look at me." Uncharacteristically obedient, I did so. "Promise me you'll trust no one."

I smiled with an effort. "Not even you? Very well, I promise."

"Not even me. Excellent. You take orders better than any Irish Trooper I've ever had."

This made me so unreasonably cross that I got up and went over to the door and wrenched it open. "Out!" I said, and he grinned and went.

. . . *Down to see Lady Tyra, I daresay,* was my thought as I bolted the door again. My little spurt of energy had tired me more than I suspected. I made my way across the room to the bed, held tight to the bedpost and rested my forehead against the cool wood of the post. The ache at the back of my skull had subsided and I assumed it was the reaction which set in now so that my face, even my throat and neck felt weak, terribly tired. I tried to stroke my neck to relieve the pressure but my flesh was astonishingly tender, and the jugular vein felt tight and swollen as whipcord under my probing fingers.

The wretched Borgos undoubtedly struck my neck as he fell against me. All in all, it had been a dreadful evening!

I made an inadequate attempt at bathing with the now cold ewer of water left by young Draja, and not a moment too soon, dropped into bed. I reached out to snuff the candle, remembered Captain Surtees' exaggerated remark about the lateness of the hour and reached for the small, square clock in its doeskin case which my husband had used in our bedchamber. I took out the clock, stared at the Roman figures, unbelieving. The Captain had been right. It was now half after midnight. Somehow, I had apparently lain unconscious for two hours or more. How long could it have been before the girls or Captain Surtees heard of my plight and came to my rescue? Small wonder that I felt weakened now. Doubtless, the blow had been more severe than I at first supposed.

"Well, now!" I sighed, replaced the clock after polishing the gold frame and the glass face, and snuffed the candle. Careful not to lie upon my back, for my skull was still tender, I was soon fast asleep.

I awoke some time later in the night, hearing that tiresome scratching sound which I knew must be one or two of those inquisitive Moura rodents, who gave the students a subject both for trouble and gossip. This time, the horrid thing scrambled over the bed coverlet. I was so impatient I raised my hand, twisted my head around painfully and swatted at the toothy rascal. Panicked, the creature rushed across my breast and throat. I shook off the loathsome thing but not before I felt a sharp pinch between my shoulder and throat, which was due either to the swift turning of my head or the teeth of the rodent.

When I sat straight up, staring through the darkness to see whether I could light a spill at the dying fire on the hearth, the rat disappeared.

"It's poison or the trap for you tomorrow, my toothy friend!" I promised him.

Meanwhile, my neck felt inflamed by the sudden movements I had made, and perhaps too, from the bite of my night visitor. However, I did not seem yet to have fully recovered strength after my earlier encounter with the other rodent, Borgos; so I lay down again tiredly, and this time slept without disturbance on the part of the rats, or people trying my door latch, and only noticed that my dreams were haunted by the effort of night birds, or perhaps only one bird, flapping small wings against my window. It was an unsavory dream that, fortunately, ceased with the dying of the wind, a little before dawn.

XIII

After my absurdly weak behavior the night before, I had a profound desire to avoid the young ladies the next day. I was ashamed of what had happened to me, that I had, somehow, allowed hours to pass while I lay unconscious, perhaps stared at by those children, by Tzigana, and by Captain Surtees. . . .

The only possible cure, of course, was to banish that picture of me by another which contradicted it. At least I felt better this morning, my only complaint being a stiff neck and a badly swollen jugular vein where the rodent had nipped at me. I rubbed the place now and then, almost without being aware of the gesture. The side of my throat was still surprisingly tender.

As soon as I had dressed, drunk my morning tea and examined the sore spot on the back of my head, I went down through the building, across the East Front toward the gallery and the students' wing. I was determined to have my interview with young Hedi von Preysing, come what may.

It was raining heavily, so I took the indoor route. I was passing the great hall when the double doors were opened with a sudden, impetuous movement that startled me, and Maître Stavko stopped abruptly at sight of me. I recovered first, having had a few seconds more time to prepare. During my brief, businesslike curtsey, I observed that he had little of the sinister aura I endowed him with last night in the green velvet room. Evening shadows, flickering candles and my own ridiculous imaginings had made a kind of monster out of this handsome and distinguished man. At least, I thought, he hadn't spent the night in the arms of Tyra Stavko!

Far from behaving monstrously this morning, the Maître came over to me looking concerned and, as he took my hand and studied me from head to toe, I began to make out anger and indignation in that stern face.

"I am given to understand you were assaulted last evening by that drunken peasant. You have my word for it that Borgos will not molest anyone again." This latter sounded so chilling, I found myself almost concerned for Tzigana's hapless husband.

"Thank you, Sir. But I am very much on the mend this morning, and I am persuaded the unfortunate man has already been punished by his wife."

I was making an unobtrusive effort to free my fingers

and he let my hand go at once. His colorless cheeks flushed faintly and I wondered if I had humiliated or offended him by this nervous withdrawal on my part. I would not, for the world, have admitted it to this fastidious man, but when I was very close to him, as now, I became aware of a shaving scent very fashionable in the day of the oldest man I had ever known, the lord of my parents' coteen in Ireland. His Lordship was in his nineties when I knew him, and he was said to have been a great rake in his youth, which had also been the youth of the Eighteenth Century. I, having been born just prior to the opening of the Nineteenth Century, could hardly imagine anyone having lived almost a hundred years before.

It was like that now with Istvan Stavko, the most absurd memory in such a connection. Were it not for the scent of that shaving soap, or perfume, popular a hundred years ago, I should never have had such a feeling about my immaculate employer.

"You are looking pale, Miss Anne. I do not like it," he said, pretending he had not noticed my withdrawal. He smiled and his austere features warmed perceptibly. "We must feed you better."

"It isn't that, Sir. I twisted my neck last night when I fell, and later, one of our permanent Moura residents sank his teeth into me." I laughed, assuming he would guess that I was joking, but his pale eyes flashed quickly, startled, to my face and then my throat.

"What do you mean?"

I tried to make the joke clearer. "Oh no. Please! I mean—we have an over-abundance of rats in this old place and one of them scampered across my bed last night."

He relaxed his vigilant attention only slightly. "Let me see. . . ." When his finger probed the swollen vein, I winced but he went on to examine it closely, then, in a firm voice told me to come with him. "We must attend to that. I have an excellent salve which should remove the swelling, and you will be feeling much better in no time. I created it myself. At one time I thought of devoting my life to surgery and healing, but it was impossible. The Prince, my father, would not hear of it. You may imagine why."

No one knew better than I the low repute in which the surgeon is held, or I should say *was* held, in the time of my youth. In other households I had often found the local surgeon ranked socially below the steward and sometimes below the butler as well. Having once been half in love with a surgeon in Ireland I felt all the injustice of his position and was inclined now to rate Maître Stavko more highly for his appreciation of the healer's art.

Obedient to his suggestion, I went along beside him to a chamber just east of the long gallery which had been fitted up as a bookroom with, however, the addition of basins, trays, carafes and innumerable jars spread upon a long baronial dining table so that the room looked for all the world like an apothecary's shop. As he turned back the immaculate white cuffs of his shirt over his coat sleeves, I asked rather ingenuously, I'm afraid:

"Was your father truly a prince?"

He smiled and I avoided those full, curved lips of his which always troubled me in a way I could not begin to analyze.

"In my homeland, Miss Anne, every second landowner who is not a peasant bears the title of prince. It is not like being a son to the King of France, I assure you."

A slanting rain beat heavily at the mullioned windows, giving the room the appearance of twilight and this, combined with the fact that no fire was laid in the ancient stone fireplace, made me anxious to be quickly done with Stavko's well-meant ministrations. He must have known my feelings. He was extremely perceptive and while I looked around the room, secretly picturing it as the pleasant parlor it had been in my husband's day, the Maître began in his efficient way to work with a powder that had healing properties, and with an ointment of a dusty-brown color.

"Now then," he said, motioning me closer. As always, I

was made uneasy by his nearness, the faint whiff of that century-old perfume, the mesmerizing effect of the long, lean fingers as they caressed the side of my throat and neck with the ointment he had concocted. It would hardly have been flattering, I thought, had he known that with little effort, he could put me to sleep by means of these medical caresses and the steely look of those pale eyes. I applied my mind urgently to other things, among them the very different effect of that rogue, Captain Surtees, who boasted of a murderous "accident" to a girl and doubtless slept with Tyra Stavko; yet he had seemed, for a few minutes last night, the only tender, warm protector I had at Moura.

So much for the spell Edward Surtees could weave! When all was said, his spell was probably far more dangerous than the mesmerizing influence of the Maître. With this in mind I was better able to show my gratitude when Stavko, after carefully massaging the swollen vein and the flesh of my neck close by it, stood off and observed me thoughtfully.

"You will do, I think. How do you feel?"

I said in the sprightliest tones I could muster, "Excellent, Sir. Quite the thing. I shouldn't wish you to think I behave in this idiotic fashion upon my arrival at every post to which I am engaged."

"Not at all, Miss Anne. But I shall not be content until that fine, healthy color has returned to those cheeks of yours."

I was beginning to think this was what Mr. Shakespeare calls "much ado about nothing." And so it was! I thanked my employer, explained that I had many things to do in the students' wing, and after bobbing a quick curtsey, I went across the room to the corridor.

In several long, deliberate strides, he managed to stop me there. "What is your opinion, Miss Anne, of the young ladies' passionate cry for a Waltzing Party? Do you approve?"

I knew quite well the guardians of our students would not approve the waltz, which was still shocking during this time of my life, but he seemed not to care for their opinion and certainly, a knowledge of the waltz would be of service to the young students. In view of the curious events since my return to Moura, I found this question naive in the extreme. As I turned back to look at the Maître while I answered him, Tzigana, the gypsy, passed me in the corridor. I would like to have noticed her expression, and whether she revealed any emotion either at my presence or at my good health after last night, but by the time Istvan Stavko had asked me his question about the Waltzing Party, and I answered with the noncommittal "That should be your concern, Sir," the gypsy woman was gone.

"Not entirely, my concern," the Maître reminded me, with an authoritative tone I could not ignore. "This is the sort of thing no male can organize. Such a thing as a Waltzing Party requires endless adaptation." I looked surprised and he came out into the corridor, which, unfortunately, prevented me from going up the steps past the North Parapet to the gallery. "My dear Miss Anne . . . are you avoiding me?"

I was embarrassed; for he had been kind and seemed to have cured my swollen throat. Although it was awkward now to be stopped when there was so much to be done, I stopped and took a step backward to oblige the gentleman. "Certainly I would not avoid you, Sir, upon any account," I lied. "Please ask me any question you like. I will be more than happy to answer you. If I am able."

He came up the steps until he stood beside me, very tall, very straight and overpowering, and a little frightening by that very shadow he was able to cast over my face. Yet he was cheerful, in a pleasant mood.

"By far the greatest problem is the males, wouldn't you agree?"

"The mails, Sir? I don't—"

"No, no. The young gentlemen for our young ladies. Where are we to find them?"

You may account it strange, but although I had given an occasional thought to a party or ball requested by the students, I somehow assumed that they would dance with each other, as in the academies I had been used to. Not an especially practical training, to be sure, nor was it a preparation for the Polite World outside, but that was how these academies have always operated. And the Maître had touched upon a very real problem. Where, in this small oasis among the rugged hillocks and forests, would a dozen to fifteen young gentlemen be found as partners for our young ladies?

I said hesitantly, "Perhaps a visit to the village might suggest some possibilities, Sir. It will be necessary to order materials and patterns for gowns from a mercer's shop there."

"What neighbors would be likely prospects in this countryside?" he asked.

All unconscious of self-betrayal, I considered his question. "Not many, Sir. They were, for the most part, passionate Imperialists who followed m-Moura into the Grande Armée." For a breathtaking moment I had been about to say "my husband." I wondered if he was aware of the stammer with which I caught myself. He appeared to be ignorant of it. He said with a peculiar little smile:

"And now, those same Bonapartists are buried under the snows of Russia and Poland, or they are in exile. One does not envy them."

I could not resist the sharp reminder. "They gave their lives for France, for what—someone told me was the Declaration of the Rights of Man!"

"But what heat, Miss Anne! An Irish Bonapartist?"

Mother of Heaven! Would I never remember to guard my tongue? I got out of this by venturing the suggestion that as my throat and neck were quite well now, and I was much obliged to him, I would go about my work.

"As you say. But later, you will oblige me by joining Miss Kate and me for a discussion of this matter of a little social gathering. There is no doubt our students will profit by this foretaste of their social future."

I agreed that I would be happy to do as he asked, more especially as his mention of Kate Moura suggested to me that her original suspicions of the Stavkos did not fit into this picture of a public affair. If the Stavkos were committing unholy acts, they would hardly open the doors of Moura to strangers, especially young strangers who were likely to be curious.

He leaned toward me. I stood firm, with a set smile. In every respect, he had been kind to me as a person, generous as an employer. The faint, creeping malaise that gripped me when he was close seemed completely unjust. I was determined not to show him the least disrespect. It was scarcely the fault of Istvan Stavko that the drunken husband of his daughter's maid had knocked me unconscious. Even so, I felt in retrospect that the pain of that headache had prejudiced me briefly. The man, Borgos, had done nothing deliberately to harm me. Nor had the gypsy, Tzigana, been the evil-eyed, evil smiling sorceress I thought her during the few seconds before I lost consciousness.

"Anne, my dear—"

I looked up, startled. Something in my face may have warned him of an indiscretion. In any case, he added smoothly, with a quality in his voice that held an unexpected gallantry:

"My dear Miss Anne, you have been here so short a time; yet you bring your bright Irish beauty to my life . . . to our lives. . . . And our drab world is quite different from that we knew before you *returned* to Moura."

He knows, I thought, stiffening under the blow which had come so unexpectedly, and even slyly. Whatever his knowledge of my real identity—and I was sure it came from Kate—all my Irish stubbornness came to the fore. I bobbed my curtsey which put me further from him, and retorted with every evidence of respect:

"You are too flattering. But I believe you meant to say—my *arrival* at Moura. Will you permit me—?" I made the bland, smiling assumption that he did not wish to further delay me. I was retreating as I did so, but I wanted him clearly to understand that he had not frightened me away. He was playing some game, right enough, and I no longer doubted that he knew I was Edmond Moura's widow. That question about the neighbors at Moura had not been innocently asked.

I left him on that note and went up the stairs and across the long gallery. He must have returned to that curious experimental room of his; for I heard the door close once more on the floor below me. I found myself slowing my normal swift step as I reached the opposite end of the gallery and looked down at that place where several hours of my life had been unaccountably lost. There were no signs of the mishap now. It was difficult to believe it had actually happened to me. I felt of the place on the back of my skull and found it still slightly tender, but I have always had a tough skull, and a tough constitution which I inherited from my County Wicklow forebears.

A door opened somewhere in the students' corridor beyond, and I could hear the chatter of many high-pitched, girlish voices. It had all been real, including the belated presence of the girls when I came to consciousness. I must remember to ask them what they had really seen last night, and why it had been so long before they came. I was still haunted by those hours in my life.

Suddenly, I recalled the conversation between Stavko and his daughter in the velvet room last night. How had the Maître been so sure of Captain Surtees' very correct relationship to me on the coach? He must have gained his information from that weird, muffled old Moura coachman whom the Captain and I first met at the time of the accident to the Moura tumbrel. The tumbrel had carried a dead body in a coffin. . . .

Where is that coachman now? When he left me at the East Front of Moura that night, did he then vanish in a clap of thunder?

I went to the students' salon and was gratifyingly received by most of the girls. Effie Swiversedge had clearly been my good will ambassador; for when she came across the pleasant room to me, clattering in her badly tied sandals, she brought several agreeable young ladies who wanted to know whether I felt more myself today. I told them I was feeling so, very much. I was also pleased to note that Effie had somehow decked herself in a flattering green round gown, a trifle out of the current mode, but the pretty lace collar and the puffed short sleeves with the green silk sash placed low, at the natural waistline, were all charming. I had high hopes for her. It would be a pity if we could not organize a small social affair in which Effie and her schoolmates might gain the necessary further poise and training.

Kate Moura was at the window in the far end of the salon, having completed a teaching course to the girls, I supposed. I wondered if she was aware of my presence. As Effie and a lively, black-eyed girl questioned me about last night's fall and its aftermath, I thought I saw Kate raise her head and look around at us. Though remarkably curious about her, and disappointed as well by her growing antagonism to me, I ignored her, letting her make the first overtures. I suspected she knew about my recent interview with Istvan Stavko. Perhaps she could even have seen us in the corridor of the East Wing, from this window where she now stood. I could scarcely ignore the fact of her jealousy; yet the absurd thing was that if she had been present, she would have found little to feed that jealousy.

"We thought you were dead last night in the corner of the gallery," Effie chattered excitedly. "And we were so frightened, you can have no notion!"

Seeing the chance after they had reverted to the subject, I asked, "How long was I unconscious, do you know?"

The dark girl shrugged and she and Effie buzzed briefly between themselves: "It was half an hour before that we heard the Captain walking through the hall. That was when he found the housekeeper lying there . . ."

"But no! You forget. Tzigana said she went for help and found the servants gone from their parlor. And then—"

The dark girl rolled her eyes. "In any case, that handsome Captain stomped by our door and made such a disturbance, fetching water to soothe Miss Anne's feverish brow that he woke us all and brought my headache back."

"Oh, Hedi! You and your tiresome migraine!" cried the healthy, unsympathetic Jessie Tynford.

I looked sharply at the dark girl, seeing her quite herself, apparently untroubled by any aftermath of her long siege at Tzigana's hands. So much for Effie's absurd suspicions that the gypsy was poisoning the Austrian girl to keep her from betraying secrets! Still, it would be valuable to know what the Austrian did know about her former roommate's death.

I glanced from Hedi to her present roommate, Effie Swiversedge. "Miss Elfreda, you thought Miss von Preysing might wish to speak with me. I wondered . . ."

The dark girl took a breath, started to say something, then hesitated. I was sure she was about to blurt out an unthinking, honest confidence, in the way of orphaned students starved for an adult relationship in which to confide. Then something happened to cut off all her spontaneity. She was abrupt, curt, and even snobbish. "Effie tells stupid tales about all of us. It is nothing. Nothing!"

I was so surprised I was not aware for a few seconds that the young ladies and I were not alone. But an overpowering perfume warned me. Kate Moura was close enough behind me to overhear our conversation, and especially Miss Hedi's rude answer. Kate looked magnificent in another of those very new styled gowns whose fuller purple skirts and decolletage about the throat and shoulders were created for a woman of her voluptuous attainments. I was not so naive as to wonder why she wore such gowns in teaching young female students. She obviously had the expectation of seeing the Maître soon. I think of all the things I regretted about my return to Moura, the loss of the old trust between my cousin Kate and me was the most painful. A velvet throat band studded with small amethysts set off beautifully the heavy, golden flesh, but I could well imagine the calamitous effect of all this richness and splendor upon the tastes of our young ladies. If the Stavkos were not careful, the girls would soon be appearing at breakfast in these sensual evening garments. The possibilities, disastrous and otherwise, were endless. I wondered who would warn Kate. Not Anne Wicklow! I could well imagine the hair-pulling!

Kate made an attempt to be her old amiable self, but the effort was palpable. "Ah, Chérie. I imagine you've come to discuss the Waltzing Ball with our girls. And have you discovered a source for the males we sadly lack?"

The Tynford girls and Effie giggled, but Miss Hedi's sharp, set face did not relax. She looked at us with such contempt that when she turned away abruptly and started out of the room, I found my attention wandering to her and the curious business she had confided in part to Effie. But only in part. Whatever Hedi von Preysing had wanted to confide about the illness and death of Cléa Raines, she had certainly changed her attitude in twenty-four hours. I wondered if either my presence, or Kate Moura's had prejudiced her.

Kate noticed my inattention and its subject. "Underbred little creature. Never has a civil word to say for herself."

"No matter," I said with a pretense of unconcern. "You are right, Miss Kate. Our immediate problem is to produce several young gentlemen. Perhaps, since you know this countryside, you will be so good as to consider the matter with me." I started out of the salon, having made it clear that I wished her to follow me. I believe she would have refused if she dared, but she may have been influenced by fear that I would betray her as I suspected she had betrayed me. I was tired of her nonsense and I meant to settle things between us very soon.

The girls looked after us curiously, so I waited until I had closed the salon door between them and us before I asked Kate in a low voice, as firm as I had ever been in my life, "Why does your presence frighten those girls, Kate?"

She tried a laugh, but it was a feeble attempt. She knew exactly what I meant, though she professed ignorance. "But what heat, Chérie! And for nothing. I am one of them. You saw how all those children adore me."

"All of them?" I repeated bitterly. "Not quite all. Kate, what's happened to you? Why was the von Preysing girl frightened away the minute you came near?" Her brown eyes, usually so frank and challenging, looked tired, heavy-lidded. Not like the bold Kate Moura. She shrugged eloquently at my question, but her gaze wandered, avoiding me. I persisted because her whole manner demonstrated to me that she was not yet completely hardened against me. "Kate . . ." I tried again. "Why will you let this thing happen to you? Each time I see you, you more nearly resemble Tyra Stavko."

This time her eyes flashed with the old fire. "Liar! I am not yet like that. Not yet . . ." Then the fire died. I hated to see it. It was like the death of a once dear friend. She laughed with a hint of hysteria. "You are joking, Anne. You must be. You see me now, by daylight. Here I am. Very much alive. I am not yet like—that one!" She moved a trifle closer, raising her voice, though I don't think she was aware of it. "You don't understand what I am saying, do you, my poor, foolish, innocent Anne? You don't even understand why you never see Tyra by—" She broke off, looked over her shoulder.

"What do you mean?"

"My poor Anne," she repeated, shaking her elegantly coifed dark head. "You pity me. I can see it in your eyes. But don't you know the reason for that pallor of yours? You are now one of us. Save your pity for yourself. It is already too late for you."

The woman was mad. There was no other explanation!

XIV

A TERRIBLE sadness gripped me. We had been friends so long, and Kate was the last human being who loved my husband and remembered him as I did. But now I knew that I could not trust this woman who stood before me rambling so wildly of the hour being too late, of my being "one of them."

I had not spoken with Hedi von Preysing yet, and with my feeling against Kate, I could not let her suspect what Miss Hedi and I would be talking about. Kate's obsession and her uncharacteristic loyalty to the Stavkos made it imperative that I be rid of her now. Not an easy matter, as I learned at once. She seemed anxious to follow me along the corridor into the room Miss Hedi shared with Effie Swiversedge.

I tried to find an excuse to be rid of her, but nothing would serve. I was about to resort to the shabby device of suggesting that the Maître Stavko wished to see her at the earliest opportunity, when Elfreda came to my rescue. She pushed open the door of the room she shared with the von Preysing girl and her plump body crashed into Kate, arms flailing the air. I set her on her feet but could hardly soothe the ruffled Kate, who called her a clumsy little butterball and stalked away, trying to restore some order to her beautiful gown.

Miss Effie waited until Kate had gone out of sight into the long gallery. Then she flashed a mischievous grin at me and tugged my hand to drag me into the bedchamber.

"We've seen the last of that one for a while."

"Yes," I said, following her. "I'm afraid so. The change in her is dreadful."

Effie looked back over her shoulder at me. "Did you know her in the old days? She's been like this ever since she and the Maître have begun to dine together. She's in love with him. Everyone knows about them. But before that, she was ever so jolly. All funny and red-cheeked and full of fun. She disliked the Maître in those days. She used to ask us questions about him and especially about Lady Tyra. One night the Maître heard her. After that, it was all changed, and she was horrid and jealous. She's forever afraid he might like us better than her. . . . That's how it is; isn't it, Hedi?"

The dark girl sat on her white bed, looking sullenly at

the doorway. I thought she was angry with me, but at Effie's words, she said in an irritated way, "Of course, it is true! It was true about Cléa as well, but nothing will be done. It never is." She stared at me directly, as if she issued a challenge and the fault was mine, that I must set it right. A trifle too much to ask, I thought, even if it coincided with my own wishes in the matter.

"May I speak with you, Miss Hedi?" I asked and saw the quick glance the girl gave her roommate.

"Alone!" the Austrian girl commanded. I tried to explain that Elfreda had done her best to interest me in Hedi's problem, but there was no need. Effie said hastily, "Don't imagine I care to listen again. I've better entertainment elsewhere." Just as she was leaving us, she stopped, swallowed hard and asked me plaintively, "Do I still look like a butterball? I thought—I just thought I looked quite nice today."

Indignant with Kate Moura on many scores, I said angrily, "You look lovely, Miss Elfreda! And let no one tell you otherwise. People do not always tell the truth and say good things. Sometimes they lie and say cruel things. Remember that."

Effie thought this over and very shortly her troubled little face brightened. "I believe that was profound, Miss Anne. I'll bear it in mind," and she left us.

Hedi von Preysing fixed her black eyes upon me. She made no effort to conciliate me, no false smiles, no youthful exuberance. She said abruptly, "I know you are her friend. Even now."

Astonished, I could only protest, "Can you doubt it? I make no secret of it. Why should I? Miss Elfreda is a—"

I was not allowed to finish. Her impatient shake of the head told me I had misunderstood her. "Please! They say you are not stupid, Wicklow. I am used to dealing with hirelings. In my home, the Schloss Preysing, there were a hundred like you."

"All like me?" I tried to keep the irony light, but young ladies with a background of castles and hereditary wealth would not recognize an irony with her description of Anne Wicklow, one of a hundred servants.

Miss Hedi waved away my interruption. "I was speaking of your friendship with that aging beauty, Kate Moura, as you must know. Before I discovered that, I thought you were my only hope. But the girls tell me that you and the Moura creature have been friends for many years. I knew then that I could not trust you. . . ." She stopped an instant, and asked harshly, "Are you going immediately from this chamber to your precious friend and betray me?"

I did not let the girl stir me to further resentment. If she had seen Kate and me together, heard the natural gossip that I was employed at her suggestion, her assumption was natural. The most puzzling aspect I found to be her fear of Kate, rather than of the Stavkos, or even of Tzigana.

I said, "Will you be taking my word then, that I will not betray to Kate Moura what you tell me?"

We looked at each other. Miss Hedi was the first to turn away. My pride made certain of that. She nodded slowly.

"I believe you. I had to be certain. Tzigana and I have known ever since Cléa went home to die. Your friend, Kate, was forever being gracious and gay with us, teaching, becoming our confidante. And when Cléa wished to explore the dungeons, Kate Moura took her."

"Through the dungeons? Impossible! Kate was always terrified of them. She would never dream of going through the cellars beneath Moura."

Miss Hedi reminded me wisely, "You see, you do know Kate Moura better than those of us here." Her eyes flicked over me with more curiosity than fear. "In any case, Cléa changed after that trip through the dungeons. The cellars, as you call them. So whatever it is that Kate does to her friends, she is still about it. But you are stronger than Cléa, Anne Wicklow. Do something—before it is too late."

Taken aback by the evidence and by the accusation, I murmured vaguely, hopefully, "It need not be Kate. Why not Tyra Stavko, or that gypsy woman, your friend Tzigana, or the Maître. Even Borgos. And—and—what of that ugly old creature who brought me from the village? Why not one of them?"

She was patient with what she clearly considered my stupidity. "Because Cléa told me the last thing she saw before she became ill in the dungeons was Kate Moura."

"It proves nothing. Nothing, indeed!" I insisted but suspicion once planted is hard to dislodge.

"Is this what Miss Elfreda wished you to tell me?"

The girl raised her chin. "I do not know what was in Effie's addled mind. I told her something of this, yes."

"And did you tell her and Cléa Raines that you suspected only Kate Moura to be this monstrous destroyer?"

"I have told you how it was with Cléa. And it is the same with you when you have been in Kate Moura's presence. You are pale. You collapsed last night. You will go like Cléa. I make no doubt that is what Elfreda told you."

I was already on my way out of the chamber but I turned once to challenge her. "Miss Effie feels very strongly against your friend Tzigana as well."

It was startling, in the circumstances, to hear her cutting laugh. "You forget, I know Tzigana. I have known her since I was a child. If she were responsible, I should have been dead years ago. No, Wicklow. It is your friend, not mine, who is guilty. Think on the facts of the matter. Good day."

Never had the words of polite dismissal been more sardonic. I did not appreciate the humor of it. This day threatened to be one of the worst, both for Moura and for me. The great difficulty was that such suspicions as Hedi von Preysing's bore a contagion with them. My own suspicions had already begun this morning before I talked with Miss Hedi. I opened the door and almost stumbled over Effie Swiversedge, who got up from her knees, grinning so guiltily I laughed at her confusion. I closed the door so that Miss Hedi would not hear, then taunted our eavesdropper, "And have you learned all you wished to learn?"

She stood on tiptoe and whispered, "Is it true? Is Miss Kate the sorceress who killed Cléa?"

I lied firmly, "We know nothing of the matter, and I think we had better not talk of it."

"Not talk of it!" Her voice raised and I tried to silence

her with a quick gesture but already two girls in the corridor had looked around, and beyond them Tzigana's trim, white-haired figure stiffened. She hesitated briefly, but when Effie and I stopped talking, the woman went on toward the courtyard steps to the west of us.

"Listen to me!" I warned Effie, scarcely above a whisper. "Do not speak of it again, unless you wish to tell me of some new development. Then you'll be telling me only. For your own safety; you understand me?"

Her eyes widened. "Can you help us?"

"I came here to help you."

"Like a Bow Street Runner," she remarked admiringly. I laughed, though the fact of the matter is I should like to have had a dependence upon those useful Londoners with their shrewd investigation of crimes and the tracking of wrongdoers. "Perhaps," I agreed. "A trifle like. But you must promise me."

She agreed, obviously proud of her serious responsibility. Hoping for the best, I went my way, but throughout the morning, while the maids and I were at our work of scrubbing down the floors and walls and attempting to add a cheerful note to the wings of the chateau commonly in use, my thoughts kept returning to Hedi von Preysing's story. I was inclined to believe the girl spoke the truth about her relationship with Tzigana, and that we might look elsewhere for the real criminal of Moura. I could not forget either, what I myself had observed of the change in Kate. Most painful of all, my own rising suspicions of Kate may have been confirmed.

The lively Isabeau was an eavesdropper, more or less by accident, upon a puzzling bit of conversation later that day and scrambled into the huge dining hall to tell me about it. I was balanced at the top of a ladder wielding broom-straws wrapped in wet cloth along the beams. The results had been negligible, save in regard to cobwebs. The removal of these was my single triumph. Isabeau came to the foot of the ladder far below and called up to me.

"Mademoiselle! Come quick and hear. It is most exciting."

"Go about your work. After we are done, then you may eavesdrop . . . until you are caught."

"No, no! You do not understand. I think the Maître is very cross. He says bad things to someone."

To save my dignity I spent a few more seconds brushing off the beams and then, holding my skirts and pettticoats close around my limbs, I climbed down. Knowing myself to be a hypocrite, I scolded her, "One day you will be caught in your eavesdropping and then—"

"Please, Mademoiselle! Come quick and listen! It is very bad, I think. I saw Madame Kate in the passage a minute ago. Could he be speaking like this to her, do you think?"

A shameful thing it is to confess, but upon that information, I went with Isabeau, to spy upon my employer. I was aware of an angry resentment against Stavko, if it was true that Kate was the object of his present attack, and this in despite of what I now suspected. Whatever these suspicions, they persuaded my head, not my emotions, which remained loyal to my old friend.

"Where are we going?" I asked Isabeau, for she seemed to be on her way to Lady Tyra's sealed off corridor. "We can't go this way. There is a door halfway down the passage and it is kept locked."

"Not so, Mademoiselle. . . . You see?" She demonstrated. The door was on the latch. We moved with a stealth that made me more ashamed of our spying; yet I could not stop myself or Isabeau. Almost immediately, I heard the low, murmuring tones of someone who might be male or female but certainly I could not be sure it was Kate. The old Kate would never dream of murmuring, so long as she had any voice with which to speak out. Still, the new Kate might be capable of nearly any behavior. And then, too, the voice may have been male, after all.

Isabeau tapped my arm significantly as a man's voice became recognizable and clearly audible from one of the rooms which may have been the chamber in which I first met Tyra Stavko. The several rooms along this section of the corridor were very similar.

The stern, unmistakable voice of Istvan Stavko said something fierce in his own language, then lapsed into French, as if to emphasize his command.

"Doubtless that is so. It is not so, however, that I have promised you that which is mine. Whatever your games—your needs, you will not again touch my property. From the first it was known that this was to be my property. Do not talk to me of temptation!"

"What does he mean?" whispered Isabeau excitedly, but I knew no more than she, and all our spying hardly seemed worth the effort. I heard a step inside the room as though someone were pacing over the creaking boards, and I rushed Isabeau out into the foyer below the staircase. We were fortunately back in the dining hall by the time we heard booted feet crossing the passage and entering the dining hall a few minutes later. I was a bit shaken by the possibility that Stavko had guessed we were eavesdropping and followed us. I scrambled up the ladder, treading on my skirts and hearing a hem rip, but I was there, in whatever condition, by the time the gentleman came within sight of us.

Isabeau's surprised giggle warned me that something was amiss. With difficulty, for my slipper was caught in my hem, I looked over my shoulder. I was almost surprised and relieved enough to giggle myself.

Captain Surtees, obviously prepared for the elements, in a handsome, concealing black driving cape with a dozen collars, gave us a "good day" and demanded to know, "Why aren't you ready? We've got very little daylight left and your wolfish friends may prove less hospitable if the rain should come again tonight."

I wanted very much to mention his own "wolfish friend" Lady Tyra, but I was much flustered by my recent guilty conduct in regard to eavesdropping, and perhaps even more by my trapped shoe and torn skirt.

"What can you be talking of, Sir?" I asked instead, trying surreptitiously to cover my foot with my petticoats. "As you see, we are busy at our work."

But the Captain came on to us, entirely undisturbed by

my cool reproof. "Charmingly put, Anne, my girl. Now that you have established your loyalty to your post, and your nobility of soul, you may yield gracefully. Come!" He raised his arms to me and I started to retreat up the ladder, leaving my shoe and part of my skirt hem in his hands. His expression of surprise was so amusing as he stared at these objects that I began to laugh and by my laughter was defeated. Under the interested eye of Isabeau, the Captain dropped my property and then swung me off the ladder. To save face I freed myself in a businesslike way, and picked up the shoe before he could do so, the while I made clear my objection.

"Monsieur Stavko did not hire me to dash about on social visits to the village. I am very sorry, Sir."

This produced only a denial. "On the contrary. I was instructed to escort you into the village, the fascinating Kate being a trifle ill. I am to have the pleasure of watching you select materials for our giggling demoiselles. For the Ball, of course."

"What? We are to go in the rain?"

"Not at all. There is a splendid afternoon sun, although I do admit the landscape is a trifle soggy."

It was annoying to leave my work half done; for it meant that I must complete it by candlelight, making my work day much longer and the dark corners harder to see and clean. Nonetheless, I was delighted to be quit of these walls, if only for an hour or two. Though I had privately agreed, I felt compelled to make one last stab at dignity.

"I am sorry about Miss Kate, but there is always Lady Tyra. I feel sure you would do better to escort her into the village. A lovely creature like Lady Tyra should just do."

I expected to confound and embarrass him by mention of his mistress, but he was not to be confounded. "Don't talk nonsense. We've only a few more hours of light. Hurry! Change to something that will demonstrate Moura's rivalry of Paris to the villagers."

I said "Ha!" to this but obeyed him all the same. Since I was close to my own bedchamber I was able to make a rapid change. My best gown, of a soft green velvet we used to call "tabby," and made in the new full skirted mode, must be reserved for my appearance in the background of the Waltzing Party. As the housekeeper at Moura, I would not, of course, be a ball guest, or appear in any receiving capacity, but there would be many responsibilities involving the wraps and outer garments of the guests, overseeing the Ball Supper, and repairing the torn trains and skirts of any young ladies whose partners pranced about too energetically.

My wardrobe was an easy matter from which to choose for the afternoon trip into the village. It consisted of the day gowns aside from the green tabby for a festive evening. For the shopping expedition I wore my lilac day gown with a little stiff white holland apron so there would be no doubt in the village of my position at Moura. Over this I wore my straight, ankle-length coat with its caped collar.

The villagers had never known my husband or me very well. The long tradition of evil at Moura prevented them from approaching nearer than the High Road, and my husband returned the compliment by sending or driving to Montemessine for any of our necessities. But there was a chance that, upon my infrequent appearances in the village, I had been remembered. For that reason I bundled my hair at the nape of my neck, instead of wearing it full to my shoulders as in the old days. I went further and wore my best bonnet, whose pale green and white striped ribbons did not clash too severely with my coat or gown, but the great asset of the bonnet at this moment was the shadow its deep brim cast over my face. It was unlikely that anyone would associate the new Moura housekeeper with the late Master of Moura, but it was well to be beforehand with the world.

When I went out into the passage I was a good deal surprised to find Captain Surtees standing there casually slouching upon his elbow against the wall. He showed every sign of having stood there in that position the while I dressed. I tried, with enormous difficulty, not to be impressed by his charm and consideration of me. No matter that I knew his violent past, his relations with Lady Tyra, his probable insincerity. I was honest enough to confess that when in his presence I felt happy, amused, protected and exceedingly aware that I was a female. Whether I trusted him was quite another matter. In point of fact, I did not.

"Why did Monsieur Stavko choose you for the young ladies' mission?" I asked as we crossed the courtyard to the Carriage-House.

"My dear Anne, you underestimate my abilities. The pupils themselves insisted, and I regret to say several volunteered to act as your duenna with me."

I laughed at that. "So they trust you no more than I do."

"Apparently. In any case, Stavko insisted that one girl should go with us, and after a good bit of blather, climaxed by the drawing of straws, a charmer named von Preysing won the honor of destroying our peace."

I would have preferred Miss Effie or nearly any other girl to the sharp-tongued Austrian, but I told him with cynical amusement, "I am persuaded the girl was your own choice."

He was in the midst of a wide-eyed denial when we entered the Carriage-House but was forced to break off as we met Hedi von Preysing, looking hard-eyed and very adult in a black velvet riding habit and a high-crowned bonnet with an enormous and positively funereal plume. She made a picture that Kate would have envied, but there was no conciliating air about her. This pleasant manner was left to her companion, Tzigana, who was soft-voiced and soft in her behavior as always.

"I will leave the Fraulein in your good hands," she said to me with a curtsey and a long, quiet look at the Captain that puzzled me. She seemed about to leave us but paused long enough to say something rapidly to Hedi in the language of the Stavkos which sounded vaguely Slavic and was unidentifiable to me. I saw the Captain paying a deal of attention to Old Chamfers, who had brought around a curricle and was harnessing the team of blacks out on the path beside the slow-moving waters and debris of the moat. Still and all, I was sure Surtees shared my curiosity over the instructions the gypsy woman gave to Miss Hedi.

Miss Hedi seemed bored and turned away from her, asking the Captain to lift her up into the seat. It was plain she meant to be between Surtees and me, and managed the trick very well. I was both amused and secretly flattered at the Captain's disappointment. As a result of this seating arrangement, we left Moura a singularly silent group, the Captain at the reins, Miss Hedi in the center and I on the outside.

By the time our tight-fitting little group had reached the High Road with no untoward incidents in the shadowed Moura Woods, the tension, particularly involving Miss Hedi, had subsided. I could see that she had been uneasy during that part of our journey, probably because of the wolves, but we had seen none, and now the girl began to talk to Captain Surtees about the upcoming Ball. I listened only intermittently. I found her presence here, the trip itself and that little warning by Tzigana in their common language very suspicious.

Occasionally, Captain Surtees talked over the head of our "duenna," making remarks like: "Customs are strange throughout Western Europe. Some are worse than others, I believe. For example, the matter of Spanish influence. I had not supposed it reached so far . . . our architecture . . . our duennas—"

I did not look at him, but his head moved and he saw by my smile that I understood him. He remarked, "You have an enchanting smile."

Before I could think of an answer, Miss Hedi replied brightly, "Thank you, Captain."

Chagrined, I let my smile die rapidly, but this time Surtees looked so intently over her head at me that I was forced to acknowledge his stare. I could hardly misunderstand that look. A little flushed I lowered my own gaze to my gloved fingers. Miss Hedi, meanwhile, rambled on, describing at length the gown, its mode, color and material that she intended to wear at the Ball while, over the plume in her very adult hat, the Captain mouthed to me "duennas!" rolling his eyes skyward to punctuate this.

We reached the village in very good time, with the late afternoon sun rapidly drying all the water puddles left by the morning's rain. Some of the buildings on High Street and around the grassy *carrefour* were half-timbered, charming in the gaudy sunlight, but for the most part, even at this lovely hour, they looked gray, stony and secretive as they had looked in the Middle Ages when they were built; for the village was one of the oldest in this part of France.

There was only one mercer's shop in the village and when the owner's wife brought out lengths of goods suitable for evening wear by young ladies who were not yet "out" as the English say, I could see that it was going to be a problem. Most of the goods were far out of the mode, being muslins, gauzes and indiennes more suited to the summer of an era five years gone by. I could see that, as I had expected, I would get no help from Captain Surtees, who spent most of the time holding tarnished-looking cloth of gold or lengths of bright scarlet velvet against me with highly inappropriate remarks about wishing to see me in them.

We did find a flattering black and white Jacquard striped silk for Miss Hedi. The material had been out of fashion so long it was now quite stylish again. I was particularly anxious to find the right colors and materials for Elfreda Swiversedge and thought I had done so with a deep, vivid blue silk that would do charmingly made in a fashion not too tight, nor too elaborate. By going into the mercer's old and seldom-used stock we found some soft tabbies, and a paduasoy that might do, though an exquisite length of changeable violet taffeta had split badly with age and was useless.

Miss Hedi provided a list of necessities for the girls which needed some common sense paring, but I was beginning to think our journey had been a success when the mercer's wife began to study me closely.

"Mademoiselle, is it possible? You bear a quite astonishing resemblance to the late Mistress of Moura."

I was deeply aware of Miss Hedi's attention directed at

me suddenly and at the same time was sure I had never entered this shop before. I avoided a direct lie by saying, "Really? And did you have much custom with her?"

"Not here, Mademoiselle, but in Montemessine where we formerly kept a draper's shop." She peered at me while I, remembering that I had done business with a draper in the other village, tried unobtrusively to keep my face in the shadow of my bonnet. "The resemblance is astonishing. Truly astonishing," she repeated. "Is it not, Gaspard?" This to her husband who was in a far corner of the shop speculating with Captain Surtees upon the possibility of further rain.

The man looked at me briefly and dismissed the idea as an absurdity. "Not the least in the world. Madame Moura was quite unlike this young . . . person. You are well enough, Mademoiselle. I would not wish to offend. But Madame was—" He blew a kiss and looked significantly at the Captain. "Exquisite, believe me, Monsieur."

Surtees glanced at me with an amused expression, but though I suspected he had guessed the truth, he did not betray me. Miss Hedi too said nothing, but her long, thoughtful stare almost put me out of countenance.

Although it was now past sunset and the shadows had lengthened grotesquely, when we stepped out into the muddy roadway, the Captain insisted that his "two charmers" must have an apéritif at the little outdoor table across the street. Miss Hedi accepted at once and though I felt we would be expected back at the chateau very shortly, I was overborne by the two of them.

Most of the villagers were indoors now on this late wintry afternoon so that as we sat at the table, under the eaves of a small tavern, we saw few passersby. Captain Surtees ordered a sweet greenish liquid for Miss Hedi, who became charmingly young and ingenuous in her enjoyment of it. He took brandy and would have ordered it for me but I had learned to enjoy the thick black Turkish coffee in Venice and reluctantly, he ordered it for me now.

"And I wanted to stimulate you," he complained.

I laughed and confessed, "I find coffee very stimulating,"

but the pleasant mood passed as I sat sipping the steaming liquid and remembering other years, other days at sunset in this countryside.

Captain Surtees, as understanding as he was charming, saw my mood and when Miss Hedi would have questioned me, he engaged her in a light, teasing conversation, only glancing at me in a concerned way now and then. I tried to lighten my mood for the sake of my companions, but while the girl chattered on, my attention was caught by someone behind the Captain who appeared to be watching us from the darkness of the tavern interior. He was muffled against the coming night and looked old. At least, I judged his age by the gray witch locks hanging lank about what I could see of his face.

I sat up stiffly. I had seen that sly, furtive creature before. The witch locks identified him. He was the evil-eyed coachman who drove the tumbrel with the coffin that first night. And he was excessively interested in us now.

XV

ALWAYS AWARE of Miss Hedi's sharp eyes, I was forced to bide my time until she became interested in the local barmaid, who was encouraging the only other customer, a grinning, mustachioed veteran of the Imperial Army. Captain Surtees looked over at me and by the fixed direction of my gaze, he understood what I did not wish Miss Hedi to know. With an ease I admired, he gradually looked behind him, appearing to take up his cloak.

In the shadow of my bonnet brim I kept watch, but even as I did so, our odd watcher seemed to blend into the dark of the tavern's interior and I knew the Captain would see very little. I was surprised and gratified when he looked back at me, frowning, in thought, and did not dismiss my gesture as some idle fancy of an imaginative female.

Almost at once he got up and jokingly said we must be leaving before Miss Hedi became a confirmed tippler. This produced a big smile on her part, but as he fastened her coat at her neck I saw that he maneuvered so as to look over her head, into the tavern. I crossed behind the table, smoothing on a glove in the doorway and dropping it deliberately. When I picked it up, I had an unimpeded view of the taproom and the entry way, but saw only the tapster, who was alone. It was no use. The ugly creature whom I had feared and detested so unreasonably from the beginning was gone. But I could not get over the belief that he had been spying on us for heaven knew how long!

As the Captain lifted me into the curricle, he asked me in a low voice, "The coachman?" I nodded and he muttered, "I scarcely glimpsed him. I've never seen him at Moura. I'd like to know what the devil he has to do with—" Before I could reply, he said, "Never mind." And I understood that Miss Hedi, at her chosen place in the center, was beginning to pay attention to our conversation. It was easy enough for me to avoid conversation on the way back to the village, however. I was surrounded by rolls of materials, packets of threads, and lengths of trims, so that I could scarcely see the two who shared the high perch with me.

It was dusk when we turned off the High Road, under the aged Moura arch and past the stone gatekeeper's lodge where Kate had once lived in a pleasant independence of the chateau itself. There were no lights, no signs of habitation, but in looking back at the lodge I became aware of something else. We had been followed from the village. The High Road was seldom traveled at this hour when the fading daylight made it difficult to see the potholes and muddy wagon ruts, but for some minutes I had been vaguely aware of a sound like hoofbeats behind us. It had seemed no more than the echo of our own team until we turned into the Estate Road and then I was sure.

Miss Hedi had advanced in her relationship with the Captain to the point of flirting, so lightly and with such self-absorption that I wondered if she even remembered how serious had been her concern this morning for the illnesses at Moura. Deep in my own uneasy thoughts, I was relieved at the girl's self-concern. Miss Hedi was saying, "You will promise me the waltz? The first one? I am excessively good at it. I learned at an Imperial Reception. Not that I was permitted to dance, but I saw it done. It was very daring, very romantic."

"Much too old for children," said the Captain. "Actually, it is a dance for very mature—that is, older personages." He looked across at me and unfortunately I did not understand for a moment. He explained with eyebrows raised, "I intend to have that dance, you know."

I smiled but shook my head. He must know I had never waltzed. He contradicted me with an insistent nod, and turned his belated attention to Miss Hedi, who was arguing that she and other students had practiced when the Tynford girls and Cléa Raines showed them how.

"And who taught the Tynford girls and Miss Raines?" he wanted to know.

While she explained that the sisters had learned from a former tutor, and Cléa was taught by her brother, who must have been a modern soul, I looked back carefully, trying to make it appear that I studied the untended, water-soaked little kitchen garden of the gatehouse. It was thus I caught my first real glimpse of our pursuer. He was on horseback, a hunched figure in a storm-cape and wide-brimmed traveler's hat, but though he kept to the side of the narrow Estate Road, sometimes completely swallowed by the creeping shadows of the Moura Woods, I did not doubt his identity. He was the sinister coachman of the death tumbrel. Of one thing, at least, I could be sure now: The coachman resided with us at Moura in some capacity. The thought was chilling.

When we reached the gloomy, medieval East Front of the chateau, Captain Surtees asked if he should hand us out here or drive us around to the Carriage-House situated at the junction of the students' wing and the unused West Wing. Miss Hedi clearly wanted to ride as far as possible with him, but I asked to be set down here where, from behind the windows of the great hall, I hoped to catch a closer look at our pursuer. The Captain lifted me down, held me a few seconds as we looked at each other wordlessly, and then let me go and almost before I was inside the hall, he had driven the girl around the corner of the building and out of sight, together with the larger packages of material I had left on the seat. With an effort I put out of my mind the memory of those seconds, of Edward Surtees' eyes, for once neither sardonic nor laughing, but looking as if, like sapphires, they had a blue fire in their depths. What would it be like to kiss him, to be kissed again, to experience his warm arms, his love. . . .

I heard myself sigh and was angered at this maudlin desire for what I could not have, Lady Tyra's lover, as I moved down the long, desolate room to stand just beside one of the windows that gave upon the narrow carriage drive. Surreptitiously, I stood there watching for the possible approach of the rider who had followed us, while I untied the ribbons of my bonnet and unbuttoned my coat. Within these nine hundred year old walls it was difficult to hear the hoofbeats or other sounds outside, until the moat bridge was crossed, and I doubted that a secretive creature like the "coachman" would come boldly over the bridge.

Dusk was now heavy upon us and when something shifted at the edge of the Woods, I straightened tensely, expecting our pursuer to appear. A lean, gray, doglike creature crossed the road beyond the bridge, followed by his mate. The two wolves disappeared at the periphery of my vision, this time at a faster lope, frightened by something on the Estate Road. Very likely that would be the person I waited for.

At such a moment, with all my attention upon the view from the long window, it is probable that I simply was not aware of my closer surroundings. Later, I realized that I had not been alone in the gloomy hall for several minutes. It was the curious little nudge at my nose that affected my backbone, and was provided by scents much subtler than perfume that told me I was being watched, even as I hoped to watch my old enemy, the coachman. The alien presence behind me carried a curious, sickening odor, like the breath of a person long ill. . . . Almost the scent of decaying flesh, I thought, and turned slowly, trying to place that scent before I looked into the inhuman eyes of Tyra Stavko.

Because I was angry at my own fear of the woman, I said sharply, "Ah, Lady Tyra! Since you are up and about, it must be nearly dinnertime." I dipped a slight curtsey, asked if I might be excused. "To see to the various dinner services."

"How efficient you are, Miss Anne!" she remarked in that metallic, almost mechanical voice of hers. "Did you enjoy the little adventure of the village with our so-charming Captain?"

"I fear, my lady, that he was very little aid in selecting lengths of material for the young ladies. He was most obliging in listening to the child's conversation, however."

"The child? I was forgetting Hedwige. And did he make love to you both in his delightful way? A man of his agility could do so quite easily. Take care, Miss Anne. You may lose your . . . heart." Before I could think of something to lead us back to cases, she said quickly, "And this evening? Will you oblige those silly little chits by working at their gowns with them tonight?"

"When my work is done, yes."

I understood at once that her jealousy had done nothing to abate the immediate dislike between us; nor could I acquit myself of a jealousy that equaled hers. Remembering this, I took up my bonnet and the remaining packets of thread and trims, and begged her politely to excuse me. Then I left her, going toward the passage that separated the great hall itself from the kitchen quarters.

I had intended going on up to my own bedchamber to change for an evening's work and have supper brought to me later, but I was halted by the fearsome red face and wild hair of Matilde, who must have heard my footsteps or simply waited for me in the doorway of the kitchen passage.

"Madame! You there!" she called to me with her usual abruptness.

I wondered what new kitchen crisis threatened as I hurried Matilde back into the kitchen to discuss it. For one thing, I knew her well enough to believe her malevolent humor would cause her to betray my identity by some sly word or other, if I let her talk to me while Tyra Stavko was near at hand. I closed the doors between the kitchen and the dank little passage.

"Now then, Matilde, what is it?"

She took up a huge, smoke-blackened pan and as she made her complaints, she emphasized them by slapping together ingredients, including an inordinate quantity of a potent local brandy, all of which she would turn out later as clean, highly edible brandy cakes.

"A first matter, Madame Moura—"

"Please . . . I am Mademoiselle Wicklow. It is important, Matilde."

"So now, Madame—" She went on. I gave up. She pursued her way, while she stirred the alcoholic contents of the big pan. "You must see to it that my wench, Isabeau, is here to do her trifling part. That other one— What can one expect of a barbarian like Lotte? She cannot even comprehend an order from me. It is not to be imagined but this imbecile does not speak very much of the only sane language in the world."

"She comes from somewhere on the Danube," I apologized. "I daresay she would find that we are as stupid at her language. What ails Isabeau? She did not remain in the dining hall when I left. She followed the Captain and me out of there."

"Very true, Madame. She came slouching in here and chewed up half a loaf of tomorrow's bread, and when she is asked a simple task—'go and fetch two bottles from the wine cellar'—what does she do, but refuse me."

I sighed and found myself tapping my bonnet against my skirts impatiently, but this was unfair of me, for I did understand Matilde's irritation at incompetent help. "Well, Matilde, you know how they feel about the cellars. Even Madame Kate is terrified of them. I do believe you and I are the only human beings at Moura who have ever spent any time in those cellars."

"Ay. It may be so. The only human beings." She grunted at my startled look. "I make no doubt the one they call the Maître, and the one they call Milady Tyra, they would not fear the cellars. They seem to like the night, and the dark."

"Oh, come, Matilde!"

"What else? And this incredible Milady, how does she exist, may I ask? She eats no more than a bird. She sleeps the day away. She would pay no mind to the darkness of the cellars. . . . But you may be sure, idiot things like Isabeau, they do not long defy Matilde. I said 'March down and fetch the wine and the brandy' and she marches. And later, I am complaining when the stupid Borgos comes in for an apéritif for his woman, and there I see the two bottles; so that lazy Isabeau obeys me."

"Good! Then you cannot want me to speak to Isabeau." With my hands full of packets and bonnet ribbons, I started to open the door into the passage but she reminded me harshly:

"I wish you to send her back to the kitchen. I need her in the stillroom, and for serving the household. To bring up the bottles and then to run away again, leaving me with Draja and that impossible Lotte, it is a stupid business! Send her back to the kitchen where she is useful."

"Yes. I understand. I will, Matilde." I left the kitchen in some confusion and puzzled out her complaint while I went to the front door and opened it, but the night was now far too dark for me to see anything of our weird coachman. I wondered if Tyra Stavko's arrival in the great hall had been planned to take my attention from the moat bridge. No matter. It was too late now. I turned and went to see if I could locate Isabeau on my way to my room.

The dining hall itself was empty and shadowed, with only two tapers on the long table, flickering in the draft. I had been sure Isabeau would not be there. She was probably playing truant somewhere after having briefly obliged Matilde by fetching up the bottles from the wine cellar. Poor Isabeau! No one knew better than I that life was not easy for girls of her domestic status. They must play truant occasionally. It was very human of them.

I looked around my bedchamber as I entered it, wondering, as always, if it had been entered in my absence, but everything was as I left it. I still suspected that whoever entered my room the morning after my arrival had been searching for my extra set of keys. I touched them where they were fastened at the waistband of my top petticoat and considered again that it was clear the person who searched my room had not been near me during my unconsciousness last night. Else my keys would have been removed.

I changed for the somewhat dismal task of completing my day's work, puzzling now and then over the footloose Isabeau. She might have her qualities of disobedience, as perhaps all of us do but her conduct with Matilde was unlike her character as I had come to know it in working with her.

Since the dining hall would shortly be in use by the family, I resumed the work of cleaning and removing cobwebs from the time-darkened beams in the oldest section of the chateau, the rooms of the East Front. I worked alone because the Stavkos' meager staff was always occupied at this hour with the dinner meals to be served in three locations, for the students, the family, and for the servants in their own dining parlor. While I was thus occupied, I received an unexpected and, I confess, unwanted offer of help. I was not familiar with the harsh, gutteral male voice and looked around in surprise, uneasily wondering if the intruder might be that evil-looking fellow, the coachman, whom I had not yet encountered in sufficient light to identify him. I was almost equally startled to find the huge, callused hand of Tzigana's husband, Borgos, reaching out for me as I stooped, removing cobwebs and a little of the soot that had accumulated since my last cleaning of this room three years ago.

"You! Miss!" he said in his halting English.

"W-what do you want? Go to your wife. She will be at dinner now. Dinner!" I repeated, hoping to send him away from me on that inducement.

For a second or two he stared at me, at the scar over my jugular vein, I thought. But when I repeated my command that he go about his business, and his gaze shifted, I realized he had been studying the small pearl crucifix I always wore about my neck, suspended from a narrow gold chain. It was all that remained to me of my parents' little property, though the little ivory cross was usually invisible, tucked into my bodice. Today, because I was bending over at my work, the crucifix swung free and he noticed it.

"The so-pretty miss is of the Faith of Rome? Not like the young ladies?"

"I am Irish," I explained. "It is the faith of my parents and of their parents before them."

"You let me see? Very pretty. Like Miss." He seemed to change the subject rapidly, to my surprise. "Now, I give aid. Take my hand, Miss. So?" He pulled me to my feet and took the cloth from my fingers. While I watched apprehensively, the rugged, bearish fellow did a fast job of scrubbing, moved on his hands and knees to the opposite side of the table and finished under that end. I saw that his big, broad feet were wrapped in strips of cloth, like the poorest peasants in the countryside when I first arrived at Moura. He looked around at me several times with his huge, toothy grin a slash of brightness in his dark, unshaven face. He had an odd way of holding his head to one side, favoring it so that I saw his left profile or three-quarters of his face. I had not noticed that when I saw him in the long gallery.

Gradually, I lost my fear of him and even responded with more than monosyllables when he asked me questions about my work and where else he might assist me in the cleaning. I refused his offer tentatively and he cleared his throat and flashed his wolfish grin again.

"I do not intend it when I hurt you, you understand. It is only that I was drunk and my feet were in my path and when I fell . . . You do understand, Miss Anne?"

"I understand." I took this chance to ask him, "Do you know what happened, who came into the gallery after I fainted?"

He shrugged. "That? No. Impossible. Tzigana and I, we went to our bedchamber; and I? What would I do but sleep!" He rubbed the hidden right side of his face and grimaced in thoughtful remembrance. On a sudden suspicion I moved the candelabrum on the table closer to him. It was then that I saw the great, raw slash that cut almost the length of his cheek from his dark eye to the corner of his thick-lipped mouth. It might almost have been made by a knife blade but very likely a whip had done the work. Was it possible Borgos' sweet-faced, white-haired wife had punished him so viciously? And if so, why? Merely because he had been seen drunk by the new housekeeper?

A door opened from the passage and as if in answer to my unpleasant thoughts, Borgos' wife, Tzigana, peered into the room without entering. She was her typically good-mannered, genteel self.

"Forgive me, Miss Anne. If you please, I must borrow that great bear, my husband. The young ladies ask that some trunks be moved from the storerooms to their chambers. Furbelows for the party, you see."

"Of course," I said. "Thank you, Borgos."

He seemed touched by my simple thanks and before I knew what he was about, he had taken my hand and kissed it in a clumsy but not unlikable fashion. Then he lumbered off after his wife.

A short while later, having finished my current task more quickly with the aid of Tzigana's husband, I returned to the kitchen area where Matilde had departed, her work day finally over, and I asked that when I had washed, Isabeau might bring up to me the late supper which had been laid upon the hob to keep warm. But young Draja, who was curled up like a kitchen cat in front of the great hearth, crawled out and unrolled himself to his full height, a trifle above my shoulder. He was at his most ingratiating, though his understanding of English and even French had not much improved.

"No possible, M'amselle . . ." he informed me pleasantly. "Isabeau—no possible."

"You'll not be saying she still plays truant!"

He did not understand this and I amended it to describe Isabeau as a "runaway" which gradually became clear to him. "But such odd place to run!" he went on in his happy, unquestioning way.

I foresaw that Isabeau and I were destined for a scene of scolding, protests, complaints and perhaps, in the end, adding an enemy at Moura to my already imposing list.

"Never mind. Would you put those cloths around your hands and take the plate off the hob and bring it to me here?" As I sat down at Matilde's old, scarred deal table I felt a surprising and unusual tiredness. I wondered if it was the result of that accident last evening and its aftermath with the rat-bite, or whatever plagued my throat and neck.

Draja good-naturedly carried out my instructions and also brought me a thick, cracked mug of mulled wine which, along with my dinner, warmed and refreshed me so that I felt infinitely better by the time I arrived at the brandy pudding and I could give some attention to poor Draja, who stood on one foot and then the other, undoubtedly waiting to be dismissed. I thanked the boy and told him he might go back to the fire or to his chamber. He shrugged.

"This is my chamber, if it please you, Miss-M'amselle." He giggled. "You are in my chamber; isn't it so?"

"Well, lie down again and go to sleep. I promise not to disturb you . . . or wake you . . . until morning."

He went to follow my advice, but as he knelt before the warm coals he looked around and reminded me mischievously, "You say what is no true. A lie, yes? You say no one wake me."

"And no one shall."

"But she will do so when she comes up out of there again.

Always she yell and talk. Walk heavy when she has anger. And being down there so long, she will have anger."

I looked around, puzzled, and with the beginnings of a dread that I tried vainly to dissemble. "Draja, tell me at once what you mean. Who is she? And what do you mean by *down there?* Who is coming up again?"

"But Isabeau, naturally. From the cellars."

"Nonsense. Isabeau went to the cellars hours ago, to fetch up the bottles for Matilde. Then she ran away."

"No, no, M'amselle. It was Borgos fetched up the bottles when Isabeau did not come back. Matilde thought Isabeau is gone through the underground dungeons and out, but is not possible. Isabeau fears the cellars too much." He grinned happily. "Maybe she loses herself down there, I think."

I got up in haste. I had the most horrid fear that this might explain Isabeau's truancy, her complete disappearance from sight for at least four or five hours. The Moura cellars had terrorized stouter hearts than Isabeau's, and if I were to believe Miss Hedi's tale, this same terror of the cellars had seen the beginning of Cléa Raines' illness as well as the ghastly change in Kate Moura. Had it now set about the same destruction of young Isabeau?

I was strongly of the opinion that this fear of the cellars was groundless in respect to physical harm. The real harm at Moura was abovestairs, from some flesh-and-blood danger. I had been through the cellars on various household matters a hundred times during my life at Moura and no harm had come to me. But the dangers to the mind, the fancies these women carried with them into the cellars had very likely been the instruments of their suffering. And poor, silly Isabeau had been driven into this place she feared so much!

"Draja," I said, pulling myself together hurriedly. "I did lie to you. You must help me. I need a lantern with a shield, and one of my shawls and—" I looked down. My slippers with their flat heels would do. And an escort? There was not a person at Moura whom I trusted wholly except young Draja. I had far rather put my faith and confidence in one of Matilde's meat axes which came under my fingers at this moment. I took up the smaller carving knife, hefted it, tried its point and blade and found them adequate.

The boy bustled about, finding a suitable lantern of the type used for fetching articles from the stillrooms and the wine cellar, and then he brought me a blood-red woolen shawl that hung on a peg beside the crockery wall. "It is a shawl of Matilde," he explained. I thanked him, threw it around my shoulders and took the lantern in my free hand. Draja's eyes were saucer-round as the lantern light played along the length of the carving knife. "But Miss-M'amselle, you will never take that horrid thing! You are gentle lady. Not like Matilde."

His horrified challenge suddenly made me aware of a deep and heretofore unsuspected truth about myself. As I moved toward the cellar steps, I said firmly, "Let me tell you, boy, there is very probably no one at Moura so like me in spirit and perhaps in soul, as Matilde. When I am her age, I daresay I shall be even more like her."

"But you do not look in the least like Matilde!"

I laughed at this superficial observation, explaining, "If you're about to come upon me in the darkness, Draja, you'll be seeing soon enough that I can use this." He looked askance at the blade but rather surprised me by coming along behind me. "You'll not be frightened?" I asked him.

He grinned. "Always I wish to go through all the cellars, and twice I go down alone, but I nearly lose myself and I come back to the wine cellar. Now I go with you and see all the rooms, the dungeons, all of it. No?"

"No, I hope! I have no wish to take you through the entire underground of Moura. I want to prove to myself either that Isabeau is down there, perhaps hurt, unconscious from a fall, or that she left the cellars by another way."

I raised the lantern and started down the cellar steps. During my years at Moura I had seen to it that this area of wines and winter food stores at the foot of the steps was relieved of its cobwebs and other nocturnal inhabitants. I could see now that, for one reason or another, no effort had been made to restore the dank and gloomy spot to the condition in which I had left it. The place was two rudely constructed rooms with floors half dirt, half stone. The walls were of great, irregular blocks of stone against which various shelves and a number of bottle racks had been constructed. I examined this area carefully but found no indication of Isabeau's having been here. Frightened as she was of the cellars, she would not, logically, have left this area.

"Unless," I murmured aloud, trying to place myself in Isabeau's position, "something distracted her."

Draja was already trotting through the passage beyond and in another minute, if I did not follow him with my lantern, he would be tumbling down another flight of steps, into what I have always considered the bowels of the earth. I hurried to stop the boy. At the same time I held the lantern in such a way as to illuminate the uneven stone flooring and the walls with their eternally blind creatures crawling among the lichen that clung like dark gouts of blood under my light. I still saw no signs of Isabeau's presence and was beginning to think the boy and I should accomplish nothing tonight. If Isabeau had not appeared by early morning, I would certainly summon every male at Moura and demand that the cellars be searched in their entirety.

Water had seeped into the earth between the stones and Draja stopped before the iron-bound door which sealed off the last flight of steps to the ancient torture dungeons below. He was staring at the mud that had accumulated and turned to me proudly.

"See? The mark of the shoe heel. I think maybe this is her mark."

It was a clear track in dried earth upon the stone beyond the mud. Part of the imprint of the sole was missing, but Draja's sharp young eyes had made out the odd triangular shape of the heel. I could not recall the heels Isabeau wore, or if she even wore slippers with heels, but certainly this was a fresh track that must have been made within the last few hours and dried in its correct shape.

"What in heaven's name was she doing down here?" I

asked myself and then glanced at Draja, who excitedly reminded me:

"We go on? See all the bad places under the earth?"

I had been ready to turn back, but knew that having found this possible sign of her I must go on, at least through the torture chambers. But the truth was, I still could not imagine why she had come so far.

XVI

I TRIED THE heavy, iron-bound door and found it locked. Draja looked so crestfallen I almost smiled at his disappointment.

"Turn about," I ordered him, "and close your eyes." He did so, obligingly taking the lantern to free one of my hands. I took out the key ring from among my petticoats and had him hold the lantern close so as to illuminate my work as I fitted the key into the door. I prepared myself for the shriek of rusty hinges but only a slight grating sound ensued as the door opened under the pressure of my hand. It seemed clear that the door was frequently used. This, when compared to the eerie, ill-kept condition of the wine cellar and storerooms, suggested to me that someone wished to frighten away the unknowing servant who ventured into the wine cellar, while the deepest quarter of the labyrinth was being constantly utilized. To what purpose?

There was one more plunging flight of steps before the dungeons were reached, and either the slime upon the aged stone or our difficulty with the locked door had thrown my bold young cavalier into quite a different and more gingerly mood. He lingered behind me, looking back over his shoulder, murmuring, "It—is very cold . . . strange," and following this came words in that language he shared with the Stavkos and Tzigana. "*Die Todten! Die Todten!*"

I did not understand the words then; yet there was grim meaning implicit in his tones. The chill of the walls and the sunken steps themselves crept into my very bones. At such moments I was usually inclined to put on a shield of anger or impatience. "Do not make such silly talk. We will look into the old rooms below and if we do not find her, we will turn back."

"Miss-M'amselle . . . hold the cross before us for to save us."

Puzzled, but more than half inclined to do so, I touched my neck absently to stroke the little pearl crucifix. My fingers felt only the bare flesh on my throat. Somehow, I had lost my precious little crucifix. It seemed suddenly an omen of ill-fortune.

His sabots clattered down after me, the clacking sound unnerving to say the least, and he whispered, "It is place for *Die Todten*. Not for us. For the dead. Please . . . I change my wish. We go back?" He set the lantern down.

"Presently." Until this second we had not seen one untoward thing, one sign of danger. It seemed preposterous that a healthy grown woman, together with a sturdy boy should be stopped by a mere atmosphere of cold and damp; yet so it was, since I had realized my crucifix was gone. When Draja whispered shrilly, "What if Isabeau lies there . . . among the dead?" I was of a strong inclination to flee up the steps with him.

"We are at the bottom now. This door is broken. Beyond it are the two dungeons. She probably did not come this far. I think"—as I reached for the door which had always hung broken by one hinge—"we would probably do well to turn back after I just see to the old torture cell here." But already the boy was clattering up the steps. Before I turned to join him, at this rate, he would be halfway to the wine cellars. I smiled, partly at his direct and very human reaction, partly to cheer myself. In a minute, perhaps two, I should go back after him.

The door began to move under my hand, slowly and with difficulty at first. I saw what the trouble was. An old threadbare strip of carpet was wedged between the bottom of the door and the uneven stone beneath. I reached down to pull the carpet through, but found it would not yield. It was somehow weighted on the other side of the heavy door. Losing patience and knowing now that I had been on a useless search, I started to rise from my knees.

To my stupefaction, I felt the door yield abruptly before me, being pulled open from the other side to reveal a light that dazzled my eyes, so that I saw nothing of the ancient dungeon cell beyond, nor the cause of this shocking light. I blinked and nearly dropped the carving knife but managed to catch it hard against my skirt while I knelt there, feeling a strange and deathlike calm suffuse my chilled body.

. . . *It is a trick,* I reminded myself. . . . *Someone human is behind the light. . . . And for what terrible purpose, God only knows. . . . God or the Devil, belike!*

I tried to get to my feet, hating that light which still blinded me, hating the creature behind it. But most of all, I was still consciously aware of a power being exerted upon me through this burst of crystalline flashes. A pair of hands lifted me to my feet while I shrank away, trying to scream, to cry for help, unable to utter any but muted sounds. The hideous thing was that I could feel myself surrender to the mesmerizing influences of those dazzling jewel lights.

Within the aura of those lights, I felt my wits and my will grow numb. A face shimmered as if seen through many facets of the jewel lights and for an instant I thought it was our nemesis, the evil-eyed coachman, but then, the features rearranged and became the austere, high-boned face of Istvan Stavko. I was conscious of the faint repulsion I always felt at his close proximity, the remembrance of a creature nearly a century old; yet the man I saw, tantalizingly, through jewel prisms, was barely above middle age. In my present state, lulled to a great calm, I remember thinking, with his head so close above mine, that he was about to kiss me and that I would welcome that kiss. It had never been so during my previous encounters with him. Why had I changed?

His deeply curved lips, which I had found repulsive, were moist and sensuous in the prism light as he bowed his head over me and those lips touched, feather-light upon my throat. A trembling pervaded my flesh. My limbs were too weak to hold me, but I was gripped about the waist in a hard-boned, painful hold, and always there were those thickened lips at my throat.

The dazzling prism lights blurred before my eyes and blurred, too, the single stab of pain where my throat was pierced by this terrible being who had made himself my master. The loss of my own will was perhaps the worst thing of all. My fingers were still frozen about the shaft of the carving knife and yet my will to use it was gone. A part of my consciousness remembered that I must scream, that possibly the sounds would reverberate through these echo-haunted passages.

And again there was a buzz of voices and the strange words: "My property. No one will touch my property. From the first moment I sighted her on the road, it was meant so."

From far away I heard someone moan and wondered if it was I. By exerting all the reserves I possessed, I tried to draw away, to free myself of this frightful nightmare, but I was still subdued by the blinding aura of crystal prisms, and the singular power of this creature who seemed composed of many terrors.

Voices shimmered as if under water, and in a language uncomprehensible. Gradually, with the draining of strength and will and blood, came a ghastly peace, a sense of weakness that must be like dying.

Whether hours passed or it had all occurred in a moment's confused nightmare, I did not know. Coming back from the nightmare was far longer, more painful than the confusion and frenzy that attended it.

Gradually, I remember, my bed in the small South Wing chamber became real to me. With all the will at my command I forced open my eyes, putting aside the nightmare with what I thought of as its imagined horrors, and thinking to welcome the bright path of sunlight which cut between the window draperies that had been improperly closed. So depressed was I by the aftereffects of my nightmare, as if cobwebs had been spun over my brain, that I decided to open the curtains wide, and let in the crystal clear winter sunlight to cheer me. But when I tried to put my feet over the side of the bed, I found myself lamentably weak. My senses seemed to swim as I moved my head.

What a dream it must have been, that left me in such a state! Even the cords in my neck were painful and the small teeth marks over my jugular vein, made by the scampering, frightened rat two nights ago in this room, had swollen and now throbbed in a nerve-wracking way. It must be like this when one awakened from a prolonged bout with the brandy bottle. I was so tired last night I seemed not to have changed to my nightgown and my dress and petticoats were dreadfully squeezed about, wrinkled and, in several places, mud-stained.

Fiercely determined to shake off the weakness that pervaded my body and even my bones, I removed my clothing and scrubbed my body with the towel and the chilly water in the basin that had been left warm and perfumed in my room last evening. I felt somewhat better when I had completed this brisk massaging of my body and limbs and was dressing for the day in crisp, clean petticoats and my blue wool gown.

As I was setting aside yesterday's clothing to be cleaned, I noticed two tiny brown stains on the collar. They were on the side, curious stains like drops of blood from a pinprick. As I studied the stains, and almost before I was aware of the significance of the gesture, I raised my fingers to my throat and rubbed the swollen vein gently, thoughtfully. It was becoming apparent that the results of my encounter with the rodent several nights ago were not ended yet. Had the tiny puncture made by the teeth of the rat opened and bled again?

The cure for this poisoning came to me unbidden. I must

go and see the Maître. . . . Yes. The Master would know how to treat it. He experimented with powerful unguents and salves. I must go to him and explain how I had forgotten the events of last night, and confused them with a hideous nightmare.

An unaccountable chill seized me, but not, surely, I thought, at the prospect of meeting Istvan Stavko. My compulsion to go and see him, to ask his help, was overwhelming, almost a physical compulsion. Mentally, I was not at all sure why I must trust him, nor why, in spite of the languor that beset me, I should still spend so much time making myself excessively presentable for him. I even felt the faint repulsion that his close presence always aroused in me; yet I must go.

I was shocked by a slapping sound on the door, as if the flat of a strong hand were being used. I called out, wondering at the weakness of my own voice, "Yes? Who is it?

"Are you all right? Answer us, please! Are you all right?" asked Captain Surtees in an anxious voice I would never have associated with the self-assured Captain.

"But, of course, Sir! Why should I not be?" I made little delaying gestures, smoothing the folds of my fresh gown, patting my hair in a very conscious way; for I had not had time to do more than brush it vigorously before I tried the door. It was locked and the key lay on the tilt table nearby. I never put the key there. As a matter of fact, I usually left it in the lock and, instead, bolted the door. It was not bolted now. I unlocked the door, surprising some noisy whispers in the passage. The sounds abruptly ceased as Captain Surtees and Draja looked at me in the most guilty way, Draja holding my breakfast tea tray and the Captain waving a hand in my direction.

"Not a scratch. She's lovely as ever. Now, will you apologize for sending me to rouse her in this rude fashion?"

Draja started to take offense at this but I cut them both short. "Why?" I asked, amused at their childish squabble. "Did you expect some calamity had struck?" I took the tray from Draja and set it on my table. Both my uninvited guests came trooping into the room, Draja protesting all the way.

"I run away last night. I leave you, Miss-M'amselle. I am much ashamed. The Captain is angry this morning when I tell him of it, and of you who do not hear me when I bring the tray and knock and call to you. He says he will go with me then."

"What nonsense you talk, Draja! I heard you—or the Captain—the minute you banged on my door. I'd have been deaf otherwise."

Draja and the Captain exchanged looks, which annoyed me very much, as if I were shut out of some knowledge that I ought to have.

"Go away, my boy," said the Captain with a brisk push softened by his delightful smile. "Say nothing of this to anyone or I'll send a *gytrash* to eat you up."

"What may a *gytrash* be?" I asked, highly amused as the boy scuttled away down the passage. The Captain closed the door, surprisingly locked it and strode over to the table to face me. I was made uneasy by his searching gaze.

"If you were a Yorkshirewoman, you would not have to ask what a *gytrash* might be. All claws and fire-breathing. Monstrous, I assure you, though not perhaps as monstrous as some I have encountered here in—" He broke away from that comparison to take me by the shoulders and propel me bodily toward the window. "Let me see you in the light."

He reached for the portieres and drew them apart. Abruptly, the room was flooded with sunshine and the instant it illuminated my face I felt a pain so intense I screamed. It was as if a thousand white-hot needles pierced my eyes. I recoiled in panic at my own reaction, but the Captain's arms reached out for me, holding me prisoner until the terror and stupefaction left and I stared at him very much, I'm afraid, as a child seeking explanations from an all-knowing adult. My lips felt parched, and it was with difficulty that I spoke at all.

"What—what is wrong with me? Have I some dread—dreadful illness?"

Although his own features looked strained to my pleading eyes, he was blessedly confident. "Not unless your belief in superstition is unshakable." He tried a warm and friendly grin. "That, I'm afraid, is something one should never ask an Irishwoman." He could see my confusion and doubt, but went right on talking, encouraging me in his own positive, humorously masterful way. "Come, now, Me Darlin' Colleen, you must eat your breakfast and get back that enchanting Irish complexion. You're looking frightful this morning."

"You did not say so when we first met not half an hour since." What he said now may have been true—I had very little doubt of it—but it hurt, nonetheless. "In any case, thank you, Sir, and I'll be more thankful to see the back of you after that insulting verdict. So go along. Follow that other silly child."

Instead of letting me go, he shook me so that my head ached, my teeth chattered, and the cords of my neck felt as if they would snap with the strain. To my own disgust, I discovered I was very close to tears and tried to turn away, yet realized too late that this drew his attention to my throat. I avoided his eyes, but heard him catch his breath sharply at sight of the swollen vein and the teeth marks of that infernal rodent two nights ago.

"You were having difficulty with your throat yesterday; were you not? And it seems much worse today."

"I know." And knew, too, as if my mind had been instructed precisely at this instant, what I must do. "There is an ointment that has great healing powers. I'll go and ask the Maître for it."

He looked as if he would argue this with me and I wondered, with a really intolerable conceit, if he might be jealous of my relationship with my master, that is to say, my employer. Curious how easily I had come to think of the austere and subtly attractive Istvan Stavko exactly as Kate did. He was called *the Master,* and stood in that relationship to us both. An admirable man, very reserved, perhaps, but I could not deny his power. As I thought of him now, I wished the Captain gone, so that I might the more rapidly bring about my meeting with my master. . . . In my thoughts I corrected myself again, but the fact of his power over my senses remained. I dared not tell him of my jumbled and fantastic dream last night, in which he appeared, and the malign and twisted coachman, and a diamond-bright prism whirling before me with a mesmerizing effect upon me. I could well imagine the contempt he would show and how his lips would curl haughtily at the idea of filling any woman's nightmare dreams. How hideous and yet how profoundly affecting that nightmare had been! So much so that it blotted out even my memory of my activities last night. This might be due, of course, to the frightful headache I had just before I opened my eyes this morning.

"Forgive me, Captain Surtees. I really must be going about my work."

The Captain hesitated, as if torn by conflicting impulses. "See here, Anne—"

"I have not given you permission to call me that. Only one person has the right. My—my employer. Please let me go. I say it to your face, Sir, you make me excessively nervous, staring at me like that as if I were turned to salt!"

He undid all my firmness by kissing my forehead in a highly respectable, almost paternal way, and then lowering his gaze to my eyes, he smiled warmly. "Well then, Miss Anne, I have a surprise for you. This will bring back the Irish roses to those alabaster cheeks or I'm a Dutchman!"

"I really must go. . . ." But before I could move away, he took something from his coat and slipped it over my head.

I did not immediately understand, even when the narrow chain dropped around my neck, but I cried out as the little pearl crucifix touched my throat and the Captain's excited reaction to my cry astonished me.

"Good God! What is it? Is it already too late?"

"I don't understand. All this because a pearl cross is chilly upon my neck?"

"Is that all?" His wholehearted laugh more than made up for his ridiculous over-reaction a moment before.

"Where did you find it, in heaven's name? I thought I'd lost it."

"That noble savage, Tzigana's husband. He must have found it. Or stolen it."

I thought over that brief time last night when Borgos helped me with the cleaning in the great hall. Quite possibly, with my exertions, I had lost the crucifix. I was grateful for its recovery, and at once the Captain seized the opportunity of returning to his former manner.

"Good. You must promise me two things: one, that you will never—*never* remove that cross and chain. Consider it an omen, a symbol of good luck. And two, that you will eat this very solid and substantial breakfast, including the entire contents of this mug."

"What mug?" Then, looking into it, I wrinkled my nose in distaste. The sour odor was sickening. "Red wine at this hour? You might at least have offered me good Irish Whisky!"

"Drink! It is said to be good for the blood."

Obedient to his command, I drank. Fingering my small pearl cross, I obeyed him afterward by eating almost all the food on the tray, including a dish of buttered eggs which were almost jellied after their trip through endless halls, followed by their long hibernation in my room as I had quarreled and made up the quarrel with Captain Surtees. It was astonishing to me that by the time I finished this endless breakfast I was feeling much more the thing and could appreciate how very much the Captain had helped me. When I awoke to a frightful sore throat, a general weakness and a mind still haunted by the most ghastly dreams, I had the strange notion that there would be only one solution, to see the Maître.

After my bout with the breakfast forced upon me by Captain Surtees, and perhaps, too, by his mingled teasing and torment, I felt infinitely more myself. When the Captain showed every intention of escorting me about the chateau all day, I explained as politely as I could that we both had our work to do and even if he was not expected in the students' wing to teach them history or how to dance the waltz, I must report to the Master for my day's instructions.

"How long will you be employed by this creature—this Master at Moura? I'll go bail you didn't come merely to oblige the Stavkos," he remarked as he unlocked the door and persisted in escorting me down toward the Master's offices in the East Front wing. I looked at him suspiciously.

"Why should I not be employed here?"

"For one reason, your Cousin, Kate, was out of reason cross last night. She suspected you were dangling about after her beloved Maître Stavko, and she confided a few choice items of your history, including why you came to Moura so recently."

I was more than impatient at this. I found it alarming. "Good God, Sir, I trust she is not so loose-tongued with everyone! And in any case, I do not *dangle about* after Maître Stavko. . . . He can scarcely be blamed if he appeared in my nightmare last night."

He gazed at me intently, so much so that I looked away, pretending to be occupied by my descent of the staircase that was cut into the side of the great East Tower. "Where did you go and what happened after Draja ran away?"

The answer was perfectly simple, I thought, as I began to recount my journey with the boy through the cellars in our search for the missing Isabeau. "We did not find the girl in the wine cellar. I had a notion that she might have slipped, and struck her head. Perhaps fallen unconscious. But we found nothing. Draja saw a heel mark which he said belonged to the girl. That was just in front of the upper dungeon door. There is one at the foot of the dungeon steps as well. Draja turned back just there."

"Yes," he prompted me. "And then?"

Through the confusion that settled over me at this point, I became obsessed with thoughts of the Maître. Each time I tried to retrace my steps back to my room last night the strange mesmerism of the austere Istvan Stavko blotted out all else. He filled my thoughts as a lover might, and yet I knew I did not love him. But I *was* obsessed by him. So much so that I could not bring myself to mention his name, for fear the Captain might sneer at his influence, or insult him again in discussing him with me. I must protect Stavko. I must not allow suspicion of any sort to be cast upon my master. I said coolly, "After that, I went on through the cellars without seeing any further signs of Isabeau, and I came out by the steps near the courtyard door where you met Lady Tyra that first night."

In a voice so reasonable I should have suspected it, he said, "And, naturally, you came at once to your bedchamber."

"Naturally."

He took my arm in a tight hold that made me protest angrily. He was no less firm in his accusation, despite my anger. "My darling child, why are you lying to me? Don't you know I care more about what happens to you than anything else in this den of tigers?"

Far from calming me, this made me terribly agitated. I could not understand the strangeness of my own behavior. But listening to him gave me the same hot, violent sense of guilt that I would have if I committed adultery. Most horrible of all, the one I betrayed had miraculously become Maître Stavko, my master. . . . *I have become as bad as Kate,* I told myself. *I do not love that strange man. He has always affected me with a tiny prick of fear; yet he becomes my master in every thought. So strongly has my nightmare overcome my senses! But, Mother of God, if it were not a nightmare—if it were truth! If all those ghastly, tangled pictures flashing before my brain were the memory of things that had really happened, what then?* . . . I would not think of it. I dare not, or I should be convinced I had run mad.

"Why should you think me a liar? You are very offensive."

His smile did not reach his eyes which considered me in the half-dark with concern and even sadness. "Anne, I was there—in your bedchamber. No one saw you all evening, so I waited. And waited. Where were you, Anne, my girl?"

"Don't call me that, please. You must not. Someone might

hear you and tell—him." My head ached abominably. I could not even remember his question. I knew only that there would be danger to him, terrible danger, if he were suspected of seeking the Master's property. Even in my confusion, though, I recognized that those words were an echo of something I heard before. *The Master's Property had become Anne Wicklow!*

I stumbled in my blind haste to escape from Captain Surtees, his questions, his prying, the danger he represented, both to himself and to me. Nothing must happen to him. Nothing! And to ensure that, I must not be seen in friendship with him. But I caught myself as we were stepping down into the courtyard very near to the turret entrance of the East Tower. At almost the same time my companion and I were shaken by an ear-piercing and prolonged shriek, followed by the utmost confusion in the cold, narrow stone courtyard between the tower and the East Front of Moura.

"Stay here!" Surtees ordered sharply, pushing me against the doorway to the turret steps. "Don't move until I come for you."

Stricken as much by that dreadful cry as by his warning, I leaned against the rough stones of the tower, wondering tiredly what new disaster had befallen those at Moura. I tried to make clarity out of the noises that came from that narrow extension of the courtyard far below the turret embrasure, but my confused thoughts were crystallized and drawn away from that area suddenly by the realization that someone was coming down the time-worn steps of the tower. I looked upward, heard the quick, sharp beat of wooden sabots, and an instant later the flushed, excited face of the missing Isabeau seemed to rush at me, out of the half-dark of the turret's twisting flight of steps. She seized me in a pinching grip.

"Come, quickly, M'amselle! What a dreadful thing! They were quarreling, fighting at the very edge of the turret, and she went over. All that horrid way!"

"Who went over? What are you talking about?"

"Madame Kate and the Austrian Mademoiselle Hedi.

Such a fight. As though they had murder in their hearts. And she went over!"

Not Kate . . . Not Kate . . . I began to run, leaving the girl to gawk at me and repeat endlessly, "All that way she fell. . . . All the way to the courtyard. . . ."

XVII

As I ran, with my head buzzing madly, I thought this was twice that I might blame my headache on Isabeau. She had not been at her duties the previous night and so sent me climbing through those dirty, depressing cellars searching for her. She looked very healthy just now, if one allowed for her excitement over the horrible accident she had just witnessed. But was it an accident?

The narrow extension of the courtyard, heavily shadowed by the tower, was now alive with screaming, hysterical girls crowded around Captain Surtees, who knelt over a huddled thing he had partially covered with his coat. The white sleeves of his shirt ruffled in the morning breeze, and his waistcoat was badly stained. I pushed my way through, scarcely aware of the clamor around me until I caught a glimpse of the thin, twisted young arm trailing out beneath the coat, as if it had groped over the cold stones in a last agony against death. And I found in that sickened moment of revelation that I could not be glad for the sparing of Kate Moura. Not when a child Hedi von Preysing's age must die in her place.

No one seemed to be staring upward at the tower which brooded over us. Even Captain Surtees was too busy at his hopeless task of trying to revive the unfortunate girl. Apparently no one had guessed that Kate had been up in the turret with Miss Hedi and Isabeau. I looked back across the wide, sunny expanse of the courtyard. Isabeau was obviously rushing toward the Maître's chambers in the East Wing. I should do likewise. I felt the strong urge to go to him at once, to betray Kate, my only relation, my dearest friend, and I was actually about to move in that direction when I forced myself to throw off this insidious and heretofore unknown influence.

It was Kate to whom I owed my first allegiance, now that this poor child could no longer be aided. I made my way back out between the onlookers, completely unnoticed, and ran to the entrance of the tower steps. I listened there for a minute or two but heard no sounds of a descent from the turret. I started up the steps rapidly, running. I wanted no one else to suspect Kate was still here in the tower and alone. At the first embrasure I had to stop to take a breath of the crisp country air. I wondered at my own weakness that seemed to linger with me long after my nightmarish fancies should have vanished upon my awakening. I listened but could still hear no sounds above me. Had the girl, Isabeau, lied about Kate's presence? If I could get Kate out of here unnoticed, though, I would be perfectly willing to lie about her presence myself, and it would be my word against Isabeau's.

I tried again, mounting the steps so rapidly the round and round ascent made me dizzy, but I kept remembering that I had found Miss Elfreda up here, and things had been better for her since. I would regard it as an omen. However, on that morning I had not been nearly so worn down as I was today. When I came within sight of the turret, I was breathless and shaking with the effort.

It was easy enough to sight Kate Moura. She lay face down upon the stone floor of the turret, huddled much in the manner of the dead Hedi von Preysing far below us. She wore one of her new and ultra-fashionable gowns with the elaborate full skirts and a fur pelisse that only partially covered her well-rounded arms. The pelisse was pulled and torn, which made me realize there must have been a struggle, as Isabeau claimed. I reached for Kate's hand. Thank God she was alive! Guessing that I would have very little time before Isabeau brought the Maître first to the courtyard below and then to fetch Kate from the tower, I slapped Kate's wrists and shook her gently until she opened her eyes.

She stared at me as if, like myself an hour before, she struggled against a blur of the senses.

"Why?" she asked vaguely, her fingers plucking at my sleeves. "She told me the Master needed me up here . . . why did she lie to me?"

"Never mind that. We must get you down from here at once. Can you get to your feet? Lean on me."

Kate struggled to do so, but observed in a way I found troubling, "You look ghastly, Anne, so pale! Have you the strength to help me?" As I did so, she murmured, "But of course you would look so. It was inevitable, once he began to—to love you."

"I don't know what you are talking about. Stand up now."

With some effort, for Kate was never a lightweight, she followed my instructions, and I saw that her forehead was bleeding and bruised from what looked like a blow. "Did the girls strike you?" I asked, planning in my mind the logical defense she must make for this dreadful business if she were accused.

"The servant girl did nothing. She came up behind us and tried to stop us, I suppose. I know she did nothing to help me. But that black-haired Austrian hussy was quite another thing entirely. She kept trying to tell me I must jump, that I'd lost my—the Maître and there was nothing for it but to jump. I didn't believe her. Little lying wretch! Probably sent by someone who wants the Maître for herself. I saw that quickly enough." We were moving down the steps now, I in the lead, trying to hurry her, but at this I could not misunderstand her as she raised her dark eyes from a careful examination of the steps and studied my face accusingly. "So you've been through the cellars, Anne! That spinning prism has overcome all those fine scruples of yours. But mark me! He'll soon tire of you. He detests pale, bloodless creatures. He told me so." She showed every sign of slowing down to get behind me, and this, combined with her jealous accusation concerning Maître Stavko, made me acutely aware of danger.

"Please go on ahead," I told her quietly. I thought she would obey me. She showed every sign of doing so, but just as she was passing me on the narrow step, I surprised her in a gesture with both hands that made me move quickly to avoid being propelled head first down those spiral steps. She looked at her hands in a puzzled way and then at me and I knew she had not really been aware of the sudden danger she had represented to me.

But all her previous rambling about the Maître reminded me of the nightmares that had so disturbed my dreams last night and when she began to rail at me again for having stolen the Master's love, I wished she would be silent. She was as bad as Captain Surtees, as though both of them were trying to make me believe the ghastly jumble of my nightmare had been real. But it could not be real! If it had been, it would be against all nature, a horror too great to be borne, and I should end in Kate's condition, full of jealousy over an incredible—and impossible relationship. How could she imagine I loved the Master, or that he loved me? I had scarcely been in his company other than upon the affairs of my office at Moura. In many ways he repulsed me as did his daughter.

I liked Kate's talk even less when I remembered my strong compulsion to see and be in the Master's presence this morning. I could only thank the timely interruption of Edward Surtees, and the breakfast I had been forced to eat, for shaking off that curious and unhealthy tie which seemed to have been knotted during my dreams, between myself and Istvan Stavko.

We reached the bottom of the tower with considerable expediture of energy, and Kate was so dizzy from that abrupt, circling descent that she stumbled against me, made a panic-stricken clutch at my shoulder and grasped my crucifix in her fingers. I freed the delicate little chain, taking her hands in mine to calm her. She did not apologize for her action but indicated my crucifix, and murmured thoughtfully, "I had a cross like that. When I was so high and mighty because I resented the Stavkos, I suppose." She sighed. "I lost it somewhere. In my bedchamber, perhaps."

Remembering Captain Surtees' insistence that I wear mine at all times—an odd fancy for a man who did not belong to the Church of Rome—I asked Kate whether she might have lost her crucifix at Moura instead. "Perhaps it was stolen."

"No. No. I had worn it to the chateau. Didn't enjoy myself that visit. Found them all strange creatures and even suspected them of devilish doings. And I recall fingering the cross as I walked into the porter's lodge. After that, I must have misplaced it when I removed it. I remember lifting it over my head. I saw my face in the mirror and found a new line between my eyes. . . . And I forgot the crucifix. God knows where it dropped to. Fortunately, the next time I came to Moura, with some absurd notion of spying on them, they were exceedingly pleasant, and the Maître— Well, you know about the Master and me."

I did, indeed, and being a person of keen superstitions myself, I wondered if the absence of Kate's crucifix could have been a factor which broke down her first, keen observation of the doings at Moura. Certainly, her passion for Maître Stavko, which amounted almost to a madness, had begun after she misplaced that small guardian angel, her crucifix. It was an explanation of sorts and the only one that had occurred thus far.

Kate went ahead of me. It had seemed for a short time that we might slip out of the tower without being seen, but we were just stepping blindly into the sunlight, when Kate stopped with a startled exclamation. As I joined her I saw Tzigana's straight figure, her white hair catching the brightness of the day. There was nothing bright or happy about her features, however. They looked drawn, and older than

I ever remembered them. I knew she must have seen young Miss Hedi, her one friend among the students. But she curtseyed to us with a slow, strong-limbed gesture, far less shaky than I felt at the moment.

"If the Maître Stavko may see you within the next half hour, Mademoiselle?"

"At once," Kate said quickly, with an urgency that was painful to hear. It put me in mind again of my own strange impulse when I awoke this morning. Had I spoken of it then, I daresay I too would have been absurdly anxious to find myself in the Master's company.

"Pardon, Mademoiselle. It is Miss Anne that the Maître wishes to see. If Mademoiselle Kate will be so good as to come with me, we will see to the wrapping of . . . the corpse."

Nothing that had happened thus far seemed so terrible as this word calmly spoken by the girl's closest confidante. I saw Kate's face, which was ashen, and said quickly, "Miss Kate is not well. I have done this—this task before. I am familiar with the necessary steps. I will help you."

"But the Maître—" Tzigana began, though she glanced in the direction of the crowd around the dead girl. I was relieved that she made no protest at the change in Kate's and my assignments. As a result of my strange attachment to Istvan Stavko this morning, I found myself anxious to avoid him now. I did not want to renew that inexplicable dependence upon him.

Kate's obvious anxiety to take my place in the interview with the Maître might well be as senseless as my own earlier anxiety. But there were more urgent matters now. I said quickly. "Tell the Maître exactly what happened, Mademoiselle Kate. That the young lady, Miss Hedi, behaved strangely, enticed you to the tower on some pretext, struck you on the head and tried to send you over the side. Then she slipped and fell."

Kate did not wait to hear Tzigana's further objections, nor how to counter whatever accusations Isabeau might have made. She hurried away as the gypsy woman beckoned to me. "There is much to be done. For me it is a painful business. I knew Fraulein Hedi in her childhood."

"Then perhaps you will be good enough to tell me why Miss Hedi did entice Madame Kate to the East Tower, only to attack her."

Tzigana glanced at me blankly, her mind fixed upon the dead girl, rather than the live and possibly malign Hedi von Preysing who had formerly existed. "Miss Anne, you say this thing of a child who has been the victim of a terrible—event? How can you know Madame Kate told you the truth?"

I could think of no reason why Kate would wish to entice the girl into the tower and murder her, but then I had not yet discovered the dead girl's motive either. And I had seen only a few minutes ago Kate's brooding and dangerous jealousy of me. Why was Kate meant to be destroyed by Hedi, or by anyone else, for that matter? This way of putting the problem seemed to suggest shadowy things, evil as my nightmares last night. Could Kate have killed that child, after all, in a defense of her own passion for the Maître?

The schoolgirls scattered as we came among them, and I was disturbed to see that Captain Surtees had disappeared. Discovering his absence, I understood suddenly how very much I counted upon and needed him. The dead girl still lay where she had fallen, covered by the Captain's coat. But as I sent the students on their way back to their section of the chateau, I was enormously relieved to see the Captain return, this time with sheets and a blanket. He made plans to carry the unfortunate girl to a suitable place in the chateau for the necessary examination by an authority from the village, or even from Montemessine.

Tzigana and I followed him with the dead girl, the gypsy murmuring, "How do such things happen? My poor Fraulein Hedi! It is too much!"

With the shock of the girl's death somewhat subdued now, I found myself furiously angry at these unaccountable tragedies and said so aloud. Tzigana hesitated, looked at me directly and asked, "Is it possible for so much tragedy to follow a family? Is that what you are thinking? That the Stavkos are in some way at fault?"

"You would know better than I," I snapped back, recalling barely in time that the woman had been a part of the Stavko family since before Lady Tyra's birth.

She looked hurriedly over her shoulder. Had I not been so suspicious of her, I would have sworn panic was in that normally placid face. "There were—things," she whispered so that I had to strain to hear her. "Lady Tyra's mother said there were things about the family. And now, oh my poor Hedi! That child!" She stumbled as we reached a step into the hall beneath the long gallery and I caught her. How frail her bones felt beneath my fingers! I saw then that she had stumbled because her eyes were closed as she whispered the dead girl's name. "I thank you," she said a minute later in her usual calm, efficient voice when I released her arm.

I said I understood as, indeed, I understood too well. I had felt the same almost motherly grief three years gone by at the death of another girl for whom I once had an affection and comradely feeling. Captain Surtees had gone far ahead of us and I was about to hurry after him when my companion's voice, broken and only half audible, arrested me.

"Miss Anne—I have seen how you act. You believe my lady is at fault some way. But she is all I have now, and I know her to be innocent. If—if you and I were to aid each other, we might stop him." As I stared at her, speechless at her audacity against the all-powerful Master, she seemed to recollect her place with the Stavkos, the danger in which such a suspicion placed her. A shadow crossed her face and she shrugged. "Well then, if I must work at this discovery alone, I do so! Only—" She broke off, ventured closer to me. "—What if Madame Kate works with the Maître in this and destroys my Fraulein Hedi at his wish? Who is to say you or I will not fall into a similar accident?"

For the first time I began to see how it was possible Kate had been used. Certainly there had been hatred for me in her eyes that moment on the turret steps. I did not believe the Maître was as guilty as Lady Tyra, but I allowed for

Tzigana's prejudices. After all, she had reared the woman from childhood.

"Is it that we count upon each other, should we fall into trouble?" Tzigana asked me finally. I nodded, only half-convinced, and we went in to do what must be done.

Troubled as I was over the appalling death of Hedi von Preysing, I was more troubled that Kate might either go the way of Miss Hedi or that in her passion for Maître Stavko she might try to destroy others at Moura, myself included. Her entire obsession seemed to have something to do with the loss of the gold crucifix she had worn as long as I knew her. All during the hours of our care for the dead girl and the examination by the surgeon from Montemessine, my mind kept returning to Kate's lost crucifix.

I was told by the breathless Elfreda in the afternoon that the school would be shut down soon. The scandal was too great. "And Madame Kate may be locked away for it," Miss Effie finished in triumph. "Everybody knows Hedi suspected her. Hedi warned everyone about her, but no one listened."

I caught my breath sharply. I had forgotten that damning bit of evidence against Kate's story. "Never you mind!" I said to Miss Effie. "You know no more than I of the matter. Above all, remember one thing." I took the girl and faced her as sternly as I could. "You'll not be discussing this in the presence of adults. Not any adults. You understand me?"

"I d-don't know. Why?"

"Because if they hear you, you may go the way Miss Hedi went." Her eyes looked enormous in her plump, ingratiating little face, but she promised me, adding, "Should we not talk to Tzigana either? I don't above half like her, but Rosemary Tynford said she cried when she discovered what happened."

I hesitated. It would be good if the Captain and I could count upon Tzigana, the only person known to and trusted by the Stavkos, but although I thought we might eventually find her helpful, we did not dare trust the children's safety to the gypsy who had been a lifetime companion to Lady Tyra.

"Not anyone," I repeated.

She agreed with a serious look but then smiled winningly. "Except you. And do not tell me you are as bad as the others; for you are not." She hugged me and then, with her arms around me, looked up into my face. "But you must promise not to be ill. That dreadful Miss Kate was a splendid romp; like a girl she was, until she got pale and put on grand lady airs. Now you look pale. Oh, don't be ill, Miss Anne! Please do not!"

"Very well then. I promise." I hugged her in turn and after assuring myself that the girls were all safely in their rooms or the students' parlor, I started belatedly to see Maître Stavko. I had not spoken with him privately all day and dreaded the prospect, ever since I had shaken off that ridiculous dependence upon him that I felt on awakening that morning.

Instead, however, I was stopped by Captain Surtees and the little surgeon from Montemessine, coming out of the room where we had laid out Miss Hedi for her coffin. There was so much about the girl's appalling death that made it impossible for the Stavkos, or for the employees of Moura to dismiss it as an accident, following hard upon the death of the first coachman who had, according to report, fallen down a flight of steps a few days ago, and the fatal illness of Cléa Raines some time before that. I was much relieved at what I conceived to be the little surgeon's concern about these terrible events at Moura. I had seen death here, and incredible things occur, and yet I could prove nothing. Whoever was responsible, whether Lady Tyra or the Maître or even Kate, I might as well not have come painfully back to my old home, for all the good I had done.

"Anne . . . Mademoiselle Wicklow," the Captain began, first in English, then in French for the benefit of the surgeon, "it seems that Mademoiselle von Preysing fell from the East Tower while in conversation with Madame Kate. Her death resulted from skull and back injuries. Monsieur Nortier agrees to it."

"Doctor Nortier agrees? With whom?" There was an edge to my voice that I could not hide. I did not want Kate involved, heaven knows! But they must investigate further. Were they going to dismiss the whole affair as Cléa Raines' illness had been dismissed? I went on, "I trust that truant, the all-seeing Isabeau, agrees to this?"

While Nortier was explaining stiffly that he was a surgeon, not a commonplace doctor as I had incorrectly addressed him, Captain Surtees said to me in English, "Nothing points to anyone but Miss Kate. Stavko agrees that Isabeau will say nothing. Do you want Miss Kate to be placed in danger of the guillotine?"

It was a timely reminder. I said no more to start the little surgeon's thought processes simmering. The Captain took my cold hand and held it briefly in his. It was a warming experience.

"I am going to drive Monsieur Nortier to Montemessine now. Will you go with us? I have a small matter of business to conduct there."

"I wish I might go with you," I said frankly. "But someone must help Tzigana with the young ladies' dinner, and to give them some occupation. Else they will be frightening themselves silly over what has happened." However, I did want to get away from the grim memories of Moura, at least briefly, and I sought and found an excuse. "Perhaps I may ride with you as far as the porter's lodge. There is something I wish to fetch there for Miss Kate. She will need it."

"Delightful," said the surgeon politely while Captain Surtees tossed my hand back to me in his quick, brusque way and the reminder, "Good. The curricle will be outside the East Front in ten minutes. Mind, now. Don't be late." Although there was one witness to this scene and there may have been more, he slapped my hand that he had rejected and then kissed me quickly but delightfully on the lips. I was dumbfounded but at the same time regretful that I had not been able to return that caress before he and the surgeon were on their way. I glanced toward the young ladies' apartments hoping Lotte would carry a message to the Maître about my delay. Lotte was coming out of the Tynford girls' bedchamber and as I called to her, she stopped, looking more frightened than I thought possible in that heavy, stoic countenance.

"Lotte, what is it? Why do you look at me like that?"

She mumbled something and I went to her, but it was now perfectly obvious it was myself she feared. She tried to retreat to avoid my touch, all of which made me more uneasy than ever. "Fraulein . . . not touch, *bitte.* Fraulein lost now."

I had never heard her speak English and her words made no sense to me. "Lost? Who is lost? What can you mean? Lotte!"

She shrank away. I wanted very much to shake the silly creature, but she avoided my touch. "*Bitte,* no. Undead! Undead!"

Of all the simpletons, she was the worst! Abruptly, I gave her my message for the Master, explaining I had to get something from the lodge and would return shortly. She nodded but would take no chance of my touching her. I went downstairs in haste pursued by my anger and more, by the fear that seemed to hover just at the edge of my senses and had done so since I awakened this morning. I really must do something about my new tendency to nightmares. I did not want to begin that unpleasant habit.

It was a shock to catch a glimpse of my whey-face and tousled hair in the pier glass of the passage, and I understood at least in part why Lotte had been terrified of me. I was certainly not in the best looks.

I stopped in the kitchen where Matilde and Isabeau were peeling potatoes, and Draja was mending the fire. I had come for another purpose but took this opportunity to demand of Isabeau where she had been last night when I searched the house for her. Impudently, she shrugged and said, "I went to Borgos. He promised me a pretty gold chain if I stayed with him and—" She glanced at Matilde sideways. "—And talked." Then she turned her lips down and added as an anticlimax. "But he did not pay me the chain. We were interrupted by the handsome Captain, and it all came to nothing."

I might have guessed how it would be. Very likely, it had been my own chain and crucifix! At any rate, I ignored it in no time at all. "I'm going to the lodge to fetch up something for Madame Kate."

The cook grunted without looking up, but Isabeau giggled at me as though none of the grim events of the day, or the previous night had occurred at all. I was preparing to give the girl a long-deserved scolding for my fruitless trip through the cellars, but Matilde complained loudly, "First, you steal my red shawl and my best carving knife. Now, you ask for another shawl. You think I am always a fool?"

Puzzled, I looked around the big room. I had not thought of the shawl or the knife since Draja left me last night and it was vastly annoying now to realize that I could not recall where I had laid the two objects. Try as I would, I could not picture myself at the moment I put off the shawl, and as for the knife, I remembered only that there had been a few minutes when I gripped its shaft with such force I could still fancy the pressure in my palm. I did the only thing I could do and begged Matilde's pardon for my carelessness and promised either to find her old property or replace it the first time I went into the village. She grumbled that no one understood the problems of a good cook, and that no new instrument could have the proper seasoning until it had been used a score of years. Knowing Matilde and that she could go on in this vein for hours, I left her as quietly as I could, indicating silence to Draja behind her broad back, and ignoring Isabeau.

Draja followed me into the passage, though, coaxing me to wear his jacket, and failing that, for he had an exceedingly ragged shirt beneath, he fetched me a young lady's pelisse which hung from a peg in the stillroom.

"How does this happen to hang here?" I asked as I threw it around my shoulders and noted its dusty condition.

Draja looked at me innocently. "When M'amselle Cléa

is taken away home, they hurry, and they leave many things. A shawl. A gown. The cloak, it is to M'amselle Cléa."

My fingers hesitated over the soft, dusty pelisse, but I did not remove it. I could not believe poor Miss Cléa would have grudged it to me. I thanked Draja and went out to the moat bridge where the Captain and Monsieur Nortier awaited me. It was an exceedingly close scramble to fit the three of us onto the high seat and the poor surgeon was none too pleased by my presence, but Surtees had for me that wondrous, warm smile that had come to mean so much to me during these harrowing days, as he lifted me up.

"If you please, Monsieur, let us move on," the surgeon suggested almost before I was seated. "It is near on sunset. I never travel in these parts after sunset."

The Captain leaped up to the perch, and shook the reins obediently, but he ignored the surgeon afterward, remarking to me, "I don't recall seeing you in that cloak before."

"No more you should. It belonged to one of the students."

He was thoughtful as we turned down the main sector of the Estate Drive through the Moura Woods. "Yes. I rather thought I had seen—"

I looked at him and he amended easily, "I had *not* seen it before, I mean to say."

Nevertheless, I was sure that in spite of all the scandalous stories about him, he was in some way concerned with the unfortunate Cléa Raines. I was most anxious to discover this connection; for it would explain much about Edward Surtees that puzzled me. I had long since discarded my original belief in his guilt as the killer of his mistress, whether intentionally or not. Why he lied about it I did not know, nor even if he was, as I had supposed, the lover of Tyra Stavko. His conduct with me, especially this morning, suggested that, like myself, he was here on some mission. Twice he had remarked upon clothing that had belonged to Cléa Raines; hence, his appearance here must be under false pretenses. I devoutly hoped this was the case.

He set me down at the Moura arch and then turned out into the High Road. He set off at such a spanking pace I suspected he would arrive at Montemessine almost as soon as I entered the lodge. This seemed more than likely; for it was at the garden door of the lodge that I discovered my keys were missing, so that I would take as long getting in as he would take on the High Road! I felt the waistband of my top petticoat, but did not find the ring, and then shook out my skirts. I thought back and it seemed to me that the last time I had those keys was during the evening, when I unlocked the iron door on the cellar steps leading to the dungeons.

I had thought the curious malaise that had overcome me when I awoke this morning was long since displaced by the very real, physical concerns of Miss Hedi's death. But it came back upon me in force now. *What had happened to me last night?* Why was my memory so much at fault? It had never happened before. Why, in fact, did I tire so easily and arouse those curious stares, the sinister comments from Lotte and others?

Mother of God! If my nightmare should have been real!

Impossible. I would not think it, nor allow myself to speculate on such a monstrous theory. I must concentrate upon something physical, like getting into this accursed lodge by one means or another. All Kate's troubles had come about following the loss of her crucifix. Perhaps this was her good luck piece. Captain Surtees had a similar notion about my own ivory cross. If I could find Kate's cross, it might work its old charm. I went off the path and walked around the house over the frozen ground until I reached the front door. The windows were, for the most part, sealed on the ground floor, but the first floor windows upstairs were unshuttered. The front door appeared at first to be locked, but was only warped and I pushed it open after a little effort.

Even though it had not been in regular use for a month or so, the house smelled of wood smoke and the sensual patchouli perfume that was Kate's signature. The ground floor, with its comfortable parlor, a small dining room and kitchen with a stillroom, was inordinately gloomy because of the closed shutters, but when I went up the center stairs to the bedchambers, the late afternoon light poured in through the west windows, the sunset just grazing the treetops of the Moura Woods. It was obviously in one of the east view chambers that Kate had slept, however; so I left the door open, and the dying sun streamed across the narrow hall and into Kate's bedchamber.

It was no news to me that Kate was a haphazard housekeeper. Her clothing was scattered over the great bed with its frills and furbelows, and though I searched through them, even shaking them out, each in turn, no crucifix and chain fell out. I looked around the room over the threadbare carpet and was just about deciding my excuse to get out of the chateau had been that—an excuse—when I remembered Kate's mention of the mirror. I moved to the desk under the mirror, and almost immediately the sunset's afterglow picked out the gold of the crucifix beneath the desk. I stooped and picked it up. At the same time the golden light seemed to have gone behind a cloud and I found myself straightening up again in sudden, heavy shadow.

Because the mirror was before me, I glanced in at it, seeing nothing but the reflection of my own face, worn, haggard and pale, perhaps due to the shadow that had crossed the light. But the shadow was not reflected. Nothing looked out of the mirror at me but my own face. It was therefore a shock when I turned around, puzzled but calm, only to see the doorway filled by the tall, lean form of Maître Stavko. I had the sensation of his pale eyes burning as they stared at me, reminding me horribly of other eyes burning into my very brain, the eyes of the huddled coachman on the coffin tumbrel that first night.

XVIII

I BLINKED, made an enormous effort to conceal my terror, and flashed what I can only suppose was a weak smile. "Were you looking for me, Sir? I had intended to report to you as soon as I—ah—completed my errand for Miss Kate."

"A pity," he informed me suavely, as though he might believe what was essentially a truth; for only my motive in recovering the crucifix was one I wished to hide from him. That and the terror he aroused in me at his sudden appearance out of nowhere. "Yes. A great pity you had this tiring walk upon no purpose. Miss Kate informed me that she herself would carry out an errand of recovery. Something to do with her jewelry, I believe."

He seemed to be much closer, his black-clad, straight figure overpowering in the little room; yet I did not see him move. Perhaps it was some mesmeric power he possessed. Certainly the faint rim of western light that silhouetted him, touching on his silvery, straight hair, cast his arrogant, high-bridged nose and too-sensual mouth in shadow; yet I was aware of a light like that in my dream, that emanated from something about him, perhaps his eyes, and made my limbs horribly weak, my body languid, receptive.

I think I must then have admitted, at long last, the reality of my night's appalling adventure in the cellars of Moura, and in doing so, forced all of my body's waning strength to resist that insidious power while still I smiled and shrugged and made small talk.

"How like Miss Kate, to send me on an errand she intends to fill herself!"

His long, lean fingers, looking like fleshless bone in the

evening shadow, reached out to touch my shoulder, at the neck of my gown whose muslin frill covered the puckered scar where I had been bitten. With an enormous effort, I did not shrink from his touch, but I prayed for Captain Surtees' swift return from Montemessine. He and possbily the ancient gypsy, Tzigana, were the only persons who could help me now if what I so belatedly suspected was true.

"Miss Kate, I fear, becomes boring as a matter of conversation. Now, let us leave this quaint little place, Anne, and return to Moura."

His touch upon my throat was gentle, the mere caress of one finger, but my flesh crawled as though a corpse had risen from its winding sheet to corrupt me with its icy touch. Again, the whiff of a century old perfume seemed to pervade my senses as he leaned closer. The fingers of my right hand still held Kate's little crucifix and I dared not raise that hand. I had some notion that he might snatch it away from me. But I managed to elude him by turning my head at the last second as though coquettishly enticing him on; all the while I had the horrid idea that his moist, deeply curved lips were not about to touch mine at all, but rather that swollen scar upon my throat.

My education was sadly lacking in such matters, and heretofore pleasantly lacking. No word of such an act had ever reached me save through the whispers of the schoolgirls at Miss Nutting's Academy who exchanged under their bedclothes at night a silly and rather dull romance called "The Vampyr" in which someone, met by the hero in Grecian travels, subsisted on human blood. I remember denouncing it to the young ladies as a highly absurd, not to say monotonous diet!

"I should feel excessively awkward if Miss Kate were to find me here with my employer, Sir. Perhaps we had better walk back to Moura now." I had some hope of meeting Captain Surtees, who, if he kept to his original pace, would be returning shortly, and above all, I did not wish to be trapped in this tiny bedchamber with all the implications of its furniture, and those lascivious lips so close to my flesh, so loathsome in their intent.

He smiled faintly, whether amused at my concern for Kate's opinion, or because he saw through my ruse, I could not know, but he drew back, almost imperceptibly, enough so that I moved past him, careful not to run, careful to appear casual, a little brisk. In the effort to conceal my panic, I brushed my knuckles against the wall of the small, low-roofed passage between the east and west chambers. Kate's crucifix dropped silently from my fingers, to lodge somewhere on the worn old carpeting near the chamber door. In my cowardly revulsion at the nearness of Istvan Stavko, I could not stop to rescue the chain, but started down the stairs, aware now of the rapidity, and worse, the silence in which the Maître overtook me.

I found myself in a state of retreat without pretense, and beside me as I reached the ground floor, was my warder, my master, the creature who seemed to weave his evil spell upon me. Yet he had not touched me since that moment I took fright in Kate's bedchamber. I wondered why I was enabled to resist the first terrible revelation of his power today and then, remembering Kate's crucifix, I thought of my own little ivory cross whose chain I wore concealed by the frilled neckline of my gown. I did not touch it for I was fearful of attracting Stavko's attention to it. I had no notion of its power, or whether there was any protective power in it, but recent events made me confident of Captain Surtees' advice.

I pretended to listen, and as I could not see out of the shuttered windows here on the ground floor, I put every ounce of histrionic power into my efforts. "Do you hear those rattling wheels of the curricle, Sir? Surely, that cannot be the Captain! He said he would hurry, but this is beyond anything." All in a fine feminine twitter, I went to the front door and looked out, lying madly. "Yes. I believe it is. Excuse me, Sir." He may have thought me mad, but he could not entirely acquit me of behaving as a normal woman would, allowing for a slight penchant toward the handsome Captain.

Thus, Stavko's jealousy, rather than his suspicions, might be aroused.

Once I stepped out, I took up my skirts and began to walk rapidly into the thick copse of the Moura Woods that lay to the south, toward the Montemessine High Road. I had supposed the Maître would follow me, but I neither heard nor saw anything behind me, once I reached the cover of the woods. I had intended to keep on following the High Road, more or less walking parallel to it through the woods, but it was dusk now and I was startled out of my wits when a night bird with the mephitic odor of a bat, swooped down almost blinding me with its thick, powerful wings, and then, as if it had peered into my face, flew off through the treetops and away.

Well now! I thought. . . . *At least, Stavko isn't following me.* . . . I could fight off an inquisitive night bird much more easily.

I had heard nothing yet on the High Road unfortunately, and I began to think of stepping out onto the road where I could make much better time when I saw a gray, shadowy object move among the trees between me and the road.

Not Stavko, I prayed, and came to an abrupt halt. I knew at once, of course, that the shadowy thing watching me from the safety of that copse ahead could not be the Maître, unless he was now possessed of the power to turn his own lean and ageless body into that of a hungry Moura wolf, foraging for a meal! The danger, then, was no less real, though of a sort I had coped with in previous years at Moura. "Go! Off with you!" I commanded in French, as it always seemed sensible to me that French wolves would, of necessity, comprehend that language better than English, and I waved my arm, as if about to toss something at the creature. Unlike most wolves, this one only started slightly at my threatening gesture, then trotted very slowly in my direction, this time looking at me out of eyes almost human in their glittering intensity. I gave my command again, louder, but it may be that the creature's acute hearing caught the panic in my voice and paid no heed. Still, he came on while I retreated, step by step. Finally, I took the dangerous chance of stopping long enough to pick up a stout, fallen branch and this I threw at him with all my strength. While he barely dodged this but was confused at my sudden attack, I turned and ran, at a right angle from the wolf, in the direction of the Moura South Gardens.

I thought to avoid the creature and return to the High Road, but the woods seemed full of life, a terrifying life at this hour close upon night. Tzigana's great, bearish husband, Borgos, pushed his way clumsily through the twilight woods, directly in my path. I turned, confusedly, glanced over my shoulder, and had the dubious pleasure of seeing the wolf slink away, its tail between its legs at the approach of Borgos. I, too, hoped to vanish before Borgos caught sight of me, but it was no use. I swung around, started to run, then was seized in a grasp that nearly pulled the arm from my shoulder. Despite my struggles I found myself tightly caught by the bear paws of Maître Stavko's creature.

"See here!" I lied sternly, trying not to raise my voice. "You must not delay me. I am expected by your master."

His great, shaggy dark face looked perplexed, but he did not release me, although I made some truly epic struggles which included the biting of his hand, a bite that drew blood.

"There!" I cried forsaking all caution in my fury. "Your precious master draws no more blood than I!" I would have bitten him again, but he boxed my ear so hard it made me quite dizzy while he dragged me over the icy ground, kicking all the way. I was hoping fiercely that only Borgos' own bad temper and sudden, momentary anger had produced this attack. If he was here to head me off, in the service of his master, then I was in great danger. But after a few minutes of growing terror in Kate's stone lodge, followed by my flight and that idiotic, stupid wolf, I was almost too angry to be frightened.

Eventually, I made him drag me every step of the way through the woods until the great, dark, medieval walls of Moura were in sight. I began to recognize the open ground.

It had been here, in the old days, that I climbed out through an abandoned well, after crossing the entire cellar system which honeycombed the area beneath the chateau.

"No!" The panic was in my voice now. I could not swallow it nor conceal it. The thought of those cellars made me recall last night's live, throbbing nightmare and I suddenly felt a cowardice such as I had never known before. "Borgos, your wife is my friend. Ask Tzigana. She will tell you. You must not listen to Stavko, but to Tzigana. You understand me? Go and find Tzigana!"

I had confused him. His great, bear's face stared into mine. "You think . . . Is it possible you think my wife will not wish it?"

"Of course. Of course! You must go and find Tzigana."

"That is true. I bring you to Tzigana. It is more safe. Safe . . . you comprehend?" he asked in French and then reverted to his native tongue for explanations I did not understand, but I stopped struggling then. It seemed possible that I had misinterpreted this abduction and if so, the object was to hide me from the Stavkos until the Captain returned. It was nearly dark now and they might be anywhere wandering through the gloomy Moura Woods.

We had reached the abandoned well and I thought that if Borgos was going to remove the wooden cover, then climb down the wooden rungs to the bottom before descending the steps into the cellars, he would have a good handful in trying to take me with him forcibly. If only I could be sure he did this at Tzigana's wish! She, at least, might have grounds for helping me.

"What do you intend to do?" I asked as we reached the well. But I was careful to speak in low tones so as not to be overheard by the Maître or his night-prowling daughter.

"Tzigana says we are to go through the cellars and come out in the young ladies' wing. No harm comes to you there. They would not dare to let the young ladies see."

This was sensible but when he motioned me to precede him down through the well opening with which I had once been so familiar, I hesitated. Dangerous as the woods might be, the cellars I had found far more hideous. I looked around, desperately hoping for some sign, some way to know that this was not a trap. The answer to my fervent prayer appeared almost as suddenly as I asked it.

The old gypsy, Tzigana, had been running lightly beneath the trees, crossing the open ground at this minute, as if pursued by the furies. There was no mistaking her urgency, her fear.

"Quickly! He is coming. Down with you both. We must not be seen, or all is at an end."

Inspired by her panic, Borgos lifted me into the well, and I climbed down with the two of them after me, expecting any second to see Stavko's face with its pale, burning eyes and the moist red mouth, peering down at us. Once we were inside the cellars, I knew the way to the steps below the North Wing. They followed me obediently and for several breathless minutes we hurried along, saying nothing, feeling our way in the dark.

There were shaded candles I had set long ago in niches of this labyrinth, and we came shortly to one that must have been lighted much earlier in the day. It had now burned down to a pool of tallow and Tzigana, taking a fresh taper from a niche, lighted it by the ruined candle. It illuminated the passage only faintly with a flickering impermanence.

The candle also showed me the roof over my head, a roof often no more than the solid earth of centuries, dripping with underground water, so that it was very like a walk through my own grave. I hurried ahead, anxious to get beyond the corridor leading down to the two dungeons which could be entered from this end, as from the broken door I had reached last night.

However, as I came to the branching corridor, I heard footsteps ahead in the direction of the North Wing. I did not notice the route taken by Tzigana and Borgos behind me. It occurred to me that, knowing the cellars as I did, I might reach help much more quickly this way, if only Matilde's kitchen, than by taking the longer passages to the girls' wing. This was especially true if it was one of the Stavkos I had heard a moment ago. After that, and after I found Captain Surtees, I was determined to flee from these creatures with their unknown evil which I had glimpsed so briefly in Istvan Stavko's face. Let others, better suited, fight the evil. I had done all I could. This thing was beyond my understanding.

I did not have time to be surprised that neither of my companions called to me, warning me I had taken the wrong passage. The hard-packed earth was cold benath my feet, and the walls so narrow that my hands, as I ran, brushed against the slime oozing between stone and earth. This time I was ready for the abrupt opening into the first of the two dungeons, but a light glowed unexpectedly ahead of me as I approached the door and I stopped, moving silently to peer in through the partially opened wooden door.

I was dumbfounded at what I saw: a woman kneeling, as if in prayer, over what appeared to be a body upon an improvised altar. A curious, many-faceted little light seemed to hang from the low roof, spinning, catching the light of several tapers and dazzling the beholder. I thought at once of the prism that had mesmerized me last night. The body upon the block of wood and metal, which served as an altar, was not dead. I recognized that bundle of shapeless clothing as the servant Lotte. Her eyes were open, staring upward at the slowly revolving prism. The kneeling woman's head was level with Lotte's heavy, corded neck and in a nausea such as I had never conceived to be possible, I realized that Lotte's throat had been pierced by the kneeling woman; that, in fact, Lotte's blood was being drained. As mine had been. And Kate. And God knows how many others, in how many other countries, for years! Scores of years, perhaps.

I was not so stupid as to imagine that I could combat this enormous strength that had already been demonstrated upon me, a strong and healthy woman, on the previous night. I turned back, as silently as I had come, but the kneeling woman looked over her shoulder into the darkness where I was concealed, and I saw the wetness upon Tyra Stavko's thick, sensuous lips. It trickled horribly down the corner of her mouth, to her chin. She made no effort to wipe it off. She was like a great spider, gorged with blood. Her eyes were brightly inhuman as she peered at me. Although I was certain her eyes, blinded by the prism, did not make out my features, I had an awful fear that she guessed my presence.

In absolute stillness I retreated, step by careful step, and at last, seeing Tzigana's candle flickering behind me, I began to run toward it. I had not yet gotten to the junction of the two passages when I saw, around a turn, the white hair of the gypsy woman. I reached out to her, and saw at the same time what seemed to be a monstrous apparition behind her, the face of Istvan Stavko, so like her in the flaring light, that I knew at last she would never have betrayed him. There was clearly a close relationship between them and, old as he must be, Tzigana was still older. His mother, in all likelihood.

I had but one protection, the surprisingly superstitious claim of Captain Surtees concerning my chain and crucifix. I knew I wore them, but thus far, I was not sure they knew. I might make a pretense of submitting, of yielding under their mesmerism, but unlike last night, I would remember, and if my pretense was great enough, I might escape death, if not the revolting practice they followed.

By Tzigana's smile, by the savage gleam in her eyes, I remembered another time when she had looked like this and I had been fooled, imagining it to be my fancy, up there in the long gallery when I cracked my head and awoke so much later, unable to explain the passage of time. And the rodent's mark upon my throat! Was this what Stavko had meant when he scolded someone, spoke of his property? *Was I, in fact, meant to be his property?*

Shuddering in spite of every effort to control my revulsion, I tried to withdraw when Stavko stepped in front of the gypsy and put out one hand to my throat. Only one hand; yet its strength was enormous. Closing as those fingers did, very slowly upon my jugular vein and my neck, there was no resisting them.

"Come," he ordered me in his quiet voice with the faint whisper of an unknown accent. He moved with me back to the dungeon light, to the presence of Tyra Stavko in her white nightgown. Or were those lengthy trailing robes her shroud? I had never known. But during these terrible seconds of our return, the Maître's fingers never left my neck and throat. His grasp never quite choked off my breath. But the touch was poisonous to me, and shameful, the effect of those fingers, now caressing, now tightening, so that it seemed to me my senses swam, as in a sensuous embrace with the man I loved. It was thus, no doubt, that creatures like Stavko and his daughter, and Tzigana had perpetuated their vile ecstasy, spreading it to others.

What I should have felt without the protection of that chain under my dress collar, I shuddered to remember. Stavko's mouth twisted with contempt at sight of the heavy-faced Lotte, whose stertorious breathing I could hear as I was forced, under his power, to cross the dungeon floor. Against the far wall my eyes, seeking the sanity of familiar things, made out ancient, broken modes of torture. They meant nothing now. They were a clean death by comparison with the horror the Stavkos had brought to this place.

"Remove that simple-minded peasant!" Stavko ordered, and Tyra, her eyes glittering, moved away reluctantly, led by the gypsy Tzigana.

Even as I felt the effect of that prism which hung from the roof and circled endlessly with the air current, I wondered if I might count upon that hulking brute, Borgos, but it was into his great paws that Tzigana confided Lady Tyra, who smiled as she saw Stavko and me, and she murmured, her mouth still wet with the blood of her servant:

"I am thirsty, Father. . . . Be generous. . . . Let me—"

"This is my property, Tyra. Later, when she has served me, this soft bit of loveliness . . . Then, who knows?" He looked down at me in that way he had which made me weak with confused desires, the loathing, but also the terrible, prickling sense of willingness. . . . A weakness I must at all costs fight off, and without his knowledge of the battle.

I wet my parched lips that were stiff with my terror. "He will follow you here. Any minute."

"Who, my son?" asked Tzigana, glancing up quickly at Stavko. So I was right about their relationship. This evil must have perpetuated from the gypsy to her son, and on to his daughter. If it were not ended with them, how far, through how many generations would it carry on its vileness?

Borgos spoke up, anxious and conciliating, with a stupidity that made me doubt he was one of these bloodthirsty creatures. Like Lotte, he was but a tool.

"This one has friends. The Captain. The young ladies. Even Madame Kate. Is it not better to go elsewhere now? This female is not special. There are others.

With a hideous little smile, the Maître stroked my face and throat with his free hand. "Ah no, Borgos. You are mistaken. I knew this one was special from the instant I first clapped eyes upon her. I have not seen such a one in many years. Not since Tyra's mother. This one should produce another like my gentle Tyra. Is it not so?"

The dancing prism caught my eyes, glazing my senses, numbing me to the horrors about me, and to the arguments of Tzigana, the creature who had spawned this terrible family.

"Madame Kate is a threat. So is the Captain. Let me fetch Madame. I have a notion how she may remove the Captain—and herself."

"Excellent," said the Maître. "Bring her here."

"And if she remembers?"

"She will not. She never has."

A minute later she was gone and the dungeon with its altar contrived from the flat-bed of an ancient torture rack, the inhabitants of this hellish place, and all else were a confused blur. I meant to resist, and was much more aware than I had been the previous night of the dangers here; yet I had run so much, and after the illness of the night, that

I now found all my resistance treated as a child's, and as easily overcome. Still, though, I had one weapon of which they knew nothing, the little gold chain and ivory cross. Whatever occurred, they must not suspect its presence. I clung to this superstition as to my life and salvation.

I found myself raised suddenly off the floor, with terrifying ease, and swung upon the altar-bed. The prism danced between my eyes and those of Istvan Stavko, and I pretended to be in the stupor that he had created around me last night. His head, silver as his gypsy mother's, bent over me and through my body I set myself to make no resistance as those teeth, sharp as a mastiff's fangs, bit into my flesh. My body shuddered but I made no protest beyond that instinctive reaction.

A commotion behind him caused Stavko to raise his head, to withdraw his hands from me. Through my lashes I saw my own blood glisten in the prism light upon his lips.

"We have her," said Tzigana with satisfaction. "Come, Madame Kate. Why were you wandering outside the walls?"

As Stavko moved away from me, I watched the scene, physically too weak to move, but I thanked God my mental faculties were active. It was Kate who looked stupefied, as if in a trance, her hair blown wildly, the pupils of her eyes dilated.

"I wanted to go—something of mine at the lodge."

"What was it?" asked Tzigana sharply.

Poor Kate looked vague and puzzled. "I don't—remember. A trinket. It must have been a trinket. Master, why have you turned from me?" This was to Stavko and the poignant, awful begging sound chilled my blood. He took a stride or two toward her.

"Katherine, my love . . . you cannot come to me. There is an obstacle in your path. You know what that obstacle is?"

She hesitated, looked confusedly at each of the faces before her. "Anne?" she asked.

"Not Anne," said Stavko with his silken gentleness. "Captain Surtees. He is the obstacle. It is he who must be removed."

"But how?"

Stavko reached over her head toward Borgos, snapping his fingers. Borgos failed to understand at first, then reached into the deep pocket of the black jerkin he wore and took out a small, black and silver pistol. It was so small I suspected it to be a derringer, but there was no denying it looked serviceable. When Stavko put it into Kate's hands I was certain she would come out of her trance, refuse it indignantly. Kate had never, to my knowledge, had anything to do with guns. She was a woman of sturdy femininity. But now, after a furtive little glance in my direction, she accepted the gun, then asked Stavko piteously, "Afterward? When the—obstacle is gone?"

"You will do as you are told, Katherine, and after, yes. I will not turn from you. But you must be wise, my love, and use that weapon before he can suspect. The head, I think. Yes . . . the back of the head. . . . And then, my love!"

I could bear it no longer. She was turning away with that gun, to destroy my Captain, my delightful, loving Captain!

"No, no, Kate! Listen to me, Kate. They ask you to commit murder—Kate!" It was no use. No use at all. Poor Kate would do murder and never know it. And my jolly, tender, so very dear Captain . . . "Kate?" I cried in my despair.

She did not hear me. Or if she heard, she failed to understand. I could no longer see her. I was once more surrounded by these gargoyles, these great, sinister birds of prey who turned back from the vanished Kate to gaze at me . . . Tzigana and Borgos, and Tyra, and the dazed Lotte. At last, Istvan Stavko.

"Anne, my dear," his honeyed voice began to spin its web about me. "How is this? How agitated you are! And yet, a moment ago you were lost in the spell of love. Can it be that you were not mesmerized as we thought? And why not? What prevented the charm from working upon you?"

He reached out a long-boned hand to me and I shrank back, but he did not touch my flesh. Instead, he turned the collar of my gown. His gasping breath warned me that he had seen the chain and cross, my last protection. My last hope. I expected him to tear it away from my throat, but he did not. He drew back as though the little ivory cross carried a plague of its own.

"Borgos!" he commanded hoarsely. "Take it off. Take it and destroy it!"

Borgos reached for the chain. Though I struggled frantically now to escape that dark and clumsy paw, the chain snapped off, cutting my neck in the gesture, and the ivory cross was gone. Before I could beg, grovel, plead for its return as I wanted desperately to do, the maid, Lotte, roused from her stupor. She pointed her fat arm at me, shaking, terrified.

"She is one of the undead. Look at her throat. The marks are there. She must be destroyed. A stake through her heart. It is the only way! Our only salvation!"

Lady Tyra laughed, her tinkling, soulless laugh, but in my confusion and horror, I saw that Tzigana and Istvan Stavko did not laugh. Stavko's eyes were speculative, considering me, as his mother said in the little silence that followed:

"I very much fear we must, my son. She knows now. There can be no returning for her. As Lotte says, our Anne has the marks. She must go in the way that will not bring her soul back to haunt poor creatures like Lotte. And my Borgos."

Borgos nodded fearfully. He and Lotte were more terrified of me than of these monstrous creatures who ordered them about.

Into Borgos' clouded eyes came a slow blaze of excitement. "Will it be done? You swear? The stake. I will fetch the stake. And then the coffin. It should be done at the burial. Where the coachman was buried four nights ago. But I must drive the stake."

Stavko looked down at me. I writhed to free myself, to make protest, call upon whatever humanity was left to them, but I saw in those terrible eyes of Stavko that it would be useless. Like Borgos, like Lady Tyra whose tongue nervously flicked over her lips, these creatures looked forward to the bloody horror that was to come. Still— "A pity," murmured Stavko. "A great pity. But it must be."

XIX

I DO ISTVAN STAVKO the justice of assuming he meant me to be unconscious at the time I was placed in my coffin. I remember nothing of the preparations. I awoke to find myself smothered in a winding sheet and being lifted into what I supposed, from the jolting and the rattle of wheels, must be the tumbrel I saw on the High Road the night of my arrival at Moura. Appropriate, all considered, that I should leave Moura by this means.

I heard myself groan again as the wagon rumbled over uneven stones and down across ruts of dried mud, but I was grateful for the headache, the racking of my body, the cold, howling night wind. The pain had awakened me. It may even have saved my life, I thought, as I began to fumble against the ghostly clouds that smothered me. I wished briefly, uselessly, that I still wore my little ivory cross. But since I did not, I must rise from my own projected death by my own efforts.

The panic had left me for the time. Very possibly Captain Surtees' life, and Kate's as well, depended upon my own wits and my Irish muscle. I was calm as I concentrated hard upon freeing myself from the shroud. The awful bumping of the tumbrel awakened me to the necessity for haste. They had apparently counted upon the success of their mesmerism with the dancing glass prism and the influence of Stavko himself, but in my case, they had not counted upon my resistance, or perhaps just my Gaelic hard-headedness. In any case they had barely tied my wrists together and already the rope was fraying. I finished my job hurriedly because the shroud's thin material, probably a sheet, clung to my face every time I took a breath, and threatened to strangle me. With my hands free, I was able to work upon the shroud itself. Though I had forced myself to calm, I could hardly control my hands. They ached and shook so much I found it hard to feel for the threads that held the sheet around me. The shroud had been hastily sewn. The threads broke at my first hard yank at them. My nightmare captors must have been very sure of my state of unconsciousness. Or—they no longer cared.

. . . Did they intend to drive a stake through my head . . . or was it my heart? . . . while the shroud was still covering me? And the coffin. What of the coffin? Perhaps I was to be buried in nothing but my rumpled blood-spattered clothing and the thin shroud. Barbaric of them! And I found myself seized by a terrible passion to laugh.

Having ripped away the shroud, I felt around me and discovered the wooden box in which they had laid me was very large and badly constructed. The coffin lid lay half off, not to be pegged on until the stake was driven, no doubt. I raised up very gently, trying not to let the wood of the box creak and warn the driver of the tumbrel. The moon had barely risen. It was still early in the evening.

Had Kate already set about her horrible task? But Captain Surtees was no fool. He would guess her condition . . . wouldn't he?

The wind had risen, groaning through the trees overhead. I twisted my head around with an effort, to glimpse the driver. My neck was sore and that part of my throat which Stavko had touched was throbbing painfully. I felt weak as a kitten, but the sight of the driver's profile, twisted and evil as it was etched against the moon, told me that he was the hideous coachman I had feared and mistrusted since the first second of our meeting. It was not for several minutes that I realized this twisted, misshapen creature had all the features of the tall, elegant and immaculate Istvan Stavko. I could only suppose he contrived to huddle himself into this ugly caricature at times in order to have a scapegoat when his deviltry failed. Perhaps, indeed, he *was* the devil!

The twisted, evil face turned slightly. Had I blinked, or made a sound and betrayed myself? He looked down at me, his strong teeth gleaming in the moonlight, reminding me of the Moura wolf who had stalked me earlier tonight. Before I could gather the strength through my tired, shivering body, one of Stavko's hands went out to hold me there, motionless.

"My poor little love!" he murmured in that suave, silken voice of his. "We are off the High Road now. We soon arrive at the place of . . ." The smile was gone, but the irony remained as he added, ". . . I was about to say, of your execution. I wish it might be otherwise. Believe me, lovely Anne, it will all be over in a moment. An instant. But you know where the fault lies. You would not be in this cart now, were it not for that unconquerable feminine curiosity of yours."

I wanted to charm him, to coax and beg and lie for my life, but my tired revulsion toward him was such that I could scarcely speak, much less exert any belated charm upon this nightmare creature. I no longer knew where we were traveling, except that we were now rattling over unleveled ground, with the dark woods nearly enclosing the tumbrel. I made one more effort, putting my weight upon my elbows and attempting to sit up, preparatory to climbing over the steep side of the tumbrel. It might all have been quite useless and I would very likely have broken both legs in that leap, but in any case, I found myself helpless under the terrible pressure of his outstretched hand.

Tears of frustrated fury and of weakness too, blinded me so that when a bright, gaudy light illuminated the little grove ahead, I knew we had arrived at the place of my death. I did not realize this until I was lifted out of the tumbrel in the incredibly strong arms of Istvan Stavko. The shroud was so wrapped around me that I could not even struggle, but I saw my grave, that deep, narrow trench in the muddy earth, and I saw Borgos and Lotte, who had dug the trench and stood there, waiting for the grave to be filled.

I screamed. I must have screamed half a dozen times, but the sounds merely returned to me, the echoes of my own terror. Stavko looked down at me. Just for a brief time those strange eyes of his had a curious light, not of pity. Of regret. But I was silent again, my throat parched and raw with the effort of those screams.

I must have fainted; for I came to consciousness deep in the earth, the coffin's ill-constructed sides marking the end of my narrow bed, and the dark, tree-laced sky still visible far above me. They had not even troubled to wrap me securely in the shroud again. Lady Tyra stood at the foot of the grave, her pale garments fluttering and whipping in the night wind, which had risen to a roar in the last few minutes. Lotte stood beside her, holding high a wooden club burning pitch, her other hand to her mouth, her round eyes at once horrified and fascinated. I could not see Stavko, but he must be at the head of the grave; for I heard him giving crisp, deep-voiced orders. Strangely enough, although I knew I should die in a matter of minutes, and horribly, I found I could not move.

"See?" cried Borgos with pride, waving a tree limb he had whittled to a fine point. "It is as it should be. There will be an end to this Undead. . . . You see?" He had to shout to be heard over the wind, and there were other words, in their own language, that Borgos poured out, but it was as if I saw and heard these creatures from the distance of a nightmare only partially recalled. Like Lotte, Borgos was the victim of the power of suggestion wielded by the three, Tzigana, Stavko and Tyra. I, and not his beloved companions, was to be the *Undead.*

Tzigana, who had spawned this race of evil, came now to stand before Borgos, looking down at me. Once more, and for the last time, I saw that gloating, hungry smile of hers that I had first surprised so briefly in the long gallery. Then she signaled to Borgos, who looked hesitantly from her to

Istvan Stavko, whose tall lean figure moved into my view between the grave and the wildly flaring torch. I wondered how I could ever have taken him for the misshapen coachman of the tumbrel, and yet they were the same. Was he also those other devils who had haunted me tonight? The inquisitive night bird? The wolf who had stalked me?

I must be mad, I thought with dull surprise. *I have run mad and now they must destroy me. . . .*

There were flashes of blinding light and the noise of the wind rushing through the glade. Then a sharp, crackling sound that was a gunshot. I saw Borgos' hands raised, brandishing the sharpened stake and something else, the flat of an ax catching the light. An ax to hammer in the stake. Under the blast of another shot he swayed grotesquely, like a performing bear, dropped the ax and stumbled back, collapsing at the feet of Tzigana. The gypsy, with Stavko, turned to stare at the narrow, unkempt wagon road by which we had come.

Lady Tyra stood as if frozen, her draperies beating madly around her, while Stavko, in such deadly fury as I hope never to witness again, warned Tzigana, "The accursed Captain! And others! Cover this one in the grave. She must be gone from their sight."

I made a violent effort to move, only succeeding in calling out in a hoarse, half-croak. Such was the confusion around the grave that I scarcely heard my own voice, but there appeared the blessed figure of Captain Surtees on the edge of the grave, thrusting between Stavko and Tzigana, holding his hands out to me. The man we had called the Maître, seeing defeat, bowed gracefully, evidently directing my rescuers to me. I was reaching up for the Captain's hand, trying to stop trembling, when I saw Tzigana's figure rise on her toes behind the Captain, with the ax blade gleaming.

I cried out, freeing his groping hand, to point at this fresh danger. He saw, almost as quickly as I did, and flung his elbow back hard against the terrible old woman. She fell backward. There was a shriek that seemed to cut through me to my very soul, but it was not until Captain Surtees had lifted me up beside him that I saw what had happened. The gypsy had stumbled over the body of Borgos and been impaled upon the sharpened stake still clutched in his huge, dead hand.

I did not look again at the blood-seeking creatures, but long after we had left the flaring, hellish scene with its outer circle of startled French soldiers, I would remember the anguish of that strange, inhuman pair, Istvan Stavko and the Lady Tyra, as they knelt beside the impaled gypsy, only to see her writhe in her dying torment.

"Did you disarm Kate?" I asked the Captain as he helped me across the glade toward the curricle whose frettish team was held by a nervous young trooper in Royalist uniform.

"No need, my lass," called Kate's well-remembered brusque voice through the dark. When we reached the curricle, there she was, perched on the seat, looking pale in the moonlight, a bit worn, but otherwise her very welcome self.

Captain Surtees lifted me up beside her and leaped up himself, taking the reins. He leaned over and kissed me, but gently, comfortingly, guessing how stunned and shaken I must be, and as he gave the signal to start, he put his arm around me. Kate grinned at us. We were a cozy fit upon that small seat, but so relieved, we were mightily glad of each other's company.

"I don't understand," I murmured, looking from one to the other of them. "I went to the lodge to find Kate's crucifix, but I was not able to give it to her. You may laugh at our superstition, Kate, but the Captain and I are persuaded that the Stavkos could not put you or me under their power while we wore them."

Kate snorted her impatience at my misunderstanding.

"Far from laughing at you, my lass, I was so convinced you were right, after our talk today, that I went down to the lodge and found my cross, in the passage by my bedchamber. I was crossing the woods on my return when Tzigana and Borgos found me. The way she spoke, her manner, everything told me she supposed I remained under that mesmerism they practiced. I was not at all certain I could fight off both the gypsy and Borgos; so I went along into the cellars."

"And saw me in that place with them."

Even iron-willed Kate shuddered. "A ghastly business. More ghastly because I understood then precisely what had been done to me upon past occasions. But I played out my little *comédie* and took the derringer. I went to search for our gallant Captain. I did a bit of running about. I caught him, belatedly, as he arrived at Moura with the detachment sent from Montemessine. They galloped to your rescue, lost your direction like the clumsy Royalists they are, and the rest you know, except how they will punish those odious Stavkos. What a pity they did not commit murder!" We both stared at her, but she was blandly conscious of her words. "Because then they could be guillotined. Instead, a few years in prison. As I said, it is unfortunate nothing worse can be proved."

There was so much I did not know and would never know of the strangely accursed Stavkos, that I felt strongly inclined to find only irony in Kate's easy dismissal of the Stavkos' punishment, and of the miraculous way in which I had been rescued. Captain Surtees must have guessed my thoughts.

I smiled. "If you mean the so-called murder of some young woman at your hands, I have long since been convinced it was a trick to gain the confidence of the Stavkos." I looked at him and felt that Kate as well had begun to study him. I said quietly, "There was a relationship between you and Miss Cléa Raines, wasn't there?"

He was silent as we drove into the High Road, narrowly missing a pair of French soldiers riding at a gallop toward the grove to reinforce the arrest, I daresay.

"Your daughter?" Kate asked in her abrupt way. "If she was your natural daughter, you may say so. We French are broad of mind."

He looked at us, and the old amused charm was there as he replied to Kate's tactless remark.

"Yes. I am aware of that. But Cléa was my half-sister, born of my mother's second marriage. We have both been orphaned since my days with the Brigade on the Peninsula. Cléa seemed in excellent hands with her father's people on the Channel Islands, but during my last leave there was talk of sending her to France for . . . polish and manners. Then came Moura, and later, she was sent home to die. I never believed it was a natural illness; so I sold out, left the Brigade, and set myself to meet Tyra Stavko. . . . The King's Prosecutor at Marseille cooperated. Meanwhile, the magistrate at Montemessine has been active. He told me tonight there is a similar history in other countries. Wherever the Stavkos have settled. God knows where—and when—they started." He flicked the reins, his mouth hard. "But I meant it to stop here. And now!"

"Did you ever hear of vampyres, Anne?" asked Kate curiously. "People who live for centuries on human blood. They are only a legend, but yet . . ." Her voice trailed off into the night around us.

I was firm, and in that firm assurance I lied about my own doubts. "What nonsense! Everyone knows a vampyre is an absurd creature between the boards of that romance Miss Nutting's pupils read."

"Of course," the Captain agreed. "But as Miss Kate says . . . *and yet?*"

We three knew there were inexplicable things that had occurred here at Moura during the bloody reign of the Stavkos. Kate could not explain why Tzigana's little friend, Hedi von Preysing, had tried to force Kate to jump from the East Tower, but I suspected it was Stavko's way of removing a woman whom he no longer found necessary to his pleasure. I wondered how long it would have been before another girl, perhaps Elfreda, was mesmerized to try to destroy me for the same reason.

We were approaching the narrow moat bridge at last, and the three of us stared up at the thousand year old front of Moura. Much would have to be done there behind those walls to scrub out the memory of the Stavkos. Would we ever really know the full extent of their powers? I asked this aloud, but I did not expect an answer.

The Captain tightened his arm about my waist. I felt warm and safe and loved, as I was long ago. How dear he had become to me!

"Well now, love," he said while he drove around to the Carriage-House. "You need hardly go in fear of Stavko's daughter, if you've some notion of jealousy." I started to bristle indignantly, but he only squeezed my waist and I subsided. "It's my belief, and I came to know her well—" I grimaced but he only smiled. "The young woman was little more than a tool in the hands of her father and her grandmother. She had some loathsome habits, I grant you, and I've never seen her by sunlight, but she was of little account. Thank God we've done with the other two!"

"Thanks be to God!" Kate murmured fervently.

But I could not bring myself to speak. Perhaps it was because I still wondered, still questioned. Was I as gullible as the students of Miss Nutting's School, after all?

Return to Moura

I

For me, the fear began on one of those nights some years ago, in the late 1820s, with the rain pelting across the narrow, cobbled London streets, and sodden tendrils of ivy outside my window twisted in a thousand eery shapes, while each splashing raindrop was a footstep creeping nearer.

It seemed no different from any other stormy night, except in one particular: those phantom footsteps did not dissolve into commonplace sounds at my door, but brought into my life such sensations as even in my hectic twenty-four years I had not yet dreamed of; and their penultimate gift was to be stark, anguished terror.

The footsteps led me far afield, but always and inevitably back to the desolate, unhallowed corner of a village churchyard, which was the burial place of the one they called "The Devil-Vicar." In the end, when I came again to that churchyard I had so often contemplated, at first with curiosity and finally with torture, I understood why the villagers were awed by the long twilight common to the north country.

For it was in these hours of the great undark that they saw the Devil-Vicar. But on the rainy November night when one life quietly ended for me and another began, my knowledge of devils and phantasms was confined to the book I read. It was past ten o'clock and I was busy at my recently inherited home on Berkeley Square, copying the more illegible pages of a manuscript for the publishing firm of Sackerby, Perth, Ltd. Old Mr. Osmund Perth desired to read the manuscript at his breakfast table on the morrow. He had arrived nearly at dusk, which may have persuaded him that an apology for such haste was in order.

"It's extraordinary to me, Miss Wicklow, as I have heard your late benefactors—Mr. and Mrs. Varney—often say, how a person may have the talent to put one word before the other, and yet write like a heathen in the jungle scratching on a drumhead. However, make of it the best you can, and try not to let its contents alarm you into fancying ghosts in the night; for it is all fustian, you know."

His wrinkled, pink, babyish countenance relaxed into its more congenial shape, and his mouth took an upward curve. His elbow jogged my ribs with that irritating familiarity that "old friends of the family" so often seem to adopt with young women. "North country clods, you know, sometimes produce prodigies, for all their talk of ghosts and goblins. One of these days we hope to strike fire with another *Frankenstein.* Excellent story if you like hobgoblins, by that wild-eyed Shelley's wife. Not published by us, worst luck . . . . So, do your best, m'dear. Pity you must. A young miss barely twenty—"

"Twenty-four," I said.

"Yes. Just so. Barely twenty-four, as I say, should have better things to do at night than to ruin those lovely eyes over copywork. But these are hard times, Miss Anne."

Doubtless he made that last remark, as though it were being observed for the first time, to dampen any hope I should have for ha-pense more the page.

My pecuniary difficulties having accumulated in part because Sackerby, Perth paid my benefactor more in praise than coin for his monumental histories—*An Emigré Views the Career of Napoleon* and *Recollections of a Child of the Ancien Regime*—I felt that no comment on 'hard times' was necessary. Little did Mr. Perth suspect, however, that I intended to broach the subject tomorrow when I returned the manuscript.

Poor Mr. Varney was a frightfully incompetent man of business. That had been one of his boasts, an extraordinary quality in a Frenchman, but fortunately, I showed his sharp-eyed wife's instinct for an honest sou. I was determined never, never to sing again to the genteel poverty of the bookish man who saw his wife and copyist support him during the major part of his life.

At the end of Mr. Perth's visit, I showed him out into the street where puddles of rain between the cobbles already reflected the stormy evening sky, then hurried to my work in the little corner room on the ground floor of the house which had been my mother's dowry.

I would have preferred to work upstairs on the first floor, which I let to a colonel's widow, for the noise of criers and sellers by day, and coach wheels almost at our doorstep in early evening, was disturbing enough; but on such nights as this in early November, when the first storms of winter swept through our little square, I did not like the irritating and inexplicable noises I was apt to hear at my window, which opened directly upon the street. I was not precisely frightened, but I did feel a distinct distress.

Once in a while I even fancied that such scratchings might be my mother or my father calling me. It was absurd, but it was all part of living alone after many years of happiness with first two and then one person, whom I adored.

On that November night I hurried through the manuscript Mr. Perth had left with me, paying little heed to the sense of it and skipping the more legible pages, so that I might concentrate upon the production of a neat, flowing hand for which I was being paid. I was more in haste than usual. I had another manuscript that I had promised to have ready for a rival publishing house within a day or two, and this manuscript was even more impossible to read. I glanced at it now and then as it lay on my desk with its wrappings half off, where I had left it when interrupted by my portly friend, Mr. Perth. Well, it would have to wait.

It was not until all identifiable human noise in the square ceased that I noted, as on other stormy nights, the dozen peculiar sounds now vying for my attention. The ancient ivy that curled upward around and above my window was certainly responsible for the curious flutterings against the shutters. And the stealthy footsteps approaching that same window were nothing more than the untidy spatter of rain. But why should I hear those odd little stirrings in the dark passage beyond my study door? The street door was bolted, and Mrs. Colonel Fothergay was long since tucked into the great canopied bed that had been my father's. Our little cleaning maid went home to Cheapside before dark, and my tenant on the second floor, an actress of some distinction, was at present touring on the American continent.

I returned to my copywork, only to find this edifying paragraph in the manuscript:

> *The furtive rustlings of unsuspected life on the moors during the long un-dark can take on monstrous importance when one lives alone among these becks and dells.*
>
> *The twisted and mangled body of the unhappy Mr. Abernethy had been found in just such a haunted place, and the inhabitants of*

the scattered moorland villages were appalled by the savagery. . . .

That was enough of that.

I stopped reading, looked up and listened again. Really, one would think I was up in darkest Yorkshire, alone in some haunted dell with "the unhappy Mr. Abernethy." The sounds in the house had definitely increased. Even the staircase outside my study door squeaked monotonously, as though one of my lodgers were tiptoeing up to the first floor.

Absurd. I was being influenced by this ridiculous story. To take my mind off it for the moment I carefully rewrapped the manuscript I was to work on tomorrow. But I could not forever put aside *The Corpses on the Moor.* They must be piled up in neat and bloodless order on Mr. Perth's desk by tomorrow morning.

I riffled the pages of the manuscript, discovered that "Mr. Abernethy" had been selected by the author as the first in what promised to be a gory series of victims of some monster called a "Gytrash," who preyed on the moorland people.

Thinking of the author, I began to consider the handwriting. It was curious—entirely written in a backhand slant so that one could not guess the sex of the writer, or indeed, any especial character. I searched in my throw-away sewing basket for the cover and read the superscription to Sackerby, Perth on a heavy type of wrapping paper upon which a shopkeeper had figured, in heavy charcoal, certain items down to the last shilling and ha-penny. The author had tried to scratch this out, but I thought I could make out on the list a man's starched white cravat and then—to throw me off the scent—a lady's bonnet. The sender's name appeared as secretive as the handwriting, for the return address was "Care of the Postmistress, Upshed, West Riding, Yorks."

Yet I could see upon close examination the almost obliterated name of the shopkeeper, no doubt: "H. Peysworth, Maidenmoor, Teignford, Yorks."

I wondered why the author had shopped in Maidenmoor, yet chose the postmistress of Upshed to receive his or her mail. I knew I was reaching for a mystery where none existed. But at least it had taken my mind off the cracks and creaks and prowlings outside my study door. I bent over my work again.

The storm beating through the square rushed to a crescendo, as though jealous of my inattention. The front door shook and rattled in an angry grip. I paid it no heed.

Because the idiotic plot, full of sound and fury, signified nothing, I found it a growing source of amusement, especially the Gytrash, which, as nearly as I could gather, was a huge ghostly animal with a human intellect. Was it possible that such an unlikely—no—impossible tale, could be printed and bound and actually bought by gullible readers? I'd dare swear there wasn't a Gytrash in the whole of England, with Scotland thrown in, and as for dozens of strong, sturdy Yorkshiremen being obliterated by this fantasy with its gleaming red eyes and teeth long as a young elephant's tusks . . . well, what was the reading public coming to?

Curiously enough, for all my mental reservations, I could not stop reading the abominable thing.

I had just reached the page upon which the monstrous Gytrash leaps to devour the helpless heroine when the storm set up such a clatter at the front door that I dropped the book and lost my place in the carefully laced manuscript.

Taking up the lamp, I decided that I had had

enough. Whether it was the storm making such havoc or not, I would have to satisfy myself on the matter. I did not like the notion; for I was not the bravest woman in the world. But when even my study door shook, and I began to imagine all sorts of hobgoblins in the dark little reception hall beyond, there was but one thing to do, and I did it, if reluctantly.

I threw open the study door, found nothing in front of me except the newel post of the staircase leading to Mrs. Fothergay's apartments, and, of course, the long mirror at which every woman, even our cleaning maid, must smooth her hair before opening the front door. I glanced at the front door which still shook under the gusts of wind, but, perhaps it was my imagination, it did not seem as noisy as it had sounded from my study. Beside the door was a long narrow strip of carefully bevelled glass which had been my mother's pride and joy; for by this, she and the maid could see who our callers might be, and thus avoid tradesmen and revenue collectors.

Outside that strip of glass which was the length of a man, I could see the rain beating slantwise across the square, causing the little trees in the center of the square to commit all sorts of acrobatics in their effort to escape the pressure. From the corner of my eye I saw my lamp catch its reflection in the mirror on the wall facing the front door, and although I had just looked at the mirror a moment before and knew perfectly well it was there, the sudden glowing image surprised me. I turned my back to the door and glanced at my reflection and that of the lamp in the mirror.

I was more startled the next second; for what looked back at me was not only my own face and the lamp, but one like a shadowy image of my face, seen through a watery, uneven surface, behind me. My heart thundering in my bosom, I turned and stared at the door and at the long glass beside it.

Something was peering in at me through the bevel-glass, in the midst of all that rain and wind outside. The night was so black and gloomy I could make out nothing but the muffled figure, a little taller than I, and the dark eyes, the windblown black hair and upper face which closely resembled one I had seen before, but I could not place it.

I gave a yelp that sounded in my own ears like a dog whose tail had been trod upon, and stood there shaking while I tried to think what to do. I knew there was no help from Mrs. Fothergay upstairs; for she would only fuss and produce more confusion, interspersed with shrill demands that I send someone to fetch the police—At Once! Since there was no one but myself to send, I should get nowhere there.

The face was close to the glass, the eyes peering in. Then a hand came up and gestured at me, and to the door. The rain slackened a little, and in that short time I saw the creature was a man, quite young, shrouded in one of those heavy traveling cloaks that we see occasionally in London, and which mark the wearer as what Mr. Perth would call "a wealthy clod from up Yorkshire and the North" . . . where the climate was reputedly fearsome.

Whether this insolent creature peering in at me was from the North I did not know, but I doubted very much if his own wretched climate was much worse than we offered him tonight. Seeing that the man was human and apparently absurd enough to want me to open the door to him at this hour, I shook my head and in the lamplight made gestures for him to go away.

He must have guessed my panic for after a moment or two I saw him smile, not an unhandsome smile, but the sight of those white teeth flashing out of the stormy night put me in mind of my friend the Gytrash, and I waved him away indignantly. He threw both hands up in the air, shrugged, and gave up.

I was very much relieved when I saw nothing but the stormy out-of-doors through the long glass.

After I had given him time to be gone, I set down the lamp on the newel post and very quietly went to the door. I listened. Not a sound. Breathing quickly, I shot back the bolt and opened the door just an inch or two, to see where he had gone.

A pair of cold, wet fingers closed around the door. I had not opened the door far enough to see the face of the creature out there, and now I slammed the door so fast it caught those two fingers and just missed crushing them completely, before they were snatched away. I heard a masculine voice swear very humanly, and then the wind and rain washed away whatever other sounds were uttered. I leaned against the bolted door and shook at my narrow escape.

Meanwhile, my scream when I caught sight of those pale fingers had roused my lodger. Mrs. Fothergay came shuffling along to the top of the stairs and looked down at me over the stair-rail. She was a sight to conquer all my fears; for nothing more ridiculous could be imagined. Greying tufts of her blonde hair were squeezed into strange little papers of assorted colors, obviously having been crimped hours before. Her stout, flabby figure was wrapped in a blanket that must have come off the bed when she did. Her face, mottled by the hot suns of the India Service, was as fiery as a sunset.

"Good heavens, child! What is it? What is happening?"

I took a deep breath, recovered myself.

"It was nothing, Mrs. Fothergay. Some fellow hanging about, peering in at windows. I think he was trying to find a way to break it. I can't imagine what we have that he wanted. But I got the door bolted in time."

"Are you going to fetch the police?"

I wanted to reply that she might go out in that dark and stormy night if she chose, but as for me, I should certainly wait until morning to inform them.

However, I managed to quiet her down, and we said good night as Mrs. Fothergay went back to bed, making sounds like "tsk-tsk" all the time. Her last words to me were, "I shall certainly lock my door, Miss Wicklow. Had I known that this neighborhood would come to have housebreakers and thieves prowling about, I should never have moved here. Who knows? One of the creatures might peer in at *me.* I always seem to attract so many ineligible, though I will say attractive, young men. Ah, well. . . ."

I made a face at her retreating back and took my lamp into the study. However, it soon occurred to me that I was at the mercy of any housebreaker who felt up to breaking in a window and some ancient shutters so, after one or two more attempts to work on *The Corpses on the Moor*, I gave up and went to bed.

It is not surprising that I dreamed all night of pursuit by a gigantic Gytrash with the head of a man—a young man with burning dark eyes and slim, cold fingers that gleamed with a ghostly light. I could have uttered a few curses myself, at Mr. Perth, for handing me such nonsense to dwell upon on a stormy night.

It was odd, though, about the housebreaker. I could not recall where we had ever been troubled in such a way before. And then too, the cloak he wore, which, for some reason—doubtless the manuscript—made me suspect the housebreaker was from the north, from the country of my Gytrash friend.

II

By well timed good fortune, for myself, not for Osmund Perth, the publisher was unable to reach his offices the next morning, having been confined to his lodgings with a bad case of the gout. When the boy who ran errands for the publishing house arrived for the Yorkshire manuscript, I was still unfinished, and sent him off with some excuse while I worked on the Gytrash, his victims, and the fiendish human monster back of the whole business. To my surprise, the human monster turned out to be a nice and a rather charming way of playing down the heroine at moments when she became too bumptious. It appeared that when the moon was high the flippant young man turned into a Gytrash, reverting to his charming self upon satisfying his desire to kill. Somewhat disappointed at this preposterous solution, I finished the manuscript of *The Corpses on the Moor*, surprised at how ineffectual it seemed by daylight, with the storm gone and a watery sunlight trickling into the study.

Seeing me at work, Mrs. Fothergay stuck her head in to inquire whether I was going to speak to the police about these prowlers who swarmed all over the place to get a look at her at night.

"For if you won't go, I shall, my dear. I'm sure it isn't anything I do, but somehow I have the most irresistable attraction for young men. In Calcutta they were forever peeping, watching me with those big grins on their faces. Hoping to catch me in my boudoir, I daresay."

"I daresay," I said drily, but could not put off the matter any longer. On the little tabouret beside my easy chair I laid the wrapped manuscript on Red Indians that I had put aside when I took the assignment for Mr. Perth and his Gytrash. I would begin to read it when I returned home, although I did not expect it to be so diverting as the Gytrash tale. I fetched my street cloak and bonnet and went off to inquire just where the Metropolitan police were stationed.

Before doing so, I paid a few visits to shops, examined carpeting for the upstairs corridor, belatedly delivered *The Corpses on the Moor* to the offices of Sackerby, Perth in Cornhill, and returned home just on tea time, in the company of the gigantic, mutton-chop whiskered gentleman from the Metropolitan Police. He wore no uniform and was dressed like a newly-prosperous greengrocer in garments a shade too snug for him, which made him look even bigger. In size, at least, I thought him a much more terrifying proposition than my intruder of the night before, but perhaps that was all to the good.

In the reception hall I pointed out to Constable Whacker just where the housebreaker had peered in, and where he had seized the door with two fingers. He examined the premises closely. I wondered what conclusions he could come to with so little to go on, but he seemed satisfied with himself, muttering several times as he pulled on tufts of his whiskers.

"Hmmmm. . . . just so. Just as I thought. . . . just . . . so."

Good. Then he recognized the technique. Doubtless, he knew the housebreaker.

"You have come to some conclusion?" I asked, puzzled at his assurance.

"No doubt. No doubt of it at all, little lady. Fellow wanted to get in. Plain as a pikestaff."

While I was trying to frame a polite answer to this astounding observation, we were both startled by the trill of Mrs. Fothergay's gurgling laughter. It came from my study, of all places, and the door was closed.

"My dear Mr. Branshaw—" my lodger was saying to someone within. A little pause and then the coy return, "—well . . . *Marc,* if you insist . . . .you do flatter me. Just a teensy bit."

"Relation of yours, mum?" asked the constable.

"No. My lodger. But I don't understand why she should be entertaining in my study. She has a very fine, large study and a ballroom on her own floor."

I went to the study door and opened it. I was about to remove my mantle and bonnet but stopped abruptly, astonished to see Mrs. Fothergay seated at my desk, one pudgy hand with its many rings only just escaping my inkstand and pen. She had flung her other arm over the back of my chair in a stiff, unwieldy pose that only an idiot would have assumed, in normal concorse.

But all was explained by the sight of her companion. Mrs. Fothergay was being sketched. The man she addressed as Marc Branshaw, astride a pantry work stool across the room, was the artist, and as soon as I saw what his profession must be, I realized that I recognized the name as distinguished in the field of portraiture. His back was to the room, and I could see only a slight man, rather disreputably dressed in shirt and trousers. A frock coat which I took to be his was thrown over the little tabouret beside my easy chair. His shirt sleeves were pushed up to his elbows, the collar of his shirt turned up at the nape of his neck until it met his black hair, which he wore rather longer than the fashion dictated in London. He was a provincial then. But I was sure I would know the lecherous, dissipated face that I should see when he turned around. I had met artists before.

"Dear Miss Wicklow," my lodger gushed upon seeing me, "do forgive us. Marc—Mr. Branshaw—insisted that he must 'do' me at a workaday desk. The contrast would be the better. With my hair and my manner, he insists I am too flamboyant in my own little world. Like a peacock, didn't you say, my dear Mar—Mr. Branshaw? My background must be subdued. Isn't that absurd?"

I would like to have agreed, but said instead that the picture would undoubtedly do her justice, and tried to get only the most complimentary meaning into the remark. Mrs. Fothergay accepted it as her due, and Constable Whacker was too busy studying the room to care, but the artist, who had stood up a moment before, raised his head suddenly and I caught a glimpse of dark eyes and black eyebrows that took a sardonic curve at my words. He understood my meaning, and although he refrained from smiling, there was a mischievous look on his face. He appeared younger than I supposed "dissipated artists" usually were, hardly older than myself, but from his free and easy attitude, I suspected he had seen a good deal more of the world than I.

"Good heavens, what am I thinking of? Miss Anne

Wicklow, Mr. Marc Branshaw," said my lodger. "Such a delightful surprise! To have the great Marc Branshaw sketch one! Really more than one deserves."

My curiosity getting the better of me, I crossed the room and looked over the artist's shoulder at the sketch in his hands. It was cruelly overdone in every way, but there was skill in the caricature. I had a suspicion Mrs. Fothergay would be pleased at this comedy fishwife decked out in great puffs of hair, with eyelashes patently exaggerated and mouth wildly overripe; for he had managed to make her look twenty years younger with all the exaggerations.

"Don't you agree with me? Surely, Mrs. Fothergay deserves no less," said the artist in a low voice. This impertinent remark eluded the artist's subject and certainly did not interest the constable, who was staring at the beautiful white paneling of the walls as though he expected our housekeeper to crawl out of them.

"I'm sure it is worthy of you," I said, with an edge to the words, but his own quick grin was so infectious that I caught myself smiling back at him.

For the first time I looked at Marc Branshaw directly. I think it was the sight of his teeth, perfectly normal and white though they were, that gave me my first sensation of alarm.

I knew that smile. I had seen it last night through the bevel-glass as the dark-eyed prowler had peered in at me. How could I find out if it really was so? I glanced at his hands, thin, not very large, with prominent bones. I could not see whether the fingers had any bruises on them, at least not this far away; so I put on a fine show of enthusiasm and said loudly:

"But where are my manners, Mr. Branshaw? It is an honor to take the hand of so celebrated an artist."

I think I put him off guard, for he stared at me in surprise, but offered his hand as I curtseyed. He understood immediately after. Instead of putting my hand in his in the accepted fashion, I seized his and squeezed as hard as I could across his knuckles. He winced and there was a whiteness about his mouth. It must have been an effort to conceal the shock of pain. His hand jerked out of mine, and he gave me a swift, furious look. I was aware that in this second he could have struck me. He was the prowler, and no mistake.

"What a pity!" I said sweetly. "Have you hurt your hand?"

Before he could reply, I untied my bonnet strings and started to turn away from him. It was only a play for time, as I hoped that there would be some way to broach the matter to the constable without seeing him snatch up the young artist and put the handcuffs on him, or whatever one did with criminals, but I was startled by Mrs. Fothergay's shrill voice:

"Well, I never! The two of you have a certain resemblance. Fancy!" She tittered at her little joke. "Could you be brother and sister, by chance?"

I don't know whether Marc Branshaw was as amazed as I was. By the time I looked at him, having not a word to say for myself, he was already the practiced flirt again.

"I shouldn't like that at all," he said, with a meaning which even I, in my inexperience, could not mistake. I flushed a little, because it was going to be difficult to arrest someone who behaved so annoyingly well.

I said, "Nonsense. If Mr. Branshaw were my

brother, I'd see that he was put to bed without his supper, for I imagine he needs a setdown."

"On the contrary, I would turn you over my knee for your sauciness, Miss Wicklow. Thanks for your permission, Bedelia. I think I shall make it my business."

Upon this embarrassing observation, I decided that Marc Branshaw might just as well be occupied with defending himself as poking fun at me.

"Constable," I said, "I don't think you have further to look for your housebreaker. Mr. Branshaw is the man I saw last night." And then, as everyone in the room, except Mr. Branshaw, tensed awaiting an explosion, I added pleasantly, "I'm sure he has some defense. It is possible I was mistaken about his . . . intentions."

Marc Branshaw put his hands on my shoulders and moved me aside, murmuring as he did so, "Thank you, little sister. That should help me." His irony did not escape me, but he seemed more amused than angry. I was only relieved that when he touched me he did not carry out his first threat.

He went across the room to the constable, but managed to rest his uninjured hand lightly on Mrs. Fothergay's frilled pink morning dress, just where the sleeves joined the shoulder. She purred under his touch and looked up winningly at the constable.

"I think—er . . . Constable . . . that Mr. Branshaw may have been paying a rather late call upon me, naughty boy! And Miss Wicklow did not perfectly understand his motives. Mr. Branshaw explained to me today that he had called once before to ask my permission to sketch me."

"At eleven o'clock at night?" I asked indignantly.

"I do my best work at night," explained the artist, looking as though he were silently laughing at me.

I ignored him and demanded of the constable, "Aren't you going to do anything?"

"Well, mum, it does seem like the gentleman ain't like to be the kind that breaks in of nights." He saw how well Mrs. Fothergay and the artist were getting on, and added, "Don't hardly seem like he needs to break in, excuse me for mentioning."

I waved my hands in exasperation and gave up. "Very well then. If people can come round breaking in at all hours and be let off, then I've nothing more to say. Now, if you will all excuse me, I have work to do, and I would appreciate having my room back."

The constable tipped his hat, plunked it back on his head and after one more tug at his whiskers, departed, having proved to his own satisfaction that my house was just the sort of rendezvous for the disgusting goings-on between Marc Branshaw and this woman old enough to be his mother.

By the time I had seen the constable out, Mr. Branshaw was approaching the door, with his coat thrown over his arm. I opened the door for him and just as I curtseyed with frigid politeness, he said, "You hurt me damnably last night, you know."

"Good," I said. "I'm glad to hear it. And it's not very nice of you to make that poor woman think you care for her, just to get into the house and steal the silver. Why, she might have been your mother!"

"Not mine. Mine was a dark-eyed pert baggage, very like you, my dear sister!" He reached for a lock of my hair and pulled it hard. I was aware suddenly of the coldness of his fingers as they brushed my cheek. What an extraordinary chill! I don't know what he would have done if I hadn't pushed him out the door and slammed it behind him. I looked out the bevel-glass to watch him cross the square with a jaunty, light stride. Although the weather was a bit nippy and storm clouds hovered on the horizon, he still hadn't put on his coat.

Mrs. Fothergay came up behind me, murmuring softly over her sketch.

"How charming of the dear boy! You see, he plainly thinks me younger than I actually . . . What a charmer! Don't you agree, Miss Wicklow?"

"No, I don't. He's a thief. He took manuscript paper from my desk for that sketch of you. I think he is a housebreaker, and I strongly suspect you will find your best silver plate missing tonight."

For some reason, my disapproval of the artist pleased Mrs. Fothergay and she smiled at some dream of her own. She was still standing there when I started to my study. I passed the hall mirror and saw my reflection. No wonder Marc Branshaw's face had looked familiar last night. It did resemble mine slightly, especially now, with my hair smoothed back from my ears. I did not know whether to be flattered or not, for he was much handsomer than I was. But it irritated me to be called his sister, and that was something I could not understand.

What I saw at once, or did not see in my study, was an absence so loud it fairly screamed at me.

The manuscript which I had laid aside in order to do Mr. Perth's story, and which I had re-wrapped last night, was missing from the tabouret. Since Marc Branshaw had laid his coat over it, I looked all around the room, thinking he might have put the manuscript somewhere else. It was nowhere to be seen.

I rushed into the hall to catch Mrs. Fothergay as she was going upstairs to her own lodgings.

"Did you see that artist fellow take a brown package when he left?"

"How should I know, dear? He had his coat over his arm. I didn't see what was in his hand."

"My manuscript!" I shouted. "I told you he was a thief. He's stolen my manuscript. What will I say to Hubbard and Wilson when they call for it?"

"Now, why should he do a thing like that? A gentleman of Mr. Branshaw's breeding! I don't believe you know his reputation, Miss Wicklow. When his paintings were first exhibited in Paris he was a sensation! My dear, the nudes he painted, the most exquisite tonal quality! Everyone in France knew of him. Three years ago they were even wearing Yorkshire cloaks and bonnets, and the ladies were painting their eyelids what they called "Noir de Marc" in imitation of his eyes. I never dreamed he would seek me out for a sketch."

"Yorkshire . . ." I repeated, thinking over the problem.

The manuscript he had stolen was about Red Indians in North America. Yet, the wrappings of the two manuscripts had been the same. Even the writing was similar to that on the Yorkshire manuscript of *The Corpses on the Moor*. Had he intended to take the Yorkshire manuscript? But why not ask me straight out? Of course, I would have refused. Was it possible he had actually come to my house to sketch Mrs. Fothergay and taken the manuscript as some joke of his own?

"Do you know Mr. Branshaw well?" I asked her.

She simpered. "Not as well as I should like to. Most mysterious young man. A mutual friend suggested he do a sketch of me but he won't tell me the name. I imagine it's someone I knew in Paris."

"Then you met this artist in Paris?"

"Oh, heavens, no. I've never seen him before. But he was arguing with that wretched little cleaning maid of yours—wanted to get in and wait for you; at least that's how your maid understood him. It turned out that he had no such intention. But you know how stupid the help is today. As soon as I saw him, I recognized him, of course. I had seen his miniature on one or two charming throats in Paris. In diamond frames, my dear, let me tell you. And I remember a rather large portrait of him done by the distinguished Vicomte de Gris and hung at one time, I believe, in the Louvre or some such place."

It was growing more ridiculous all the time. It was obvious to me now that Marc Branshaw had come here to get that mansucript and merely used Mrs. Fothergay's fawning attentions as a ruse. What a devil he was!

But what possible interest could he have in the Red Indians of North America?

No. He had mistaken the wrapping. He wanted *The Corpses on the Moor.* I wondered if he had written the novel and then changed his mind about its publication. Now that I thought of it, the charming young monster in the story was startlingly like him in appearance and manner. The idea was singular, even a little chilling. He had looked so very harmless. Except, I remembered suddenly, during one brief moment when he had given me that murderous glance.

III

THE THOUGHT of reporting the loss of the stolen manuscript to Hubbard and Wilson severely tried my nerves. Aside from the unfortunate author, I could imagine what it would mean to my own good name, my credit as an honest copyist, and perhaps lawsuits which I should lose since I was clearly culpable.

Oh, that wretched, thieving artist!

Without even waiting for tea, I hurried out again, hired a horse and cab, with mental reservations to collect the fare from Master Branshaw, and had myself driven to Osmund Perth's lodgings to ask his advice. Much good it did me; for he was sleeping off the effects of laudanum taken to ease his discomfort, and his housekeeper refused me admission to him.

I called upon several of the leading hotels in the City and the Straund, but none of them had any record of a guest named Marc Branshaw. Perhaps he did not sleep of nights. Then it occurred to me that when he discovered his mistake, the artist would return the manuscript, hoping to substitute the right one.

I hurried home, barely got through a late bread-and-butter-and-tea, and waited the interminable evening through, but no artist appeared. When Mrs. Fothergay knocked on my study door with the intention of discussing her insufferable Marc Branshaw, I very nearly ran her out of the room and myself out of a paying lodger.

I slept ill again that night. I would have welcomed my thieving "brother" in any guise, even as a Gytrash. It was far better to be chewed by a monster than to lose one's credit.

Desperate now to forestall what I clearly saw as personal ruin, I dressed quickly the following morning and was about to visit the offices of Hubbard and Wilson to discover how soon the manuscript must be returned, when Sackerby, Perth's young errand boy came by and asked me to accompany him to Mr. Perth's house. It seemed the old gentleman wished to speak to me about a manuscript.

I devoutly hoped this would be the missing manuscript about the Red Indians. Rejoicing in this rescue of my credit, not to mention the poor author, I took a cab with the errand boy and was presently ushered into Mr. Perth's Green Room, which was in every respect a most descriptive term for that glassed-in chamber. It was a jungle of growth, pervaded by a strong smell of rich soil and what Mr. Perth often referred to as his "interesting" fertilizers. It always seemed to me that I also smelled the decaying leaves and some rather overpowering scents of flowers that would have better graced the ladies of Cheapside.

The Green Room was so full of potted plants and wild Sandwich Island growths that I nearly had to grope my way to Mr. Perth, who was seated with his leg propped up on a settee halfway down the long conservatory. Behind him was a huge green-leaved plant so tall that it bent over him in a way he doubtless found protective. I shouldn't have been surprised to find that it had tentacles as well. I stayed away from it.

"My dear Miss Anne, good of you to come. So obliging."

I got to the point at once.

"It's about a manuscript that was stolen from my home. Do you have it, sir? It is extremely important. I shall be in disgrace if it's lost."

Mr. Perth scratched at the bandages of his swollen leg thoughtfully.

"No, I'm afraid I cannot help you there. But something may be arranged. Perhaps compensation to the author. At any rate, to get to the point—"

"What?" I demanded, raising my hand quickly for

emphasis and nearly knocking off my bonnet. "You mean you didn't call me here to talk about the stolen manuscript! Then I'm afraid I cannot stay. That—that horrid man whose manuscript you sent me about Yorkshire is the man who—"

He coughed, cleared his throat and generally behaved most unlike his suave self, even putting one hand out to stop me.

"Please, my dear—may I—"

"He is a thief. You apparently deal in thieves, Mr. Perth. And I strongly suggest you take action. As detestable and sly a creature as I have ever—"

"I couldn't agree with you more. A detestable creature!" said a voice behind that accursed potted palm, and out came the Detestable Creature himself, as jaunty as though he had just been picking roses, which, as a matter of fact, he had. He offered me the thorny, heavy-headed flowers and when I refused them indignantly, he agreed.

"Quite right, dear sister. White roses are not for you. Only small roses the color of a deep blush will do you justice. I shall remember that."

"Pray do not trouble. Where is my manuscript?"

"Oh, that. I sent it up to my home by the post. How fortunate!" He turned to Mr. Perth, who agreed sagely.

"Most fortunate. Most opportune."

"I don't see how. I must have that manuscript back immediately." Nevertheless, it was difficult to remain angry, for the artist did look silly, standing there with those roses drooping over his fingers, and trying his best to soothe my ruffled feathers.

"Just so. And you shall have it. You have but to accept my offer."

"We are to bargain for it now? What is the ransom he demands, sir? I told you he was a pirate, Mr. Perth."

"Oh, tut-tut," said Mr. Perth, his pink jowls joggling as he chided me. "Mr. Branshaw wishes to revise certain chapters of the manuscript that has been submitted to us. It was originally written by a friend of his. It seems that in his small village there is no one familiar enough with the script to copy as he makes the oral changes, and he suggested that since I could vouch for your good character, you might be the very person."

"Vouch for my good character!"

"But of course," Mr. Branshaw agreed with the smuggest hypocrisy. "I cannot afford to introduce any but persons of the highest character to the people of my village. You will appreciate my delicacy."

"I trust the members of your village have more character than you have!"

He smiled. "On the contrary," he said, looking directly at me with those black eyes as though we were alone in some secluded place. But his words, the last I expected in the circumstances, were puzzling.

"He often speaks like this, my dear," Mr. Perth said hastily. "It is merely his habit. Mr. Branshaw is a man of sterling reputation, above reproach. And he has offered you twenty pounds for the task before you. I explained to him the situation in which your dear friends left you. Such a fine man, but improvident."

"We will leave my friends out of this."

"I think we are going rather far afield," Marc Branshaw put in. "Possibly you had better explain to Miss Wicklow that I didn't regard my taking of the manuscript as a theft, since it belonged to someone in my—acquaintance. I had no idea, at first, that

I had actually sent home another person's manuscript."

I was too confused to ask how he discovered it was the wrong manuscript if he had already sent it home, or any of the dozen questions I thought about much later in the day.

"Mr. Branshaw even mentioned a desire to sketch you. A compliment, my dear."

Mr. Perth gave us both a paternal smile and pointed to a large, unframed oil painting which rested temporarily against the further wall.

"The crowning touch to my collection. Mr. Branshaw has been kind enough to sell it to me, and at a very moderate price, I assure you. Just look at those tonal colors." He glanced over his shoulder at the painting, then abruptly changed his mind. "No. I never thought! I believe, Miss Anne, it is not the sort of painting that should be graced by a maiden's eyes."

This, naturally, made me all the more curious to see it. I took a few steps toward the painting while Marc Branshaw, with a mischievous look, obligingly stood aside.

The background of the picture was a glade of gigantic greenery, and very much in the foreground, coyly rising from a huge clam shell, was a young woman. A trifle overfed, I thought, but obviously and inexorably nude.

Although I daresay I was the color of a fresh-boiled lobster, I remarked as coolly as I might, "You say, Mr. Perth, that I may be invited to pose for the gentleman? One never knows when one will receive so pretty a compliment. And this early in the morning, too."

The artist laughed aloud, but Mr. Perth was embarrassed and made a somewhat confused statement that there had been no intention of sketching me in anything but my street garments, or any other way I chose.

"However," put in the artist, "you may, of course, pose as Venus if you insist. I have no unalterable objection."

I should have slapped his face, but I said instead, "You will kindly send back my manuscript as soon as you reach your home. I say nothing of the cab fare and other expenses you have put me to. Good day, gentlemen."

Mr. Perth called to me but I ignored him. I half expected the artist to run after me to make his peace but the disgusting creature made no move whatever, except to call after me, "I'll wager I see you in Yorkshire, all the same."

Barely missing a prickly desert plant and one or two African thickets, I left the Green Room in a huff.

The most important matter now was to find out how long I had before Hubbard and Wilson expected the return of their manuscript. I went directly to their offices and received encouraging news. Both gentlemen were away from London, Mr. Hubbard visiting his wife's relations in Cornwall and Mr. Wilson taking the waters at Vevey on the Continent. They were not expected back until a fortnight before the Christmas holiday. This gave me more than a month in which to see that Marc Branshaw returned the manuscript, and if he did not I should certainly set the constables on him. In fact, if I had been acquainted with any local Gytrash, I would have set that useful animal to work as well.

Trusting souls that they were, Hubbard and Wilson's company had sent over another manuscript in my absence, and I kept a close watch on this one, all the while that I prepared my lunch.

I turned back to the pantry only for a moment, to fetch the vinegar cruet, yet when I returned to my tray in the parlor, this manuscript too had been moved mysteriously from the loveseat. I was ready to scream when Mrs. Fothergay interceded.

"Your manuscript, my dear. Here it is, safe and sound. And you were such a naughty girl to accuse Mr. Branshaw, when you had it in your parlor all the time."

"I did not do your dear Mr. Branshaw an injustice, I assure you. This is another manuscript."

"Oh. Well. . . . However! Come, Miss Anne, do sit here and I'll sit on this side. So comfy. I have something of excruciating importance to tell you."

She was suffing and puffing pretty badly, from which I took it that she was wearing her best corsets. She always bought them a size too small; so in charity I could hardly refuse to let her sit down. But I never had liked the loveseat, partly because it was the favorite seat of Mr. Sackerby's overgrown son when he came to call, and he began each of his proposals of marriage by archly calling my attention to his choice of the loveseat.

"Now, dear Anne . . . I may call you Anne, since we shall presently be seeing a good deal more of each other—"

I wondered what this betokened.

"Yes, you must look upon me as your moth—your elder sister; for you simply must accompany me. All is lost if you do not."

"What on earth can you mean, ma'am? Where are you going?"

Could it be possible she was inviting me to accompany her to Paris? What a dream! My dream home. The city of the Varney family. I must be very kind and polite to Mrs. Fothergay. I could not afford to lose such a chance.

"I cannot tell you of my delight," she went on, "I don't believe I have ever been so flattered. In short, about half an hour ago I had a caller. You will never guess."

I did not try.

"Yes. Just as you surmise. Dear Marc came calling. He wants me to come to Yorkshire for a visit. He has decided he must do me in oils."

I was speechless.

Mrs. Fothergay giggled. "That surprises you, doesn't it? To think I should consent when he has done so many of those—well, there is no other word for it—nudes, you know. In deference to my position, however, he wishes me to pose in a boudoir gown. Quite proper, my dear; for we shall have a chaperone."

"Not—"

"Exactly so. Yourself. Oh yes. Marc thinks of everything, the dear. He tells me that he cannot risk any scandal attached to my name. I must bring a chaperone. Isn't that touching, from such a sophisticated young man?"

"Touching is not the word for it."

"No, of course not. But then, there really is no word for his kindness to me, and his admiration; for I am just a teensy bit older than he, you know. However—" She shrugged her thick shoulders. "It was always so. Something about me appeals to young men, ever since the Colonel died. I am always being told I am too feminine to have all the worries of the Colonel's estate. Charming thought. You will come with me, there's a dear."

"I couldn't possibly. I have too much work to do.

I am a business woman, you know, ma'am. I must keep busy."

"How stupid of me! I neglected to tell you the best part. He is so anxious for me to arrive safely that he offers you twenty pounds for the journey. He says you may be handy also to copy some manuscript or other. Now, that takes care of your little scruple about money."

That dastardly villain, Marc Branshaw! Getting around me in this underhanded manner. I did wonder what on earth he wanted of me up in his God-forsaken country. I was not quite so beglamored by my own charm as Mrs. Fothergay by hers, and seriously doubted if he went to this trouble to get me up there just to seduce me, or even to paint me in the nude. What then was his purpose?

"I'm sorry. I can't leave London at this time. I'm sure there will be no problem. After all, you are a grown woman, a widow. You may surely conduct yourself as you like without duennas and chaperones. He's only teasing you. He cannot possibly need me."

"So I told him," she admitted ingenuously, "but he would not have it so. For my own reputation, I absolutely must bring you. I imagine, though he did not say so, that it may have some thing to do with the murder. Perhaps he fears something may happen to me."

"How exciting! I always suspected that fellow was up to no good. Whom has he murdered?"

Mrs. Fothergay wanted to evade the subject, but seeing that she had interested me, she finally got up from the loveseat, brushed out the feathered wrapper she had apparently been wearing when she entertained Marc Branshaw, and went to fetch one of the papers to which she subscribed. She returned with the newspaper and also a wide vase of white cabbage roses that looked a trifle blowsy and exceedingly familiar.

"From Marc. Wasn't that dear of him? A bit wilted, perhaps, but he said he picked them just for me, because I reminded him of white roses."

I became suddenly very busy and did not look at the flowers. After all, they were technically mine. What right had he to give them to her?

The murder Mrs. Fothergay had spoken of was in the oversheet of the Yorkshire Post, dated several days ago. She read the date, fumbled through some engrossing advertisements on cures for sheep disease, restoratives to manhood, and applications for posts as governess by needy young women.

"Ah, here it is:

"MONSTER ANIMAL SLAYS SHEEPMAN.

"William Grimlett, a sheep farmer resident on Maidenmoor heath, in the West Riding, was savaged to death Saturday evening last while combing the moors for stray sheep. It is believed that the brutal and bloody attack which tore out the unfortunate man's throat and worried his features until they were virtually unrecognizable, was made by some savage animal of the cat or lion breed, perhaps escaped from a carnival or a wandering gypsy caravan.

"Upon the same night that sounded the death knell for Grimlett, a child, wandering the moor in pursuit of his pet sheep, was frightened by a savage animal which leaped into a tuft of heather at sight of the child, but which the young witness later described as being much too large for a dog, and of a dun color popularly associated with the leonine family. 'He had fur,'

said the lad. 'Like ye sees at the fair down to Bradford. Happen he was a lion-like.'"

I snatched the paper from Mrs. Fothergay, who went rattling on happily.

"My dear, it's simple. Marc wishes me to have an escort because he's afraid for my safety. Since that farmer was murdered just outside Marc's own village, Marc feels, and rightly, that I should be protected."

The newspaper was dated exactly a week ago. A horrifying idea occurred to me. If the manuscript about the silly Gytrash had been written after the death of the farmer Grimlett, then the explanation was simple, a mere re-telling of the unfortunate man's death, with dramatic license. But the novel was written before the man's death, and described several murders just in the manner of Grimlett's death. Was it possible that the animal which killed the farmer was known to the author of *The Corpses on the Moor*? Small wonder Marc Branshaw had gone to such lengths to get the manuscript back.

Possibly the novel was a coincidence, an accidental foreshadowing of the real crime. Was it a foreshadowing also of the real animal that had committed the murder? Too much coincidence. In any case, this horror was no inducement to me to visit Yorkshire and a man who knew about savage killings before they occurred.

"I'm sorry, Mrs. Fothergay, but I don't think Maidenmoor is a place for either of us to visit at this time."

"I see." Mrs. Fothergay took back her paper, folded it several times, as though pleating a skirt, and then stood up ponderously. "In that case, my dear Anne, I think you had better advertise for a new lodger."

Mrs. Fothergay was not the only one who "saw." I had planned to buy carpeting with the next quarter's rental. I wanted to repair the shutters, and get twenty yards of a bewitching striped *barège* which would give me nineteen yards for one of the new full skirts that flared out with style.

"Perhaps you are right," I gave in ungracefully. "I will leave the arrangements to you, ma'am."

She brightened at once. "I knew you were a sensible girl. We will stay at the inn in the village, of course. Mr. Branshaw will meet us at the Teignford rail stop and take us on to Maidenmoor." She went on making all sorts of plans about schedules, prices, wondering about the virtues of the new fast schedule mail coach versus the old and infrequent stagecoach route, and finally came to what she considered the most important instruction.

"You will call me Bedelia, my dear, and I shall call you Anne. That will make us truly sisters." She went off, happily carrying her vase full of my roses.

I stared after her. She had not evinced one flicker of fear or nervousness about the doings on those mysterious, impenetrable moors which, as I understood from the manuscript, completely engulfed the little village.

But then, I knew something of which she had no knowledge. Somewhere in that village, and undoubtedly known to our host, was a man or a woman who, weeks before it happened, knew that a savage animal was going to kill a man, and in just such a manner, almost at the very spot pointed out in the manuscript.

I was selfish enough to turn to a question even closer to me. It was obvious that this whole stratagem of "painting Mrs. Fothergay" was an effort to get me up to Yorkshire. What did I have to offer

Maidenmoor and Mr. Branshaw that required such elaborate staging to get me there?

IV

I WAS ALONE, as solitary as a wanderer on the face of the moon, and the realization was unnerving.

I stood on the hilltop, catching my breath, and stared at a vast green world all around me, in which I could not make out one sign of human habitation. Yet there was a curious life of sorts in this emptiness of the rock-studded moors; for the thick, deep green turf, wet with late rains, seemed to throb somnolently, like a great serpent curled around me in many humps and twists, waiting . . . faintly breathing, but not yet aroused. The moors were not flat and brown as I had thought, but endless, bleak rolling hills separated by tangled folds of still deeper green that carried pretty little becks whose trickle of water, hardly wider than a human finger, made their criss-cross way over and under the back of that great green monster.

It was my fault that I was alone. I had come this far along the road from Teignford toward the isolated village of Maidenmoor entirely on my own initiative, paying no heed to the innkeeper in the town who tried to dissuade me.

An hour before, it had been just as I might have predicted. Mrs. Fothergay and I arrived on the Leeds and Bradford stage from London only to find that our host, Mr. Branshaw, was nowhere in sight, had not been expected, and undoubtedly had forgotten all about us—or else was playing this trick for some humorous reason of his own. Worse than all, every bedchamber in the Teignford Inn and the other two hotels was let to visitors for the Woolens Market Day.

It was past sunset and we could not wait here indefinitely. I inquired of the innkeeper the distance to the village of Maidenmoor.

Like one or two other Yorkshiremen we had encountered on the mail coach, he had an over-the-border burr in his speech that did not make his broad Yorkshire accent any clearer.

"Ay, mum, a wee step, but up a stout hill or two, then down in the bottoms, crossing a beck here and there, and nothing around ye but the moors. Then up another hill, and ye be there. Bide the night, mum, and happen y'll find some'ut here with the gig or yet a nag."

As the innkeeper could make no adequate provision for sleeping quarters during the night, it seemed to me that his advice was not very sound.

"Is it safe to walk to Maidenmoor at this hour? Is it often done?"

He looked surprised.

"Ay, mum. Done it myself times out of mind. But then, I'm born to it. The moors is no surprise to me. It's different-like with an outcomer."

Rightfully applying the "outcomer" to myself, I asked, "Why?"

I didn't really want to go. In the first place, I am not an inveterate walker and in the second place, the world outside the inn had began to look passing dour, as did the whole town. A glorious sunset, feathered with many hues of orange, red and pink, as seen through the pall of smoke from the Teignford Woolen Mills, was now gone and we were apparently in for the long, gloomy dusk of the North Country, that time of night referred to in the manuscript of the *Corpses on the Moor* as the un-dark.

To compound the unpleasantness, there was rain in the air. Even within doors, before the cosy comfort of an open fire, I could smell the acrid, wet odor of the great unconquered heaths that surrounded these Yorkshire towns, often encroaching on the villages themselves. But I was determined not to satisfy the detestable Marc Branshaw by sleeping on a hard, cushionless settle in the Public Room, or some other grisly method devised by our goodnatured host. Besides, he would be sure to charge us dearly for any little "comforts" of this sort that he added to our reckoning.

No, indeed. Master Branshaw had promised me twenty pounds for this journey, and to provide shelter at the Maidenmoor Inn which was, if the innkeeper told the truth, "only a wee step." I was determined that the artist should be made to pay. I could see him now, smirking at our discomfort, never dreaming we would have courage enough to come after him and face him in his lair.

Mrs. Fothergay fanned herself with her handkerchief, and occasionally stopped to rub her poor swollen toes, which were encased in town boots much too narrow for the short, squat shape of her feet.

"Dear Anne, what can be keeping him? Frankly, I don't understand this at all. Could he be ill? I do believe that must be the case."

"Oh, nonsense," I said. "He is about as ill as—as our host here."

Our host looked from one to the other of us. He was an enormous man, like most of the men I had seen in this part of the country, except Mrs. Fothergay's Gay Romantic, Marc Branshaw, and the host's leathery countenance with its high, red cheeks and twinkling little blue eyes, looked eternal as the moors.

"Best be making yourselves do here, such as can be. It's no time for a lady like yourself on the moors. Now, mum, what'll be for supper? Boiled mutton and turnips. Ay. We'll fix ye all right and tight. See if we don't. Bessie!"

Whoever Bessie was, all this sounded expensive. He had obviously seen us coming and took us for green ones.

"Never you mind that," I said. "Just set me on the road to Maidenmoor and I'll fetch Master Branshaw or know the reason why."

A little thread of a frown crossed our host's leathery brow.

"Now, mum," he began soothingly, like a great mastiff licking one's face. " 'Tis a long way for such a little lady. Ay, and dark afore the hour's gone."

I looked out through the one open shutter.

"It won't be dark for two hours yet. I know a little something about this country." I didn't tell him that I had garnered my information from sundry books.

"Well then—" he shrugged and gave me up.

"Really, dear, are you sure you're doing the right thing?" Mrs. Fothergay asked me. I wondered if she was concerned with my welfare—an unusual quality in her. She soon disabused me on that point. "Do you think I shall be quite safe here . . . all alone?"

The innkeeper and I looked at each other almost without intending to, and I caught the faintest of smiles on his pleasant, homely countenance. I assured Mrs. Fothergay that she would be quite safe. No one had designs on her. I suspected that she wasn't too sure, and she proved this by whispering as I said good-bye, "When I prepare for dinner, I shall take care to make myself as plain and—er—

unobtrusive, as nature will allow me. No need to encourage their pretensions; for I have already seen two of these rustics eying me in a certain way."

I assured her gravely that if she tried very hard to disguise the great endowments of nature, it was possible they would not find her irresistable. I left her by the fire, still uneasy that her fatal charm would crack a few local hearts.

The innkeeper walked with me to the cobbled street and pointed to the road which wound up over a hill and vanished. Along the upward slope of the hill, lining the road, were many gray York stone workmen's houses slap up against each other, like lean-faced, hard-working men, united in a huddle against the cold and misery of the world.

"Yon's the way."

I started off but he caught my cloak.

"Don't ye maunder to one side or t'other and ye'll get there afore ye knows it. Ye looks ahead and walks straight as a lance. Mind now. The moorland's a passing strange creetur. He don't pay no mind to his own, but them as is outcomers is not made t'home. Happen a man could die out in them moors, lost and feared of such false creeturs as the Gytrash and all. Besides all else, there's the pot-holes. So ye best keep the road, mum. No matter what! For I tell ye here and now—if ye tries to cross the moorland without ye has a man of the countryside along of ye, there's many a thing can happen. Now, give ear t'that!"

With this cheerful piece of advice ringing in my ears, I left him.

I felt a drop of rain upon my head as I proceeded up the hill alone, but I was prepared for such weather in November, and was wearing a mantle and hood which were very nearly waterproof. I climbed the hill rapidly, from flagstone to flagstone, reaching the top almost before the innkeeper had gone back inside his warm taproom. But my haste was at some cost, for I was soon out of breath, and on descending this hill on the further side, I paid no attention to my surroundings but stepped onward until the gray, time-polished stones underfoot seemed slowly to dissolve into the stark earth of the wagon-rutted road. Once the house of Teignford ceased to line my route, I was not aware of any impediment to my view on either side of the road.

From the blue-gray light of the cloudy heavens that illuminated my way, I seemed surrounded by open spaces. I paid no heed until a little trickling beck crossed the road in front of me and vanished in the undergrowth of a gully on my left side. I had to pick up my skirts to cross the water. Even then the toes of my shoes got wet and I could feel the sogginess creep into my stockings.

The road wound around over the next hill and at its peak, already tired, I stopped to get my breath and study the surroundings. The intermittent sprinkles foretelling a shower turned gradually to a fine misty spray. The scent of the green moors and the blackened heather was pervasive.

It was then I knew that I had never been so alone in all my memory.

I tried to make out the countryside through the mist, but it was difficult, for a stiff breeze blew the spray across my face and made the whole scene appear blurred, as through a freshly washed windowglass. I thought I made out the topmost lines of a bell-tower across the narrow valley that dropped off from the right-hand side of the road. But the rest of the tower, and apparently the town, were tucked behind a hill even more steep than the one I stood on. By peering hard through the mist I saw the steep descent of my road probably half a mile beyond me, down into the valley on my right, and then climbing that impossible hill which I supposed must lead to, and conceal from my present sight, the village of Maidenmoor. My friend, the writer of the Gytrash tale, had not exaggerated when he described the location of the village in his story. Nothing could be further cut off from "civilization", unless it be a vessel at sea.

The walk from here to that formidable hill across the valley was certainly more than a "wee step" and I was greatly provoked with myself for having taken the innkeeper's description at face—or foot—value. I should certainly not reach Maidenmoor before dark, upon my own feet.

After studying longer the wider expanse of moors around me, I began to see at last the faint signs that man had made some effort to conquer this green monster. At spaced intervals the bleak, empty scene was riven by low, black stone walls that rose and fell over the distant prospect and which I took to be the indications of private property. Still, it seemed to me that the blackened heath, blending into the green of the moorland itself, looked no more fit for human habitation than those sections on the far horizon that had no York stone boundaries. Man might fancy he had conquered nature, but I was inclined to agree with the innkeeper of Teignford that the moors were still no place to wander alone. If there were, as I had read aloud to my father in learned chronicles, certain dimensions beyond ours, certain places where Man was not yet the master but only a puny, poor little visitor, then I had come to one of these places. But if Man did not command here, then what intelligence, under God's, ruled these vast, unconquered moors?

I suddenly remembered that preposterous Gytrash, and wished I hadn't.

At the same moment, it was almost as if my thoughts took form. Somewhere among the wet green verdure at a short distance on my right, below the road, I made out furtive movements and saw a bird fly upward, as though startled by a higher animalism in the heath. A fleck of dun color gleamed above the high vegetation, as a drop of rain glanced off the surface of some beast. The creature was hidden, for the most part, behind a curious formation of solid-packed turf and brush that at first I took to be a very large tuft of heather but which I realized must be a man-made shooting butt. From the careful movements I assumed the animal was one of the solitary and aloof breed which knows no allegiance to man. It could not be, then, as I had at first hoped, a large dog of the neighborhood.

I began to panic. If this thing mounting the moorland hill to the road was actually, as the Yorkshire papers had said, "of the leonine family", a rapid motion on my part would be fatal. But every second's delay made me tremble the more. I lost all caution and started to run, with all my skirts and petticoats flapping about my ankles. Then I looked back. The beast was coming into view. I gaped at it.

The dun-colored creature of the moors was nothing more terrifying than a dainty-footed mare, an animal not likely to be found in these parts where more serviceable breeds were needed. Behind the mare, taking long leggy strides with more force than the animal, was a very tall, well-built man in his middle years.

I felt more than a trifle foolish, for I had been so obviously running away that even a blind man could read my panic. Unlike myself, the gentleman, as his first words proved him to be, was not in the least surprised to see me.

"Ah, there. Delightful weather. I say, you must be devilish fond of capering about in the wet, madam. Carriage broken down?" Although the situation warranted curiosity on his part, I could not but feel that he spoke in a sardonic way, as though my plight was amusing to him. His blue eyes were a trifle weary, his face just a shade puffy beneath the ruddy complexion that he appeared to share with most Yorkshiremen, but I suspected from his voice that he was not a native of these parts. I could only sum up the general impression he made on me by a quote from my father who had a friend "with a pleasantly dissipated face." And so it was with Sir Gareth Owen, as he introduced himself.

I explained briefly that a lady and I were to have been met at Teignford, and finding there had been a mistake somewhere, I was now walking to Maidenmoor to discover what had gone amiss. I added acidly, "I had no notion just how far this wretched village would prove to be."

"Wretched indeed," he laughed, and I thought a little of his boredom was lifted as he looked me up and down. I had not traveled in Mrs. Fothergay's company for nothing. I was becoming quite a female coxcomb, yet I could not but be flattered, although I took him for a man who spent his life making himself agreeable to women, so practiced and yet with that aloof indifference which was always a challenge.

While I was beguiling myself with the notion that he found me attractive, he took the most peculiar interest in me. At last he said, "Would you oblige me, madam? Just raise your eyebrows and stare at me as though you could cut me down at twenty paces. Stand on tiptoe. No, no. Keep the hood of your cloak around your face, just so."

Utterly confounded, I did as I was bidden, feeling like a schoolgirl, while the mist swirled around us and this towering man, with his only half-concealed insolence, considered me.

He murmured after too long a time, "For a moment you put me a little in mind of. . . . May I ask the name of the person whom you were expecting at Teignford?"

"An impudent young artist named Marc Branshaw."

He was satisfied, but puzzled too. "Now, what the deuce is his object? Personal, of course. Hmm. No matter. Come madam. Let me make amends, for the sake of the family, as it were."

"Are you—?"

"Gad, no. But it was a near thing. We were fortunate. My sister Catherine escaped his designs. In short, he jilted her. I knew his mother. Sort of thing she would do. Piquant charmer, was Moyna Branshaw. Broke many a heart, I daresay. And such a faithful, devoted mistress, so loyal to a tender memory! Touching, I'm sure. Don't know how she came to produce her revolting offspring. . . . Here. Here. What am I thinking of? Your shoes are wet through. Come! Up on Jassy here. Won't hurt you in the least, ma'am."

I stood uncertainly in the muddy path, only to be swept into his arms and up onto the back of the quiet mare who gave me one look of mild interest before snorting in a gentle way. I was not sure that I approved of these masterful ways of Sir Gareth, but at the same time, I did not approve of walking another hour in wet feet either.

"How do you find young Branshaw, Miss Anne?"

"I find him odious."

"Ah! Always pleasant to have one's own judgment vindicated."

I thought I could plainly see why Sir Gareth and the young artist would always be in dispute. The peer seemed to me very like his blue eyes—bored and disillusioned, perhaps early indulged, and now despising the more commonplace virtues of humanity, such as Moyna Branshaw's fidelity to her husband, as I suppose he had meant to imply. Sir Gareth was surely a man whose character was easily read. On the other hand, I remembered Marc Branshaw's eyes with their dancing blackness against his sallow olive complexion. Those eyes, I thought, were as unfathomable as a deep pool at night. Sometimes, in my memory, they seemed ageless, as though they had absorbed and then concealed a whole lifetime of experience, at great variance with his look of youth.

Even in general configuration, Sir Gareth held all the cards. He was so very big and ruddy, so very Anglo-Saxon. Everything Marc Branshaw was not. Why then should he interest me less than Marc?

As we jogged along down the road toward the valley and the beginnings of what appeared more and more to be an appalling ascent of the hill leading to the hidden village of Maidenmoor, I studied the man walking ahead of me, leading the patient Jassy.

Sir Gareth was dressed, like so many men of the district, in leather breeches and leather jerkin, as well as what appeared to be a homespun shirt and an expensively cut but none too new jacket. Instead of wearing boots, as one might have expected of a sporting man, his limbs were encased nearly to his thighs in well-rubbed leather.

Either he had no taste for the expensive garments of the gentlemen, and this seemed unlikely, considering the cut of his clothing, or he had come upon bad times and was playing the gentleman without a gentleman's purse. I remembered the prosperous, if Bohemian, look of Marc Branshaw. It must have been painful for the aristocratic Owens to lose both a husband for his sister and the Branshaw money.

Why had Marc Branshaw jilted Sir Gareth's sister? It did not set him in a very pretty light. Probably there was no betrothal at all, merely an understanding. Anything else would be unforgivable in a gentleman.

As we approached the flagstones at the foot of the road that mounted to Maidenmoor, I became aware of the sudden snuffing of the last blue-gray streaks of light in the sky. How dark it was!

With the wild expanse of moors everywhere rising around us in even darker shadow I saw something dotting the distant hills like insects, with flaring, fiery wings.

"What are those odd lights?" I asked, pointing to those curious little flames that came and went, up and down, sometimes disappearing, then rising again on a further ridge, against the stormy night sky.

"Oh, that." Sir Gareth glanced at it in his supercilious way. "The lights of the searchers, I should imagine."

"Searchers! After what?"

"My dear madam, why do you suppose Branshaw did not meet you at Teignford? He is playing the hero, a party to the search. Not from choice, you may be sure, but because it would be worth his neck to commit a suspicious act at this time. Missing girl, you know—daughter of one of the sheep cotters.

It seems she was out where she shouldn't be, on the trail to Marc's cottage across the moors. He paints. Women, you know. Doesn't live there all the time, but visits the place for his work. Desolate, Godforsaken. Roof falling in. Frightful inconveniences. His mother died there, though what she was doing in such a rat's nest I'll never know. Probably saving pennies."

"Yes, yes. But why are they searching for this girl?"

He looked at me in his bored way. I could not see his features too well but I guessed his manner from his voice.

"Because she is missing, naturally. Left her father's cottage before the rains yesterday and never returned. Marc Branshaw claims he wasn't expecting her. Cowardly little pup would claim that, in the circumstances. Still, only thing to do, I suppose. Girl's probably lying in some pot-hole with a broken limb. Pity. Beautiful limbs."

I was somewhat uneasy. Surely, a girl living on the moors would know her way well enough to avoid pot-holes. Was there foul play? Horrid thought.

"Then that is how you happened to be crossing the moors on Jassy, sir? In your search?"

"Gad, no. What do you take me for—a blasted hero? I was doing a little shooting."

Curious, that explanation for his only weapon was a large pistol carelessly stuck in Jassy's saddle, its barrel cold and wet even through my skirts. It was the kind of implement one associates less with field sports than with highway robbery, or perhaps self-defense. Was Sir Gareth afraid of something?

As Jassy put one dainty foot before the other, mounting this incredible hill paved in deeply scarred old flagstones, I reminded Sir Gareth that I must returned to Teignford tonight with a horse and a gig, or at least be at the expense of hiring a trustworthy local tradesman to fetch Mrs. Fothergay in his conveyance. I will admit I was hoping that Sir Gareth would offer to furnish the gig himself. He did better than that.

"Don't give it a thought, ma'am," said my new friend. "Fetch her myself. Sounds just in my way."

Good Lord! I thought. Was Mrs. Fothergay about to be wooed in very earnest, and by a peer of the realm?

Although the first stone buildings of the village loomed up now ahead of us, I could make out very little of the particulars. I was surprised to discover that, although the two-story houses appeared austere and even forbidding, they were like guardian walls between the life within the town and the encroaching green monster that sprawled all about them, licking at every little vacant space where the stone walls and fences had worn away.

Another reassuring thing was the loud clap of bootheels ringing on the wet, shining cobbles of the street as the residents went about their business, probably home to supper. There seemed to be some sort of iron-clad rule that all should be dressed in black; for I never saw a man in the streets who did not wear a black jacket or coat, sometimes of leather, and those solid, noisy black boots, either ankle high or nearly to their thighs. The women, except for a few old ones with daringly scarlet cloaks, were for the most part swathed against the rising cold in black as well. I was surprised to note that their footgear made even more noise than the boots of the men, and discovered that the older women were shod in furiously clanking iron-patched wooden shoes.

This was no deserted village, but an up-and-coming little town with a not undistinguished past, known in the North, as the inhabitants soon told me, long before the woolen mills of Bradford and Leeds robbed them of their skill at the hand looms by substituting machinery. Still, it was grim. When Sir Gareth lifted me off uncomplaining Jassy's back and set me on the stoop of the Yorkish Lion Inn, I glanced up the street, which glistened under the smokey glow cast by the outside lamp of the inn, and I thought how much more cheerful the village might be with pots of bright geraniums in some of those wide, empty-looking windows.

We stepped into a passage that held the warm glow of the fireplace we were approaching in the old-fashioned parlor with a taprail at one side. Several men, all in black, and calmly smoking smelly pipes between long draughts of spirits at the taprail, turned to eye me curiously. I noticed that although their glances at me were indifferent, they were not hostile. So much could not be said for their treatment of Sir Gareth, whom they plainly disliked. Nevertheless, they addressed him politely enough.

"Evenin', mon."

Sir Gareth was expansive but I fancied he overdid the politeness, as though he found something amusing in these surly villagers.

"Jolly fine evening, Cutter. But I am surprised to find you here. Have they found your pretty playmate then?"

"My playmate?" thundered the man at the rail, turning red. "Now, what'll ye be meaning with that? I know'd Abbie Hinchley, as did a mort of others, not to be naming no names."

The other two men at the rail looked uneasily at each other, from which I reflected that the missing

Abbie had a wide acquaintance. For some reason, I was relieved to know that Marc Branshaw, detestable as he might be, was not the only man concerned in her affairs.

"Manners, gentlemen," said the woman behind the taprail, and I saw a female of thirty-odd years, with delicate features and a manner as quiet and incisive as the tone of her voice.

Sir Gareth brushed aside the subject of Abbie Hinchley.

"Hallo there, Rose. I've been out beating up custom for you. The young lady is to stay the night. After that, I imagine our dashing young local celebrity will have other arrangements to make. I believe she is employed by him."

Apparently Miss Rose knew who the "local celebrity" was. I tried to enter into an explanation, but saw that it would only make matters worse. All three of the men looked at me, obviously thinking me another Abbie Hinchley, and as for that tiresome Sir Gareth, he looked at me as well, in his lascivious way which I was beginning to find irritating, and remarked that I must be lonely as he would return presently with my friend. He did not explain to those in the taproom that my friend was a female and I knew perfectly well what they thought, but I was tired and annoyed and the woman behind the taprail guessed as much, for she raised the bar and came around to me.

"Come, Miss, let me help you. The side chamber is not occupied. It should do for you tonight, at least."

I thanked her for her courtesy, but actually, I was thanking her for her quick acceptance of me without foolish questions. On the way up the newly painted white stairs behind the taproom, she explained to me that her name was Rose Keegan and that she and her nephew owned the Yorkish Lion in partnership.

"What? Both of you?" I asked, laughing a little.

She smiled. "You will find that Jamie is quite as responsible as I, though he is only eleven."

The upstairs hall creaked like a thing in pain as we crossed the ancient planks to the door of the side chamber, but I liked the atmosphere, for there was no mistaking the home touch of Miss Rose: a rose-tinted lamp on the flat newel post, a pretty little side-table against the wall, tiny touches of delicacy and charm in this grim village.

My room was small and bitter cold, but in other ways adequate, with a neat bed that I was happy to see had no moth-eaten testor and dingy curtains—merely a hand-loomed coverlet, spotless pillows and four well-carved sturdy posts. There was a commode beneath the cracked but clean mirror, and on the commode, a polished jar and basin, completely free of the soot or coal-dust I had observed everywhere in Yorkshire.

I was drawing back the starched yellow curtains in order to see what lay beyond my window when Miss Rose spoke up.

"The front bedroom is permanently let, miss. Else I shouldn't have put you here. The view is—"

But I had already opened the shutters. Marching right up to the very walls of the Yorkish Lion was the community graveyard. When I was able to take my eyes off the truly horrifying gravestones, some laid out flat, the exact size of a human corpse, some standing up like a ghostly army in the rainy night, I saw the outlines of the village church which formed the opposite boundary of the graveyard. The church itself was gothic, forbidding, and of course, formed by the omnipresent York stone. A kind of diseased, grasping ivy crawled up the stone walls to the bell tower. Fearing the contagion of that ivy, I looked straight down at the sides of the Keegan inn, and found more of the same crawling up toward my window, its tendrils extended and swaying in the rain as if blindly seeking me.

I said "Good heavens!" and pulled the shutters to and then the window.

Miss Rose made no apology beyond saying that if I did not think about it, I shouldn't be troubled. This was undeniably true, only the doing was harder than she apparently thought.

"Supper is served sharp at half after six," she said, and with a pleasant smile left me to my solitude and my companions in the graveyard.

I was combing my hair in a curlier style about my face and studying the result in the cracked mirror some minutes later when a voice spoke to me out of nowhere, it seemed. My scalp tingled. The voice was young, light, phantomlike—not the voice of anyone I had heard in the tavern.

"Happen you're one of them, be ye?"

I looked into the mirror. A small, sturdy boy of ten years or so was standing there watching me. He was a handsome boy, slightly resembling his attractive aunt, for I took him to be young Jamie Keegan, her partner in the ownership of the inn.

"I don't know," I replied, turning around and receiving his polite handshake with what I hoped was a matching grace. "Am I? I am from London."

"Ay, ye be. They're from York and Leeds and all over since it happened. Come to see if they can fetch out the Gytrash."

I smiled, thinking he spoke in fancy, but then covered the smile, for I saw that his smooth young face looked troubled. His blue eyes, studying me, were as grave as an abbot's. Childlike, he had apparently salted the broad tongue of the West Riding with half a dozen other brogues, so that I had to listen hard to unravel it all.

" 'Twas me saw it, love. Sir Gareth's sister, Miss Catherine, she give me a lamb, by name Gambol, and it maundered out on the moors. Can I sit on your bed? I been over far as Mister Marc's cottage 'cross the moors. We didn't find her though. Marc said for me to go home to supper. He's good, and he's thoughty-like."

I wondered if the boy and I could be thinking of the same Mister Marc.

"He's my best friend. He's a love, that he is. And so's Miss Catherine. Not like her brother, Sir Gareth. You don't catch him looking for poor Abbie. . . . Gytrash's got her in his lair."

I began to understand. "Then it was you the newspapers quoted. You saw the tawny-colored thing like a lion that attacked the sheepman. That was very brave of you."

"Ye might call me 'love' if you're a mind to. You're a dancey lady, with dancey eyes. I like that."

"Thank you. But don't you think it's possible what you saw was a lion escaped from a fair in some village or other? Or perhaps a large dog that belonged to wandering gypsies?"

He had seated himself comfortably on my bed and was getting his bottom settled after a good deal of sliding back and forth, while he looked at me in the style of a very mature man trying to teach an untractable pupil.

"Now you're talking like Sir Gareth. Come, mum, you didn't see the Gytrash. He's a great flaysome brute, with a mane, I think. And great, long claws that's curled up—like this—"

He made the requisite gestures, which caused me to back off precipitously.

"I understand. I see it, vividly!"

"—and he jumps into the heather and away. He's half man, half beast. That's what he is. Some's said he walks like a man when he chooses. . . . I fancy I seen him t'other night out yon in the graveyard where the Devil-Vicar's bones is buried, but I can't be sure. I'd had a Shandy Gaff after supper and I might a been a wee bit dipped in the nob. Besides, there's a heap a live ones to eat. For why should he be hanging about the gravestones? But if ye sees him out there tonight, ye must let me know. Promise, now."

Jamie leaped off the bed, jarring the uneasy floor as he landed in his iron-tipped boots. "Come. It's suppertime. I'm to take you to supper. Ay, and time, too. I be that starved."

Wondering who the Devil-Vicar might be, I thought of the graveyard outside, the ivy climbing up to my window, and Master Jamie's friend, the Gytrash, lurking about in the wet darkness among the gravestones, and I asked myself if I could ever eat again.

Clearly, Jamie had no such doubts. He took my hand, once more my very correct host.

"You're a tiny thing, for a fact. Not much bigger'n me. Well, ye come along a me, love. Mark me, though. The Gytrash was feared a me; so ye see, you're safe with ol' Jamie Keegan."

He was so convincing, I very nearly believed I was.

V

Through the early portions of my meal I was the solitary diner in the little back parlor which had been newly whitewashed and the shutters firmly bolted behind freshly dusted drapes. The flagstones were so cold they seemed to carry ice clear through my morocco shoes. There were three tables in the small room which barely accommodated them, and although the tables were covered by charming old clothes freshly laundered, stiff and clean, the tables themselves were unpolished deal tables—practical, functional, and enduring, like the Yorkshiremen themselves.

Young Jamie kept me company for a few minutes, but then he saw someone of greater interest in the taproom and scampered out to where the excitement was, the searchers having begun to straggle in for their "pint" to give them sustinence for the long, bitter cold night of searching still ahead.

I was joined briefly by one of the searchers, the Reverend Frederick Niles, curate of the local church, who proved to be a quiet, attractive, blond young man.

"Are you visiting us for long, Miss Wicklow?" he inquired as he ate a quick meal standing up, ready to rejoin the search at any moment.

I explained that I expected to be gone the next day, if not sooner, and when he looked surprised, I did not bother to explain further. He said after a slight pause, "A pity you were not able to visit us earlier in the season. I cannot recall when the heather looked lovelier."

"Are people often lost on the moors hereabouts?"

"Yes, yes. Quite cooked, I assure you. Nothing but the bones remained. Poor devil never got out of the house. Everyone had thought he was gone, you see. But it wasn't so. Probably knocked unconscious beforehand by some idiot. Let us hope so, at any rate. Which explains the talk about monsters. One always hears that after a murder."

"They do say, dear, there was talk when the Owens moved into this district, about five years after the fire. From Wales, you know, Miss Wicklow. Very odd people, the Welsh."

"Emily, I put it to you. Could anyone in his right mind mistake Gareth Owen for the Devil-Vicar, or even a Gytrash, when it comes to that? Why, the man's too dashed lazy. Almost the antithesis of our Devil-Vicar in looks. It's all balderdash. The Devil-Vicar's bones are snugly buried in the ashes where the parsonage stood, at the southwest end of the graveyard behind the inn here."

I said, "Is it not a little odd that the very villagers who must have been present at the burning of the parsonage should once more fancy they see men in the form of animals?"

Miss Rose came in before the Vicar could answer, and, apparently familiar with the Vicar's ways, she brought me a fresh plate, this time with a potato and a turnip as well as a slice of beef in its own juice.

"You must pay no mind to the Reverend," she told me, before the Vicar himself, who grinned widely. "A legend began this business on the moors, and now children and mischief-makers are carrying it on. Believe me, Miss, they enjoy talking about Gytrashes and the like."

"But your nephew saw it first," I said.

Miss Rose smiled, although I could see that she was not too pleased.

"My nephew is only a lad. He tells what people want him to tell. We've had people lost on the moors before. In summer we are always setting out to find them. Outcomers, for the most part."

"Will Grimlett was no outcomer," put in the Reverend.

"Will Grimlett drank," said Miss Rose succinctly. "My own tapster has tried to persuade Will to give it up on many a night—and taken him home safe to bed as well. No. I shouldn't use Will Grimlett as an example."

She swung the door to behind her.

Reverend MacDonnachie chuckled.

"What a pity! She'll spoil every fine tale we conjure up to frighten the natives."

In spite of his horrid stories, I could not help being amused by him. I said with a smile, "I suspect, sir, that you have a little of your martyred predecessor's love of deviltry."

"Oh, more than a little. I confess it. A delightful rogue he was. I have tried to spread the rumor, to no avail I am afraid, that I am actually a rebirth of my friend, the Devil-Vicar."

"My love," his wife chided softly. "How foolishly modest of you! Everyone knows the Devil-Vicar was the veriest dab of a creature. Dark foreigner from Wales, you know, Miss Wicklow—moody and mysterious like all the Welshmen. Handsome enough in his way perhaps. We were all very struck by him, I do confess. But he was nothing compared to Cadmon. Cadmon would make two of him."

"What a pity!" sighed the Reverend MacDonnachie, taking out a huge handkerchief and blowing his nose like a trumpet. "I've always suspected the Devil-Vicar was burned, not for his religion, but for his success with other men's wives, and one lovely widow in particular. Rather fancied her myself."

"Really, dear," his wife protested feebly.

Miss Rose came in with the MacDonnachie supper and a word for me.

"Marc Branshaw's come, Miss. He would like to see you, when convenient."

I went on eating indifferently, but I noticed after a few movements of my hand that I was unusually nervous. That rogue managed to get the better of me every time we met. I was resolved it should not occur this time.

"How curious!" said Mrs. MacDonnachie. "We were just talking of the Devil-Vicar, and now, out of nowhere, Marc Branshaw's name is mentioned. One's heart goes out to the dear boy. He's not precisely well, my dear. I have often felt that I could be of some service to—"

The Reverend burst into this plaint, "She wants to mother the fellow every time he has a headache. Thinks to take Moyna Branshaw's place."

"Now Cadmon, you know the Keegan lad saw him quite ill once, and I saw him recovering another time."

"That's as may be. But since he refuses to let a doctor touch him, you can be sure it's nothing more than artistic indulgence. We are dealing with a painter from Paris, m'dear."

I did not doubt that. "Was he so fond of his mother then?"

"How could he be? He never saw her after he was six or seven. Reared on the continent. But you see, Moyna was a beauty, and most of the women hereabouts were jealous of her because she attached the Devil-Vicar."

"Cadmon! Your language, my love!"

"How did she die? Mrs. Branshaw, that is," I asked.

"Fell into a pot-hole, just about a year ago. Sort of thing that happens to the merest visitor to these parts."

"My love, you will give Miss Wicklow an entirely false picture of Moyna Branshaw. I assure you, ma'am, the lady in question was a faithful and honorable widow. Her husband died a year before the Reverend Morgan—that is, the Devil-Vicar—came here to St. Anthony's in Maidenmoor. She'd only just returned from taking her son, Marc, to the continent for the cure of some ailment—lungs, I believe. At any rate, she'd intended to sell out her property, the Branshaw mills and Branshaw Hall, and rejoin the boy. But after she met the Devil-Vicar, she never went back to France, even when he was burned to death. So there was her son, reared alone, in foreign parts, and behaving in such a fashion, never returning until she's under the sod, not but what he is a love, in many ways."

"Which brings us back to your beginning, m'dear. You'd like to take Moyna's place. You're long of wind, as usual."

"You aren't interested in Marc because you just don't like the lad," Mrs. MacDonnachie reminded him, in the first tone I had heard her use that held a faint edge to it.

"You are partially mistaken, m'dear. 'The lad,' as you call our very sophisticated artist, interests me profoundly. I am curious concerning . . . oh, many things about him. But to get back to our Devil-Vicar—"

I could not but feel that the two were somehow connected in the Vicar's mind.

"Why? Are they related?"

The Reverend MacDonnachie guffawed into his food, but Mrs. MacDonnachie flushed rosily.

"My dear, what an idea! Marc was born in Maidenmoor and duly enrolled in St. Anthony's Register here as the first-born son of Josiah Branshaw."

"Wouldn't be the first time an old gaffer's been cuckolded by a pretty young wife," put in the vicar, who appeared to know a great deal about such worldly matters.

"How can you say so? The Devil-Vicar arrived in Maidenmoor some seven or eight years after Marc's birth, and as I recall, the Devil-Vicar seemed too young and too serious to have sired anyone eight years before—dear me—what am I saying?"

The Reverend MacDonnachie was overjoyed at having trapped his wife into an indelicacy.

"They mature fast, those Welsh males."

"You say he was serious," I remarked. "I think he must have been nonsensical to play such tricks about devils and Gytrashes and all."

The vicar looked at me with his big head cocked on one side.

"There is nothing more serious, I assure you, than a trick played by a very gloomy and romantic young man whom all the world thinks incapable of displaying a sense of humor. As to his having been rather young eight years before he arrived in Maidenmoor—well, that is not a problem. We have no real notion how old he was when he arrived here, only the hair-brained ideas of a pack of gossiping women half in love with him."

"Yes, but where could they have met before he came to Maidenmoor?" murmured his wife. "I'd swear they met here for the first time. It was I who introduced them in the chancel of St. Anthony's one Sunday night at service. And Marc was seven years old at that time."

"Ah-ha! But what of Moyna's summer outing

eight years before—in fact, the year before the boy's birth? Miss Wicklow, about three years ago, the villagers caught a look at a miniature Moyna's son sent her from Paris, and when they saw that miniature, how the busy tongues of the village ladies wagged. Such delving into old records you have never seen, lassy! It seems that our dear Moyna spent the summer before Marc was born in Wales, of all places, where the Devil-Vicar came from. His name was Ewen Morgan, by the way."

I said, "And he waited seven or eight years after . . . conceiving the boy, before returning to the village of his lady-love? It doesn't sound very passionate to me. And a vicar of the church, at that."

Mrs. MacDonnachie coughed delicately.

"My dear, even a servant of the church may sometimes fall into temptation—especially when he is extraordinarily attractive. I could tell you of the temptations Cadmon has been forced to resist! As for the boy, Marc, let us not forget Josiah Branshaw had accepted the child as his own. I am convinced Marc is Josiah's son, no matter what they say about idyllic summers in Wales and the like."

"And wouldn't you say," put in the vicar, "that seven years later, when Josiah conveniently died, the Reverend Ewen Morgan arrived on the scene more coincidentally?"

"But Cadmon, there is no proof whatever that Moyna had ever met the Devil-Vicar before, in Wales, or anywhere else."

"None except Marc's own extraordinary appearance."

Mrs. MacDonnachie lowered her voice to what was almost a titter. "Dear Miss Wicklow, they say even worse about poor Marc. Some people wonder if he is the Reverend Morgan come back to life, and that would make Marc a being returned from the dead. Absurd, is it not? Only if he really were a devil could he manage such a trick."

I did not know what to say. Her words made me shiver—her words and the memory of Marc Branshaw's chill fingers.

The Vicar waved his fork at me. "When you've the time, you might visit my office in the church. If you've any interest in our Devil-Vicar, there's a striking portrait of him I resurrected from Moyna Branshaw's property. Hangs over my desk . . . as an inspiration to deviltry, you know."

"Sir Gareth Owen had ambitions to marry Moyna last summer before her death," Mrs. MacDonnachie added as I got up to go and meet Marc Branshaw. "But she wouldn't have him. Not Moyna. Loyal to her memories."

"I wonder if she died for that refusal," her husband remarked and was hastily hushed by his wife.

What? I thought. Two jilts from one family? Small wonder Sir Gareth had no use for the Branshaws.

As I went to the taproom I tried to imagine what connection there could be between the young man in his early twenties, as I took Marc Branshaw to be, and a murdered vicar who died in agony almost twenty years ago.

I supposed Mr. Branshaw would meet me in the taproom but there were only Jamie Keegan and a close-packed crowd of men in black, all talking and blowing pipe smoke and drinking at the same time. I wondered if, among them, were the men who had years ago accidentally burned to death the vicar of their church.

Jamie pushed out of the crowd and joined me on the lowest stair, eager to escort me to my room. Somewhere upstairs the night elements were worrying a loose shutter. It made me aware of the great darkness outside.

I said sternly, "You'll not tell me he's the impudence to be in my room!"

"Come, mum," said Jamie, holding out his hand. We went up the stairs together, and the boy left me at the door to my room.

When I walked in, I saw Marc Branshaw blowing on his cold hands, and clapping them together to restore the warmth. He was in the grass-stained garments common to the countryside, his boots badly scuffed, his jacket collar pulled up around his throat as though he were still cold. He seemed very tired, with sallow smudges of weariness under his eyes and below his cheekbones, across the thin lower half of his face. I found my anger evaporating, and could not suppress a kind of protective instinct at sight of him. Surely, he could not have slept for several nights. Under the bright fire of the lamp on the commode, he appeared somewhat older than I had remembered. His slender build, his easy, impudent charm, were deceptive.

Forestalling what I felt sure would be a lie, I said, "I daresay you wouldn't be in the least sorry if your guest were out on the road now, being eaten by Gytrashes."

Outside my graveyard window a shutter banged to and fro. It disturbed me but seemed to have no effect on my uninvited guests.

Marc Branshaw was nonchalant.

"But you aren't out on the road, being eaten by Gytrashes, I am happy to say."

"Your guest, Mr. Branshaw, is a lady named Bedelia Fothergay. And she is, at this moment, on that very road, somewhere between here and Teignford."

"Dear old Bedelia. I had forgotten her entirely.

How tiresome of her to be so prompt!"

He moved away from the bedpost and came toward me. I did not know what he was about to do, and suddenly shifted. I saw that his aim was for the center of my bed, where he settled himself comfortably.

"Now come and sit down beside me."

I backed away.

"Don't be tiresome. If I wanted to make love to you, as I suppose you are thinking, I should do so. But I don't."

I approached the bed in a gingerly way and, seeing that he apparently meant what he said, I sat down tentatively, ready for instant flight. He began to take off his jacket. I started to rise and was stopped, not by the quick motion of his hand, which knocked my hair loose from its pins, but by the sight of the nasty deep scratch across his throat, and another, crisscrossing that, upward toward his chin. Both had bled but the blood was now dried, and he must have forgotten them. He had certainly been in some wild country today. I began to perceive how rough the seach for Abbie Hinchley was.

"Jamie says Gareth Owen has gone to fetch the delectable Bedelia. How did you happen to meet Owen?"

I explained and he grinned.

"What a happy couple! Gareth and Bedelia! How divinely suited by providence!" He added after a moment, with an insistence that puzzled me, "You saw Owen first on Teignford Brow; did you not? Do you recall the exact time?"

"Now how should I do that? But never mind. Tell me what you want with me," I demanded, while my mouth was full of hairpins and I was torn between this, the banging shutter, and the necessity to keep one eye on my companion.

"I want you to come to my house, properly chaperoned by Gareth's sister, Catherine, and take down what she tells you. In short, to collaborate in the revision of a manuscript she has written."

So it was his jilted betrothed who wrote *The Corpses on the Moor!* No wonder she had chosen Marc for her villain. I did not begin to understand it, for if she had chosen him for her villain, why were they now friends again?

"Will you give me back my manuscript about Red Indians of North America?"

"Solemn promise," he said, looking anything but solemn.

"And Mrs. Fothergay?"

"Ah, the ubiquitous Fothergay. That presents a problem. Well, we must see that Owen makes himself useful. Catherine shall tell him the lady is fabulously wealthy. Her late lamented husband was an India Nabob."

"Yes, but—there must be many ladies in London, or in York or Leeds, who might do what you require of me."

I was hardly thinking of what I said; for my mind was upon those long, ugly scratches on his face and neck. Surely they were painful. I longed to apply an excellent salve which had been my mother's recipe, and was most efficacious in such matters.

He frowned when he saw the direction of my glance and changed the subject in the rudest way. "There's no use in looking like that. I'm not going to, you know. Haven't time."

I committed the shocking blunder of understanding him. "I never asked you to, and wouldn't permit you to touch me if you did!"

That put him in a good humor again, and he stretched and yawned. I thought for one horrifying moment, during which my heart beat very rapidly, that he would stretch out on the bed behind me, as comfortable as you please. He did not, however.

"Leave your hair alone, you foolish girl. Wear it long while you are here in the village." It was puzzling, the inordinate interest he took in my hair.

He got into his jacket as he talked, but managed to reach over and knock my netted hair down again. I could have slapped him. "Wear it down, I said!" This time he saw that I had my hands full and basely took advantage of me. He leaned over me, saying, "Well . . . if you insist!" though I hadn't uttered a word.

I was used to being asked for a kiss, followed by a rather inept aim at my lips. There was nothing inept about Marc Branshaw, who had all too evidently mapped out his destination while we talked. I put up a pushing resistance but the bastions soon crumbled. He wasn't nearly so tired as I had thought him. I felt excited, light in the pit of my stomach. I remember the look in his eyes and then the dark lashes very close to me, and me closing my own eyes and thinking, "How odd! I feel all prickles."

I wondered why he did not kiss me. Then I heard his laugh and felt myself pushed away like an importunate child. I opened my eyes, outraged. He reminded me, "You said you wouldn't, but I think you would."

The man was a cad. No two ways about it. I did what I should have done much earlier. I slapped his detestable face.

I am happy to say that he winced, but in spite of the hard little glitter that had come into his eyes, he smiled and got up as if nothing had happened.

"As I was saying, Catherine Owen will come for you tomorrow. Now, be a good girl and go off to bed before you go about getting into more trouble. Next time you may find yourself teasing the Gytrash and not a gentleman."

The "gentleman" in question crossed the room with his light, almost noiseless step, and went out the door to the accompaniment of the banging shutter across the room. He left only just in time. I was feeling around for something to throw at him. He had done it again, got the better of me.

Of course, I would not visit him tomorrow, or any other day. His conduct had made that quite out of the question.

I was, however, curious to meet Catherine Owen. It appeared now that in writing *The Corpses on the Moor* it was she who had written a guidebook for a bloody crime, but the association of ideas was ridiculous, even as I considered it. The animal that killed Will Grimlett certainly could not read.

I wondered about Catherine Owen. How could she be so complacent about her jilting lover? I should have died of shame and humiliation, if not sheer rage. Perhaps she considered it revenge enough when she made Marc the villain of her manuscript. But knowing the hold the scoundrel could take on one's emotions, I thought Catherine Owen must have extraordinary self-control, for I should have been undone by his behavior.

Eventually, I located all my hairpins and having decided after due thought that my hair did look better down, I rolled it as best I could, and went over to fasten the shutter. This entailed looking out over the graveyard, and I was sure, after the Reverend MacDonnachie's tale at supper, I should see at once the corner where the martyred Devil-Vicar's bones lay buried—if, of course, he wasn't out prowling the countryside in the shape of a Gytrash.

What did a Gytrash look like? In spite of Miss Owen's graphic description in her novel, I still couldn't consider the notion without laughing. Preposterous, the superstitions of these northern people.

The window opened stiffly, thanks to the rain which had warped the casement. I reached around the corner of the window to take hold of the shutter and after I had felt the latch, I realized that it had not been broken, but simply locked improperly, and come unfastened under the pressure of the weather. It was impossible for me to reach the entire shutter, so I took hold of the bottom of it and began to pull it toward me.

In spite of my resolutions, my eyes wandered out over the patch of graveyard just to the left of my window, which marked the burning of the old parsonage, and the bones of the unfortunate young vicar. How cold and dreary it looked, with the white mist rising from the sodden ground! Not at all the sort of bed for the romantic trickster and charmer that I pictured the Devil-Vicar to be. I forced myself to look away from that ground and carelessly glanced beyond at the gray tombstones crowding the yard like witches huddled in the misty night.

Come, Anne, I told myself; *you will dream of this for sure.*

I pulled the shutter toward me, reaching far out to do so. The act was difficult and forced me to look downward at the vines under my window, and the muddy ground below that. I was chilled and shocked to see a woman huddling on her knees there against the wall of the inn, a little to this side of the bare place which marked all that remained of the Devil-Vicar, and the parsonage. The woman was huddling just as my witch-tombstones had seemed to huddle a few seconds before. Her youthful face was staring up at the heavens, her eyes wide open, though the mist swirled around her. She must have been sunk several inches in mud, and wretchedly uncomfortable.

I called to her, "What is it? What are you doing there?"

She continued to stare at the sky in that motionless way until a sudden gust of wind flung me against the side of the window and wrested the shutter out of my hand so that it started banging again. The same gust of wind struck the woman below my window and, to my horror, she toppled stiffly over on her back, still staring up at the heavens, ghastly white and unmoving.

She lay now upon what I took to be the Devil-Vicar's unmarked grave.

I knew then what my senses would not credit before. Either she had been dragged there, or she had crawled to that place, kneeling in that horrid suppliant position for death to encircle her.

Did *he* know, there in the unhallowed ground beneath her? Did the Devil-Vicar know that she lay there, like a human sacrifice to his corrupt and tragic spirit?

My throat closed and what I had meant for a scream came out a mere whisper of itself. But at last I got the sound out, and kept on screaming until the room was full of people. Live people.

VI

BEDELIA FOTHERGAY could not have timed her arrival more opportunely to suit her tastes. For at least an hour that night I kept thinking she would run out of breath, which is clear proof that I was not acquainted with her enormous reserves. Despite the horrifying discovery of Abbie Hinchley's body on the barren ground traditionally assigned to the Devil-Vicar, Mrs. Fothergay surprised me by showing no fear, but only a highly developed sense of her own dramatic role in the tragedy.

"To think, my dear Anne, only to think that poor creature should have been discovered precisely as Sir Gareth and I arrived! And attacked by the same creature that killed the sheepman! Why, had we arrived an hour earlier, I myself might have been the victim."

"I doubt that," I put in drily, when I could get in a word. "You are not sufficiently acquainted with the Gytrash. I understand it was he—or it—who killed Miss Hinchley."

"Dear me, dear me! Nor do I wish a closer acquaintance. Truly now, haven't you noticed that women of that sort usually have some prior . . . er . . . dealings with their murderers?"

"Murderers? How can you call an animal a murderer?"

Mrs. Fothergay put one pink finger to her lips and looked coy.

"Never you mind. But someone—some charming person who shall be nameless—told me, on the way to Maidenmoor, that he suspects a human intelligence behind the death of that dreary little sheep farmer and the disappearance of Miss Hinchley."

"And did this nameless person say whom he suspected of going about in a lion's skin, murdering sheep farmers and the like?" I wondered what would have been her reaction if Sir Gareth, in his natural antipathy to Marc Branshaw, had named Mrs. Fothergay's beloved artist as the Gytrash.

"No, but it should be obvious. The Hinchley creature was murdered by some man with whom she had played the jilt."

"And the sheep farmer?"

"Oh, well," she shrugged, "I can't be expected to furnish the answers to all the questions that disturb this heathen place." She had begun to divest herself of numerous and expensive cloaks, pelisses, jackets, and I was hoping she would proceed to her traveling gown and so to bed, but she stopped at this crucial point and sat down on my own bed instead of retiring to her room. Indeed, my bed had become the rendezvous for half of Yorkshire tonight.

"Fate, my dear Anne, that's what it was! Fate! I do have that effect upon events. Some sort of cataclysmic aura. I no sooner arrive at my destination than strange things occur. I cannot begin to explain it."

She did, however, at length, while I alternately huddled in a corner of my bed with my eyes closed, trying not to think of what was occurring beneath my window, and then sat up and rubbed my hands and feet, wondering if it were my imagination or if there actually was a thin coat of ice congealing my room. There was no carpet on the floor; probably these sturdy north people found it superfluous, a mark of the effete Londoner. But for me the damp cold seemed to ooze out of the floorboards when I set my stockinged feet down, and when my elbow accidentally struck the whitewashed wall, the chill of it froze me to the marrow. Perhaps it was because only that wall separated me from the witch-tombstones out there, and from that other place, untended, unhallowed, where the Devil-Vicar slept.

At one moment during Mrs. Fothergay's endless

discourse, I wondered what the Reverend Ewen Morgan had been like and, in spite of the denials of both the Reverend MacDonachie and his wife, I subscribed to the theory that he was humorous, quick and satiric, with a highly developed sense of the ridiculous. He must have been so, to have told such tales about devils and Gytrashes. The truth is, his tragic history and his doomed romance captured my fancy, and I gave him rather more of my thoughts than one customarily devotes to an uncharacteristically bad servant of the church who has been under the sod these fifteen or twenty years.

If he was not a humorist and actually believed in the horrid things he preached, then the mere thought of him lying out there under the muddy ground, no doubt directing the acts of this killer-animal who roamed at large, was too dreadful to contemplate; for in that case, he must have directed his Gytrash (or was he himself the Gytrash?) to lead poor Abbie Hinchley to his grave for her own demise. We torture ourselves with such fearful imaginings by night, where the same impetus by day would merely make us smile at the preposterous thought. But it was now close on midnight and I was no more immune than the next person to the influence of that witching hour.

I shuddered and tried to concentrate on Mrs. Fothergay's ramblings.

"Well, I know you are frightened here alone, Anne," she said at last, yawning delicately, "but I really do need my sleep. I'm afraid I must leave you. I am a person who manages with very little rest, in spite of a fragile constitution. But . . . there comes a time! Good heavens above! What is that?"

"That" was a stiff knock on the door. A moment later I heard Miss Rose's quiet, confident voice.

"I thought some hot tea might not be amiss, ma'am, seeing that the whole village is congregating beneath your window."

I welcomed her gratefully.

"Yes. Do come in. Thank you so very much."

How good it looked, the steaming teapot, and the sturdy, shining blue cup and saucer! There were also two thin, delicate slices of buttered bread. As for Miss Rose herself, one might have thought she discovered dead bodies beside her inn almost any day, for she was so unruffled as to give the whole room a glow of warmth and peace.

Mrs. Fothergay made some ado over the tray, but Miss Rose carefully set it near me and told my companion, "You will find a tray in your room, ma'am."

Mrs. Fothergay looked flustered, appeared as though she might take this as an insult, but then decided aloud:

"Of course. You must have known I crave solitude after this ghastly experience. How kind of you, I'm sure! For you must know, I only escaped your savage beast by the matter of minutes."

Miss Rose looked at us with justifiable surprise and I explained. She did not look amused, but her eyes might be said to have smiled. Mrs. Fothergay bade me good night, with one last apology for leaving me, which she would never have done except for the delicacy of her constitution. Miss Rose was about to follow when I asked her to stay.

"I thought perhaps you were tired, ma'am."

"Nervous, yes. But I doubt if I could sleep yet. I keep thinking of what they are doing out there."

"Oh, that." Miss Rose waved her hand. "They'll be removing the girl presently. Most of them are out there now smoking and recounting, each of them, the exact location at which they stood in the village when the word of the girl's discovery reached them."

"Why," I asked her suddenly, "hasn't the community ever built another parsonage for the Vicar?"

"We are not a rich village, ma'am," she reminded me.

"Yes, but you have a very old church which does you credit, and it would seem to me that—"

"It is, perhaps, a superstition," she explained after a little pause. "Since there has never been enough money, and since the Vicar seems quite happy in his own apartments here at the inn, the years have gone by with no action in regard to a new parsonage. But I think, also, the village feels its guilt in the matter of the fire, and in some way this is a punishment it has brought down upon itself." Then she smiled. "However, when all is said, money is probably at the root of it. It usually is."

I listened, hearing telltale sounds outside the window.

"I should have thought they would be pursuing the creature instead of standing out there gossiping."

She looked at me rather oddly, I thought.

"The Gytrash, or whatever it is," I explained.

"They are doing that too. But, miss, I did not think you believed such a witches' tale. Of course the thing was done by a human being. Perhaps the girl was savaged by a dog, as Grimlett was. But the deaths were certainly inspired by human agency. You must have guessed that."

I sat with my mouth open, staring at her.

"Who?"

She raised her eyebrows, and gave no other reply.

"I can see why a man might kill Abbie Hinchley," I went on. "For . . . well . . . for the usual reasons. But what have they to do with the sheep farmer?"

She watched me pour the tea and drink it, scalding

hot as it was. The tea brewed here in the north was much stronger than the London tea I was used to, and stimulated me almost like strong spirits. At the moment I welcomed its effect.

We both heard the Vicar's booming voice below my window.

"No question but that she was dead some hours before we saw her. Wouldn't ye say now, Billy-boy?"

"Ay, sor. Stone dead. Likely was dragged here. They's marks in the wet, mostly smeared."

One of the men gave a yelp that unnerved Miss Rose and me. She went to the window and thrust it open. Neither of us had closed the shutter yet. I did not want to linger there long enough to do so. She called down to the men:

"What is it? Have you found something?"

The young curate, Frederick Niles, answered her in his calm way.

"We were discussing the curious nature of the wounds. The hands and limbs had been badly savaged, as though she were defending herself against a creature that clawed at her."

"Mebe so," said another voice, "but no dog done all o' this. Crushin' blow to the head here."

"Big dog perhaps," went on the Reverend Niles. "Tooth-marks here. But it may have been a large cat."

"Ay, but what a the nasty bit a work on the back o' the skull? What o' that nasty work, I'm askin'?"

There was muttering among the men and stout Vicar MacDonnachie called up to Miss Rose:

"It's the same as Will Grimlett. Remember, Miss Rose? Lost on the moors, you said. What do you think now?"

"Ay, mon," said another voice, "but what o' the bit a business on the back o' the head-like?"

Miss Rose closed the shutters and the window. She turned back to me.

"You mentioned Abbie's sex, Miss Wicklow. But it had nothing to do with these crimes. They'd do better to concentrate on that bruise or whatever it is that they've found on the back of her head. In my opinion, these crimes are all part of something that happened here years ago. You recall the story the Reverend MacDonnachie told you at supper?"

"Yes, yes. The Devil-Vicar's love affair with Mr. Branshaw's young widowed mother, and all the suspicion that came of that. But Abbie Hinchley is too young to have been involved; isn't she?"

"Abbie used to hint that, as a child, she peeped in the parsonage window and saw the person who struck down Ewen Morgan. The story made her important. But she would tell none of us who the murderer was. It was Abbie's secret, and considering the blood guilt of the village, no one wanted to press her for the name. I say 'murder' since it was this attack Abbie witnessed which prevented the Reverend Morgan from escaping when Will Grimlett and the others set fire to the parsonage."

"Will Grimlett set fire—"

"And Will Grimlett had been killed by the Gytrash."

There was a little silence in the room. Outside, the voices of the men grew fainter. I hoped they were through with their conjectures and going about their business.

I said finally, "Why should the murderer wait so many years to kill Abbie? And who is the murderer?"

"I have no notion, in either case."

"Could it be—" I hesitated, feeling foolish, but I had to have her denial in good, plain terms. "Could it be that the Devil-Vicar himself has somehow succeeded in avenging himself? Perhaps he felt that Abbie was guilty too and must die."

"And the Devil-Vicar's theories were true then? He could return after death? In short, he could turn himself into a Gytrash because—he *was* the Devil? Is that what you mean?"

How ridiculous it sounded, brought out into the light by her matter-of-fact voice! I blushed for my fears. I had never felt more nonsensical.

"No. Of course not. I don't know what I meant, really."

"Because, Miss Wicklow, that is what the village ponders. In my opinion, it is what the murderer wants the village to think. And so long as they believe that, they are not going to find the real demon. I'll say only one thing for our people: at least they do not believe the obvious, the efforts to make Marc Branshaw look suspicious."

I drank the rest of my tea in silence and chewed the thin, delicious slice of bread. One moment I was reassured, the next I was uneasy again. I wished she had not said that. I almost preferred to believe in the Gytrash.

She saw my indecision and left me shortly after.

I did not sleep well that night, which is understandable, but I managed to dream inordinately, and always of the Devil-Vicar. There was no sense to my dreams—no beginning, no end. But I was aware that I dreamed. It was curious, for I had only the vaguest idea of what the Devil-Vicar looked like, and yet I was sure it was he whose pale and shadowed face haunted me. I promised myself that as soon as the opportunity afforded, I should go to look at that portrait of Ewen Morgan in St. Anthony's church across the graveyard.

I detest being watched by some people as I sleep, and it was in no very pleasant mood that I awoke the following morning, to find Bedelia Fothergay's mottled, pink-powder face gazing down at me while I lay in bed.

"What the devil?" I cried and sat straight up in bed, furious.

Mrs. Fothergay was a good deal astonished, not so much at my conduct as at my use of that naughty word.

"Up-up-up, my dear. Time for tea. Your tray was left before your door, whole ages ago. I took the liberty of bringing it in. Then, breakfast and away we go."

"Away we go where?" I asked, not thinking very clearly. When I awaken suddenly everything has cobwebs on it, and for the first hour or two I do nothing but ask people to repeat things.

"To visit that handsome artist who took such a fancy to me in London, my dear Anne. Why else are we in Yorkshire, after all is said? He insisted on doing me in oils."

"I'm not going," I said firmly, drawing my cold feet up in the blanket almost under my chin.

"Now, don't be tiresome. Of course, you are. That is what you are being paid for. Besides, you cannot disappoint Sir Gareth and his charming sister. The poor thing. And so in love. So—hopelessly in love." From her tone, I imagined that she regarded herself as the chief obstacle to "poor" Miss Catherine Owen's love for Marc. With less self-confidence, *much* less since my scuffle with the artist on the bed the previous night, I also felt that Miss Owen held very little place in his mercurial affections. However, I was not ready to sympathize with her just yet. She may have been deeply in love with Marc, but even if she were as charming as Mrs. Fothergay said, and as extremely forgiving as Marc implied by his present relationship with her, this bird of so much perfection was not altogether without malice. I had read *The Corpses on the Moor* and her portrait of her villain, while charming and likeable, turned pretty savage before the end.

I knew all along that I would have to see her. My curiosity was too strong for me.

In the little back dining parlor I met Frederick Niles, who was finishing breakfast as I entered. He arose and bowed to me politely and looked as though he might be conversable if given a chance.

I asked if I might join him and upon being accepted with flattering promptness, I inquired if any new discoveries had been made in connection with the recent deaths.

"Nothing of consequence, ma'am. We are in hourly hopes of tracking the beast, however."

"You think it was a beast, and not a man?"

He looked at me, his blue eyes for the first time a little disconcerting in their direct gaze.

"Why do you say that, Miss Wicklow? You cannot think a man made those horrible wounds."

"What if a man used the beast to—to finish the task?"

He gave my idea an unwilling smile.

"Such theories require a savage imagination, and, I am afraid, not a very Christian view of mankind."

"Still, it would not be the first crime committed in this village. If these people suspect their murdered Devil-Vicar has come back for revenge, why don't they admit it?"

He said stiffly, "It is true these people murdered a man once, inadvertently. They feel that they owe it to themselves, if not to their fellow men, to go warily this time. If you mean to suggest some blood tie between the dead vicar and Marc Branshaw, I must tell you, most of the villagers like young Branshaw. He has a way with him, as you may have noticed." He added, seeing my surprised look, "You must not believe the misguided humor of—persons in high places."

"Like your own vicar, sir?" I asked maliciously.

He looked uncomfortable, but whether from indignation or embarrassment, I could not tell.

"The Reverend MacDonnachie had the advantage of a personal acquaintance with the late so-called Devil-Vicar. I don't doubt that, with his peculiar sense of fun, he amused himself in teasing you about the Reverend Morgan's conduct. But I am sure the Reverend MacDonnachie does not condone it. Just prior to the Devil-Vicar's death, there was a movement afoot to remove him." He finished his ham and eggs and arose from the table, saying with a gentler look, "The fact that Ewen Morgan boasted he could change into a Gytrash or a devil, has nothing to do with young Marc Branshaw. It would mean another disaster here if such a line of thinking were pursued, and whatever may be the policy of the Reverend MacDonnachie, I assure you that I for one would make a strong protest if such a threat were made."

I respected him for this defense of Marc.

"Then you like Mr. Branshaw? He is an odd man, but very clever and talented, I believe."

"I dislike him profoundly," said the young curate, not mincing words. "I am not a humorous man, and can see nothing admirable about a propensity for paganism. He is supercilious, irreligious, and amoral. I have not seen him at one service in St. Anthony's since his return last year."

I was somewhat crushed by this severe observation

and could find no defense, but he finished less sharply: "Nonetheless, I doubt if he is a rebirth of the Devil-Vicar, as some persons hint. And I shall continue to say so, in spite of all humorous efforts to the contrary."

The Reverend Niles was fairminded, I had to admit, after he was gone. I wondered, however, if his dislike of Marc was based solely on moral grounds.

I had barely finished breakfast, eaten rapidly because my mind was on so many things, when Jamie Keegan came clomping in to announce:

"Miss Catherine and that old Sir Gareth's out with Miss Catherine's horse and gig. They'd be obliged was you to join them, love."

Mrs. Fothergay, who was standing over my table by this time, urging me to hurry, assumed at once that Jamie's term of endearment was addressed to her, and replied as she patted his head, "Dear boy! He's a love, too. Yes, he is, calling his dear Bedelia a love! Children are always so fond of me."

Under her ample arm Jamie made a face at me and grinned. I could not but grin back. I appreciated his feelings. As we passed Jamie on our way down the passage to the taproom and the street, however, the boy clasped my hand and squeezed in beside me.

"Watch yourself, will ye now?" His seriousness was not like him and I stared at him, upon realizing the change in his voice. Even his little-boy face with its endearing nose was troubled.

"Why must I watch myself?"

He said nothing, just looked at me. I did not like it, not half. Jamie was too wise, too intelligent, for all his talk of Gytrashes and other demons. He meant something or someone in particular by his warning, and I couldn't fathom exactly what it was.

Certainly not too much damage could be done to

me or anyone else, when five persons were included in today's outing. I did not know what Marc Branshaw would do when Bedelia Fothergay arrived on the scene, but I thought it might be well worth the expedition just to see how he contrived to divide his charm among three women of assorted sizes, ages and temperaments.

Harnessed to a black gig, and nervously pawing the wet cobblestones in front of the inn, was a small, long-haired horse little larger than a pony, yet with those hard prominent bones that made the other citizens of Yorkshire so durable and formidable. He tossed his head at sight of me, or perhaps it was at sight of Mrs. Fothergay, elaborately bedecked in her frills, and crowning all by a huge hat like a catherine-wheel, tied with a large, gauzy bow under her chins. Small wonder the horse was upset.

I was glad, for the sake of the hat, if nothing else, that the weather had cleared to a certain extent. When I say cleared, I mean that the mizzly climate of last night was now more or less obscured by a thick gray overcast that shrouded the houses on the steep main street of the village, but only made the distant prospect the more green and desolate by contrast.

Outside the confines of the village I could see no sign of human habitation. The villagers under direction of the vicar and the curate Niles, looking for the killer, whether man or beast, of Abbie Hinchley, had been absorbed on the moors as if swallowed in a thick green quicksand.

It was with relief that I turned to the very human face of Miss Catherine Owen, who sat in the gig. Her brother, Sir Gareth, was waiting to greet us, looking not quite so bored as yesterday. Behind those pale blue eyes he appeared alert. I had been expecting his sister to be big-boned, husky, ruddy haired as he, with the look of arrogance that Sir Gareth never troubled to hide. Catherine Owen was unlike her brother in almost every detail. Her hair was dark, thick, worn in a style that was some fifteen or twenty years out of the present mode—puffed too much on the sides, and with a knot in the back, so that it accentuated the broadness of her cheeks. Her eyes were hazel, large and honest. I suspected they could light up with laughter, given the right impetus, but that laughter would not be pointed and cruel. She was solidly built, with a becomingly small waist, but I felt that her dull, dark paisley-print gown and short pelisse might have been more wisely chosen. In short, she endeared herself to women by being friendly, modest, a trifle dowdy, and with an inclination to submissiveness. Her voice when she spoke was young, sweet and girlish, and it suited the sweet, broad-cheeked, childish look of her face, although she must have been in her late twenties, if not older. It was not that, like Mrs. Fothergay, she strove for a semblance of youth, but rather, I thought, that her face had never quite caught up with her intellect.

"How very nice to meet you, Miss Wicklow!" She held out one hand in a neatly darned black mitt. Her clasp was strong and almost as firm as a man's. I was surprised but could not help liking her.

"I do trust you will forgive me. I am afraid there's only room for one other in the gig. If you don't mind walking with my brother as escort—"

"My pleasure, I'm sure," put in her brother gallantly.

Miss Catherine glanced downward at the thick folds of the hem of her gown. She brushed aside the folds. I saw nothing unusual in her two neat, motion-

I asked, discourteously avoiding pleasant topics.

He flushed a little at my changing the subject and replied with a sincerity that almost made me smile, "Believe me, ma'am, Miss Hinchley's mysterious accident, if accident it was, has us all baffled. It is much out of the common way, believe me."

What a pedantic young man! But oddly touching in his sincerity.

Presently Miss Rose Keegan came in with my second course, which proved to be a slice of well-turned roast of beef, and as she set my tray down she indicated the two persons entering the little dining parlor. At the sight of them, for some odd reason, the young curate gulped down the last of his tea, bowed briefly to the newcomers and departed in haste. Rose Keegan smiled at his swift exit and nodded to me significantly, so that I could only conclude the young curate was not on the best of terms with the man and woman who entered now.

"The Reverend MacDonnachie and Mrs. Emily," said Rose Keegan. "We have let the front parlor rooms to the vicar since there is no parsonage, and the Reverend's grown used to those rooms. He has had them now for well on sixteen years."

I wondered what circumstance it was that left the local vicar without a vicarage, but soon I felt my curiosity on that matter as well as the obvious coolness between him and his young curate would be satisfied in short order, for the Reverend MacDonnachie proved to be a huge, red-bearded, talkative man who insisted that, "if the lady would do him and his good wife the honor" he would share my table.

"Please, by all means," I said, and began to push the dishes and teapot about to get them out of the Reverend's great hands. When he moved things you could almost hear them crunch under his prodigious paws. His wife was the very opposite—a frail, wistful, breeze-blown creature with a faraway look, a sweet, absent smile, and extraordinarily pink hair whose texture, if not its color, reminded me of cat fur.

She looked toward the door. "Poor young man," she murmured, meaning the curate, Frederick Niles. "Always a little in awe of my dear husband. They are so very different."

I believed that. Nothing could be more ludicrous than the contrast between the esthetic-looking young Reverend Niles and his superior, the stout vicar, who was obviously a good trencherman.

Mrs. MacDonnachie sighed contentedly and sat down beside me. I poured her tea and waited with many questions I was anxious to ask. The Reverend MacDonnachie plunged into everything on the table, and I was almost afraid his questing fork would steal the very slice of beef off my plate. In fact, the fork did hover over my plate for an instant before he thought himself of manners.

"Ah, there, Miss Rose. Food for the gods, I see. Be quick! Be quick! Or I shall eat this pretty thing you have served me."

Mrs. Emily leaned over me, saying in her faraway voice, "My dear, he means you."

I thanked her with a smile and abruptly went to another topic. He was rather overwhelming, like a gigantic cliff overhanging one.

"I am given to understand that we are fellow boarders here at the inn, sir."

"Yes, yes. Fortunate, eh? Eh? By George, that beef does look good. What say I slice off just a wee . . . wee . . . morsel. . . . Ah! Um! Good! By thunder, that's good!" I looked down ruefully at my denuded plate. What a pity! And it had looked delicious, too, swimming in its own juice. Mrs. MacDonnachie patted my hand.

"Never mind, dear. Think how good it is for the figure. And poor Cadmon, he does require more food than the ordinary man." She smiled at him fondly. "Of course, that's because he is not an ordinary man. Dear me, no. Not like that tiresome young Reverend Niles, always preaching continence and abstinence as though we were in eternal Lent." I suspected she was quoting from her husband. She looked like one of those dreary women whose opinions shifted like weathercocks, to suit whatever man was present.

Getting back to the non-existent vicarage, which these Yorkshire people persisted in referring to as a parsonage, I said, "But I don't understand. Surely, with such an imposing church, you have a vicarage."

The red-bearded gentleman threw back his great head and roared with laughter. "Had a parsonage once, you know. Yes. But they burnt it down. Twenty years ago, must have been. . . ."

"Nearer fifteen, love," put in Mrs. MacDonnachie faintly, but he ignored this interpolation.

"Since then, the vicars have lived wherever the townspeople could find room for them."

"Yes, but how did it happen that the original parsonage burned?"

"Had a wee dispute concerning Holy Writ. Occupant of the parsonage disagreed with the congregation. Taught them all that the Devil could appear among them as a dog or a cat or in any form. Preferably, as himself. Had them so terrified they wouldn't venture out of doors after dark. Some of the congregation disapproved. Riots. Clubs. Blood. . . ."

"Please, dear, not at the table," murmured his wife.

"Ah, just so. Now you put me in mind of it, delicious juice to this meat."

Let us not get off the subject again, I thought, and ventured, "In short, the vicar preached that the Devil could appear in the form of a . . . Gytrash."

"Precisely." He beamed at me approvingly, while mopping up the dribble of sauce on his healthy red lips. "All nonsense, of course. I do believe the fellow was mad. I was one of his curates in my beardless days, you know. At any rate, he planted the idea. Gradually, it occurred to his congregation that if he knew so much about devils, and about men who could take the form of an animal, he must be the Devil himself. It was just after a time of great strife, you understand. The Dissenters had crept in everywhere. Every second preacher was a Methodist. Church of England fighting for its very existence in these parts. So—when they thought our handsome Devil-Vicar was elsewhere, some of the good folk burnt the parsonage—like the purging of an animal's lair, you understand. Then they tore down the foundations, stone from stone. After that, it was quite some time before anyone dared mention a Gytrash again. Matter of fact, even the Devil is not as welcome in church as he once was."

"And the Vicar—and his family?"

"Oh, them. Emily, would you call his . . . er . . . connections . . . a family?"

Thus questioned pointblank, the lady looked up in panic, her watery eyes wavering helplessly from object to object in the little dining parlor.

"I—I believe not, love. Such a painful subject. They found what was left of the . . . the body of the Reverend Morgan, you remember."

less feet, carefully shod in low kid boots, until she added, "I do not walk. An accident on the moor last year. Mrs. Fothergay, would you oblige me by riding with me?"

Mrs. Fothergay was whispering to me behind her hand, "No wonder he jilted her. Good heavens! What a dowd!" but I turned my head away, pretending not to hear her. Sir Gareth had bowed first over Mrs. Fothergay's hand and then mine, languidly acknowledging my curtsey, but now he said with firmness:

"I don't like it. Damned if I do, Catherine. Why the deuce should that little whelp have any business with you? After what you've been through. However—"

Mrs. Fothergay nudged me. Annoyed, I stepped away from her and crossed the cobblestones to the other side of the gig while Sir Gareth lifted her into it, amid her flutters and little cries of panic. She was soon safe beside Catherine Owen, who looked across her imposing form and gave me a warm smile before taking up the reins in her capable-looking hands.

"Did you read my manuscript, Miss Wicklow?"

I was thinking that it was a curious kind of manuscript for a woman of Catherine Owen's temperament to write. I should have thought a high-spirited person with a vivid imagination had written all that nonsense, and here was this calm, quiet, strong-handed young woman, crippled yet capable, acknowledging she was the author.

"A little, here and there," I replied. "I re-copied certain pages. I'm afraid I don't have time to read entire manuscripts," I explained as Sir Gareth began to walk beside me. I found it difficult to keep to his great stride. When I lagged a moment, his heavy arm came under mine to lift me along, and it seemed to me that his fingers pried more than necessary along the underside of my arm as he did so.

"Yes," said Miss Owen. "I noticed you had not rewritten the last sixty pages. But perhaps you did not have time to read them. It must be tedious, copying badly written manuscripts."

I shrugged and she sat back comfortably. I saw now that she was relaxed and realized what I had thought to be a firm control of the reins a few minutes ago was actually a severe spasm of the nerves. One would never have guessed that her kind, phlegmatic constitution was so susceptible.

Sir Gareth said to me, "I hope you do not expect to do much business with Branshaw, Miss Wicklow. He is extremely unreliable and I shouldn't be surprised to find that he has forgotten you entirely. . . . You must then let me show you around our countryside. I'll show you a time you won't forget, will she, Catherine?"

I did not doubt it for a minute. Already he had made an impression upon me, particularly upon my arm and now and then my waist when he conceived the road too difficult for me.

But I said innocently, "He would indeed be forgetful then. He was very set upon our coming when he spoke to me last night."

I saw something shadowy out of the corner of my eye and knew that either Catherine Owen or Mrs. Fothergay had looked at me quickly, but I could not tell which.

"Oh, well then, if you had had a *tête-à-tête* with Branshaw already—" He lowered his voice romantically. "I shall see that there are no more between you. I'm your man for that, Miss Anne. You want a man for good company, not a frippery fellow who's lived among the French all his life."

I sensed that the two women in the gig were waiting for my indignant denial of the *"tête-à-tête"* so I said nothing, only raised my skirts to keep from dragging them in the dirt of the lane, for we were now on top of Maidenmoor Rise and had lost the security of the cobblestones.

Mrs. Fothergay twitched around on her seat, muttering, and then squealed.

"Ah! What am I sitting on? Good heavens! I have crushed the box. What can it be?"

By this time the sheets of Catherine's manuscript were scattered over the seat and her dress, and several fluttered across my vision, into the blackened heather at one side of the lane. I ran to pick them up, feeling the thick carpet of wild vegetation underfoot, and with Sir Gareth's help we finally located all the scattered pages.

"Gad! What drivel, Catherine!" Sir Gareth bellowed, studying the loose sheets as we approached the two in the gig. "How's this, ladies, to frighten you into a fit of the fidgets?" He began to read from the top pages in his hand, in the manner most calculated to drive the author out of her mind:

" 'She shrieked at him in a fury, and indeed she was a fury! Well-made and tiny-waisted. Seeming human, but a cruel enchantress. Her Irish eyes snapping. . . . And then he saw her hands, held to him like claws, and she made as though to tear at his face. . . . She was no longer his little Monanne, his precious Irish enchantress, but a demon. Possessed—' " Here Sir Gareth gave out in the trumpetry of a bad actor: " 'He had known all along, and yet, fool that he was, he loved her. She it was; who had worn the habit of the Gytrash. No! Said he so? She *was* the Gytrash!' " Sir Gareth shook his head. "Oh, come now, Cathie, surely this will never reach the printed page."

"Well!" said Mrs. Fothergay. "I never! It's enough to give one the shivers. And out in this lonely country, too."

Miss Catherine smiled at her criticism as she had smiled at her brother's.

"What do you think of it, Miss Wicklow? Do you agree that it is pretty poor stuff? Or perhaps—?" she ventured with a waver of hope in her voice.

I started to say something and realized that my hand was at my throat. I felt dry as bone; for this page had never been in the manuscript that I read, and the description of the Gytrash, allowing for a bit of self-flattery, might have been myself. It is true that my name had not been used, but "Monanne" was near enough to "Anne" to be annoying if not downright alarming.

Where could she have gotten my description but from Marc Branshaw? It was like what I had suspected of him, too—cruel and wicked and perverse. He probably thought it a great jest. I had an appalling instant when I almost cried with the hurt of it, but then I looked up and, hating her and the rest of them, said calmly, "It is quite in keeping with the popular mode."

Mrs. Fothergay took the conversation from me at once.

"In keeping with this horrid countryside. Yes, indeed. If it were not for the keen disappointment to that dear boy, I should turn around instantly and take myself out of this dreadful place. One never knows when a blow will come, to wipe one out precisely like that unfortunate girl last night."

Catherine said, "Oh, no, ma'am. I hope you will not let my nonsense disturb you. It was only made up out of my head, you know."

"From living in this wilderness. I can well believe it."

With that lovely, childish voice, Catherine remarked to me, "I know you will understand, Miss Wicklow. From what Marc tells me, you appreciate the things I appreciate. You can see the beauty in this landscape. Can you not?"

I smiled at her.

"I should think we might share many of the same tastes, ma'am. And you mustn't underestimate your ability with a pen. One can do a great deal with such an instrument. I do a little work of my own. However, I am afraid I have no brother to keep my pens sharpened. I sharpen them myself."

My animosity seemed to surprise her. I could not get her to reveal her true nature. There she was, bewildered, behaving as though she did not understand any more than her brother and Mrs. Fothergay were meant to understand.

"Now you can see it on the Brow yonder, the Hall. Moyna Branshaw's house," Sir Gareth announced as the horse and gig jogged across the rutted lane and entered on a path even narrower.

I did not at first hear him. I was still puzzling about Catherine Owen.

"What an actress she must be!" I thought; for I could have sworn that her innocence over the manuscript was not assumed.

VII

Mrs. Fothergay and I looked with interest across the high, rolling plateau with its color like the heart of an emerald, and made out the rectangular two-story gray stone building set attractively on a slight eminence above even the plateau on which we stood. Settled around the main house were various small outbuildings housing poultry and appurtenances to a house of the prosperous merchant class, neither too grand nor too gothic for the old Yorkshire family it had housed these two centuries.

It was about ten minutes' walk from us and I liked its look of a gentleman's house—solid, respectable, with the gracious air that so many homes built in the seventeenth century seemed to acquire. I think Mrs. Fothergay and I half expected a ghost-ridden haunted castle, that being more appropriate to the desolation around us. We were very much relieved.

"Why," said she, "It's quite—quite unexceptionable."

"All of that," Sir Gareth agreed drily. He had given his sister her manuscript and was reaching for my arm, but I had other things to think about and made the fatal mistake of crossing a gurgling little stream without relying on his outstretched hand. I had a suspicion, from the way he seemed torn between fixing his interests with me and with Mrs. Fothergay, that he was weighing our respective charms in his mind. Whatever else we might have offered the roving eye of a bachelor, certainly Mrs. Fothergay's comfortable little fortune should have been taken into account, and I think it was.

"How very odd," said Mrs. Fothergay suddenly. "There is no smoke coming out of the chimneys, and on such a day."

"Not odd at all, ma'am, for that fellow," said Sir Gareth. "The miserly beggar has a positive aversion to wasting fuel on the firegate. Never saw such a penurious dog. And if one wants a fire, one must provide it, and light it oneself. Isn't that true, Catherine?"

"Well, yes, but he likes it a bit . . . cool."

"Cool! He always has the place cold as ice. And what's more, when you touch him, he's cold as a tomb himself. If he's that cold, why doesn't he light a fire?" He broke off suddenly to tighten his grip on my arm. "Come now, Miss Anne, why should you tremble? Don't tell me you're frightened of that puppy."

"Heavens, no!" I said quickly, attempting a laugh that was more nervous than convincing. "It's just that I really am cold."

I may have been cold but I was also nervous over how I should behave without doing bodily harm to that horrid Marc Branshaw. Yet, from the first moment when he peered in at me in London like some resurrected ghost, to a moment ago when I began to suspect he gave my description to Catherine for such a mean, malicious joke, he had made it all seem reasonable. If there were some deep motive, I might understand, but from what I now knew of him, he had a naturally cruel sense of humor. Small wonder that I was nervous.

We came to a hollow outlined by several heavy chestnut trees, one of which overhung the lane, twisted precariously by the years and the harsh winters, until Catherine Owen's gig barely crept past the hungry black branches without being entangled. As we mounted to Branshaw Hall beside a low stone wall in good repair, I saw the slender figure of a man standing on the wall at the top of the hill, feet apart, motionless, but in the oddly graceful position of a schoolboy about to leap off into space. He saw us and waved, then actually did leap off the wall and come down to meet us. I was walking close beside

Catherine Owen and saw her hands tremble noticeably upon the reins. Without having the right to, I pitied her. But then, I was very nearly as nervous as she—and I had less excuse, for I was the merest acquaintance of our fickle young man.

"Insolent pup!" Sir Gareth exclaimed. "Catherine, the fault is yours. Why do you permit him these familiarities, as though he might run to you like a lad to his lass, whenever he may choose?"

"Please, Gareth, be quiet," said the lady, without, so far as I could see, losing her temper. I stepped back and she leaned out of the gig to call to Marc Branshaw. "Good morning, Marc. How are you?"

The gentleman, in excellent humor, took her hand. "I needn't ask how you are, Cathie. Sweet as always." His glance flicked over her brother with a brief, malicious, "Ah! Ever the attentive escort, eh, Gareth," and his glance at me was just as indifferent except for a little crooked smile at the corner of his mouth. I wondered what he found amusing about me. "Good. The lady from Sackerby, Perth. We need that fine Italian hand of yours." He reserved his effusive greeting for Mrs. Fothergay. I could not understand his motive, although I knew there must be one.

"Bedelia, ma'am, radiant flower! How kind of you to come! Did you have a pleasant journey, ma'am?"

He walked on up the hill on Mrs. Fothergay's side of the gig and as we passed the carriage block and reached the walled garden gates of Branshaw Hall, it was he and not Sir Gareth who lifted her to the ground. A groom from the Hall came to take the horse in charge. Sir Gareth, angrily chewing his lip, picked up his sister and carried her into the entrance hall, which was pleasantly carpeted in worn but rich green and gold drugget. All the time that Sir Gareth was muttering his disapproval to his sister, Marc Branshaw was chatting animatedly to Mrs. Fothergay. Once only, when we entered a large main room on the right and saw at the far end of the room a great Jacobean fireplace, unlighted, but stacked as though ready for burning, our host spoke to me. I was by this time inured to the indifference of all concerned, and thought at first there was a mistake. He spoke almost in my ear, very low.

"Come, don't look so cross. I'll be rid of them. Bide a moment." He must be mad. I, of course, said nothing to such effrontery.

Catherine was seated comfortably in a heavy chair decorated with Jacobean carvings like all the furniture in the room—solid, very old and worn, but of excellent workmanship. The windows opened out upon a delightful view of the little garden, where a thorn tree was surrounded by rose bushes and some green foliage with red berries still dripping from the morning dew. Beyond was the garden wall and then the lane back down past the ravine of the ancient chestnuts and up to Maidenmoor Rise.

"Whole thing's preposterous," Sir Gareth was saying. "My sister's manuscripts are no concern of yours, Branshaw, and as for Mrs. Fothergay—" The more attention his host paid to that lady, the more attached the baronet became to her. He had obviously made his choice between her and me.

Marc looked from one of them to the other.

"But—I had no notion. Are you acquainted with Mrs. Fothergay?"

The lady fluttered.

"Oh, indeed, yes. We are old friends, are we not?"

"But not such friends as the lady and I." Marc argued in that tone of sweet conviction most calculated to irritate Sir Gareth.

"Rubbish! The lady and I journeyed from Teignford together."

"Good Lord! But that was only yesterday. I have known her this age; have I not, dear ma'am?"

Mrs. Fothergay protested laughingly but I saw how it would be in the end.

Sir Gareth grew more cutting and determined, until there was only one thing for it. Marc retired gracefully from his position, yielded his prior claim on Mrs. Fothergay and ended by propelling them both out to the garden. He suggested that it was a pity Miss Catherine's gig could not be used by Sir Gareth to show his charming companion the countryside—

"—while we three get on with such dull stuff as musty manuscripts."

"Certainly I may have the use of my sister's gig!" cried Sir Gareth, rising instantly to the bait. "One would think I have nothing to say in my own household. Catherine, I am driving Mrs. Fothergay to—to—"

"Why not try Upshed?" suggested his sister.

Sir Gareth favored us all with an indifferent glance from his cold, blue eyes, and a few minutes later we could see him out beyond the garden gates, taking the reins from the hands of the groom and turning the gig while Mrs. Fothergay chattered happily at his side.

Catherine laughed.

"And if you had asked Gareth to leave with that woman, he would not have budged from this spot! You are quite incorrigible, Marc. You are determined to make that poor woman believe she's broken your heart. Must you pretend with everyone?"

After giving me a sheaf of paper, during which brief contact I realized his hands were excessively cold, and seating me beside an inkstand on the great dining table in the center of the room, Marc sat down on the table's edge.

"Not everyone, Catherine. Perhaps she merely leaped to a conclusion, as women often do. They have the invariable habit of believing everything that is said of them in their praise. It's a dangerous habit."

She blushed and looked discomfited.

"You are right," she admitted reasonably.

He seemed more annoyed than pleased at her sweet disposition.

"Well!" he said after a pause. "Let's have a go at the manuscript. Have you made the changes I suggested?" He began to rifle through the pages, now and then looking down at me, although he addressed no words my way. I was wondering how I could reproach him for the wicked description of me, since he here confessed that the changes were of his own devising. Once, when I caught him looking at me, he smiled in such a way that it was painfully difficult to resist smiling back, so I ended by catching myself in a ridiculous grimace which had begun as a smile.

After an hour had passed and we were all tired, he skipped through and glanced over the climactic pages. He frowned.

"What is all this, Cathie? What the deuce made you change your villain?"

Catherine said faintly, "I—I thought people might take you in dislike if he were as much like you as you said."

"I said change the details about the Gytrash nonsense, so that it shouldn't be traced to what's going on here, or we shall have mobs taking matters into their own hands as they once did. I didn't say it was necessary for you to shield *me*. That is not, and never was, your job, Cathie."

She was frightfully hurt. I knew that. I wished I might vanish for it was painful to witness this scene. I had no business here. I looked down at the sheaf of paper on which I had jotted certain changes as he dictated, and began to draw meaningless little checks and figures.

As he read on, he was less and less pleased. He laughed shortly. It was an ugly laugh.

". . . Irish-eyed Monanne. . . . Now I wonder who that might be."

I kept my gaze fastened on the sheaf in my lap, but my cheeks, I am sure, had bright red spots in them. True, I had eyes almost too dark to be called green, but the implication and the further description, were there. He went on in that cuttingly polite way.

"You have outdone yourself, Catherine. Half the good citizens of Yorkshire will recognize Moyna, my mother. You conceive that to be an improvement, I take it."

She quailed in embarrassment.

"No—no. I made up that description. I scarcely remember Moyna's eyes. Were her eyes Irish?"

Marc moved off the table and walked across the room. When still some distance from the great fireplace, he stopped and studied a portrait over the mantel. I did not know how he could see it so clearly, and wondered that he did not move closer, for it was dim in the November daylight. He said, with his back to us:

"Pale green, I seem to recall. I am surprised you did not mention her height—she was quite tall for a woman—and the red hair as well." He turned suddenly, looking at Catherine Owen in the way of a black cat about to spring. His voice was silken and made me shiver. "But then, you must remember her eyes. You were with her two hours while she lay dying. Did you never look in her eyes during those hours, my dear Cathie?"

Catherine's answer was a pained outcry.

"Marc! I could not walk. You know that. It was the shock of seeing her fall like that, I think. Or perhaps when it took so long to save her. You know I was injured as well, in trying to rescue her."

"Moyna was familiar with every pot-hole on the moors. She knew every bog, every fallen place. She would never have taken that last step herself."

"You don't know! She was willful. She went where she chose. She—she said the place had old memories. She had been on that trail so many times with the Devil—with Ewen Morgan."

"And she wanted to take you?" he asked ironically. "It was not like her to share her memories."

"I wanted to write about her and the Devil-Vicar. She knew the silly passion I had about the memory of him. I knew him when I was a girl in Wales. He scarcely knew I lived, but I remember him. Moyna was amused. She said it would avenge her upon the village if I wrote about him. She agreed that I might accompany her when she walked up to the cottage. She even mentioned that I would be amused at the contents of those journals she kept. We were speaking of them when she—"

It seemed to me that Marc was suddenly very much interested, but I could not be sure. It was natural that he should have an interest in his mother's journals. Miss Catherine went on.

"And then she fell. The earth seemed to give way. It was very boggy there. I tried to get her out . . . but I discovered I couldn't walk either. I think I'd got my legs caught in those horrid submerged tree limbs where the ground and turf collapsed when I tried to help her. My legs were numb . . ."

I could not contain myself longer. This was a terrible scene with which to tax Miss Owen.

"Please, Mr. Branshaw, surely the lady has suffered enough for the accident. Can't we talk of something else?"

I don't believe Miss Owen really thanked me for the interference. She gave me a quick, straight look from her large hazel eyes and then smiled apologetically.

"I do not often discuss my infirmity. I hope you will believe that, ma'am. As for Marc, we know each other so well, we can make allowances. Marc, my dear friend, can't we have tea? That should cut the gloomy atmosphere."

I could see that her kindly defense of him and her assumption of the hostess role annoyed him but he shrugged and reached behind him to pull a worn bell-cord. When a pert young woman with an Irish face appeared in answer to the summons, Catherine spoke before Marc could do so.

"Tea, Dilys, and, if we may, a few slices of that delicious parkin that Cook makes."

"Ye'll be meanin' the moogin, mum?"

"Muggin or parkin, or gingerbread!" her employer cut in sharply. "What does it matter? Go along, Dilys." But the girl did not take Marc's tone amiss. She merely looked from him to me, grinned and said, "Ay, sor. It's parfectly clear. Tea an' moogin for the lady . . ." She glanced briefly, insolently at Catherine. "Ladies, what I mean to say," and left.

I was surprised at her apparent animosity to Miss Owen, whose forebearing nature under her affliction should have commended her to everyone. Everyone, it would appear, except Marc Branshaw and his servants.

What a queer-tempered creature he was! In the clouds one minute, chattering and casting a spell with his smooth tongue, the next minute down in the depths and cross as a cat.

When the tea and gingerbread came, Dilys set the tray on the table near me. I was dumbfounded and pushed it toward Catherine, not knowing what else to do, but Marc interfered.

"For heaven's sake, will someone pour!"

I poured.

Catherine's cheeks were flushed, but she managed to look pleasanter than she felt, I daresay.

No one said anything for a time, and Marc, trapped between one woman who was looking injured and noble, and another who was scowling at his shocking display of bad manners, finally broke down.

"All right, Catherine. I'm sorry."

True, he did not have to be so excessively sorry. He stepped over to her chair and, leaning over her, kissed her lightly upon the cheek. It was so quickly and carelessly done that I hardly thought it warranted such rosy confusion on her part. In fact, I thought the whole episode a little overdone. I doubt if Marc did, though, for he went back to the plate of "parkin" or "muggin" and began to eat.

As for me, I felt clearly now the chill of this great room which, with a fire burning in the grate, would have been an ideal place. I reached for my cloak, forgetting that it had been removed when we came into this room. Catherine saw my gesture and seemed to be thinking busily. She was looking directly at me, yet she did not appear to see me at all. She said, after she had reached her decision:

"Marc, our—your guest is chilled. Don't you think

we might have a small fire? I see there's one laid."

He did not glance at the grate, or the huge fireplace itself. To my surprise, although he had been happily eating gingerbread a moment ago, he was now very much occupied with Catherine's manuscript.

She began again. "Marc. . . ."

"Yes, yes. I hear you. Miss Wicklow, if you will do this page over, I think it will save us all from wearing spectacles."

I took the page he handed to me, and we looked into each other's eyes. His dark brows curved in a puzzled frown.

"Do you really want a fire? I feel quite comfortable."

Nevertheless, his fingers, when they touched mine, were colder than my own. I stared at his hand. There was nothing in the least odd about it, but he snatched it back and looked at it. I don't know what he expected to find on it. Apparently he realized that it was its unnatural coldness which had interested me. He smiled.

"I suppose you think I am cold-blooded; is that what you would like to say?"

"That goes without saying," I remarked tartly.

He laughed and went over and summoned Dilys. I had turned my attention to the manuscript pages when I noticed Catherine's arrested pose. She was watching the Irish girl and Marc Branshaw with an attention that the act of lighting the fire certainly did not merit. The moment Dilys came back with a lighted spill from the kitchen Marc turned his back to her and to the fireplace and went to the great baronial table at which I sat. He leaned forward over a page of manuscript, with two fingers of either hand tightly clutching the carved table edge. Behind him, across the room, Dilys started a sputtering light in the grate and left us. Catherine looked up at me. As I watched her, she deliberately extended her arm as far as she could reach, and pushed the burning newspaper off the coals. The fiery paper went on burning but, of course, it would not catch on the coals. I gaped at her, ready to say something, too amazed to know what to say. She put her finger to her lips.

Marc, sensing our abnormal stillness, raised his head, but he did not look around to see what we were up to.

Catherine exclaimed suddenly, "Oh! What a pity! The flame's fallen off the coals. . . . Marc!"

He did not turn around, but his head was still raised. He was tense as though there had been a gunshot. He put out one hand without looking around at me.

"Miss Wicklow, would you be so good as to—"

I think the thing that almost unnerved me was his hand. Just for an instant, it trembled. Then he seemed to recover himself and took up the manuscript pages again.

Astonished at what I could only suppose was a humiliating display of cowardice, I went to the fireplace and kicked some of the coals into the little blaze so that they eventually caught. As I rose from the fireplace I exchanged a look with Catherine. Her eyes were all sympathy. She touched her temple significantly and nodded in Marc's direction, as one would say: "It is a madness."

If the scandalmongers were right and Marc Branshaw was the natural son of the dead Devil-Vicar, then his abhorrence of fire was more understandable, for he must often think of that agonizing death his father suffered.

I ignored Catherine's expressions and said calmly,

"Shall we resume the reading, Mr. Branshaw?"

His stiffened form relaxed. When I came and sat down facing him, his eyes had such an expression of anguish and shame in them as was almost heartbreaking to see, and I could have cheerfully slapped Miss Catherine for putting him to this ordeal. His face was damp with the cold sweat of his effort to conceal his panic from us. Then he got hold of himself and managed to say, as though nothing had happened:

"You haven't seen the house yet, have you? Suppose I show it to you while Catherine makes the changes. It's rather an interesting old relic, fortunately built in a day when the architecture wasn't quite so monstrous as these presentday horrors. Can you get on alone, Catherine? You will probably welcome the peace and quiet in which to work."

She hesitated just a moment before saying in her pleased way, "Thank you. I shall be quite content. There's so much to do on this silly manuscript. Just so that the bell-cord is within reach."

"Will you come?" he asked me, holding out his hand. I was put in mind of Jamie Keegan using the same gesture. I took Marc's hand. It was warmer after we had gone a few steps. I thought, with the conceit of all womankind, that if Marc Branshaw saw very much of me, I might thaw out that appalling physical chill of his flesh; for there was nothing chilling about his look or his manner to me. I was sure that, despite his taste for cold rooms, his lips were not cold, as I very nearly knew from experience, and his eyes, in my company, were not always haunted and suffering.

I remained with my illusion for some time that day.

VIII

NEITHER OF US said anything for the first few minutes. He cast sidelong glances at me now and then to see how I reacted to his curious display in the drawing room. When I did not speak, he said defensively:

"I don't always behave like such a complete and utter fool, you know."

I said, "Don't talk about it. We all have things that annoy us."

His fingers tightened their grip on mine. I had a notion the gesture was to reassure himself that there was someone near.

"Frightfully oppressive place," he went on, referring to the walls around us. "I always feel like a very small intruder who may be booted out if he's caught."

We were walking up the great carpeted staircase, which I found pleasantly grand, but it was only afterward that I remembered anything about the interior of the house. I was too much absorbed in my companion. Perhaps he felt the inadequacy of his excuse about the fire. When he spoke again, he was back at the thing that really troubled us both. He was still fearfully nervous when he mentioned it. I could sense the tension in his body, and for that reason, I tried not to let him suspect I considered his behavior to be an act of sheer cowardice.

"It was because you were watching—that made her fire trick a little more ghastly than usual. I knew you were watching. Even so, I—I couldn't. You won't believe it, but I tried. I really tried."

Attempting to cover the little break that came with his last words, he cleared his throat, but that naked, betraying emotion lay between us in the silence. I was conscious of a twist at my heart which was more than sympathy, though less than understanding.

"It doesn't matter in the least. Don't talk of it unless you wish."

"Why does she do it? *Why!*" He paused, took a deep breath. I tried not to notice the strain in his voice and his face.

"Miss Owen? But that's nonsense."

"She's done it before, but always when we were alone. . . . This time—" His eyes opened wide. He struck the polished oaken balustrade with a ringing slap. "Of course. It had to be so. That you might spread the story."

I did not agree with him aloud, although I suspected he was right. But I recalled that she had grounds for her behavior. While I was wondering how I should venture onto the boggy ground between him and the girl he had jilted, he pointed out to me several portraits of severe-looking Branshaws, or the handsome Rivercombs who were, he explained to me, Moyna's people. There were no pictures of his legitimate father, Josiah, and I supposed that if there had been, Moyna must have removed them in the long years she lived here alone.

The bedchambers were on this floor and Marc pointed them out, showing me one or two which were nicely kept, dust-free and clean, but somehow rather sad, for it was impossible to prevent them from giving off a curious, unused odor, like the musky scent of costumes in an old trunk.

He did not show me his own room, except to point it out, which was not surprising, for from my observation he seemed never to sleep. We came presently to his mother's room, and he showed me around it, watching my reactions I suppose, because he was proud of the room. It was indeed attractive—all white, with low, whitewashed cross-beams, dimity curtains, a lovely canopy over the bed, and carefully chosen furniture, done in elegant *petit point.*

My eyes went back to the bed. I don't know what I would have thought eventually in connection with it, but at the moment I was innocently considering what type of material had been used in that tester which was still kept so clean and neat.

Marc's mind obviously did not run along the same path.

"I imagine that bed could answer a number of questions that still puzzle the villagers. My mother used to say 'My bedposts could tell many a story that the gossips would like to hear.' "

I was embarrassed at his bringing up such a thing, but in order to save face, I pretended to be as sophisticated as my French ancestors would have been.

"Do you think she and the Devil-Vicar met here, in her husband's house?"

He started to answer me, stopped suddenly, then shrugged and called my attention to the portrait on the near wall, which was of an exciting red-haired beauty with green eyes. I knew that it must be Moyna Branshaw herself, yet it puzzled me. Something in the face, or the eyes, made me recall an idea I had formerly held. Why did I think that Marc Branshaw's mother was Irish, brown-haired and dark-eyed? Where had I heard that other description? And why should someone lie to me about Moyna Branshaw's appearance?

"She's beautiful," I remarked, unnecessarily. She was also selfish and charming and sparkling with sly humor, I guessed.

To my surprise, he studied the portrait thoughtfully, and then said, "I suppose she is. When I was young, I thought so. An enchanting companion—I've been told. But . . . one's ideas change, as people change. So I cannot say now."

"Anyone that beautiful must have been a little selfish and she may not have given you the attention you thought you merited as a child." It was curious how little she resembled her son, except in her nature perhaps.

He was amused.

"How old you sound! But you needn't bother making excuses for her. She never expected them. That's one reason why she was always teasing and worrying Catherine Owen. She used to write to me of the girl with her sweet fawn's eyes. They troubled Moyna, who was more salty herself. But Moyna was Moyna. The village forgave her very rapidly. It was her wicked seducer—our Devil and Monster—they blamed."

I could not help reminding him, "They certainly treat him with deference today. No one has an unkind word for him. Everyone seems to think he was the pride of Maidenmoor's past."

"Pity he didn't know that, while he was burning," said Marc.

I felt a little sick at his words and changed the subject quickly.

"From the look of her, I wouldn't put it beyond her to have seduced the poor Devil-Vicar."

He laughed at my female wisdom. "I don't doubt you're right."

He took my hand and drew me out of the room, whether I wanted to go or not.

When we came out upon the narrow side gallery, we stood there a few moments, staring at the vista of far, green rolling country that looked so harmless from his height.

"Do you ever feel smothered by all those moors?" I asked him.

"I loathe them!"

The furious passion in his voice startled me.

"You can't mean that. These people are human. They have tried to make amends to you and your mother for their crime. You must wish them well for that."

"Wish them well! I wish them at the bottom of a bog!"

"Not all of them, surely. I met the young curate, Frederick Niles, last night. He is a good man."

"Detestable creature!" exclaimed Marc, with one of his self-derisive smiles. "He is a constant reminder of the kind of man I should have been and am not. If only he were righteous, or even pompous and absurd, like MacDonnachie. But no. He must be kind and understanding, and intelligent . . . and," he ended on a laugh, "of course, I detest him for it."

I changed the subject. "But it is a beautiful country, in its way."

"And its citizens are beautiful, in their way," he mocked me. I stared up at his face. Now and then I seemed to glimpse another soul behind the light-hearted, gay, mocking young man I thought I had known in London. It was a bitter, hardened soul that had gone through fires of which I knew nothing. It was older, as old as his bitter world, and the gay, mocking young man was—at these times—devoured by that other creature lurking always behind the facade.

The curious thing was, I found myself drawn to that hardened soul fully as much as to the gay, mocking young man. Perhaps because I sensed he needed me the more.

"I can understand your feelings, because your mother had such an unhappy romance with that . . . that man. But even so, they are your people, and this is your own country."

"Much you know about it."

"Then why did you come back?"

"I wanted to discover if they had hounded my mother to her death as they hounded that poor idiot who was her lover. Now you know."

"And did they?"

He turned away.

"I can't say. If I could find her journals, I feel sure I would know. Catherine mentioned them, you remember."

I decided I might as well ask my question now as later. "May I ask a question you might not wish to answer?"

"Certainly. If I may give you an answer you may not wish to hear." When he smiled in that way, half his face looked different, so that his mouth and his eyebrow curving upward gave him a kind of cruel, mocking cynicism. I was learning to be uneasy when he looked like that. I wished I could dislike him at such times. I went on being uneasy, hoping the quick mood would pass.

"Did you jilt Catherine Owen?"

I don't think he expected that at all. He had the decency to redden a little.

"Not . . . technically."

"No. But literally?"

He sighed in a bored way. "Must we talk about that tiresome great creature?"

"She was crippled trying to save your mother."

"Still," he said, in the most cutting way, "she did

not *quite* save her, did she? And she has played on that ever since. From the moment I reached Maidenmoor, I've been reminded by all and sundry of my debt to Catherine Owen. So I was friendly to her, hoping to discover what she really knew. But then, her creep-mouse ways, and her pawing! Good God! She makes me shudder sometimes at her sheer goodness!"

I began to be frightened. Was no one ever allowed to express any emotion over this curious man? What if one could not help it?

I said, "If you'd ever been in love, you could not feel this way. Think of your mother. She knew what love was. Can't you make allowances?" I began to wriggle my fingers in his grasp, afraid he would think I was like Catherine, cloying and clinging to him.

"Good God!" he exclaimed. "Do you think I'm averse to love? But why doesn't she stand up to me? Those ways of hers. That grimy, sweets-filled paw of hers! No, I thank you! Not my sort, and never was!"

He felt my attempt at retreat and laughed.

"Oh, come now. Don't flatter yourself. You are neither sweet nor pawing. You're as prickly and as salty as Moyna was, I'm sure." I was wondering how to take this dubious compliment when he went on, firmly. "Catherine doesn't love me. She loves some idiotic conception of me. I feel as though I were a ghost; and she were looking through me at something—or someone—else. Besides, it's quite possible she did lead Moyna to her death. It was either Catherine or her brother. I am . . . I was convinced of it."

"But why?" He had let go of my hand and I decided that if I wanted to keep his good regard, I had better not make any "sweet" gestures.

"Why?" he repeated. "Because of Moyna's letters to me. She said she was amusing herself, playing a game with a person she suspected of attempting murder long ago. That would not likely be Catherine, of course, but suppose she had found out something about Catherine's brother?"

Moyna sounded as devilish as her Great Love, I thought.

He took a deep breath. "How glad I'll be when this thing is done and then it's back to France again, to work! I don't belong here. I hate them all too much."

"Not quite all, surely."

He smiled. I'm sure he thought I was making an exception of myself. But he did not answer. I went on.

"Jamie Keegan worships you."

Frowning, he stared at the countryside that lay all around us. He had probably caught sight of several men in the distance, moving quickly through the blackened heather, crossing the Branshaw grounds to the north. They all carried weapons—clubs for the most part—and I thought I made out one or two hunting rifles.

"Jamie," he repeated thoughtfully. "That lad knows something."

"Naturally. He saw the Gytrash. He is a witness."

"My dear girl." He turned around and took me by the shoulders, shaking me for my stupidity. "My girl, there is no Gytrash. There is no animal, unless it be some wretched hound or other. There's a human intelligence behind all this, and Jamie knows it. He told the Gytrash story to conceal something . . ." He stopped rocking me back and forth, for which I was only half grateful; I liked the sensation of his hands upon me. He added in a whisper, ". . . something worse."

He let go of me, behaving almost as if he were alone. "Now, what can be worse to a boy like Jamie, than a Gytrash?"

"Why don't you ask Miss Catherine?" I said, remembering suddenly. "She invented the Gytrash for her novel. Probably that's where young Jamie got his idea."

"Ah, yes. We return to the delectable Catherine. . . . I had to post to London once, to snatch up that stupid manuscript. She was so obliging as to tell me about it—after she had sent it. Heaven knows what made her change her mind. Conscience, perhaps. All apologies, she was. She wanted to know if it might do me any harm—as though I cared for that! But the Gytrash, that had to be changed. I think she was writing about someone she knew. That's why she asked me to get the book back . . . not to protect myself, but to protect someone else."

Behind him I could see the men in the distance, crossing to the north, where the country looked darker and more boggy. Two men had broken away from the main group and were hurrying toward Branshaw Hall.

Marc turned and leaned over the stone balustrade. "What is it, Sam? What the deuce is all that running about?"

A big Yorkshireman looked up and waved to us from the garden gates before opening them and coming around to the side of the building. Behind him, trotting along as fast as his girth would permit, was Reverend Cadmon MacDonnachie.

"I say, Marc, old chap, we need you. We've treed him."

Sam, the other one, made motions.

"Huge great sheep dog, Mister Marc, like we all said. He belonged to an old weaver from Upshed—old Danbery—died some weeks ago. The poor beast been lone an' lorn-like ever since. Half-starved, poor creetur. Must've been what young Jamie Keegan saw. We got the beast treed over past the Brow, in the Wind-Rock."

"I'll join you. Go on."

The Vicar called up to us: "Is that a lady with you? Ah, just so—Miss Wicklow. Can you spare us a bit of your time, ma'am? We've got the boy, Jamie, to identify the beast, and it's too far to go back and fetch his aunt. He's a bit skittish. Seems he needs a female to give him countenance."

Marc went back to the balcony. "Don't be ridiculous, Cadmon. I'll not have Miss Wicklow caught up in this thing. There may be danger up there. My housekeeper is over in Maidenmoor, but I'll get Cook to go with Jamie. She'd frighten any self-respecting beast."

"No, no. Ma'am!" trumped the Vicar. "Ma'am, the boy knows and likes you. There'll be no harm to you. We've got twenty men with us. Will you come?"

I looked at Marc. He shrugged and we left the balcony together.

"Don't blame me if the damned thing chews you up," was his consoling remark as we returned to the upstairs hall.

I must say, I would have preferred that they send Marc's cook or someone else, but after privately thinking of Marc himself as a coward, I could not commit the same folly. Marc found some of his housekeeper's heavy walking shoes for me and, after stuffing one of Marc's handkerchiefs into each shoe to fill up the hollows, I felt ready for the moors.

I did not know too much about the quirks of the

human brain, but it seemed odd to me that he should not be afraid of searching the moors for wild beasts, as he had done now for several nights, and yet be terrified of lighting a simple fire in his own grate, merely because of the fate that had befallen his supposed father. Perhaps a man could be only half a coward. I supposed some women would shun him for his half-cowardice; I despised it, but it did not have any effect on my feelings toward him. Rather, it seemed to augment them, since it was obvious that he needed someone, if only to light his accursed fires for him.

He considered me.

"Will you be warm enough? No. Of course not." He asked Dilys to fetch one of his own short hunting coats and then helped me into it in Moyna Branshaw's bedchamber, pushing my arms into each sleeve with the usual male carelessness for such things as linings and fingernails. I liked being bundled into his coat, especially when he smoothed the shoulders, turned up the cuffs, and raised the collar around my neck, then stood me there while he inspected me. When Dilys had left the room, he moved me about as though I were some toy.

We were both standing in front of Moyna's exquisite long mirror. He turned me around, pushing me this way and that, and then unfastened my hair. He swept it straight back above my ears in a fashion almost boyish, pulling the long strands so tight I was flat as flat can be. As to the other features, I winced.

"Hold it there!" he commanded me. I reached around, under considerable strain, and did so while he played with the tendrils of hair over my brow, trying to make it stand up, but it was too soft, and he gave it up, taking my hair out of my hands and loosening his grip a little. I still saw nothing in my looks to excite either of us. If he thought my hair might resemble his for some practical jest, he was mistaken, for it was lighter than his. His, being perhaps not so fine, was inclined to wave, and his hair curved naturally upward from his brow while mine saw not the slightest similarity. It must have been only a quick—very quick—impression that had made Mrs. Fothergay, and later, Sir Gareth, see something of a resemblance.

This matter of my hair occupied him a great deal more than it occupied me. I wondered if he had forgotten about the savage beast the villagers were going off to capture. But I was quite willing that he continue his playing forever.

Standing immediately behind me, with one hand holding my hair and one on my shoulder, he studied both our reflections and, although he frowned, he seemed satisfied. Then he turned me with my back to the mirror, and again looked at my reflection. I could not imagine what was so interesting about my back, unless it was his coat, which fit me surprisingly well except in the shoulders, and the sleeve length.

His own coat was very old, almost threadbare, and of a cheap plaid cloth such as the poorest man in the district might have worn. It did not have the quality and grace that most of his clothing suggested. I wondered at his ever having purchased it, and for what cause.

Finally, he gave me a little push, and said, "Now, do your hair up again. Ready to go?" He half-dragged me out into the hall and downstairs while I was still pinning up my hair, raining pins as we went.

I had had such tricks played on me before, but always for some ulterior purpose, such as the chance to embrace me. But Marc Branshaw showed no signs of wanting to do so. I was just a tool to him. I could not conceive then what his purpose was.

IX

In the drawing room as we passed the open doors, we saw the red-bearded Vicar MacDonnachie leaning over Catherine Owen, apparently trying to persuade her of something. He stood up as he saw us.

"Marc, my lad. I can't get this charming lady to go with me. Thought Mrs. MacDonnachie might drive her home; she has her carriage and our wretched nag out on the road. But Miss Catherine is faithful to her vows. Said she's promised you she'd finish the manuscript."

Marc had been about to pass the doors without going in, but he stopped long enough to say indifferently, "By all means, Cadmon. Persuade her. We shan't be back until quite late, I've no doubt. Come!" he said to me.

We were arrested by the Vicar's voice.

"No use. Stubborn child." He pinched Catherine's full, childlike cheek and she smiled at him, but gave Marc a little glance to see how he took this. The Vicar sighed, left her, passing me in the hall and going on out to speak with his wife, who was waiting in an ancient covered carriage.

Catherine called softly, "Marc! May I speak with you?"

He let go of my hand and crossed the room quickly.

"Marc . . . do you really think I should go? I mean —would you rather?"

"I think you'd be more comfortable in your own

house, don't you?" He looked around at the handsome interior of the drawing room. "You can't possibly enjoy this lonely place, and we shall probably be very late."

"Well . . ." She sighed. "Perhaps you're right. Would you oblige me?" She put out her hands. For just an instant he hesitated. Then he picked her up in his arms and carried her past me in the doorway. Looking back over her shoulder, Catherine smiled at me and held out one hand. "Dear Miss Wicklow, I am so glad to have talked with you. Please come and see me often, won't you?"

Looking impatient, Marc stopped while I shook the hand she extended to me. Again, I was impressed at the warm, solid strength of her hand. What a pity such a healthy young woman, with so much to live for, should be crippled in this way! I felt that Marc behaved badly to her. She let her arm drop around his neck, but a quick motion of his head, whether by accident or intention, threw off her touch. She looked straight ahead afterward.

He took her out, set her in the carriage beside Mrs. MacDonnachie, and waved them both goodbye, which they correctly took as a hint to be off.

Marc and I started across the thick, wet turf to meet the distant group of hunters. I could understand his cross behavior, but it did seem excessively rude by comparison with his sudden change of manner now. His scowl had disappeared and he was behaving in the friendliest way, like someone who has observed the proprieties and almost expects to be thanked. It was difficult to be cross with him, no matter how he deserved it.

The trail we followed after crossing the Branshaw fields was hardly more than a sheep track, twisting, winding and rising all the while between the dying heather and the bracken that grew more heavily on the slopes as we ascended. More frequently now, giant slabs of naked rock masked an occasional cave but gave us no shelter from a biting wind. I huddled further in Marc's coat, thankful for its high collar.

"Ay, mum," said the big man called Sam, seeing me shiver. " 'Tis wutherin' this day," and he pointed into the face of the wind.

"I told you you shouldn't have come," Marc reminded me. He put his arm around me, which was not much protection against the wind, but I let him think so.

I soon found all this climbing hard on my breath and limbs. I was little used to walking in London, and not really constituted for the long country strides of these Yorkshiremen, and I would soon have turned back but for the knowledge that everyone except Marc Branshaw seemed to expect strenuous efforts of me.

He laughed when he helped me after I had stumbled a second time and said with mock severity, "You would play the heroine!" It was a relief when I perceived that he was not ashamed of me, for I had begun to realize the immensity of this task I'd set myself. Then we saw Jamie Keegan running down the sheep track toward us.

"Marc! Marc! You're come now. I'm that glad to see ye. They said it was a female I was wanting. But I said I must see you first. I'll say no word of the beast til ye tell me." He shook Marc's hand like an adult, winked at him, and then looked at me.

"He's half a mind to snatch you from them London men; he told me so. You've a mind to let him snatch you, mum?"

Any other man might have been either cross or embarrassed at this disclosure. But while I tried hard to look indifferent and ignore the question, Marc Branshaw ruffled Jamie's hair, thus completing the wild job already begun by the bitter wind.

"That's the chatterbox!" He laughed. "Now you've ruined any chance of my discovering whether Miss Anne would let herself be snatched."

"What a magnificent view! I had not thought we'd come so far," I cried suddenly, so that I should not be said to commit myself.

Jamie stopped on the brow of a hill in the less side of a great, overhanging boulder, and pointed out what he claimed to be my own room in the Yorkish Lion Inn. Looking back over the glens and rolling landscape below us, broken by outcroppings of rock, nettle and black peat, I could see nothing beyond the distant spire of Maidenmoor church and decided Jamie's vision was fanciful.

"Where did you see the Gytrash?" I asked him, thinking of the relief to the countryside now that the starved and savage beast was cornered.

Jamie said not a word. When the silence became a little oppressive and I could hear only the wild roar of the wind whipping through the bracken and against the ageless rocks, I looked at him. He and Marc were staring at each other in a curious way, both alert, keenly pitched, as though they waited. For what?

Marc and I glanced at each other. I was remembering what Marc had said two hours ago—that the murders were not the work of an animal but a human intelligence. He had been proven wrong almost immediately. Yet he said now, gently, to the boy:

"Thats what we must be sure of, Jamie. Don't you agree?"

Jamie's eyes looked a little wild, trapped. I had an inexplicable sensation that he was undecided which way to jump. "If—if there's no more killing . . . then, does it matter?"

I could not help saying, "It matters a great deal, Jamie. If a beast kills a man, the beast should be destroyed."

"Even if he never kills no one else?"

What ailed the boy?

"This is very silly, Jamie. I'm surprised at you. Your Aunt Rose wouldn't believe a murderous beast should be spared. He might kill again."

"But—if a beast don't know? What if somebody—something I mean to say—is punished and then . . . then it . . . ain't the one?"

Marc said pleasantly, "Do you mean there are two savage dogs loose in this Godforsaken wilderness? Come now, Jamie lad, you've already testified that you saw the beast." His voice was gentle but I sensed the dagger sharp attention he was giving to his words and to the boy's reaction.

Jamie did not say anything. He began to walk. We saw then that he was crying. He made no attempt to wipe away the tears. The wind whipped at his face and the tears dried in streaks. Marc and I followed him. He was facing some sort of a problem that came even before his devotion to Marc. I was afraid to interfere further between them.

On the north side of the great jutting boulder we received the full impact of the wind, and although it was unpleasant in its furious gusts, it carried the wild, half acrid, half sweet odor of the wilderness that lay now all around us. Where, in the heights and glens of the Maidenmoor country, there had been sheepcotes peppered about the landscape, almost but not quite hidden from view, here the country which led down to a noisy stream and over toward Moyna Branshaw's cottage on the opposite hill, was even more rugged. I could see no sign of habitation except the Branshaw cottage, which I now beheld somewhat dimly, as clouds came and went over the watery November sun. The path meandered around clumps of heather and bracken, now and then soggy, so that one's feet nearly bounced over the dark turf that was the remnant of ancient bogs.

The Reverend MacDonnachie came puffing back up the trail to meet us. He had with him a quiet, gentlemanlike man whom he introduced as Dr. Ralph Lowther from Upshed, the physician the old weaver had been visiting when he died of a heart seizure.

"Yes," said the doctor, upon Marc's questioning, "it's the old fellow's dog, right enough. I never thought him savage. But he was a one-man dog, as the saying goes. When he lost his master and wasn't fed, I daresay he took to savaging whatever he could lay teeth to. Must have met old Will Grimlett on his forays and Will tried to stop him robbing the sheep-cote of the poultry yard—something of that sort. The beast is just down below the brow of the hill, in an old hollowed passage in those crags yonder. A couple of sheepmen trapped the creature there before dawn, and lost two dogs to the beast. Can't get him to come out."

The Vicar rubbed his red beard as though it itched, and said, "Damnable thing is, the creature's very liable to find another way out, and then it's the Devil to pay."

Half a dozen voices broke from the confused gathering at the mouth of what I took to be the passage worn into the rocks and perhaps leading far to the other side of the hill. The passage was directly below a trickle of water that must have been a gushing torrent in spring, sweeping across the bracken-covered brow of the rocks and then descending, to wind its way through the narrow passage and empty itself into the Maidenmoor country on the other side.

Many of the men and boys, with one or two warmly-dressed women, were strangers to me, and from their greetings to the group from Maidenmoor, I took them to be from Upshed.

One or two boys had tried to wriggle their way into the narrow passage, hoping to get a shot at the animal, but hastily scrambled out when we all heard, inside the passage, the gutteral growl of the beast who had already murdered two people. Hearing the warning sound, the wounded dog began to whimper, and the Reverend Niles took a shawl offered by one of the women and spread it over the suffering animal.

"I couldna get a line to shoot on," complained one of the boys. "Yet I heard un."

"We all heard him," Dr. Lowther agreed. "The thing is to get near enough to shoot the creature."

The Vicar turned to Marc, who was studying the situation with what I could only hope was simple curiosity, not the careful eye of a man who intended to go into that horrid place.

"Ye'll have no trouble with the light. It's light as a lamp inside," explained one of the boys, encouragingly. "All the daylight comes in, like in a cave."

"A great help to the beast as well as to the man who must flush him," murmured the doctor.

The Vicar seemed to find Marc's progress interesting, for Marc had climbed the side of the boulder and was examining the higher, more open crevices some six feet above the ground.

The Vicar called up to him:

"Miss Moyna knew this passage, didn't she, laddy? She met my late predecessor here now and again, if legend serves me. Did she ever mention it to you?"

The crowd grew still. Everyone was staring up at Marc except Jamie, who knelt with his head down, picking wet bracken that grew on the outside slope of the path. I saw that his breath was suspended, however, and he was waiting for Marc's reply like the rest of them.

Marc called down to us, "I imagine she did. I have some vague recollection. . . . The beast is not in sight—I can see that much. He must be hidden in a recess behind the cave."

"Was there any other way out?" asked Dr. Lowther.

"Now, now, doctor," put in the Reverend MacDonnachie. "How would Marc know that? It's only Moyna and the Devil-Vicar who would know." He winked at me but his joke was in bad taste, I thought, and I looked stonily ahead.

"I believe there was another way out," Marc said, as he moved up further to the top of the boulder, getting a handhold rather precariously, I thought, from the tufts of dead ling and bracken. "It may have been sealed up by the bogslide on the Maidenmoor some years ago."

"But you can't be sure," said the Vicar.

"Have a care, Branshaw," murmured Frederick Niles.

The others began to buzz about the danger. Someone said, "He's got to be got out; that much we know. If we can't see to shoot the bugger from here, we got to go in and do it proper. Who's to flush him?"

The Vicar examined the opening in the rock, which was certainly not large enough for a man of his girth to penetrate, although I thought perhaps either Frederick Niles or Dr. Lowther might make it. But the young curate appeared a trifle clumsy and I doubted if Dr. Lowther would be a match for a beast that had killed a rugged sheep farmer. Holding tight to his hunting gun, the Vicar fingered the crevice with his free hand, attempting with ludicrous results to force an entry which would give room to his great stomach and hips, as well as his weapon. What he attempted was so impossible that I almost suspected the good Vicar of merely making a brave show.

I was surprised at the laughter among these rugged men, even in the face of this danger. Some tried to push and crowd the Vicar into the aperture, and, failing, joked about his size and how he would have to starve and come back another day, with less belly to handicap him. But the women murmured, as I would like to have done, at the notion of any man going through that ghastly crevice, at the mercy of a savage killer-dog. I would have voted to camp here until the dog became starved enough to come out, or, at the worst, to place some poison handy. But the men seemed determined to do things in their own way.

"You'd best give it up, sir," said the Reverend Niles to the Vicar, offering a handkerchief. The Vicar wiped the sweat off his brow before the wind could chill him, then climbed back out, stamping his feet to restore circulation. "Thought I caught a glimpse of the beast's eyes blazing at me in there, but I may have been mistaken. It'll take the Devil's own spawn to squeeze in there—and then he might not be got out. Besides, he'll get but one shot."

As if by common consent, all heads moved slowly upward, upon the Vicar's careless words. I looked with them, yet hating the inclination that made me betray my thoughts when "Devil's spawn" was spoken. One of the villagers was not so careful.

"Ye've hit on it, Reverend-sor. They's none but the Devil's spawn can do it."

Marc looked down at us from the brow of the crags, and then descended easily to within a few yards of the Vicar's head. He said quietly:

"There's another way—just over the brow. Give me your weapon."

"Now, lad—" began the Vicar, but Frederick Niles pulled at his sleeve.

"Someone must go. I believe Mr. Branshaw is the logical one. He is fast on his feet. Do you think you can manage it, sir?"

Marc did not reply. He moved back up the brow of the crags and down the other side. Several of the men climbed up after him, and Jamie suddenly ran up the trail, retracing his steps, with me hot behind him, in a tempest of anger and concern to keep him, at least, from running into Marc's danger. Jamie came to a stop not far from where the men stood, watching Marc as he tore away great handfuls of dead nettle and tufts of bracken, to uncover a hole the size of a wagon wheel in the rocks. This hole, apparently torn away by erosion of water and wind through the ages, opened straight down into a section of the rock passage some six or seven feet below. Marc swung his legs over the side, and dropped through that repulsive hole. His feet touched the earth below so silently that we could not hear the sound. The men looked down through the hole, breathing fast, but keeping absolute silence for fear of disaster to Marc. I glanced in, between two villagers, and saw Marc move through what was, as had predicted, an extension of the cave-like room we had glimpsed from the aperture, where the Vicar and the others now stood ready, should the animal be driven out. I saw an item even more odd—a ring set in the wall of the passage, and, beneath it, the frayed end of a coil of rope. Had the dog been kept prisoner here and had he worried his way free of the rope? But how would that explain the fact that the villagers had treed him in this spot? Probably, upon their giving chase, he had returned to the place which was at the same time his prison and his haven.

Suddenly Marc stopped, backed up stealthily, and we could see him raise the gun to his shoulder.

The angry snarl of the beast before him in the passage reached us on top of the crags and we shuddered. Marc took aim, fired. The sound reverberated underground but our own shock was covered by the Vicar's voice on the other side of the crags.

"Got him, by George! Good shot!"

Jamie pushed me aside and peered in so that I could not see. "No, Marc! He'll leap! They don't die sudden-like. . . ." He broke off to scream.

Jamie's cries mingled with the shouts of the Vicar and Dr. Lowther, trying idiotically to advise Marc.

I was only just able to see Marc raise the gun as a club before the maddened, dying beast sprang at him. While I closed my eyes, too horrified even to pray, I heard the sudden gasp of astonishment around me, and looked again. The paw of the beast—a large black and white, long-coated dog, of a kind seen commonly around the sheepcotes—had torn a great gash across the breast and shoulder of Marc's coat, but then, either because he was dying or for some other obscure reason, the dog dropped before Marc and, in his last struggles, managed to crawl to Marc's boots and crouch there, sniffing at Marc as at a friend.

One of the men behind me raised up after watching this eery sight. He traded glances with the others.

"Quite a power over beasts, has our Mister Branshaw."

Marc looked up at us.

"Over and done, or just beginning?" whispered a male voice behind me. "Remember that Other One? He said he had power over savage beasts. Ay, but Mister Marc proved it."

"Like father, like son," said another voice.

Unsteadily, Jamie clutched my arm, but I looked at him with as much stern resolution as I could summon.

Frederick Niles had joined the group and was briskly scoffing at their suspicions, but I saw him cast an occasional puzzled glance down into the Wind-Rock passage.

Marc called, "Jamie! Fetch someone to get the carcass. One of you, give me your hand up."

Three or four of the biggest among the men hesitated, but when Niles and I reached for Marc's hands, the others were finally shamed into helping the man who had, alone, destroyed their murderous Gytrash. Marc pulled himself up before we could help him, and by the time the Vicar came lumbering over to give a hand, Niles had retreated, and Jamie and I were dusting off our hero. Marc grinned at Jamie, pulling the boy's hair and behaving as though the curious incident of the dog crawling to his feet had never happened.

Niles stared at Marc, especially at his jacket, and presently I glimpsed a smile on his sober features. He must have found an answer to the mystery of the dog's behavior that escaped the rest of us.

I was thrust aside by the well-wishers who did not share the view of the superstitious, that Marc Branshaw had revealed some of his supposed father's Devilish powers over the dog. It was only when the Vicar smacked Marc hard on the back and shouted that he was the "preserver of Yorkshire" that I noticed the slight signs of strain in Marc's face, and his occasional circular exercise of his shoulder, as though it bothered him. I wondered how deeply the dog's paw had gashed through his clothing, whether, in fact, it had touched his flesh.

Meanwhile, as Marc received congratulations with an indifferent and almost sarcastic air, two of the boys in the crowd had brought up the dead dog and laid it on the bald crown of the rock. Marc looked at me as the others buzzed around it, studying the muzzle, the great canines, the paws, amazed that such an ordinary animal had done so much harm under the impetus of starvation.

He said, "You aren't dancing a farandole over the body, I see."

"No, nor am I like to do so. Did you notice how starved the dog was? It looked as though he'd been kept prisoner in that place. I found all the signs, including an iron ring in the rock. How could the dog be starved, since it has, presumably, been wandering about all these weeks?"

"Ah!" he smiled. "If we knew that, we should know . . . a great deal more than we know now."

At this unsatisfying answer I could not help making a face at him. He seemed in a humor to tease, but a flicker of pain crossed his features, and he massaged his shoulder mechanically.

"Are you hurt? Let me see. Perhaps I can oblige by—"

To my surprise, he drew back out of my reach, and then, apparently realizing that such modesty did not suit the stories about him, he said brusquely:

"No need to fuss. I'll attend to it later."

I was more puzzled than angry at his rebuff, and he could see this. He must have felt that some explanation was due, for he said after a moment, and with a look which promised all sorts of forbidden pleasures, "But if you insist you may come to Moyna's cottage with me. Who knows how you may oblige me there?"

"If you're going to be insulting—" I began, but Jamie cut me off sharp, saying quickly,

"You're to go to the cottage with Marc and me. It's a fine place. I learn to play chess there—ay, and to paint pictures like Marc. You'll come, love?"

I laughed. "Shall I come with Jamie, Mister Branshaw?"

"Certainly. And if you ask very prettily, I may even allow you to sit for us."

At this invitation I was prudently silent.

"See here, young Jamie," called the Vicar. "Come and identify your monster. . . . What do you say? Is he your Gytrash?"

The boy left Marc and me reluctantly, shuffling his feet along the nettle, as he walked up to the body of the dead dog. He licked his lips and squatted beside the animal, staring at it.

"Well, Jamie?" Dr. Lowther prompted him.

Jamie looked around helplessly.

"Must I?"

"Yes," said Marc quietly. "You must, Jamie."

"Ay." Jamie appeared to be thinking as he pretended to examine the dog, touching the long hairs, but he was gazing blankly into space. "No. It wasn't this dog at all. This un's got black on it. I said the Gytrash wasn't black at all. Not a bit black. It was—it was—like a lion. Not black."

Everyone began to look uncomfortable, casting

exasperated glances at the boy, and Dr. Lowther said soothingly, "I think we may account for the boy's confusion by the frightful experience he underwent that night. Are we all agreed that this is our celebrated Gytrash?"

"But he was bigger," cried Jamie. "He was bigger and he was dun-color and not black or white."

They all seemed in agreement to disregard this, although one or two of the men, who had whispered about Marc, now gave him odd looks and nudged each other. I was surprised, however, when the Reverend Niles came strolling over to us, with a frown.

"It seems odd, to say the least. You would do well to train your young freind to be more observing. We had had enough of careless suspicions in this village."

Marc nodded. "I have thought so for some time. Jamie fancies he may have seen me as a Gytrash, and doesn't like to say so. I'm afraid his loyalty is only making matters worse."

Reverend MacDonnachie and I, who heard this, were both startled. The Vicar said gruffly, clearing his throat, "Then I'd advise you not to be so free with such talk. Niles is right. Great Giliad, man! Do you want to arouse the village as they were aroused over your—over that Other One?"

"Later," said Marc soothingly. "He will know later that it was not me he saw. And now, if these good people will clear out to wherever they are going, I think I shall spend a quiet evening at Moyna's cottage, without all this disturbance."

The Vicar seemed half of a mind to challenge this. "Do you think that's wise? If any harm should befall you as a result of the boy's careless talk, well. . . . You know what happened to my predecessor. And you alone in that forsaken cottage!"

Marc smiled in the way I had learned to mistrust. "But I thought your influence had civilized them."

I could not blame the Vicar when he puffed angrily to get breath, but as the young curate touched him warningly on the arm, he completely reversed himself.

"Now, see here, laddy—I like you, but it's not right to hold the whole village responsible for the actions of a few hotheads fifteen years ago. That business with the Devil-Vicar was started by some malcontents, ruffians. The villagers did more to put out the fire than start it."

"Shall we talk of something else?" asked Marc idly.

The Reverend MacDonnachie, still upset at these unkind reflections on his Christian work, turned and stamped off.

As I started to go after Jamie, Marc took my hand. I was surprised at his gentleness after the recent display.

"I don't want these people to know that I've asked you and Jamie to come up to the cottage. Come as far as Upshed turning, and Jamie will pretend to lead you back to Maidenmoor. Instead, he will take you to me. Do you understand?"

He saw my dubious expression and added with some amusement, "It has nothing to do with 'obliging me' and the rest of it. Word of honor. But I do need you."

I assumed that his shoulder must be hurting him, and he needed me to apply bandages or something of that sort, and of course I agreed.

When Jamie came to us and Marc told him what he was to do, the boy looked glad, but there was still a hang-dog air about him. Marc slapped his cheek in a friendly way.

"Here, Jamie, what's this? You told them the truth. If they won't believe you, that's no concern of yours."

Jamie said nothing. His fingers idly twisted and untwisted the button at the throat of Marc's coat. Suddenly, he looked from the coat up into Marc's face, and to our consternation, his eyes grew enormous and he whispered, "I did right, didn't I? Please say I did right."

Marc brushed back the boy's windblown hair and said in a caressing voice, "Of course, you did; exactly right."

X

THERE WAS a good deal of milling about, relief expressed on all sides that the beast was dead, and one or two glances in Marc's direction, which hinted that news of his odd behavior had spread among those not fortunate enough to have witnessed it. I thought Marc might be upset by it all, but, on the contrary, it seemed to me that he almost welcomed their suspicions. I supposed he thought it funny, just as the man thought to be his natural ancestor, the Devil-Vicar, had gone to so many pains to present himself as a devil and weird phenomenon.

I would like to have mentioned the ring I saw in the Wind-Rock passage, the signs that the dog had been kept confined at one time, but I was afraid to interfere with Marc's plans. Obviously, he knew these people better than I.

Dr. Lowther and a number of the Upshed people walked on down across the lowlands, through what they referred to as Heaton Clough, treading on the thick, boggy surface of the ground as though it were firm paving stones. I found the peat first amusing for its bouncey qualities, and then slightly more sinister as I perceived that if the rains came heavily, this area would all be bogs and mud, with the ability to draw one down into its horrid depths. Here in the sheltered glen where great trees grew thick in clumps and long processions, Jamie pointed out to me that the place where Moyna Branshaw had lost her footing and stepped off the turf into a bog-hole, was very like the uncertain ground we traversed. It was at the junction with a sheep trail winding upward toward the wind-swept moorland where her cottage stood in the direct path of the rushing storms.

"Up there it was," said Jamie, pointing to the green hillside above us. "Rare boggy it is, too."

"Mind that shoulder, Mister Branshaw," the doctor warned him at parting. "You'll be bandaging it, I trust."

Marc did not look at his shoulder but I could see that fringes of blood had seeped through the shirt and the torn coat, and it made me nervous to see him neglect the scratches. Heaven knows, it must have been painful. I was about to suggest that he stop and apply a cloth to it, when Jamie suddenly pointed out a horse and gig in the distance, rattling along from Upshed. It was trouble of sorts, for Mrs. Fothergay was at the reins, and upon seeing Marc, she stood up, waving her enormous ruffled hat at us and calling in embarrassingly loud tones to Marc:

"My dear boy, how nice! Come to meet me, have you?" Her clumsiness on the reins naturally confused the little horse, who began to shuffle and start.

Under cover of the chuckles and laughter and rib-nudging of the Upshed people, Dr. Lowther came to her rescue so she could devote her full attention to

Marc. Like the villagers from Upshed, I could not help laughing at his discomfiture, but Dr. Lowther did handsomely by him. He looked from Marc to the lady and shook his head sadly.

"Ma'am, Mr. Branshaw is taken ill. I fear all this exertion in such freshing air is too much for the gentleman. He is about to retire. Are you not, Mr. Branshaw?"

Marc, however, showed a sudden interest in the lady, or her absent suitor. He moved through the listening, sniggering crowd to take Mrs. Fothergay's hand. When he made a pretense of kissing the gloved fingers, his lips only just missing them, there were perceptible murmurs of amusement among the witnesses, which did not stir him in the least.

"My dear Bedelia! How do you come to be alone? I had no notion Owen would be so ungallant."

"Wretched, odious man! He left me in Upshed. Some local person told him he was needed to capture that great, awful beast, and off he went."

"Impossible," murmured Marc. "to leave you with so little ceremony." He looked around at the moorland, as though seeking some trace of the missing knight.

"Bedelia, *cherie,* he was a fool. Did he go with others, or alone?"

"Alone, I think. But what is this, Marc? Am I being quizzed?" Then she observed the stains on his coat and fluttered maternally. "You're hurt, dear boy! You will be needing me. Here, one of you"—she looked around with an officious manner—"take the reins. Marc, it's clear you need a woman's hand."

Marc was melancholy, noble, but firm. He even staggered a little, and the busy, listening crowd responded with a quick buzz of sympathy. At least two dozen hands reached out to catch him.

"I couldn't permit it, Bedelia. . . ." He seemed to become aware for the first time that he was being overheard. "Ma'am, that is—you embarrass me. I cannot inflict myself upon you in this ridiculous condition. Imagine how it would be if you came with me up that stony sheep track, on those enchanting little feet of yours. You would stumble. You would be worn to a fret. And I should be the cause."

She looked uneasily up the forbidding trail.

"Well . . . perhaps . . . But are you quite sure you can get on without me?"

"I must," he assured her firmly, kissing the fingertips she uncovered to him. He motioned to Dr. Lowther let this continue a few minutes but he was eying Marc steadily. He broke up the crowd's fun after a suitable time.

"I think you'd best have those scratches attended to. And at once."

Marc grinned but said a little faintly, "Thanks, I shall," and, pushing his way through the crowd, said a loud and public goodbye to Jamie and me, before he started on the sheep trail up to Moyna's cottage.

Jamie took my hand and hustled me out of sight of the others. It was not difficult to find another sheep track that crossed the trail of Moyna's cottage, and almost immediately, we began to climb.

We joined Marc a few minutes later, without anyone being the wiser.

This trail was the most uncivilized we had come upon. We seemed to be in the very belly of the great, seething monster which was the moorland. Once again all was green in every direction, with occasional outcroppings of primeval gritstone and rock. One twisted fir tree stood guard before the low stone walls of the cottage, and we could now see the gaunt limbs, like fingers, groping for the mottled sky. I wondered if there could be any other human beings in all this desolation.

"Are you sure we shouldn't have gone on to Upshed?" I asked. "It seems so isolated here if we need any—assistance."

"My dear girl," Marc told me sharply. "it's the merest scratch, if that was what you had in mind!" I saw that Jamie clung to his arm more in the effort to be of help than to seek support. I did not dare lend my own assistance, but had to be satisfied with finding the correct path among several that criss-crossed the boggy moorland at these points.

Jamie did not lower the sinister atmosphere when he said, as he stopped suddenly, "Here it was Miss Moyna took sick. Fell into that bog there, behind the nettles."

I could see how it might have happened, for a sheep track crossed directly over the dark, swampy place which was masked, as Jamie said, by nettles and decaying foliage. It was not quite on our trail, but I supposed that Moyna Branshaw, being in a hurry, and perhaps thinking she knew the boggy moorland better than she did, stepped into that stinking black ooze, and her companion, Catherine Owen, found it impossible to get her out.

"I might have walked into it myself," I said, and tried not to look at the dreadful place.

"Ay," said Jamie, " 'twas a mucky day, with clouds hanging that low ye could fair touch un."

Marc stared at the place deliberately, and we stopped, hoping it would not revive other old memories. He said harshly:

"Yes. It was a gloomy day. If it had not been, she would have seen that the cover of rock and board had been removed."

"Removed!" I looked back at the place, realizing

that there must have been something of the sort there originally; for the alternate trail, now grown over, cut directly across the boggy place.

"And Moyna's back was broken, and Catherine—so she says—was paralyzed."

Jamie and I started to speak almost together, hoping to drive off these vindictive thoughts, but they must have been embedded even before Moyna's death; for he answered us coldly.

"These people haven't changed. You saw them today."

"But the Owens an't our people," Jamie put in hopefully.

"I wonder," said Marc, "where Gareth is now. That I should like to know. Someone in this village is wearing a disguise, perhaps only mental. If I could rip off that bloody damned mask! Which of them is it? Which one is pretending he never saw me before? Well, lad"—he cuffed Jamie lightly across the cheek—"when we know that, we'll be a trifle less popular, I fancy."

Jamie peered around at me. He looked scared and I did not quite blame him. But then, I could scarcely blame Marc either, in the circumstances. He was looking tired, his features drawn and pale, older and somehow distant. The change may have been due to his troublesome injury, yet I wondered if the other man had always been there, unobserved because of his surface charm. I was nearly afraid to speak up, but remembering Jamie's young face, so loyal and so deeply concerned for his friend, I said:

"I hope you won't confuse Jamie and me with the people you hate. We . . . we like you."

"You know nothing whatever about me," he countered deliberately. "You may fancy you like Marc Branshaw, perhaps, but you can't possibly like *me*. You don't know the first thing about *me*."

I tried to explain, with a lightness that was out of place, "We don't think you control savage dogs, or turn into a devil at night. We don't think you made that dog kill the girl and the old farmer."

"No!" He favored us both with a grim smile. "But I wonder if your precious loyalty would go further—would cover *me*—myself!"

Jamie shivered but kept tight hold on his friend's arm. I felt much the same. Marc's senseless protest did not touch us, for we didn't understand it. We saw one man, the one we both loved in different ways. His words about "me" and "myself" were so much nonsense. He might even be off his head, but we certainly knew he was Marc Branshaw, whatever crimes he might fancy set him apart.

We reached the great fir tree outside the low, broken wall of the farmhouse garden. Marc stopped a moment, pressed his hand against the torn place on his coat, and relieved Jamie and me by saying more softly:

"I'm sorry. I'm grateful to you both—I really am. Don't know what I should do without you." Grimacing a little, he made a flourish with his free hand. "Miss Wicklow, welcome to the cottage—Moyna's haven. It isn't very respectable, but then its guests have not always been respectable either. One of them was said to be a devil."

The iron gates in the crumbling stone wall stood open, swinging back and forth and creaking as the wind circled the barren hilltop. All around the two-story farmhouse, the perpetual wind had shaped every growing thing to its own ends. Even the seedlings of the ancient fir twisted frantically away from the wind. Although the afternoon had not gone, the sullen sky made a kind of early dusk over the scene, and I wondered how we would find our way back to Maidenmoor tonight. Jamie boasted of knowing the moors as well as any man. But so had Moyna Branshaw.

There was no porch. When Marc unlocked the solid oak-studded door, we stepped from the moist ground into the living quarters of the house. The main room had a huge, comfortable fireplace, apparently used for cooking as well as heating, and the usual pieces of furniture of mixed age, period and worth, that are accumulated from the more fashionable "home residence." The floor was of stone, covered here and there by worn drugget, miserably cold to me even through the housekeeper's stout walking shoes. On the left of the heavily timbered room was a narrow staircase leading up to what I supposed must be the bedchambers.

Jamie volunteered quickly, "I'll light the fires, if you please, Marc. And maybe a smidgeon of tea for Miss?"

"Ay, love," Marc agreed in broadest Yorkshire, apparently determined to improve his disposition for us. "Do that, and I'll oblige Miss Anne by changing this sad coat. Hardly the proper attire for entertaining a lady, eh, Jamie?"

Jamie went through a small door at the further end of the room and then I could hear him rustling about, in what must have been the peat room, as he loaded fuel for the fireplace. Marc was looking at me, smiling in a half-melancholy, half-humorous way.

"Are you sorry I stole your precious Red Indian manuscript? You little thought you'd be tramping over the countryside a week later in a housekeeper's boots and a coat belonging to a bad-tempered chap so ill-natured he nearly forgot to say how much he needs you."

"I'm sure you need me for those scratches of—" I began.

He said without a change in his whimsical manner," "But not for those scratches of mine." He started up the stairs. "Don't go away. Jamie will find some fresh baked bread, I expect. At least it was fresh yesterday, when Cook baked it."

"But why won't you let me help you?" I asked him, perplexed.

He leaned over the stair-rail and explained, "Hadn't you guessed? I am a very shy fellow when it comes to my own flesh."

I laughed, because he doubtless expected me to, and besides, I was happy that he was in a good mood. A minute later I heard the creak of boards, as his footsteps passed overhead. Looking around for little signs that would give me a clue to Marc's true nature, I examined the room in which I stood, and more especially the good-sized window at one side of the room. Outside the window was a fairly clear view of enormous distances, only slightly cut off by the dormant branches of an old lilac bush. It was impressive, that view, but cold.

Closer to reality were several female portraits and one or two male sketches of local faces. These works of art were stacked idly, against a leg of the old deal table in the center of the room, or lying on an oversized bed or sofa under the window. On the sofa, still attached to a heavy board I took to be his easel, was one of the best and most revealing portraits, of a yellow-haired young girl with a common, but, I should imagine, enticing face. The creamy throat and breasts were bare. I should have resented the portrait more if I hadn't detected the same cynical artist's hand as appeared in the London sketch of Mrs. Fothergay. It was inconceivable that Marc could care for a woman whose sly appeal he caught so mercilessly.

Engrossed in my thoughts, I was startled unpleasantly by someone who was sneaking up behind me, and I turned, breathing fast, not knowing what to expect. It was only Jamie. I had not thought he could walk so silently.

"That'll be Abbie Hinchley, that there picture," Jamie told me as he started a smoldering fire among the peat, the dead tree limbs, and a bundle of ancient Yorkshire Posts. He used an outmoded little firemaker and managed so well it was obvious he had much experience in that line.

"Ye must pay no mind of Marc," he told me wisely. "Once he fair broke his arm catching me when I slipped off Heaton Bridge, but he wouldn't let me nor nobody put him to mends."

Jamie and I were pouring tea when Marc came down to join us, and I was forced to admit privately he had changed his blood-stained clothing, and taken care of a painful bandaging job, more rapidly than I should have been able to manage. Marc had much better color now and seemed quite fit. Taking up one of the ugly ale mugs we used for tea, he sat down on the sofa and gestured with his forefinger for me to join him. I wasn't sure what he had in mind by that gesture, which was accompanied by a look that had more influence over me than I cared to own.

"Me too?" suggested Jamie, trying to worm his way onto the side of Marc.

" 'You too' over on the hearth, my lad."

Jamie raised his tawny eyebrows, but did as he

was ordered. He sat there, however, watching us as we drank our tea.

"Ain't you going to kiss Miss Anne?" Jamie asked, somewhat puzzled by the extraordinary behavior of his idol.

I said quickly, "How nonsensical you are! I haven't said I'd kiss anyone. Do be serious, both of you. Why did you say I could assist you in some way, Marc?"

He shook his head and spoke to Jamie as though I were invisible.

"Such a head for business! One shudders for her dismal future. She will become the richest old unkissed lady in London."

"Well," said Jamie, joggling the tea grounds around in his mug. "I'd at least give it a try, that I would now."

As Marc appeared to think this reasonable and turned to me, I stiffened with apprehension. However, Marc removed the tea mug from my nervous fingers and brushed a kiss on my cheek. Then he calmly replaced my tea mug in my hand.

"Oh, poor stuff, that!" cried our audience disdainfully. "I'd do better if I was of a mind to do such mulling things."

"When your saucer-eyes are occupied with things more fitting to your age, I'll see to Miss Anne properly. Now, you've both had my tea and my bread, and Jamie, I see, has spice cakes which he's not had the politeness to offer us—"

"They're that hard, you'd break a tooth on un," Jamie excused himself, with his mouth full.

"—so you must pay me now," Marc finished. "I want it to be thought that I'm still inside the cottage, when, in point of fact, I shall be outside, observing the noctural habits of the local fauna."

So this was why he had gone to such lengths to make everyone believe he was alone here! I did not like the idea of being used.

"Ay, let's play at it!" cried Jamie, clapping his hands, one of which held a buttered piece of bread. "We'll make out your're here. . . . But how, Marc?"

"You, my boy, will not be seen at all. You must contrive to hide yourself in here. It will serve very well if there are no lamps to give you away. Just the distant glow on the hearth to suggest my presence inside—in outline, one might say."

"And I—" I guessed without enthusiasm—"am to be the outline of Marc Branshaw. Impossible." And insulting, too, I thought, to be suggested for a male role.

"Do you remember what I was doing to your hair earlier today? Can you sweep it back and somehow let the ends be covered by the collar of one of my hunting jackets?"

I said I supposed I could, but I felt little enthusiasm for the scheme.

"Because," he explained, "someone wishes it to appear that I'm capable of several brutal murders. When I'm alone in that chair across the room, at night, busy daubing, I am often watched. You will notice the window behind the chair. Sometimes I've heard sounds but have never been quick enough to catch my visitor. It's precisely upon these occasions that the Devil-Vicar is seen about the neighborhood—an hour or two later. And since I bear some resemblance to our late Clergyman, I know it is meant to appear that I am committing these crimes."

I glanced at Jamie, who was listening now in a perplexed way. I had a feeling that he still doubted, but was willing to accept any reasonable explanation.

"How could anyone be so fiendish?" I demanded,

only half believing that Marc's view of the world was the correct one.

"How else explain that the murders and these mysterious appearances of the Devil-Vicar have always occurred on the nights when I was alone here, so that I could never prove my innocence, should it be necessary? After all, there are many times when I have not been alone in this cottage." (He need not have mentioned that!) "Yet no apparitions are seen, no murders occur, when I have someone who can testify to my presence here. Consider! Every night that some sheep farmer, some frightened farm girl, reports having seen the Devil-Vicar floating about the moors, *I have been here alone.* It took me some time to read the signs and to decide that the mysterious sounds I have heard on those nights were not my imagination, but deliberate spying, to make sure I should not have a witness afterward."

I said hurriedly, "I think you're wrong in imagining that the people suspect you. If so, they would have had you up on charges before this."

"Oh no." His mouth twisted in sardonic humor. "You forget. They think I'm the Devil-Vicar's son. They murdered him upon flimsy evidence and they're not going to chance it with me. They do have consciences, of a sort. One day, of course, if I cannot find out the identity of my mysterious spy, they will have enough evidence. . . . That's why I asked you to help me. I thought of it that day in London when dear Bedelia mentioned that we might be brother and sister."

"And you want me to sit here and be spied upon while you are out—heaven knows where—and up to no good, I daresay."

There were times when I strongly suspected he did not hear me because he did not wish to.

"Come. Let's see. You aren't tall enough. No matter. I think if we raise your height somewhat—"

"Sit her on cushions," Jamie put in helpfully.

"Yes. I think, providing Jamie stays out of sight, near you in that dark corner beyond the window, we might satisfy a passerby that I was here as usual, sketching or painting."

I looked at the window. It was just high enough from the ground to accommodate a spying face. The notion of turning my back to it was exceedingly unwelcome to me.

"Why wouldn't your spy kill me, fancying I am you?"

"Because that's not his—or her—plan. I'm to be the culprit, not the victim."

"Oh, rubbish," Jamie said quickly. "Marc wouldn't let no one hurt you."

Marc had gotten up and begun to arrange an old, heavily upholstered chair, whose insides were already spilled upon the floor. He placed it just far enough into the room so that a man peering into the large window might see the outlines of the person in the chair. I liked it less and less.

"Jamie, you sit on a pillow in the corner. See to it that the fire is kept low so that it doesn't illuminate you. In that position, you may make out anything at the window without being seen. It's not at all certain that the spy will come tonight. Still, it's well to make our plans."

"I foresee that I shall spend an exciting evening," I prophesied "Either nothing will happen, and I'll have sat a whole evening in a dark room, or—even more charming—I will have been the target for some monster because he fancies I'm you. Delightful entertainment you offer your guests, Mr. Branshaw."

Marc laughed at that. "Good work. You're in

a pleasant humor again."

"Stuff and nonsense!" I said stiffly.

During our banter Jamie had grown thoughtful. He tugged at his friend's hand finally.

"It wasn't you but t'Other One I seen on the heath the night of the Gytrash?"

Marc looked at the boy and raised his chin with one hand.

"I am not the Gytrash, Jamie. Is that what you were thinking?"

Jamie swallowed convulsively.

"I—I never thought so. . . . Only that ye was maybe—worse."

"Good heavens!" I demanded crossly. "What could be worse?" I had begun to rearrange my hair, because I felt I should be a shabby thing indeed if I failed to cooperate, but I was nervous of the whole stratagem.

"Well . . ." Jamie murmured, avoiding his eyes. "Only—t'Other One's dead."

"What does he mean?" I asked, fearing the worst.

"He's talking nonsense, aren't you, boy?"

Jamie bit his lip and appeared to consider. When he looked up at me, he was fairly reassured. "Ay, mum. It's nonsense. Aunt Rose says so too. Only, I saw . . ."

"Yes, Jamie?" his mentor prompted him very softly.

"Nothing." The boy finished his tea in a great gulp, which appeared to revive his flagging spirits, and he became eager to go at fooling whatever it was they expected to come prowling about the cottage.

By the time they had arranged me absurdly in the chair, with my back to the window, they seemed as pleased with themselves as two children. I said stonily, "You realize, of course, Mr. Branshaw, that this gives you considerable more freedom yourself, for you are the only one who can be said to have been in two places at once."

"Very profound. Lean a little forward. There's the girl—just so." He had made me change to another one of his hunting coats, and now turned the collar still farther up to disguise the nape of my neck.

When he had finished re-arranging my clothing, he knelt before my chair to view the results. Then he covered my hands in my lap with his own and looked up into my eyes. Whatever influence he had over Jamie, I could feel now in his effect upon me. He was desperately sincere. What his motives were, I could not perceive, but I did believe him when he grasped my hands in his anxiety to make me understand.

"Anne, no one knows better than I that you're being treated abominably. But you must do this thing for me. *You must.*"

"Did you bring me clear up to Yorkshire for this?"

"I did, and stole your manuscript as well. I swear to you there's no danger, as long as you stay indoors. You don't think I'd risk your life and Jamie's do you? Do you?"

I did think so, for I was half afraid my confidence in him was bolstered only by his presence. He let go of my hands and took my face between his palms. Before I knew what he was about to do, he kissed me, and in a way Jamie could not possibly have improved upon. Behind Marc I heard Jamie catch his breath, but the warm, pulsing effect of Marc's lips on mine, and my own response, drowned out any further thoughts of Jamie for a minute or two.

He looked into my eyes then and murmured a little huskily, "I knew it would be so."

This curious remark left me with nothing to say, even if I had the strength to say it, but Jamie was prepared for anything.

"Is she better to kiss than the ladies in your paintings?"

Marc's fingers moved gently along the line of my cheek. He did not look at Jamie as he spoke.

"She's not like ladies in paintings, Jamie. My Irish love has a soul. And Anne," he added simply, "it was not only to get you up here for this purpose that I wanted you. I'm sorry I've teased you, but you are such a happy subject."

I studied my hands in embarrassment, and Marc slapped them in parting, before he left us by the low-hung door to the peat room. He said in the doorway:

"Remember, keep the door bolted and don't venture out, whatever you see or think you see. Ten to one it'll be imaginary. And in any case, I shall be close by. Jamie, you'll watch over Miss Anne. And Jamie, when I've gone, remember to make sure every door is bolted, including the laithe and the mistal. Then take out the gun we used for the grouse. Just be quite sure it's not me you're aiming at."

I said lightly, "Now, that would be a fitting end to this nonsense."

He laughed, and a moment later was gone.

A pity I hadn't asked him what Jamie should do if the spy he did *not* expect should shoot me through that accursed window! I decided that he would only have talked me out of my fears as he convinced Mrs. Fothergay and so many others. Was he no more sincere with me than with them?

Still, I had a warm memory that I felt instinctively Mrs. Fothergay and the others had not known. I could forgive him much for those few moments.

"Ah," cried Jamie mysteriously, "we're waiting—Spies and All Such! Come now and face your match."

"I'll thank you not to encourage All Such," I said, only half joking.

Jamie scoffed. "Don't be cow-hearted, mum."

Alas! To borrow Jamie's elegant phrase, that is precisely what I was—cow-hearted—for I could not rid myself of the notion that already there were eyes peering at my exposed back.

XI

JAMIE BUSIED HIMSELF bolting doors throughout the house and outbuildings, creating such a furor that I should not have been surprised if we would find it more difficult to get out than intruders to get in. With tremendous energy he ran upstairs and rattled around with the dormer window and one or two other places unknown to me.

He came down presently, waving something in the air which could only be a female's white cotton stocking, worked with peculiar pink clocks. "Belong 'a' Abbie Hinchley," he informed me with airy indifference. "Marc's going to be that cross! He told her not to take off her things here."

"Not to!" I repeated in surprise. "I thought . . . that is . . ."

"Oh no. Not Marc. Sir Gareth in town, he does them things now and again, and I hear Miss Catherine saying 'tis wicked, but Marc—he laughs at them and says when he's through with putting them on the canvas, they're no more use to him." He cocked his head to one side and regarded the stocking with interest. "They get mad as fire, but though Marc kisses them, it's not like he kissed you. Not with me about."

"Very obliging of him, I'm sure." Nevertheless, I could have kissed Jamie himself for the news.

"Now I think on't, I best be burning the thing. Marc'll be cross if he knew you saw it."

"More like him to flaunt it in my face, thinking it a very funny joke."

"May be. But he told me he'd met *the* girl when he was down London way. You don't think he could maybe mean the old lady with the big hat, do you? For he laughs at her. Marc does."

"Very likely. . . . What else did he say about meeting *the* girl in London?"

Jamie scratched his head with the stocking.

"Very odd-sounding it was. Said he was like Nar-Narcis . . . them posies . . . that he'd feel like them if he fell in love with this girl, but he didn't care a farthing for that. You make a sense a that?"

I hoped I read it right, but explaining it to Jamie was something else. I was feeling a little more confident of Marc's behavior to me, and blessed Jamie for it.

"Narcissus was a . . . well . . . call him a Greek. He fell in love with his own reflection in a pool."

"Oh." Jamie's mouth made a big circle and he tossed the stocking into the fire in the most careless way, but I don't think he quite understood me yet, and I had no mind to explain further. I thought it rather delicate and charming of Marc to put his interest in me, if he was sincere, in the form of such a mythological parable.

"Coming on dark, mum. I'll sit here like Marc said. No. Don't you move. You're to sit still. What a shabby thing if there be no spy at all!"

I did not agree, but I could see that nothing would convince a boy of Jamie's age that peace and quiet were preferable to weird eyes peering in at one's undefended back.

Having attended to his chores, Jamie sat down in the corner, facing me so that he might keep one eye on that horrendous window behind me. I had a brief glimpse of it when I turned, Jamie not having his warder's eye on me at that moment, and one glimpse was really all I needed. Outside, the dusk had become black as peat, and I remembered too well the great open space there, the hint of another, unhuman, world that lay behind us in every direction. The darker it grew, the more I sensed that world was pressing in upon us, and what more natural entrance could it gain than the window behind me?

Jamie settled comfortably, rubbing his bottom, which had apparently received the full impact of the snapping fire.

"I'm that pleased Marc likes you," he said. "He laughs, but I don't think he likes many folk. He said there was one he liked once, but then they were only friends after. He said he'd learned ever after not to give himself, but only what they wanted."

"And what did he think they wanted?"

"Well now . . . that I don't rightly know. He said I was never to give my soul away, but to give them what they wants, he said. I asked him what that was, but he said when the time come I'd know."

I refrained from expressing my disapproval of Jamie's education at the hands of a *roué* like Marc Branshaw.

He read something in my face that I hadn't intended to show.

"You've no call to look so, Miss Anne. He says you've a soul . . . he thinks. He must find it out, he said. Do you now?"

"Yes, I have a soul," I said crossly. "But whether

I shall reveal it to Marc Branshaw, I haven't the least notion."

"Ay. Sometimes you talk and act just like Marc. No wonder you're good friends. I thought maybe Miss Catherine might have a soul, but Marc says she's a silly one, loving what don't be real. Howsomever, he was kind to Miss Catherine till I told him what I'd heard."

"What you'd heard?"

"Her walking, I mean to say. Aunt Rose says to hush up, that the doctor says it ain't so. But I heard 'em say it was Miss Catherine—ever trying to walk when no one was about. The servants say she tried it now and again. And crying over a stupid handkerchief she found. It was the Devil-Vicar's, Marc says."

I was chilled to the marrow.

"You mean—someone saw Miss Catherine walking?"

"Well . . . Aunt Rose says it's the same as me seeing the Gytrash. I didn't see that, of course. But I said I did. I knew it'd be better'n truth."

"Wait. One thing at a time. You say *someone* saw Miss Catherine walking. And you did *not* see a Gytrash?"

"Well now, not like that, mum. Myself, I never seen Miss Catherine walking. It's only the talk. And the Gytrash was no beast but on a sudden become some-ut like them robes that's worn in the church. Like maybe it was . . . t'Other One."

"What other one?"

His big blue yes looked up at me, round and innocent. "But the Devil-Vicar, mum."

"Never mind that. You saw Miss Catherine walking?"

"Well now, as to that, it's not certain. It's whispered. She's trying to walk so's to meet the Devil-

Vicar—that's the tale the lads tell, because they never knew a lady that couldn't walk after such a little thing as tugging another out of a bog-hole. . . . Watch, mum, when you sit back. The spy, he can see in and see you're not Marc."

In panic, I glanced over my shoulder, but Jamie leaned forward and grabbed my shoulder.

"You'll drive it away! Marc wants it to come."

I tried to restrain my mingled terror and anger that Marc should expose this child and me to such preposterous horrors.

"Listen to me, Jamie. The Devil-Vicar has been dead for twenty years."

"Sixteen," he cut in politely.

"All right. Sixteen. What is left of him is buried in the rubble of the old parsonage. Dead people do not walk at night. Or any other time!"

"Then what's Miss Catherine in love with?"

"With Marc Branshaw, that's what."

Jamie considered, but shook his head.

"It weren't no Gytrash I saw on the heath that night. It was—like I said. The robes and all."

"And you called it a Gytrash because you were afraid someone you liked, Marc, or Miss Catherine, might be implicated in the death of the old sheep farmer. That's the whole story, isn't it?"

"Ay."

"Then why were you afraid of that dog today?"

"But mum, I wasn't afeered of poor old Chaffer. I used to run with that old dog. Only he was sick now, and savage. When he crawled to Marc, it was like the days of the Devil-Vicar they tell of. And just there for a little, I thought maybe Marc had the soul of the Devil-Vicar. Or maybe the other way round. For Marc is cross with me at times. One time he's Marc, my friend; another time he's like somebody else—like t'Other One."

"Some people are very moody. Marc is like that."

The boy's pointed concentration on the window behind me was frightfully unnerving. I found myself watching his face for a telltale expression of sudden interest or fear, but it remained its eager young self. I considered what he had told me, especially the appalling notion that Miss Catherine's injury might be the cover under which she committed crimes.

"Jamie, what precisely did you see the night you were looking for your stray sheep?"

"Just at first it was dun-colored, like I said. It leaped fast-like into the bracken. I caught a glimpse of fur—red or dun-color. But then, when I hid behind a rock and looked again, and it was far off, I saw a great, floating white sleeve, like the Devil-Vicar's in the painting at the church. And it moved away. But you're not to think it was a real beast. It was a thing that turns from a beast to a man—or a lady. It turned after I saw it first and lost it. When I saw it later, far off, it was t'Other One."

"Really, Jamie, I do think you have the most extraordinary imagination. Miss Catherine cannot walk—both your aunt and the doctor say so. And as for what you saw that night, you must make up your mind to one thing or the other. Either you saw a beast or you saw a person. You didn't see one change into the other."

He paid no heed to me. His jaw had fallen and he was staring hard over my head. I felt myself beginning to tense again, and wondered what I should do if he actually did see something at that window.

"What is it?" I whispered.

"Hush."

We were as silent as in the tomb.

Presently he relaxed. The most annoying thing was his quick giggle at his own precautions.

" 'Twas the lilac bush. No more'n that. And here's me thinking it was maybe the Devil-Vicar."

I felt like booting him for the scare he had given me, but it was by no means his last such mistake of the evening.

It must have been near nine or ten o'clock when Jamie, looking up from the chessboard he was studying in the corner, to some point I had learned to ignore above my head, lowered his glance quickly and was silent. This time he had seen more than just a lilac bush at the window. Full realization stunned me. Damn that Marc Branshaw! I thought. What shall we do now?

"What is it out there?" I whispered nervously.

He said, "It was there and then gone. Kind of a face. Not too close. I can't make it out."

"Is it still there?"

"I think so, but back. Not too close. Trying to look in, I daresay."

"I daresay. What are we to do now?"

His eyes sparkled. "Better than the circus in Bradford! Wait till Marc finds we've seen the thing."

"He'll find our bodies alongside it, I don't doubt."

"Oh, Miss Anne, you're poor spirited! It's adventure, like the storybooks."

"I know. I'm cow-hearted."

He grinned and whispered a little louder, "That's it. Make out you've no notion it's out there."

"Is it still there?"

He shifted his glance above my head, then looked casually around the room.

"Just the hand. The fingers, pressing against the window."

"Good God!" I said. "How long must we sit here?"

I felt so jumpy that I did not know if I should be able to remain in this position without screaming or turning around, or doing something else rash and foolish. I tried, with faint success, to recover. "What—what kind of hands? Are they big or small? A man's or a woman's?"

"Can't say. Oh. They're gone. But he's there. Back a way, I'm thinking."

I did not know whether to rejoice that our caller might be departing, or begin to worry about the various locks and bolts in this isolated farmhouse.

"Is it still there?"

"Wait. I can see its shadow. Now I can't. Oh, it's gone!" He seemed terribly put out at this news, which I could only greet with relief. "I wonder now, does Marc know it's been and gone? Maybe we should let Marc—"

This sort of thing was precisely what our night caller would like, no doubt, and the very thing Marc had taken pains to warn us of.

"It can't be Marc himself we hear?"

Jamie shook his head. "Listen. I know Marc's footsteps, and they're lighter than this. Ay, and quicker too." He listened with his ear against the door. "It's going away. I can hear the steps."

"Good!" I said with gusto. "Now let Marc follow the creature and we're rid of both of them."

"I do think we ought to tell Marc. Maybe he don't know."

"Have you taken leave of your senses? You'll stay snug in this room or know the reason why!"

He grinned, not the least frightened of me.

"You talk like Aunt Rose. But Marc's got to know, so he can track un." He gave this some thought while I was edging back into the shadows under the window to see if I could satisfy myself that no gleaming eyes or groping hands remained there to haunt me. At that angle, of course, I still saw nothing. Our visitor should have been halfway down to the glen by this time.

Jamie said thoughtfully, "Marc must be about. If I could get track of the spy and show un to Marc . . ."

"Well, you can't, so sit down and mind your elders!"

"Miss Anne, don't you care if we lose the track?"

"Not if it means going out in the night when we were expressly forbidden to do so."

He looked at me with admiration.

"I'd no notion you're so biddable to what Marc says. You'll make him a good wife, that you will."

Already, he was edging across the room to the door of the peat stores. Suddenly, he stopped. For the first time this evening it was he who was petrified, stiff with apprehension. It must have been the strange bird-call I too heard in the near distance.

"Gorm! Hear that!"

Across the desolate emptiness of the moors enclosing us, the sound came to us once more, plaintive now, almost like a human cry.

"It's one of those moor birds, isn't it?" I ventured hopefully. "Those curlews, or whatever they are."

"No, no, mum. They're earlier in the season. And they're nothing the sound of that. That's a man."

I stood up in one panic-stricken motion.

"What can be happening to him?"

"The bogs, mum. He's trapped in the bogs. When they're trapped so, they make sounds—different—you know it in a minute!"

The sound came again, a hideous, wailing, dying away on the immense open spaces.

"But we must do something!"

"Suppose . . ." He turned to me, his eyes wide. "Suppose he's the one was at the window."

That gave me pause.

"Well, can it be false? Can he be making that sound to lure us out for some reason?"

"Oh, no. It's the sound of a trapped man. I know it well, mum. We had a man from Scarborough over, searching for queer bones and such, from days afore our own. He went down like that, with just such a sound."

"Did you save him?"

"Ay. But he was dead, poor soul. . . . There it is again, mum."

I did not know what to do. I was absolutely sure that in any other circumstances we should remain locked indoors. But I knew too that neither Marc nor I had counted on this kind of life-and-death disturbance. I should never forgive myself if we let a human being die in such horrible plight, without putting forth the effort to save him.

"Why must they fall into bogs in the middle of the night?" I demanded of Jamie, who hadn't the least notion. "Why can't it be in bright daylight? At noon!"

Jamie took this for assent to the rescue and ran for his coat and a hunting rifle belonging to Marc. Being an exceptionally provident boy, he also arrived on the scene a minute later with a coil of rope and a storm lantern of no mean proportions.

"Best I go through the laithe," he suggested in a low voice. "If the Thing is about the cottage, it's best I know afore it sees me."

I could not have agreed with him more. Even now I was ready to hold him back, for I had been listening and heard nothing more. I could not help telling myself that the first cries had been a bird of some sort, or even an animal unfamiliar to Jamie. I wanted to believe that with all my heart.

At the last, I volunteered to go with Jamie but was voted down. Jamie seemed bound to act in place of Marc Branshaw and I was amused at his orders, and his assurance that "Marc wouldn't never forgive me if any harm was to come to you, mum."

"I suppose it's quite all right if you should be swallowed up in some evil bog?"

"Who? Me?" Jamie scoffed at the idea.

I decided, however, that he might be right about checking the bolts, and followed him through the dark pet stores, which smelled of plant decay and fresh earth. Beyond, we passed through a barn of sorts. This had a door broken and open to the elements. Upon Jamie's advice, I retreated to the peat room, shot the bolt, and returned to the "houseroom" of the main building, dropping the bolt on the peat room door and checking the one at the front.

Then I sat down to wait. I suppose I was intimidated by Marc's instructions for I sat exactly as he had told me and, having nothing better to do, I picked up Marc's canvas of Abbie Hinchley and studied it. I could hardly be jealous of the shabby, overblown charms of the girl, but beyond that it seemed to me there was a calculating, cruel quality in those small, protuberant, pale eyes.

I stopped now and again to listen, but heard nothing more except the roar of the wind as it whipped the lilac bush against the window. I started to throw down the portrait of Abbie and, in doing so, saw a sheet of paper fall from the frame where it had been stuck, either for safekeeping or to get it out of the way.

It was a torn half-page of letter and, since it was

open and lying before my eyes, I saw no reason why I should not read it.

—boy's description, I should say, you have been subject to an attack of some severity. My dear Branshaw, these things are not to be shrugged off. One day, such an attack may well be your death, for others may not know the symptoms, nor how to treat them. Permit me to say that your fear of personal examination is beyond my comprehension. I can only call it fear—and a cowardly one—that you should shun a doctor who is as much a part of this countryside as your family were. Trust me, Branshaw. I may be able to help you, more than you guess.

You fancy that it is strength that gives you this energy. Believe me, it is more likely to be a kind of nervous compulsion and will inevitably lead to one attack too many.

Your obedient servant,
James Lowther.

I wondered at this warning, hoping that Marc had taken it seriously, but before I could think too much about it, I saw the charcoal sketch on the back of the letter. I should say *sketches;* for, to my overwhelming surprise and delight, I saw my own face down over a half dozen ways, with as many expressions, and as I examined all these little sketches, I was touched to see that his stick of charcoal had been much gentler than my mirror. One of the sketches nearly made me laugh aloud. It was my face as seen by Marc through the long, narrow window of my London house—frowning, frightened, but with something wistful and young in its expression which I am quite sure only Marc would have observed, for I had felt neither young nor tender at the moment.

Another sketch was almost insulting, if one had no

sense of humor. There I was, looking exactly as though waiting to be kissed, as I sat on my bed the previous night and he so rudely disappointed me. Even in this, though, he had put into my features a kind of endearing quality which only he saw, and I was more touched than I had been, even by Jamie's comment that Marc had liked me as long ago as the London encounter. This was clearer proof than mere word. I could have kissed the sketches for what they revealed of his feelings about me.

I thought of something then. Had Marc gone directly from the inn last night, and his encounter with me, to spend the night in this out-of-the-way place, instead of at home in Branshaw Hall? Did he never sleep? And if he hated the moors as much as he pretended, why was he always to be found, like one of the moorland creatures, alone in its great silences?

The world about me had been still for several minutes. Now the wind, dying down, made me aware of many sounds outside that I had not previously noticed. I wondered how the lilac bush could make those scuffling noises, like boots on gravel. Keeping my head forward, as though I were studying the painting of Abbie Hinchley, I listened. Behind me, outside that window, were sounds other than the lilac bush trembling in the now somnolent wind. There was no mistake this time. A body, perhaps that of an animal, had jarred against the wall of the cottage.

There it was again. Something approaching the window—cautious, but making mistakes in the darkness. My heart thudded, and to calm myself, I kept thinking.

"It must be Marc. Or Jamie. Yes. Of course. Jamie might do something like this—a boy, thinking it very funny to frighten me. . . ."

But I could not quite convince myself.

I raised the big portrait of Abbie and turned just a fraction, with the portrait concealing my face, as though I sought to study the portrait from a different angle. I was just able to see the vague outlines of something at the window. The face was not pressed against the glass as I had expected, but it was far off—a kind of floating thing that I could not identify—yet I knew it had not been there before. It was watching me.

Casually, I kept the portrait before my face and moved back into my original position, frantic with fear for my exposed back. What was it out there? If I had not known better, I should have said it was dun-color, as Jamie claimed when he saw the Gytrash change into the Devil-Vicar. But that was nonsense. This was no animal staring in at me. What animal was so large that it could peer in at that high window?

There were no fingers this time, nothing telltale. Only that floating, curious thing that might be a face, far back from the window. I sat stiff and silent, waiting.

Marc! I thought . . . Why don't you come and catch this thing? Where are you? Take it away!

It was too horrid. Suppose it vanished and Marc did not discover what it was? Suppose Marc was not looking in this direction now and missed it altogether? Using the portrait as a shield, I stole another glance.

The thing was gone now—swallowed up in the immense dark outside. Then I heard it again, pressing close against the house, moving around through the overgrown nettles toward the front of the cottage.

No. It must be Marc. The other thing I heard, the screams from the bog, they were the creature we feared. After all, hadn't Jamie seen it at the window? What was I thinking of? I opened my mouth to call Marc, and stopped myself just in time. Heavens! I must be growing hysterical. What harm could come to me in here? Why, the doors were all bolted and a stout poker would do considerable harm to anyone who broke in through the window.

The thing outside brushed sharply against the wall, so close to me that it seemed almost in the room. Without being able to control the sound, I cried out, then hushed, with my hand over my mouth, waiting. Had my involuntary cry given me away as a woman? I could hardly imagine Marc crying out like that.

While I watched, with every emotion suspended within me, the latch on the door moved up and down, and again, gently. Then a push, testing the strength of the bolt. This time I screamed, very loud. Surely, Marc would come. Where in the name of heaven was he!

After my scream, the thing outside no longer feared to make a noise, and the door rattled furiously. Then there was a pause.

I thought with a twisted humor: "I must tell Jamie. Gytrashes rarely try the latch of a door. It takes human beings for such refinements.

I rushed to the fire and was about to pick up the poker when I saw the long barrel of a shotgun behind the sofa. I took it out, not knowing what to do with it, but assuming that its mere presence and size would be enough to give an intruder pause. Behind me, there was a terrific crash against the door—a crash, I thought, that could not have been made by a human being.

Silence followed, and I stood still with terror. The creature was moving along the house to the shed, the barn, the storeroom—any of which was less sturdy than the front door. I listened. Yes. Already he had gotten into the peat room. The door beside the fireplace was being tried, stealthily. It would not take long to come through that frail and ancient barrier.

I called out, shrill as a harpy, "What do you want? I have a gun. I shall fire." And then, in a voice that broke with my terror, "*Who are you?*"

The peat room door, which had trembled under an onslaught, was suddenly still.

I did not wait longer. Somewhere outside were Marc and Jamie. They were my only hope. Frantic to put space between myself and this monster, I shot back the bolt of the front door and then, with the gun in my trembling hands, stepped out onto the moors.

XII

NEVER IN MY LIFE had I been so keenly aware of the hostile and unknown space around me. The stars were under fleecy clouds and the entire firmament was momentarily shrouded in Stygian darkness.

I sped over the ground, careful to step where the nettles tugged at my skirts rather than where the ground seemed easier on my feet but was more treacherous. I was aware of being, for the first time, a part of the infinite world of the moors where, for miles in every direction, there might be no human being except myself and the thing that had driven me out.

I seemed to be beyond the sound of the blows at the peat room door, or perhaps they had stopped. I found myself on the worn sheep trail we had taken up to the cottage so long ago this afternoon. There was no shelter ahead of me for several minutes, until I should reach the beginnings of the bog where Moyna Branshaw had received her mortal injuries. This made me completely visible as I ran, for there were no trees in sight.

I had run for several minutes, keeping close watch on the narrow sheep track, when I heard, from the direction of Moyna's cottage, a fierce and savage growl. It sounded like one of those enormous moor dogs, so useful with sheep. The barking was interrupted by several peculiar, piercing yelps. I tried to run faster. Then I fancied I heard winging sounds of pursuit behind me. In the great dark of the night, I was sure I heard the sounds of the Devil-Vicar—the great sleeves like wings on the wind, the skirts of a robe flying out as the thing hurried after me. I knew I should never outrun it. Faster, and faster came the sounds behind me.

The particular sounds at last parted from the roar of the wind, and they became the even tread of a four-footed beast. I could not believe this. Even the intruder at Moyna's cottage had had human sound, had displayed human characteristics. I cast a terrified glance over my shoulder and paused, involuntarily, dead-tired, and almost frozen with horror. It was a four-footed beast, and no mistake—a great, dark beast whose rough, thick-coated silhouette loomed up behind me on the horizon, rushing ever closer and closer. I began to run again but, in my mounting panic, tripped over a root in my path and fell headlong into the black heather. I covered my face with my hands, the long-barrelled shotgun wavering overhead. I had some feeble notion of using it to ward off the beast—the Gytrash, I reminded myself, still half-unbelieving.

I could hear the awful thump of its paws upon the

ground, skimming along, until at last it shook the earth under me and the great creature came to a pause. Fearing the worst, my hands clutched the shotgun and I waited. I was prepared for a sudden leap and the tearing of my flesh by the fangs of the beast. But what I received was quite a different sensation. The beast came close upon me, halted, and sniffed around my face and head curiously. I made no move. The animal, which I now perceived to be a large, red-haired dog, satisfied his curiosity and was about to proceed upon its way when it paused again, standing almost at point, listening. Cautiously, I raised my head and watched it. The dog's dark eyes were focussed upon the darkness out of which it had raced. The beast, I understood at last, was as frightened as I of something in the direction of Moyna's cottage.

Apparently hearing what was silent to my own ears, it took off again on a tearing run down the slope, and headed to what I imagined must be its home among the sheep farmers on the moors. I only wished I might take such speed myself, for if this big beast were frightened, I saw no reason to be brave.

I got to my feet and ran straight down the long, steep hill, hoping against hope that somewhere in the night I should meet Marc Branshaw, or Jamie at the least. Since the earlier sounds of the man caught in the bog had come from this direction, it was my only chance.

The bogs, with their wonderful cover of foliage, presented also my greatest danger. I paused to get my breath and to see if I could hear any sounds of pursuit, but the wind managed to conceal any hint of the thing which had been separated from me only by the wall of Moyna's cottage.

I took the sheep track again, for I could make out the faint light from the window of a sheep-farmer's cottage, not far up the trail. As I hurried by, keeping to the center track so that nothing hidden in those boggy depths should snatch at me, I saw the signs of a recent struggle.

The mudbank had given way, its cohesiveness thinned by the late rains, so that the unfortunate traveler, whoever he might be, had slipped. His struggles to free himself from the entangling bushes, water-soaked foliage, and the filth of centuries, must have served but to draw him further into the slime. Great chunks of the mudbank had broken off afresh. But I was not so concerned with this evidence as I was over the problem of Jamie's disappearance. It was plain, whatever the discomfort of the traveler who had fallen into the bog, that he had been dragged out and was doubtless safe. I wanted to know what had become of his rescuer, as I took Jamie to be.

Close by in the thickness of the trees I heard the bubbling, gurgling noise of the bog, and paused, wondering what caused that unpleasant sound. Then I heard faint squeals, telltale sounds of a tiny moor animal in distress. I winced, wishing I might be of help, but when I took a step into the darkness and felt the yielding turf underfoot, I realized I would have to leave the poor creature to its hideous fate.

There was a choice of several sheep-tracks now. I took the one that appeared most heavily trodden. When I made my way beyond the bogs, it was faster going and, although I could now be seen by a pursuer, I could also see behind me. Nothing moved except the nettle and bracken, drifting with the wind. The sounds of the tiny moorland animal died away. In a few minutes I was at the door of the low, one-

and-a-half-story cottage somewhat off the main track up to Wind-Rock. I was just about to knock when, to my amazement, Jamie appeared beside me, coming around from the barn. He looked me up and down.

"You shouldn't have left the cottage, mum. Marc'll be that cross. Sir Gareth fell in a bog and near drowned, he did. It was him we heard calling. But Marc saved him. I followed the trail him and Marc made coming up here to the cottage. Marc said I was to stay by Sir Gareth, just in case he needed me."

"Oh, he did! Naturally, Sir Gareth would need you more than I, beseiged by monsters and Devil-Vicars and I don't know what all! And is Mr. Branshaw here too, by chance?" I went on angrily.

Behind us, the cottage door had opened and a farmer stood in the doorway, trying to discover what was all this noise at his front step.

"Come in, come in," he said, more crossly than enthusiastically. He proved to be a lean, grizzled specimen of rugged manhood, with piercing gray eyes. His wife, from what I could see through the slit of light revealed by the half-open door, was a strong-armed, sturdy woman who looked formidable even in her present state of undress.

"May as well," she muttered, adding her gracious invitation to that of her husband.

I found myself in a low-roofed cozy room, where Sir Gareth was fastening a coat that fitted narrowly in the shoulders while the farmer's breeches, which were homespun and home-cut, did not suit the airs of the baronet at all, and I was hard put not to smile at the sight.

"Damnable impertinence," he was muttering. "I could have gone on with Branshaw. But no, he had to leave me here—to dry out, he said. Dry out, indeed. What's the man up to? Where was he off to in such a hurry that he could not await me?"

"He saved your life," Jamie put in loyally. "I'd never have reached you in time. It was great sport, Miss Anne. Marc saw Sir Gareth a-peeking in the windows of the cottage and followed him. Then he heard Sir Gareth scream when he fell in the bog."

"I was not 'peeking in' as you put it," the baronet said sharply. "I thought, if he weren't in the cottage, I might stop in and borrow a glass of something to heat me on my way. I'd come all the way over from Upshed to help them tree that savage mongrel, but I lost my way. And I was in no good mood when I reached Moyna's cottage, I can tell you. Especially finding Branshaw at home."

"Why didn't you stop?" I asked, remembering how he had frightened us earlier in the evening.

"What? And pass the time of day with that rascal? Thanks. I prefer to have as little to do with the pup as I can. I saw him in there and—but pardon, ma'am. He was wearing the jacket you have on. Is it possible it was you I saw? Then how was it he came so quickly when I slipped into that accursed bog?"

"Because," Jamie told him in triumph, before I could shake my head at him, "Marc was watching the cottage. And when he saw you hanging about, he followed you. He thinks you're the Devil-Vicar, the Gytrash. Are you?"

"Oh, Gad, no! I've better things to do, I can tell you, than go about in sheets, frightening women and curly-headed tots."

I was studying the faces of the people before me, wondering if I should mention the creature who had visited Moyna's cottage after Jamie left. It seemed to me now that if I told them of my encounter they would connect it at once with Marc Branshaw, who had delivered Sir Gareth to the farmer's house and then vanished. Sometime shortly after that, I heard the unknown and monstrous intruder around Moyna's cottage. The creature was going softly, perhaps only spying, until I made the mistake of crying out, thus informing it that I was not Marc Branshaw. I reasoned that the creature, discovering I was not Marc, feared I had seen it at the window or guessed its identity—and that I must be destroyed like Abbie Hinchley and Will Grimlett. But then, the pounding on the doors mysteriously stopped when I asked the question which I now believed had saved my life: "Who are you?"

This was all conjecture. Only one coherent thought leaped out of the terrors of tonight. Either Marc was lying from the beginning, or the creature had done as Marc predicted: it had tried to commit its crimes at precisely the time and place which left Marc with no defense. It was better to say nothing of all this to people whose minds would undoubtedly behave as Marc had predicted they would upon hearing fresh coincidences that bound him with the terror of the countryside.

While the farmer's wife brewed us some hot tea, Sir Gareth announced that, come what may, he was going past Wind-Rock and back to Maidenmoor tonight. I admitted I should prefer that, without explaining that I felt we might all be terrorized if we returned to Moyna's cottage. That was a story I would tell Marc alone so that we could make his defenses against accusation.

We set out, Jamie carrying Marc's rifle, Sir Gareth the shotgun which had proved so useless to me, and I, at my own insistence, carrying Jamie's lantern. I wanted to be absolutely sure of where we were going.

It was a trifle lighter, with more stars out, when we reached Wind-Rock and I paused to get my breath. Even Sir Gareth found the slippery, twisting journey more than he had bargained for. While Jamie waited a little impatiently, scuffing at the growth of dead heather in the path, the baronet heaved a sigh and propped his tall body against the Wind-Rock entrance.

"What a curious thing, sir," I remarked to him, "that your accident should occur so near that which led to Mrs. Branshaw's death, and your sister's misfortune."

"Well, don't be saying it's divine retribution!" said Sir Gareth acidly, "for I'd nothing to do with that, I assure you. Although I might have been tempted, sometimes. Moyna did have a way of making one think she might yield, and then when one expected her to— At any rate, she could turn from devil to nun in a moment. But I daresay she lost the one love of her life and just wanted to torment the rest of us. Gad! She told Catherine just the day before she died that she had one particular heart on a string, and had just discovered she'd kept it for fifteen years. Thought it extremely funny. Or so Cathie says."

"What did she mean by 'just discovered?' "

"Who shall say? Queer girl, Moyna." He added after a moment, "Don't imagine she was talking of me, pray, Miss Wicklow. As I told Cathie, the cream of the jest was that, in a sense, it might have been a female's heart she kept on a string. Perhaps she knew a secret that would hurt some female who . . . well, an enterprising man might make something profitable of that. We'll never know now."

I was heartily glad when we reached the gray cobbles of Maidenmoor, but on the fog-washed stoop of the Owen house we were met by the Owen maid servant. She was a prim, humorless woman in night curlers and a shapeless flannel robe, who beckoned to us with one hand while the other clutched the high neck of her robe. She said sourly:

"Miss Catherine's been askin' after ye. She's been up since all hours, poor lamb, worrit sick for fear ye'd fallen in a bog or the like, Mister Gareth."

"Good Lord!" Gareth exclaimed. "Well, we're for it now." He glanced down at his borrowed finery. "No explaining away that wretched farmer's raiment."

Behind the maid, in the narrow, dour hall of the old stone house, I made out the shape of Catherine Owen in a wheelchair. She waved to us. I wanted very much to get home to my icy bed in the Yorkish Lion, but there is no denying my curiosity about this woman had been piqued by the gossip of Jamie's friends, that she was trying to walk. Catherine took my hand in her familiar, pleasant way, remarking that I must be dreadfully chilled and then asking her brother what he meant by keeping me out until all hours.

"What a buzz the village will be in, Garrie! How could you be so thoughtless? I suppose you lost your way again."

"It was all the fault of that Branshaw pup," he told her. "If I'd known he wasn't indoors, I'd have stopped. How was I to know he'd follow me? As though I were a damned sharper!"

"He did save your life, sir," I pointed out, but Catherine was looking from one to the other of us in a puzzled way. "Sir Gareth fell in a bog," I explained, "and Mr. Branshaw rescued him."

"I'm afraid I must be frightfully dense. I don't understand how Marc could have been in Moyna's cottage, and still be here in Maidenmoor tonight."

If the roof had fallen upon me, I could not have been more astonished. That is to say, astonishment was my first reaction. The burning fury came afterward.

Sir Gareth contradicted her, but without my cause for emotion.

"Come now, Cathie, what's this? I saw the man myself. Saved my life, I'm bound to admit—but he did it in no friendly tone, I can tell you. Acted as though he thought I were a murderer or something equally nasty. He almost threw me back in."

"Then why isn't he with you now?" asked his sister patiently.

"Why he—he said there was something he must attend to, and off he went. Good Lord!"

"Just as I say," Catherine went on. "He returned to the village."

Leaving Jamie with a man he suspected of being a murderer, and me in Moyna's desolate cottage, the prey of all sorts of wandering intruders!

"Where did you see him exactly, Miss Owen?" I asked, trying to reflect on this thing calmly.

"He was in the mistal over at Branshaw Hall. He appeared to be searching for something. It was quite dark and Nettie only saw him in fits and starts from her lantern. She thought she was seeing the Devil-Vicar and set up a cry for me that must have sent the neighborhood into the shivers . . . unless, of course—Oh, no!"

We were all startled at her change of expression. She put her hand to her mouth. "But could it have been the Devil-Vicar after all?"

"Are we off again on the trail of two Marcs—twin brothers, or father and son?" Sir Gareth asked in a bored way.

Catherine nodded thoughtfully.

"But the truth is, one has a fairly clear view of the Hall from the back of our house. And Nettie and I did see someone over there who was dressed much more in the manner of the Devil-Vicar than in one of Marc's familiar jackets. The Other One is alive, as I've always believed. This proves it. But have we been dealing with Marc, or the Devil-Vicar? His fear of fire should tell us. Sooner or later it will break him down to an admission of his identity. Don't you agree?" She looked at me hopefully.

This preposterous theory did not wash with me any more than with the baronet. If Catherine had seen a figure like the Devil-Vicar among the outbuildings of Branshaw Hall, then it was Marc, and no nonsense about that.

"Miss Wicklow," Catherine called to me as I turned toward the Yorkish Lion. "Abbie Hinchley's funeral is for this afternoon. Then will come the Arvills before nightfall. Will you be so good as to attend the funeral with me? I would appreciate it."

I did not know who or what "arvills" were, but I was still curious about Catherine Owen's ability to move about, and I thought it would do no harm to see more of her, and perhaps discover her secret, if there was one.

"Very well, if you wish it. You know where to find me, ma'am. Come, Jamie."

I was snappish all the way home through the village, for I seethed at the thought that Marc Branshaw was over prowling about, searching for heaven knows what, while Jamie and I risked our lives to give a false impression to all who passed. Marc's entire campaign to get me up to Yorkshire must have been waged for this purpose. It was very lowering. I had been led to believe that there was something personal in his interest, but I had only been used. Like Catherine. And I daresay, like many another of his females.

As Jamie left me at my room, he said hesitantly, "You mustn't think Marc lies. It's just that—he has reasons."

"On that we're both agreed!" I said with glacial politeness and added, "but it may interest you and Mr. Branshaw to know that Sir Gareth was not the spy he is trying to trap. There is another, who came to the cottage tonight after you had gone. A very dangerous Other!" With that I closed the door in Jamie's surprised face.

XIII

I DID NOT undress for bed in the ordinary sense. I tore off the garments borrowed from Marc Branshaw and hurled them into a corner. Then, too angry to shiver in the ice-cold room, I dressed in my London night clothing, which was scarcely warm enough for Yorkshire, but that was also of no consequence. I was perspiring with my own heat of fury when I climbed into bed and slid one naked foot and then the other down over the cold sheets.

I lay for a few minutes, quietly burning, annoyed with the ruffle of my nightgown around my neck, for it seemed suddenly too warm and too tight. But the cold bed finally soothed me, and I went into a restless sleep.

It must have just turned dawn, for I recall that the room was already light when the door from the hall opened, and with very little ceremony. In fact, the noise of its opening awakened me and I sat up to demand fiercely:

"You have the wrong room. Out of here at once! Do you hear me?"

I hadn't the faintest notion to whom I spoke until the door slammed behind my uninvited guest, and he crossed the room to draw aside the worn, clean drapes that closed out the sunrise. It was Marc Branshaw, looking muddy, dishevelled, unshaven, and rather the worse for wear. I was glad that I had used the correct tone when he entered my room.

He turned to me, quite as furious as I.

"*Where have you been?*"

There is nothing that reduces one to complete self-possession like the shouting and temper of one's opponent. I said insolently:

"As you see—in bed. But in my own bed. I do not ask others to pass themselves off as myself while I leave them in danger and go off and play my games elsewhere."

He came to the foot of the bed and leaned over it, raising a hand with all the fingers outstretched, as though he were about to choke me.

"In your bed. *In your bed!* Do you know that I have been into and out of every bog, every pot-hole, every cursed trap in the entire West Riding, searching for you? I left our prowler, the good Sir Gareth, drying out at some farm, and hurried back to see to your safety, and what did I find? The cottage door unbolted, and no sign of you. Do you know that I have spent the last few hours imagining every conceivable accident had befallen you? Didn't I tell you not to leave the cottage, under any circumstances?"

"Including my own murder?"

"I had already found the man who was spying on me. And neither he nor his sister is very likely the murderer."

"I beg to differ. The murderer, or spy—as you choose—was at your cottage, in your absence, very busy trying to get at me. That's why I ran out—to find you, who had deserted me."

"I know all that. Jamie told me. But even so, it might have been the very thing he wanted, to have you driven out into his hands. It was a stupid thing to do. I came back for you as soon as I could get rid of Owen."

"It's curious that you didn't see me as I ran down to the bogs, and then over to that farmer's cottage—if what you say is supposed to be true."

He said with cutting politeness, "May I point out that the moors are rather spacious and that it was night?"

I slid back under the covers with an attitude of nonchalance. To tell the truth, I did not believe him. I thought this was a tale he had concocted upon hearing of my danger from Jamie. If he had left Sir Gareth in order to hurry back and see to my safety, then who was the Devil-Vicar person seen searching the outbuildings at Branshaw Hall? I refused to believe Catherine's romantic theory that her precious ghost still lived. . . . Was it possible that the thing which had tried to get at me in Moyna's cottage had had time to return to Branshaw Hall for the search? I supposed it was possible, but hardly probable. What was probable was that Marc had made up this story to explain his negligence. I decided to try him on it, and said smugly:

"At least I cannot be accused of being in two places at once."

He dropped his hands upon the bedpost. His fingers tightened around it until they were white at the knuckles.

"What do you mean by that?"

"Oh," I said pleasantly, "I didn't mean to be obscure. I meant simply that I don't ask my friends to take my place at home so that I may be seen by romantic young ladies while I masquerade at the opposite end of the county."

He slapped the bedpost.

"Good God! So that's what this is all about! Dear Catherine has managed to trade off a few lies about seeing me tonight. Did she tell you that the Devil-Vicar was floating about, making mad love to her? If she hasn't, she undoubtedly will. And what has all this to do with your leaving the cottage? Everyone told you it was worth your life. The countryside itself is dangerous, and then Abbie's murder . . . Will Grimlett. . . . Don't you know there's a killer loose in this district?"

"I ought to know; he very nearly got to me in your house. So don't come blustering in here expecting to find him under my bed. And furthermore," I added, growing more and more upset at his blaming me for doing the most natural thing, "you are as cold and hateful and cruel as—as your precious Devil-Vicar. At least Sir Gareth loves and cares for his sister. So I'll thank you to get out of my room."

"Is that your last word to me? After what—"

"Don't tell me what you've gone through," I said haughtily. "Come back when your manners are better. And don't think you can sweep into my bedchamber as though it were your fine friend Catherine's, either." That was uncalled for but by now I could hear stirrings in the chamber next to mine, which was Mrs. Fothergay's, and, even worse, low voices in the hall, which could only be the Reverend MacDonnachie and his wife. It was frightfully embarrassing. And I did not like it any better when I heard Mrs. Fothergay's twittering comments as she joined the Vicar and his wife in the hall.

Marc paid no attention to them.

"Very well! Run to dear, good, kind Sir Gareth! He's just the sort for you—a weak, great slug of a creature, who—"

"Weak!" I cried, and managed a fair imitation of a nasty laugh. "I am sure, if the necessity arose, he could beat you within an inch of—"

"—who, for all I know, has murdered three people!" Marc went on, deaf to my interruption. "Go! By all means! I make you a present of him." He swung around the bedpost and stopped in front of me, his dark face livid with anger and the strain of what must have been a very difficult night. "Marry him! Do! But I advise you at least to pretend to some of Bedelia Fothergay's money, for that is all he wants of you!"

This was beyond contempt.

"Thank you! I shall certainly do so. And when I've married Gareth and you have married Catherine, then, think how cozy it will be! You and I, from having looked alike, will then be truly brother and sister. Nothing could be happier."

Why this should have provoked him beyond endurance, I don't know, but for an instant I thought he would slap me. Instead, however, he struck the bedpost so hard the whole bed shook.

"The Reverend Niles said you were selfish and irreligious and amoral. He might have added you are surly and have dreadful manners!"

He threw up his hands.

"This is all that was needed. That you should talk about me behind my back with that mealy-mouthed curate! I suppose you'll say he sets me an example. Everywhere I go, every move I make, there is Frederick Niles to remind me. The good, the noble Frederick! And there am I—all that is despicable."

This time I was amazed. What was there about the young curate's sincere good works in the village that should shake Marc like this? How could Marc be jealous, a man with all his abilities and attractions?

He went out and slammed the door so hard that it swung open again, and, of course, awakened those who might have slept through his previous tantrum. It must have been maddening to him when he was stopped in his furious progress by Mrs. MacDonnachie, who said in her sweet, die-away voice:

"Marc, my dear! What is it? You must calm yourself."

Even more annoying was Mrs. Fothergay's fussy twitter. "My dear Marc, what an hour to call upon one! What business had you—er—here?"

Marc's voice cut her off harshly.

"No business at all, ma'am. Now or in the future. I am too unworthy! It was all a very bad mistake. Good day to you!"

"Come now, lad. Don't go off in a huff," the Reverend called after him, with his fat man's breathy laughter. "These things pass over. . . . Ah, Jamie-boy, did our impetuous friend awaken you?"

Jamie's voice came sleepily. "Aunty wants to know what's amiss."

"Nothing, lad. Just a lover's quarrel."

"Hardly, that," Mrs. Fothergay interposed. "Mr. Branshaw mistook the door, that is all—and Miss Wicklow was probably alarmed."

Jamie was endearingly quick to ask, "Is she all right? Miss Anne?"

The Reverend MacDonnachie sounded playful but fatherly.

"Yes, yes. Don't disturb her. And you need sleep,

you young rascal. I heard you get back in the wee hours of the night. Been out looking for Gytrashes? See the ghost of the Devil-Vicar?" He gave out a loud and audible shiver. "Damn—pardon, ladies. But it's cold as a tomb out in this windy hall. Well, is it back to slumber? Busy day ahead, what with the funeral and then the arvills. I do hope someone has bespoke some decent liquor for the arvills. Can't have a real funeral without a little refreshment, you know."

"Special best!" Jamie put in proudly.

"Really!" said Mrs. Fothergay, echoing my own slight shock.

Mrs. MacDonnachie was apologetic. "Cadmon's little jest, ma'am. The arvills in a home or the local taproom are a tradition here after funerals. But we do not take funerals lightly. It's a method of making the whole painful business easier for the bereaved."

"In this case, Abbie's father, that drunken sot, Abel Hinchley," put in the Vicar. "How he'll look forward to it!"

I looked out into the hall about this time and inquired severely: "Has that awful man gone?"

"Oh, come, my dear! Not 'awful.'" Mrs. MacDonnachie made vague gestures but was cut off by her husband, with whose views, I must say, I agreed.

"Gone, Miss Anne, and in a fine rage. You must have sent him packing, with a flea in his ear."

"I did."

"Exactly so, ma'am. And now, may we bid you good night."

He took his wife's arm to escort her down the hall. They were an absurd couple—she all wispy and waving ruffles, he in a robe of the most violent sunset hue below and above which peeped hems of his woolen nightgown.

Once back in bed, unnerved and yet excited by my battle with Marc, I realized that I still didn't know whether Catherine Owen was telling the truth or not. Had Marc been in two places at once last night? Or was it possible for both of us to have seen him within a few hours?

Of course, Catherine's other claim, that there must be two Marc Branshaws, was in the realm of fantasy. It did present some interesting, and rather frightening ideas to me, however.

It was nearly noon when I awoke to see Rose Keegan trying to close the portieres in silence so that the bright sunlight should not pour into my eyes. I smiled and told her that the sun was as welcome as it was unexpected.

"We shall have a pleasant day for the funeral and the arvills afterward," she said.

I asked her if the arvills were a kind of noisy wake. She was not offended but assured me that she had never known a person to die in this area—least of all one of Abbie's character—who wouldn't have approved the social gathering in the Yorkish Lion taproom in honor of the dead, and financed by the nearest living relation or his friends.

"To my knowledge," she went on, "only in the case of the Reverend Ewen Morgan's death, there were no arvills."

"Didn't they think it worth celebrating the Devil-Vicar's murder?" I asked ironically.

Miss Rose arranged the drapes and curtains, picked up Marc's jacket, which I had unceremoniously hurled to the floor, and came back to the bed. While I got up and into a robe, she said to me, with that quiet conviction of the truth that was so much a part of her:

"Believe me, ma'am, the villagers had no notion of murdering Ewen—the Reverend Morgan, I mean to say. An enemy, jealous of him, committed the crime. It was intended by the village that he should be driven out by the fire. Instead, from all we have learned since, he was struck down secretly and left to die. There could be no 'celebration,' as you call it, over what the whole village felt to be a monstrous crime. And although my brother, Jamie's father, was the first in the ruins to try and rescue Ewen Morgan —for he was against the burning in the first place—we all knew that as the crime was committed by one of us, so were we all to blame." She hesitated, picked at a spot of mud on the coat, and then added, "I believe, for some reason, the murderer of the Reverend Morgan has returned—if, indeed, he or she ever left Maidenmoor—and is at work again."

"Then you're quite certain Ewen Morgan is dead?"

She looked at me in an odd, speculative way. "My brother found the bones. Surely, he cannot have lived through that inferno."

I went over to the window and looked out. A thought occurred to me when I saw that bare, desolate patch of ground. "Where is Mrs. Branshaw buried?"

She came to the window and pointed out the most elegant group of tombstones at the north end of the churchyard. One had only to glance at those great gray slabs, presided over by a modestly nude white marble statue of Eternal Life, roughly the height of a man, to recognize the pride of the Branshaws, and the family's place in Maidenmoor's social life, even after death.

"How dreadful!" I murmured. "He died partly for love of Mrs. Branshaw, yet they can't even be together now."

She surprised me by smiling, as if at a memory. "I doubt if they would wish to be. I suspect Moyna taught the young man a great deal. But beyond being instructress and pupil in certain—if I may call them—*arts*, I think, had the affair not been interrupted by his murder, they would have drifted apart."

I was startled. "But if they were not everything to each other, what of their—of Moyna's son?"

She seemed to be caught unawares but recovered quickly. "Ah! Moyna's son. He was always a sickly boy—all the Branshaws were. It used to trouble Moyna a great deal."

"Aside from being afraid of fire, which I can understand because of what happened to his supposed father, what *is* wrong with Marc Branshaw?" I asked.

"With Marc?" she repeated in a surprised voice, as though we'd been discussing occupants of the moon and suddenly returned to earth. "Why, nothing, indeed! He is a little nervous. I'm given to understand that most artists are. And Jamie saw him taken ill once, after a bad headache, I think it was. He told Jamie it was nothing, and laid the blame to a severe shock or injury of some sort in his earlier years. But it's certainly nothing fatal. Even I have been known to faint upon occasion."

"Was that what was the matter with him as a child?"

"I really couldn't say. Will you be going to the funeral?"

That reminded me of my obligations and I began to dress hurriedly. "Yes, I must. I promised to go with Catherine Owen."

Miss Rose stopped in the doorway. "There's an unhappy woman. Something troubles her deeply. She had best have a care."

"What on earth do you mean?"

"Miss Catherine has some extraordinary ideas—unhealthy ones. But it's more than that. It may be that she's had something of my own odd sensation, that somewhere in Maidenmoor I sense a mask on a familiar face, or rather, a familiar mask on a face that is . . . not one of us."

I remembered suddenly. "Good heavens! Marc said almost the same thing."

"Yes. I thought he would feel it. Has he said whom he suspects?"

"Not to me. Surely, you don't think Catherine . . ."

"If Miss Catherine is not guilty, then she certainly knows who is. Her entire conduct—that book she and various villagers have discussed up one street and down the next—yes," she mused thoughtfully, "Miss Catherine knows. And if she isn't guilty herself, then she may precipitate the very thing she fears most."

I laughed, more to reassure myself than because I saw anything humorous in the situation. "I know she fancies herself in love with a dead man. But you can scarcely call that guilt. It's no worse than young ladies in London who fancy themselves in love with some actor at Drury Lane."

Miss Rose said without emphasis, "But those actors have not committed two and perhaps three murders."

She went out. On the whole, her exit line was worthy of Drury Lane.

XIV

A SHORT TIME later I met Catherine Owen outside the church of St. Anthony's, she having arrived here by her own efforts, in her wheelchair. She was justly proud of this accomplishment and, no matter what people said of her, I could not help joining in congratulations at her own initiative.

"I suppose I seem very foolish to you," she apologized, "but the truth is, I have prayed for strength, and am hoping that one day, not too long from now, I shall be able to stand without assistance."

I told her I thought she was very brave, and meant it with all my heart.

"For I freely admit," I said, "that I shouldn't like to spend any more time in this strange, murderous village than is strictly necessary to recover the manuscript Mr. Branshaw stole from me."

"Murderous?" She looked up at me as I wheeled her into the vestry of the church. "But they've killed the dog who did those things, haven't they?"

"Nonsense. It was a human being who did it," I said, not being at all sure, but anxious to see if Rose Keegan was right, if Catherine did know something about the crimes.

Her long fingers, dainty yet strong in their little knitted gloves, dug into the arms of her chair.

"No, no. I don't believe it. It was the dog." She peered up into my face with a pathetic hope in her wide, hazel eyes. "The horrid scratches . . . the . . . mangled flesh. . . . Well, everything indicates a dog."

She was certainly distressed.

"Yet a dog might be set on a human being who had been struck down by a cudgel let us say. However, that wasn't the way it happened in your book, was it, Miss Catherine?"

I expected her to grow angry, but she surprised me by covering her face with her shaking hands. "That accursed book. It was only done in revenge. And then, when I changed it, I thought he would be amused. I never meant it to be seriously taken for

Moyna. You see . . ." She got hold of herself, aware that others in the church entry were looking our way. She lowered her voice and finished, ". . . he's so different from the way I imagine him. When I'm away from him, I think of him as the Other One—Ewen Morgan, whom they called the Devil-Vicar. But when we're together . . . well, you saw how he acted to me. But suppose it were not he but the Other. . . ."

"Do you honestly think he's two people?" I asked her, trying not to smile. "That's a very difficult feat, to be two people and still seem to be one."

"You didn't know the young Ewen Morgan as I did when I was a girl in Wales. I went to all the services he took. I adored him. I never believed what they said when he came to Maidenmoor. His portrait is in the Vicar's offices. If no one is in there, perhaps you could manage to get me over there now. To the left."

So there was a connection between the Owens in Wales and the late Devil-Vicar before he came into Yorkshire.

"And was he in love with you in Wales?" I asked, burning with curiosity.

She smiled wanly. "Heavens, no! I was a child then. I doubt if he knew I existed."

Several villagers made way for us and I pushed her along the narrow, gloomy aisle behind the nave. Despite the presence of clear glass panes instead of stained glass windows, the interior of the church was dark, and as damp-cold as the tombs beyond its windows, but I was not surprised that as we approached the vicar's study the air grew appreciably warmer. I could well imagine the Reverend Cadmon MacDonnachie was no suffering saint. He enjoyed such comforts as a small enclosed stove would give him.

The vicar was no doubt elsewhere encouraging his

flock, so that for a few moments we had his office to ourselves. It was as typical of him as his red beard. Scraps of paper were scattered over the floor, which had been covered by a cheap but serviceable carpeting, and, to contribute to the general untidiness, an inkstand had been overturned and dripped slowly into its own soggy stain in the carpet.

In spite of its slovenly look, the room apparently served as a vestry as well as the Vicar's office, for there were a number of benches scattered about.

All along, I had put off looking up at the portrait, about two feet square, above the Vicar's desk, but finally I steeled myself to see the image of the creature who had caused such havoc in the village that he had to be burned to death.

At first, it gave me a start to see the surface resemblance to Marc Branshaw; yet the spirit behind those surface similarities was so different that I was at the same time amazed that anyone should have mistaken the one man for the other. What looked down at me—and those eyes seemed to stare directly into my soul—was an extraordinarily bitter, humorless face, so handsome that one could well understand Catherine's penchant for it, but otherwise alarming in its intensity. The hair, worn long in the back and rather longer in front than the current style, was black and glossy, the eyes shadowed by heavy lids and lashes, but penetrating in their power. Wherever one stood in the room, there were those eyes peering down, watching. The mouth, which might have been full and even passionate, was twisted into a thin, bitter line, unnatural even to the lips themselves, which appeared capable of violent passions.

I tried to decide how old the face was. But for the bitter, humorless quality, I should have said it was exceedingly young; yet those qualities made it seem about Marc Branshaw's age. It lacked the look of strain and of maturity around the eyes which occasionally betrayed in Marc's face an age not first evident. But in place of that, and above all, by comparison with the humor, the quick, effervescent personality of Marc Branshaw, there was the brooding Celtic quality of a man at war with himself, a man who must have hated his life and everything in it. Small wonder that he took out his hatred of the universe in such ridiculous tales as that he could turn himself into a Gytrash, and that he was the Devil come back to earth.

I considered the proposition that this portrait of Ewen Morgan might serve for a portrait of the Devil. But it was not so. I was quite sure no devil would ever appear so unhappy. This was a man, and if he had no other future than the one that appeared to haunt him in this portrait, then he was better dead.

"As you see, it's not finished," said Catherine, noticing that I wasn't able to tear myself away from it. The surplice had been only sketched in below the face, its white purity a violent contrast with the subject's eyes and shadowy hair.

"Does anyone know who painted it?"

"I don't believe so. The Reverend MacDonnachie found it somewhere. He adores it. Probably has a suppressed desire to be taken for Ewen Morgan." She glanced at me, and giggled, a young, uninhibited giggle that was rather winning. "If you can imagine anything more preposterous than Cadmon MacDonnachie emulating that man in the portrait—in anything."

"I don't know," I said defensively, trying not to be aware of those magnificent eyes watching and watching. . . . "If I were in trouble, I should certainly prefer to come to the Vicar MacDonnachie."

She raised her eyebrows at what she felt was my absurd prejudice, but I don't think she was sorry to lose a rival.

"I was mistaken in thinking Marc was my Ewen Morgan returned from death."

"And he knew nothing of you in Wales?"

"Oh no. How could he know anything of me? I was thirteen when he left Beaumaris for Maidenmoor. He was twenty-two—a brilliant young man, but much too young and too serious for such a post."

"Too serious?" I repeated, remembering Marc's light touch in almost everything. Certainly, the two men might be said to have violently opposing souls. "And yet you loved him. How then could you love Marc? They are nothing alike."

She shrugged and smiled sadly.

"He was a figure of romance, the Reverend Morgan. There wasn't a girl in Beaumaris who didn't share my feelings. Only I never outgrew them. Years later, when Garrie's expenses outran our income and we had to sell out, I told Garrie that we had to move to Maidenmoor. I'd heard about the Devil-Vicar and his unhappy romance with Moyna Branshaw, and the rest of it. And I wanted to be where he had—perished. When I saw the miniature of her son that Moyna proudly displayed to the town a year or two ago, I fell in love with it. I half convinced myself that Marc was either my Ewen Morgan reborn, or perhaps, through some strange quirk, he was Ewen Morgan himself. Of course, he wasn't." She studied the portrait. "Ewen is quite different and—I believe—alive as well. . . ."

She put her hands to her cheeks and closed her eyes. I daresay she was dreaming of this man in the portrait, alive, and her very own. But I told myself he was much too humorless for me. I should have been quite overpowered by all that demoniac grandeur. Nevertheless, I was finding it difficult to take my eyes off Catherine's great love.

Catherine finally tore her attention away from her oil and canvas lover.

"The service will be beginning. Shall we go?"

I had a sudden, stabbing memory of the unshallowed ground out at the end of the church graveyard. To think that all that remained of the creature in the portrait was a handful of bones! It was a searing realization, more searing because it should have meant nothing to me.

I willed myself not to look back at the portrait.

We were joined after the service had begun by Sir Gareth, who was forced to step over Catherine's chair to get into the pew. Although we tried to make no noise, our entry had been noticeable, and a buzz of attention went up around us.

Up in the pulpit the Vicar stopped, for he had been in the process of extolling the virtues of the deceased girl, and there were several titters from the congregation. I stared at Reverend MacDonnachie's big, hairy face and tried not to think about the unfortunate girl lying to one side of his pulpit, in her simple wooden coffin. I felt the insincerity of the Vicar's words, his effort to enlarge upon certain qualities that the dead girl had not apparently possessed. Once more my thoughts returned to Abbie Hinchley.

Was Rose Keegan right? Had the girl died for some secret she possessed, the identity of the man who had struck down and murdered the Devil-Vicar sixteen years ago? If so then the girl was indeed to be pitied, and I understood the Reverend MacDonnachie's attempt to make her a virtuous heroine.

Meanwhile, something was happening beside me. Sir Gareth had slipped a folded and sealed paper into his sister's hand and I heard him say in his hoarse whisper, "Nettie tells me it was on the hall table with the cards this morning. Addressed to you, as you see."

Catherine took the note, quietly ripped the sealed place, and then, a moment after, dropped the note into her lap and put her hands to her cheeks in a quick, nervous gesture. Her brother started to pick up the note but she whispered sharply, very sharply for Catherine:

"No. It's mine. It's nothing."

Sir Gareth resumed his sleepy contemplation of the Vicar. Out of the corner of my eye I watched Catherine. She seemed in a stupor. Her hands trembled now and then, and she quieted them with an effort. Her dreamy eyes were upon the Vicar, but I do not believe she saw him, for every minute or two she closed her fingers on the note in her lap, and held it tight, as though reassuring herself that it existed.

I was relieved when the entire service was over. It was selfish to be so little concerned over the unhappy Abbie Hinchley, but I had not known her, and I reasoned that even if she had died for what she knew, she must have been exceedingly selfish or perhaps a blackmailer, not to have revealed the murderer of the Devil-Vicar.

When Sir Gareth arose with the congregation and Catherine picked up her old-fashioned reticule, to do likewise, she dropped the note from her shaking hands. I picked it up for her, nearly dying of curiosity to open it, but could not do so under her trusting eyes.

Outside the church, Sir Gareth bade us good day, saying he was going to look for that "old charmer," Mrs. Fothergay. Catherine looked at me apologetically.

"Garrie seems to have taken a sudden fancy to your friend."

I laughed and agreed. Perhaps, because I had been influenced by Marc's maligning comments, I was sure it was the inheritance left to Bedelia Fothergay by the late Colonel that attracted the penniless baronet.

Catherine said, "It's no matter. Come nearer." I bent over her. To my surprise and faint discomfort, she reached up and hugged me. "Dear, dear Anne, I must tell you. It's come. He is really here in Maidenmoor. Read this."

Feeling the supreme hypocrite, I tried to refuse, but when the little note was pressed into my hand, I read the cryptic line:

Ten at Moyna's stone. Then the flourishing single initial *E*. The writing and the initial looked familiar.

"What is Moyna's stone and who is *E*?"

I was remembering Marc Branshaw's quick handwritten changes on Catherine's manuscript. No doubt of it. There was a similarity. She was evidently so enthralled with her notion of meeting the Devil-Vicar that she had not noticed the resemblance.

Catherine said softly, "Can't you guess? It's as I said. Why do you think people have taken to seeing Marc in two places at once, and all that nonsense? There are two of them. *He* has returned."

"Who? Not—"

"Ewen Morgan. Surely it must be he remembers me from the old days in Beaumaris."

I was genuinely anxious. Even if Marc was playing some trick on Catherine, I hoped, for his sake as well as hers, that she would not abet him.

"The Devil-Vicar! My heavens, Catherine, even if it were true—and of course it's not—why, the man would be a demon! He is dead. You must remember that."

She shook her head. There was an obstinate sweetness about her that was as annoying as it was unnerving.

"No, dear. Whether he is dead, or was dead, I don't care. I've loved that man since I first knew him in Beaumaris. I talked with Moyna about him for hours at a time. The only reason I thought I loved Marc was the silly resemblance. I was always attempting to prove he was Ewen Morgan, who would well be afraid of fire, after what he'd undergone. But now, if I meet the Devil-Vicar himself, there will be no need for all those fire tricks. Marc's fear will have some other explanation."

"Ewen Morgan is dead," I repeated patiently.

She was just as patient. "I don't care. I shouldn't care if he were the Devil himself." She gave me a funny, pitifully flirtatious look. "I rather fancy this note puts that quite out of the question, though. You can see that it's real—as I'm sure the Devil-Vicar is."

People passing us on the street had begun to look at us oddly, I thought, and I rolled Catherine's chair back up toward her house.

"You realize," I said, "that if he really is alive, he must be the murderer of these people. Out of revenge."

"Impossible. He can't be, because you see—" She stopped suddenly.

I looked down at her, but her expression was unreadable

"Well?" I prompted her.

She shook her head. "It doesn't matter. Nothing

matters but that he is alive and wants me to meet him."

Remembering Rose Keegan's warning, I ventured, "If you do know or suspect something, shouldn't you tell the Vicar, or the police in Teignford, or someone?"

She looked up at me, her great eyes dazzled by her love affair with an oil painting.

"Why should I know anything? I thought that dreadful dog did it. I still do."

"Suppose the murderer kills your precious Devil-Vicar—and this time really kills him!"

Her head snapped up. I thought for one breathless moment that she would tell me something. Then she smiled.

"Nonsense. It was the dog that did it, I tell you. There wasn't a sign of anything else."

We had reached the ugly stone exterior of her house now, and I left her with a parting reminder.

"On the other hand, your lover may decide to kill you instead. But that's entirely your problem."

"So it is," she answered me gaily. "So it is."

XV

As I passed the graveyard I very nearly walked into Mrs. Fothergay and Mrs. MacDonnachie, who were coming out the iron gate that opened upon the street.

"Anne, dear child!" bubbled Bedelia. "You have utterly missed the most enchanting excursion. Yes, indeed. The dear lady has been conducting me among the tombs. Edifying, edifying."

"But not—alas!—profitable," put in the Vicar's wife. "I so hoped to recover Cadmon's warmest woolen stock. I believe he must have lost it on the trail yesterday." She hesitated, looked around in a conspiratorial way and, just as I was prepared to be her confidante in a murder confession at the least, she said, "Could you possibly cast an eye over the heather and bracken just off the path around Wind-Rock Rise, next time you go to Moyna's cottage? Possibly you might catch a glimpse of—"

I was outraged.

"I? Go to Marc Branshaw's cottage? Indeed not. I'm afraid you must ask someone better acquainted with the gentleman." What gave her the idea that I visited young men's out-of-the-way cottages? No one knew I had been there. Ah, but good Sir Gareth! He would talk!

I don't know which lady was more astonished at my outburst, but Mrs. MacDonnachie was the first to recover. "Yes, yes, dear," she said soothingly, after which she whispered something in Bedelia's ear.

It was Bedelia Fothergay's turn to be short with the lady. "You forget, madam, it was all a mistake. The young man confused Anne's door with mine. He wishes to preserve me in oils, you know."

"Oh," said Mrs. MacDonnachie doubtfully, and changed the subject.

As for me, I went up to my room and stood a very long time staring down at the wretched, forsaken ground where the Devil-Vicar's bones presumably had fallen to their rest.

I agreed with Catherine on one matter: no ghostly vicar, dead sixteen years, had written that note of assignation. But if those were not the Devil-Vicar's bones lying under the sod . . .

But such speculation was profitless. I did not, for the life of me, know why I didn't simply pack up and hire some conveyance back to Teignford and London. I had no emotion other than common curiosity about the events here in the West Riding, no feeling for the people except a liking for young Jamie and a furious dislike for Marc Branshaw, who had used me abominably. The difficulty was that I couldn't very well ask Marc for my manuscript on the Red Indians until we were on speaking terms again, and that, of course, would be never.

The men of the village and neighboring hamlets were now gathering in the taproom downstairs for what I supposed must be the arvills of which I had heard so much mention. It was not that they were unseemly, but rather that the occasion seemed to them, to judge by all the greetings and chatter, a social moment of no mean importance. Since I did not want to pass these men when they were doubtless full of the best liquid refreshment from the Keegan cellars, I sat in my room, wrote letters to Mr. Perth and other friends in London, and pondered on the strange events of the past few days.

Some time later, Mrs. Fothergay knocked on my door and called to me, but I didn't feel that her irritating voice would help matters, so I pretended not to be in. She tried the door and for an instant I thought she might have the presumption to walk in. I held my breath and she went away.

Later in the afternoon I heard a man's boots on the creaking boards of the hall. Having knocked on Bedelia's door and received no response, he presently stopped by my door. When he called to me, I recognized the voice of Sir Gareth Owen.

"Miss Anne! Rose tells me you've been up here all afternoon. Come and join us below. No one's going to force you to drain a mug of Dog's Nose, you know."

Good heavens! I should hope not. Dog's Nose sounded most unpleasant. I was about to keep silence when the baronet added:

"Your friend Branshaw's below as well. Got his audience in the palm of his hand but I daresay you're not foolish enough to be taken in."

I pricked up my ears. I did more. I went to the door and, thanking Sir Gareth for his invitation, replied that I had better things to do than to watch Marc Branshaw make a drunken fool of himself.

"All of that, ma'am. He must be drunk; he's giving imitations of the Devil-Vicar. Several ladies tiptoed in from the parlor to watch and he's been putting them into screaming fits."

That would be worth seeing. What did Marc Branshaw mean by laying himself open to further comparison between himself and the late unlamented Devil-Vicar?

I went down with Sir Gareth to see this amazing sight. At the foot of the stairs we found two old and bearded combatants rolling half on the stairs, half on the floor, kicking and gouging and otherwise behaving as though they had never heard of the laws of fisticuffs. I stepped carefully around them and then moved more slowly to the open taproom. I could hear Sir Gareth behind me, encouraging first one and then the other of the two men to "have a go at it" and "not to give up like a damned townsman" and other helpful advice.

In the taproom, behind the rail, and leaning on it as though it were a pulpit, was Marc Branshaw, with his hair dishevelled and his face rather pale instead of its usual olive color. Except for these trifling differences, I don't believe I would have guessed that he was drunk. Perhaps he wasn't. I watched him, almost ashamed that he should expose himself to people whom he despised. But the longer I watched, the more I understood that he was enjoying himself.

The actor, the artist in him, was in full command. He liked the exhibition he was making, and I must confess, it was bloodcurdlingly good.

"Behold! Sinner all! The Devil turns himself into a Gytrash! But the turning . . . stay, ma'am . . . the turning is only in your eyes, not in myself." He pointed at an elderly woman who was retreating rapidly under his sardonic gaze, and now stood there, clutching her shawl and looking terrified. Indeed, there was something fearful in his ability to create a mood, with his burning eyes, his dark brows that were so eloquent in expressing disdain and sardonic humor, but above all, in his astounding resemblance to the face of the dead Devil-Vicar. "Says not the Book that the day of the Beast is at hand? For hear me!" He stretched out his arm dramatically. "The Beast is in Man, and Man in the Beast. As was always the way. How came the victim to die to whose memory we drink today? It was she who saw the Beast, and in seeing had to die. Isn't so, Jamie? Jamie saw a Beast turn into a Man, didn't you, Jamie?"

But the boy was huddling against the wall behind Marc, as though to avoid his touch as Marc swung around to confront him.

"No—no. Please, Marc. Not here. They'll think . . . Ye know what they'll think."

"Ay, mon!" cried a voice, only half coherent, from one corner of the taproom. A shoddily-dressed old man shuffled forward. Even I could see that he had already consumed his pint for the day. "What've ye done a my Abbie? Kilt her, ye did. Ye devil!"

Marc paid him no heed. He had chucked Jamie under the chin and was taking another drink.

"Hush, man," said one of the other natives. "It's

only a game. Ye know young Branshaw when ye sees him."

But Hinchley went on, with drunken persistence.

"Well an' good. But that's not what Abbie told me. 'He's the Devil-Vicar.' Them's her words, poor Abbie. 'He's come back from the dead, and if I play my game right, I'll have him, dead or no.' That's what my Abbie said. She loved him. And for that, she's got to die. Was it you done it, sor?"

The crowd in the taproom seemed to break into component parts, the men looking at each other, echoing the remark of the pitiful Hinchley.

"Ay, mon," said one of them suddenly. "Explain that business with the beast in the Wind-Rock. If that weren't the work of a devil."

Hinchley nodded with alcoholic wisdom.

Marc smiled at them all. He leaned forward over the taprail, and they receded from him as from a wave that might engulf them. I could not blame them. It was not a warming smile.

"That's my secret. It's so simple, to. I'll wager you the Devil-Vicar had just such secrets to explain his powers. And you never guessed. But then—you are simple men."

"And you, sir, are offensive," said Sir Gareth, coming from behind me and approaching the taprail. "Whatever else you may be, and I'm sure that's the least of it, I doubt very much if you could charm so much as a flea-blown mongrel, much less one of the feminine gender with whom you make so free."

Marc had taken up his mug of some dark, thick liquid that did not look appetizing to me, but as he put it to his mouth, he caught sight of me over the lip of the mug. He glanced from Gareth back to me as though he read something in our presence together. This stupid and wilfull misunderstanding annoyed me. Then he set the mug down slowly and, still smiling, asked in a way that suggested the purr of a tiger:

"What might you mean by that?"

"You know what I mean. Playing fast and loose with my sister. You'll not bandy her so."

Marc laughed. "Good God! I thought you were insulting quite another—but of course. It was dear, saintly little Catherine all the time! I would never dream of—how did you put it in your delicate way—'bandying' Catherine."

"Nor any other decent female, by God!" said Gareth, now losing all patience.

"Well," said Marc reasonably, while some of the men began to laugh, "you can't lay claim to the whole lot of them, can you? Be specific. What ladies do you not hold claim over? I shouldn't like to think I was disobliging that distinguished man of means, that noble patron of the poor!"

Several of the men to whom, I gathered, Sir Gareth owed money, clapped each other on the back, and dug a neighboring rib or two to indicate that this was a palpable hit. It naturally served to infuriate the baronet.

"You cur! You little whelp! You mongrel, degraded . . ."

"A pity," said Marc in his friendly way, "that my sex prevents you from adding 'bitch' to all the rest of the canine family you've dragged out of the kennel."

"Your sex!" Sir Gareth, who was by now apoplectic, managed a momentary triumph of calm over temper. He looked Marc up and down in that sneering way I did not like, and added, "My dear Marc, that would appear to be your most . . . impotent defense."

A woman gasped. All laughter stopped. The silence fell so suddenly that I heard my own pulsebeat in my ears. The next second it seemed that a lightning bolt must have struck the house. Marc vaulted the taprail and caught Sir Gareth a shocking blow that only just missed his cheekbone and struck him hard across the chin. The sound was horrid and made me shudder; I, along with the three or four other women who had been foolish enough to enter the room, retreated in disorder.

But not before I saw that Sir Gareth was temporarily incapacitated. As both men were equally to blame, I felt that I should have gone to the baronet's aid, but for some incomprehensible reason, I turned at once to see whether Marc was hurt. He was not, except for the damage to his knuckles; he was holding one hand in the palm of the other and still looking furious, as the men, who thought it great sport, congratulated him, added the rider that they hadn't thought he had it in him.

I moved into the passage, and glanced back. I saw that Marc was watching me. The hot color had come into his face. We stared at each other for a long moment. Neither of us would give a cubit, and my last view of him as I turned away was that uncompromising look which did not auger very much for the future.

I met Miss Rose who was on her way to find out what the pleasant arvills had come to, and I explained somewhat incoherently. Her reaction astonished me.

"Good! They've been meaning to have it out for some time. Now, perhaps, they'll be civil to each other." She, however, shared my relief when we saw the Reverend MacDonnachie come into the inn and make for the taproom. "Come, Miss Wicklow," she added, and took my arm. "You'll see. It means nothing. The Reverend will attend to matters."

"Well, lads," said the Vicar. "I'm challenging all comers to a match that says I'll thrash the both of you and any as cares to join in." As he spoke, he was helping Sir Gareth up from the floor, and by the time he had finished insisting that he could beat both men though he gave them ten to twenty years in age, he had Sir Gareth, at least, muttering like a civilized person again.

As for Marc, he finished the drink in his mug and then quietly made his way through the crowd toward the side door that opened near the graveyard gate. He had to pass Miss Rose and me in doing so. I looked at him but said nothing. He was about to leave, but stopped long enough to say to me:

"I wish you joy of your precious champion! Much good he may do you!"

"What a tiresome young man!" I remarked to Miss Rose, and heard behind me the slamming of the door.

Miss Rose smiled.

The Reverend MacDonnachie was laughing in his fatman way, so that others joined in from sheer contagion.

"Gytrashes! Devil-Vicars! Now, gentlemen, I put it to you! Does that bad-tempered young man strike terror into your hearts? Oh, come now. . . . Is he the kind of creature who goes about changing into animals at night or seducing fair ladies in ghostly guise? Why, he wouldn't hurt a flea! Present company excepted, Gareth."

Everyone laughed. Even Gareth managed a watery, bruised grin.

Then one of the sheepmen who had come in shortly before the fight started, spoiled the scene.

"Ay, mon, but what if he *do* them things? He's a

fair one for the ladies. They made to-do over him. And ye say he don't command the beasties. But what of yesterday in the Wind-Rock? What of that, ay?"

The Vicar scratched his beard.

"Well, there you have me, laddie. I must think on it. But at any rate," he added staunchly, "he's a well-meaning young man and when he's in a rare humor there's none you'd rather have to tea or stronger drink, for the matter of that."

"That's it, sor," said another of his parishioners. "But how does ye know when he's in a rare mood? It's a problem. That it is. Fair gives me the freezing marrow, he did just now, lookin' that like the Devil-Vicar when he was set on mischief."

"Not to mention what young Jamie saw," added Hinchley, with harsh emphasis. "My Abbie was murdered. I stand to say so now and in future. And it wouldn't surprise me none if it was a man behind the beast what done it. I'm mentionin' no names," he added fairly. "We done that before an' let a innercent man be burnt. No more a that, I say."

"No, indeed," the Vicar agreed jovially, and they all went to drinking again.

Exceedingly sorry I had allowed myself to be enticed out of my room in order to have that almost silent encounter with Marc, I started back up the stairs again, but Miss Rose asked me to join the ladies at supper in the back dining parlor. This seemed preferable to forging my way through a noisy group of men on the stair landing, so I joined Mrs. Fothergay and the Vicar's wife, and—somewhat to my surprise—Catherine Owen.

They were arguing over the possibility that a man, and not a dog killed by Marc Branshaw, had committed the two recent murders. I must confess that Catherine was the staunch upholder of the dog theory. When I had heard most of the arguments which, womanlike, were based on personal encounters with dog and man which were supposed to prove conclusively the argument of the speaker, I could not help suggesting to Catherine:

"If a dog killed the Hinchley girl, then did he drag her all the way from his lair up around Wind-Rock to drop her on the Devil-Vicar's grave? It does seem rather more clever than I would take the old beast to be."

Catherine flushed a little.

"It was pure coincidence. Probably the girl dragged herself there."

"My dear!" murmured Bedelia Fothergay happily, "you forget that the poor girl was so badly bruised and—er—mangled—that if she had been wounded, say, at the back of the head, it would have been difficult to find at this stage."

Mrs. MacDonnachie made a polite little face into her dinner plate, obviously wishing we would all change the subject, but Mrs. Fothergay was in her element.

"If I have said once, I have said a hundred times, one cannot be too careful of men. No one knows better than I. Had difficulties with them all my life. The poor Colonel, my late husband, used to say that he married me over the corpses of my admirers."

For the first time, I saw a streak of malicious female in Catherine, who smiled at me as though we shared a secret, while she remarked, "Heavens, ma'am! Had you that effect upon them?"

Mrs. Fothergay giggled.

"Lord, child! I was referring to the figurative corpses which the late Colonel left in his wake, in order to win me."

The Vicar's wife took this opportunity to change

the subject, and we did not get back on it until late in the evening, when I volunteered to push Catherine's rolling chair up to her house—since it was apparent Sir Gareth had joined the men for the night.

The air was cold and crisp. Catherine began to count the stars as we moved slowly past the church and up the cobbled street. She gave up soon, for they were too vast and overpowering in number.

"The moon will be up soon. What a night! What a glorious night!" She shivered pleasurably in her heavy coat and shawl.

I said, "I hope you've given some thought to that message today."

"I have, I have," she assured me, giving the wrong interpretation to my words.

I reminded her again, "It might be dangerous."

"Are we to go into that again? Really, Anne, one would think you were jealous."

"No," I said, trying to keep my voice low. "I'm not jealous of your Demon Lover. But I think you ought to show a little common caution. Bedelia is right in one respect. That poor beast that Marc killed yesterday would hardly drag Abbie Hinchley so far just to drop her conveniently on the one grave that would be most appropriate."

"What do you mean by that?"

I could hardly explain, but put it in the best words that presented themselves. "It's like an offering. A dead offering to the spirit of the murdered Vicar. It's the sort of thing the Devil-Vicar might conceive of doing, if he murdered the girl."

She objected crossly, "If he is dead, then how can he kill Abbie Hinchley?"

She did not reply. "You say he is not dead."

After a pause, during which we had negotiated the long roughly-cobbled surface leading to her doorstep, she asked me finally, "Are you going to tell Gareth?"

"I suppose not. But I ought to."

She shrugged and laughed quickly, without the young, rather poignant gaiety I had noticed in her before.

"Oh well, I shan't do anything tonight, in any case."

I was surprised. "I thought the note was for tonight."

"No, no. For tomorrow. At ten. Under the bright sunlight. So what is there to fear?"

Although it should have been nothing to me, one way or the other, I was relieved. I could not help feeling that an encounter with the Devil-Vicar or any of his imitators, at this hour, would be unhealthy in the extreme, and if Marc were the culprit, this act might precipitate his unmasking. Anything would be preferable to that.

"Shall I ring for your servant?" I asked.

She hesitated. "No. It's such a lovely night. Don't disturb poor old Nettie. I think I'll just rest here a moment." She held out her hand to me. "Good night, dear, and thank you for being my friend."

I curtseyed, taking her hand, and feeling thoroughly ashamed of myself—of my jealousy earlier in the day, and of my suspicions about her condition—all the things she did not suspect when she called me her friend. I left her in the starlight, the fingers of her tow hands now tightly laced together, as though she held in some powerful emotion.

Poor Catherine. To devote one's life to the adoration of a portrait! Why should it hold such a fascination for her? I had seen it once, with no earth-shaking results. A very ordinary . . . well, not quite ordinary, portrait.

I was so sure the portrait held no fascination for me that when I passed the doors of the church, which were still ajar, I dared myself to peep inside, just to prove that I had no fears of its effect on me.

There was a lamp glowing in the Vicar's office and I remembered his invitation to me on the day we met, to come and look at his precious portrait of the man of whom he—to quote the Reverend MacDonnachie—"wished he might be the rebirth." Anything less like the Devil-Vicar of the portrait could hardly be conceived.

I stepped inside, feeling the dampness rise from the stones under my feet as I walked through the shadows toward the glowing lamplight.

In spite of the lamp, no one was in the Vicar's office. It was just like his untidy habits, to leave the light burning like this. Then I realized that without the Reverend MacDonnachie to give me countenance, I was a trespasser. I started to leave but could not help glancing up at the portrait of the Devil-Vicar just once. Due to the flicker of the lamp, the highlights and shadows cast by its glow, it seemed to me that the dark, shadowed eyes of the portrait gleamed like coals when a breath of air disturbs them. I shuddered and turned away, feeling the terrible attraction, and resisting it with all my common sense.

At that moment a loud, grating noise from the front of the building informed me that the sexton had shut and locked the doors. In a panic—for I had no intention of spending the night with the Devil-Vicar, however attractive he might be—I scurried out behind the nave and tried the doors. The great, vaulted interior of the church was dark as a coal-pit and I very nearly called for help. It seemed to me each time I turned in the silent church, the Devil-

Vicar must be somewhere in those gloomy shadows, watching me. He had preached here long ago. He had died so close by, and his ghost, if there were such things, might very well be lurking behind the damp, stone pillars that supported the main nave.

"Be calm," I told myself. "There are always side doors." In fact, Mrs. Fothergay and Mrs. MacDonnachie must have gone out a side door today, for I found them just leaving the churchyard after their instructive tour of the local tombstones. If I could find that side door locked from the inside, I might cross the graveyard and reach the gate behind the Yorkish Lion. Nothing would be more welcome than that inn.

I crossed behind the nave and passed the Vicar's office again, feeling my way, until I reached the south window of the church. Faint starlight entering the clear glass gave me light by which I made out the door. I tried the door but it was locked. I paused to consider the direction of the other doors and could recall having seen but one on this side. As I made out the outlines of the family pews before me, and decided to cross down by the chancel rail, to see if there was a door at the back of the altar somewhere, I heard a scraping sound, as of a footstep among the rushes near the chancel rail.

Remembering that the Vicar might not have gone home yet, and hoping nervously that it would be he, I spoke, in an ordinary tone, not wishing to call the attention of the sexton.

"Is it you, Reverend MacDonnachie? I was looking for you—to see the portrait."

No answer. I had not seriously believed the Vicar was locked in with me at this hour, not at least the familiar redbearded Vicar of the present day.

My voice, which had begun almost as a whisper,

echoed in a hoarse and unidentifiable way through the vaulting space overhead. I could scarcely have recognized it as my own. But the echo was the only answer I received, and I began to hope it was the sexton whose footsteps I had surprised.

Well, if it was the sexton, there was no need to play the innocent now. I had to explain and get out. I moved away from the south wall, toward the back of the church, retracing my footsteps to the nave.

Then I heard it again, the grating of a shoe among the dry rushes. It was as though someone were playing a silly trick upon me, and I knew of no one with that sort of humor —except perhaps one person.

At the head of the main nave, I stood trying to focus upon the dim, almost impenetrable dark before me, straight down the aisle to the altar. My eyes gradually made out the objects—the great pillars, and even the cruciform altar cloth. I recalled suddenly that the altar cloth was not, in fact, cruciform, and did not have white among its colors. What I saw must be something, or someone, standing before the altar, silently facing me down the long nave, a figure shrouded in the black of his surroundings, with just that balance of color provided by the full white clergyman's surplice.

It was impossible to make out the bodily contours at this distance among those clergical robes. But as I stared through the hollow darkness, I remembered the note of assignation Catherine had received, and that the handwriting resembled Marc Branshaw's.

Who but Marc would play such a trick? Who but Marc had this sort of twisted humor? This must be the trysting place he had chosen in which to meet Catherine. It was nearing ten o'clock. Catherine had lied to me. Her assignation was for tonight, after all.

Forgetting our quarrel this morning, and the unpleasant scene in the taproom of the Yorkish Lion, I spoke into the darkness that separated us along the church aisle.

"Marc! How can you? I suppose you think you will fool Catherine. What are you doing?"

The figure at the altar moved restlessly, the white of the cloth shifting in the dark against its black background. Then came a whisper, a strong enough sound so that I made it out, but as indistinct as my own voice had been a moment ago.

"Anne! Come here."

I was beginning to remember now that we had parted very bad friends, and it was a relief to hear him at least call me by name. I hesitated, then moved down the aisle toward him, demanding to know what he was doing, and what he thought he should gain by posing as the Devil-Vicar to win poor Catherine's love. I did not think so at the time, but long afterward I was convinced that, although I talked much to myself about his deceiving Catherine, I was chiefly concerned that he had been about to deceive me. I could not call my emotions anything other than jealousy.

Behind me, on the street, I heard the old sexton's voice as he spoke to some late passerby. On the spur of the moment I hesitated, turned, and almost went to the door to summon him. I though my gesture would send Marc packing by whatever manner in which he had entered the church, and his little masquerade would be over. Instead, I wrestled with the thought, and my own jealousy, then turned back and proceeded toward the altar. He had stepped away from the altar now and was below the chancel, hidden by the shadows of the pews.

When I reached the chancel rail, I discovered that I could not make out his figure at all. He was playing tricks, dissolved in the darkness and watching me, a thing I particularly disliked.

I stopped at the chancel rail and said sternly, trying to pierce the darkness on both sides:

"This has gone far enough, Marc! Stop playing games or I shall call the sexton. Marc? Where in blazes are you?"

There was not a sound behind me. I do not know why I started to turn. Some instinct, I suppose. Then I saw his arm reach out around me, passing before my eyes. I recognized the white cambric over the black sleeve. From behind my body, his arm moved gently closer to my face, and I thought, for an instant, that he would take my chin in his hand and kiss me, as he had that other night. I was torn between my desire for that caress, and anger that he had tried to fool me with his stupid games. I raised one hand to touch his arm, perhaps to ward it off in some belated attempt at coquetry. Suddenly, his arm pulled tight across my throat in an embrace I was far from expecting.

I gasped and tied to cry out his name:

"Marc!"

My hands clawed vainly at the sleeves of his robe. Even then I didn't quite understand that this was not my Marc Branshaw, until his other arm came up, and I felt my throat released long enough for me to gasp for air before both his hands drew a knotted cord up tight against my throat and pulled back upon it, strangling me. In the most intense and shattering pain, I felt the blood coursing against my temples, and my breath escaping through that corded vise in tiny, gurgling sounds.

In the far, far distance there was a noise of grating doors, and the sexton's complaining voice. "What's about? Now, who left the lamp so?"

The cord that had been drawing the last breath of life out of me, slipped off my throat and my assailant moved away swiftly. As I fell, I could hear faintly the flutter of robes as he ran.

"It can't be my own Marc," my shattered senses told me. "There's a mistake. I've made a terrible mistake."

I lay on the rushes, struggling to make some sound besides a groan, until I heard boots upon the floor of the nave, and the sexton's voice over me. He was holding the lamp from the Vicar's study.

"What's this, mum? What ye doin' there? Ay, and like ye was bad-drunk?"

I sat up, no thanks to him, for he stood helpless, shocked that I should be found in these sacred precincts. I touched my throat and muttered hoarsely that I had come to see the Vicar and had been locked in and someone had tried to strangle me.

"Impossible, mum," said the sexton seriously. "Nobody'd strangle ye here in the church. Indeed, no. 'Twas the dark, I daresay. Confused ye."

"And my throat?" which I exhibited as proof of my claim. "I suppose that was confused too."

"Ay, it's red. Right enough. Musn't rub it like that. Makes it red, as ye can see. Well now, ye've had a bad time and no mistake. Can ye walk, mum?"

Oh, this incredibly stupid villager!

"Listen to me!! The person who tried to strangle me—and I daresay killed those other two people—is somewhere in this church now. Go and find him."

The sexton raised the lamp, gave a quick, sweeping perusal of the surrounding darkness, and made out nothing more suspicious than the shadows of the pillars.

"Not a thing, mum. Must be ye mere thought there was some'ut in here with ye."

By this time, my assailant could have gotten out of the church in a dozen ways, for I had no doubt the scene was more familiar to him than to a stranger like myself. I was too tired, and too near being nauseated, to care. . . . Besides, what if the fiendish creature with the knotted cord were actually Marc Branshaw? Should I then testify to my suspicions?

I did not know. I had to think. Were there any signs that proved it might be Marc? Any peculiarity of touch?

At the open front doors of the church I saw Catherine Owen in her wheelchair. She had paused before the doors and looked perfectly astonished at sight of me.

"If you're coming to your appointment with the Devil-Vicar," I told her hoarsely, "you had best give up the notion. He's been rather busy for one night."

She was all solicitude.

"Anne! You look as though you've seen a ghost!"

"You were right," I agreed. "I saw your ghost. Whatever it was, I met it by accident, and it very nearly strangled me."

"I see." She looked down at her gloved hands, and her disappointment was so keen, I nearly felt like offering her my own experience with her beloved Devil-Vicar. "Then it's no use my waiting."

"Not unless you have a taste for a knotted cord applied to the throat," I told her.

She took my hand. "I'm sorry it happened to you, dear, but don't you think it possible that you startled him? That he was, perhaps, disappointed, and reacted violently when he saw that you were not—"

I rolled my eyes heavenward and brushed off the restraining hand of the sexton as well as Catherine's thick, sweet courtesy.

"Take him. I make you a gift of him, Miss Owen.

And if you find that he is also Marc Branshaw, when he has nothing better to be, you may have that one too!"

"Who is giving me away so freely?" asked a voice on the starlit street. Catherine and I turned, aware suddenly that several persons had collected outside the church to discover what Catherine and I were talking about so heatedly, and the curate, Frederick Niles, was calming them.

Catherine smiled at the voice we heard, but I did not, as we beheld Marc Branshaw crossing the cobblestones and making his way through the crowd to us. Although he joked, I saw that he was in a hurry, and he pushed his way toward us without ceremony.

The sexton hastened to say severely, "Lady was locked in the church, that's all to it. Good night to ye, mum. Next time, rap at the door to be let out. I'll hear."

"Nonsense," said the Reverend Niles. "Miss Wicklow seems to be hurt. Perhaps you can get the story, Mr. Branshaw."

Marc came to me and I studied his features, wondering if it were possible he could have tried to murder me only minutes before. In the starlight his face looked so like the Devil-Vicar's, and yet there was his smile, and the way he drew me to him, forgetting that we had been furiously angry on our last encounter. I don't know why, but I was reassured by a small thing—the fact that the sleeve of his short jacket was so obviously not the black robe and covering surplice I had seen in front of my eyes just before the knotted cord was applied to my throat. He managed to move me away from the gawping bystanders, and we got as far as the graveyard wall before he asked me what had happened.

"I thought we were not on speaking terms," I challenged him, getting down to more essential matters.

He laughed

"Still wish to be brother and sister?"

He reached around and took down the hand that I had pressed to my throat, where the pain was beginning to reassert itself in a nasty, throbbing way. He examined the aching red marks.

"Who did that?"

I said, "If you can tell me, you will do a great favor to the village. I stepped into the church to see the portrait of the Devil-Vicar and he paid a personal call upon me."

"Good God! That tiresome portrait!" he exclaimed. And then, as he fingers gently traced the bruises left by the strangling cord, he added, "Did you see this Devil-Vicar?"

"No. Furthermore, I have no wish to. If that is Catherine's idea of a lover, I can only say I pity her taste."

He smiled and then, when I was totally unprepared, leaned over and kissed me. I was almost too exhausted to respond, but I made a valiant effort. It was comforting to make myself believe in him, whether I had any proof or not. I felt that his very presence was essential to my nerves and my morale, and was perfectly ready to risk whatever danger was entailed in loving him. The moment I returned his kiss, I felt convinced of his innocence. Infallible intuition!

"I do think," he went on, when we were not so busy, "if we are going to spend our lives quarreling, we would do better to spend them elsewhere, in greater privacy. Don't you agree?"

"I wish you would explain," I said, "because as it is I don't know whether this is a proposal of marriage or an invitation to slap your face."

"I suggest you don't slap my face, or I might change my mind—since it is a proposal."

At this, the Reverend Niles began to clear everyone off the streets, with a smile at our doings.

But I did not feel capable of pursuing Marc's banter. I was trembling with the excitement of the night, my narrow escape, and the cold, sharp northern air, and Marc regarded me with concern.

"Great George and the Dragon!" cried a familiar voice. Stalking up the street from the inn was the Reverend MacDonnachie, followed by his wife. "What's all that noise at our Cathedral of the Almighty? Never heard such a babble!"

"My love," ventured his wife timidly, "I think you've interrupted a—a—well . . ."

"No, blast it!" shouted the Reverend. "Not this. Anybody can see what *this* is. I'm talking about all that babble at the church. What is it? Another wild dog they've treed and are wanting Branshaw to exorcize with his magic?"

It was nasty of him to bring up again the queer business of Marc and the killer-dog, but Niles explained to him, in his quiet way, what had happened. His voice was punctuated by loud, explosive and unbelieving ejaculations from the Vicar.

Marc had just picked me up in his arms when we saw Jamie Keegan looking down at us from an open window of the Yorkish Lion.

"Thought you was goin' home. What kept ye?" he demanded of Marc.

"Yes," said Marc, "but I was busy."

Jamie looked down at me. "Why must he carry you? Can't you walk, Miss Anne?"

Marc grinned. "Never mind. This is my affair."

"Well," said Jamie. "I always thought Miss Anne could walk right good for a female."

"True. But you see, I was proposing to Miss Anne."

"Oh, that. I thought it was something important."

"I'm afraid," Marc told me apologetically, "that our news isn't of importance to anyone but ourselves."

Well, I've done it, I thought. I've burnt my bridges, confessed I don't wish to live without him, and for all I know he may strangle me in my bed some night.

But if I had it to say over, I should still have said yes to him, I knew.

XVI

ROSE KEEGAN CAME to my room the following day to tell me that Marc had arrived with Dr. Lowther, but I was a great disappointment to the doctor as well as to myself, for he announced that he could find no mementos of my encounter worth mentioning. Even the soreness was leaving my throat muscles. Tea, and more tea, was prescribed, along with some choice gruel. Poor substitute for the coddling I had dreamed of from Marc, and no consolation for my dreadful experience.

While Marc stood behind the doctor, making silent fun of my chagrin at not finding myself a heroine, the doctor spoiled his entire diagnosis by warning me of another attack.

"You understand, of course, ma'am, that two of our people have died violently, in the recent past."

I wished he would not remind me. It only made my throat ache in sympathy with my renewed fears. These had been lulled to sleep today, during the few hours since Marc asked me to marry him. Marc's presence did more than that. It lulled me out of any suspicion that my mysterious assailant might have been Marc himself. I had only to look at him, to see his smile, and the way he regarded me with an expression, at once tender and warm, to banish all my previous fears that the Devil-Vicar was Marc Branshaw.

I told Dr. Lowther that I knew of the other deaths.

"Well then, I need not warn you, Miss Wicklow, that the attack on you today—that is to say, last night—might prove fatal on its next dosage. I advise you to take care. Extreme care. Perhaps it would be best if you trusted none of us, until you are on your way back to London." He patted the bedclothing in a paternal way. "And now, may I wish you a pleasant rest? I will not say recovery, for you are quite recovered now, I believe. In any case, I must be off. Some typhus cases in Upshed. Very unfortunate."

He packed together the horrid instruments of his trade and, in doing so, studied Marc rather carefully. Marc was uneasily aware of his survey and yet I could see that he pretended not to be.

"As for you, my friend, hadn't you better see me one of these days? One never knows, eh? You can trust me, my boy. No? Well—so much the worse for you. Good day to you both. Remember, Miss Wicklow, I prescribe rest and quiet. That means . . . no visitors, for the moment."

When the doctor had gone, I laughed. "What a cheerful note on which to leave me! Does he expect some giant Gytrash to leap into my bedchamber and devour me?"

"He's a fool. Pay no attention." Marc kissed me goodbye, then paused before leaving. "But let us say I'm a jealous dog. Don't find yourself alone with *any* man. Promise?"

"Females too?" I asked with mock-seriousness.

"Especially females. Forgot to say so. Even if they—don't walk."

He left me prey to a thousand fantasies, each worse than the other.

That evening, during my supper of nauseous gruel, Jamie Keegan presented me with a bundle which, when unwrapped, proved to be the manuscript Marc had stolen from me, the one about the Red Indians of North America. With it was a note:

Darling Anne, I used this to entice you up here. Let us hope I will have no need of such methods again.

I hardly care whether they ever find their monster of Maidenmoor if it means danger to my dearest. I am done with my quest for knowledge in that department.

So it is back to London or wherever, as soon as we can dispose of Moyna's property, which she so foolishly left to me. Let me know when you feel up to another heated quarrel. The "making it up" is the best of it.

Have I told you? . . . I love you.

He did not sign his name, or even his initial, but I suppose he assumed that I should recognize it on the grounds that at the very most, I received only one proposal a day.

Studying his handwriting and trying to recall the note to Catherine, I convinced myself that there was only the most superficial resemblance. But to be sure, I asked Jamie:

"How long was it last night between the time you said goodnight to Marc and then saw him again with me on the street?"

Jamie ruffled his hair in thought.

"Ten minutes. Maybe twenty. He might've stopped in the taproom."

"But no more than twenty minutes?"

"Ay. No more."

The horror of those minutes in the church with the Devil-Vicar had made them seem an eternity but I felt that twenty minutes was too short a time for the strangler to perform all that had been necessary. Thank God!

As for Marc, he was as good as his word. When I thought it would be the proper thing to see him the day following his proposal, I learned that he had gone into Teignford to arrange for the sale of Moyna's property.

Mrs. Fothergay took the news of our engagement surprisingly. She said to me at once:

"How like the dear boy! Well—" She paused to sigh. "It was not to be. As I told Marc myself only a day or two ago, 'You and I can never be,' I said. Now, Gareth, there is a dear man, just the sort to suit me best. He wants to take care of me. So protective, you know. He asks me innumerable questions about my affairs, anxious to be of any help that he may. Charming man . . . and then too, I shall be Lady Bedelia. It has a ring to it."

I confessed that it certainly did. We were up at the local stationer's, I to send the Red Indian manuscript back to its publishers in London, and Mrs. Fothergay to order a quire of writing paper for her voluminous correspondence.

Just when she was hesitating between the lavender and the green paper to express her personality—"which is so changeful, so illusive"—she explained to me, Jamie Keegan came hurrying into the post office side of the shop.

"Ay, it's like I said, Miss Anne. I know'd whether to find you. Miss Catherine sent me to ask you to come to a party tonight. Not a big one. Just a comfortable one, she says. You and Marc, and the Reverend and the Missus, and one or two others."

"Myself, of course," said Mrs. Fothergay familiarly. "I was the first to be told, you know." She took the two packets of paper to the open door and stood there, considering the colors.

Jamie whispered to me, "Miss Catherine would be that pleased if ye'd accept, Miss Anne."

"Has Marc accepted?"

"He will if you will. He was busy goin' over some old things Miss Moyna's thrown out in the mistal. Never saw so much trash in all his life, he says."

"Yes, but what did he say about Miss Catherine's party?"

"Made a face, he did, like this." He wrinkled his nose. "But he's to come if you will. Says it's one last chance to take the size of them that might've killed Miss Moyna and the others."

"What a romantic reason!" I exclaimed, somewhat put out.

But it ended with Marc's fetching me that evening and telling me about our future as we walked up to the Owen house, so that when we arrived I was in a flush of good humor. I had never been in love before, although, upon several occasions I had fancied I was, and I supposed that treading-on-air feeling, with no worries, no problems, only the all-consuming question: Does he really love me?

We stopped at the door and, as he raised his hand to the knocker, he looked at me. I realized only then that all his charming banter on our way had concealed what he was really thinking. His face, by moonlight, appeared to me dark and brooding and sad.

I said, "What is it? Are you quite well?"

He laughed, but I sensed that it was forced.

"Of course. Why do you ask?"

"Nothing. I thought—it was almost as though you were a different man somehow." I wished his eyes did not look at me like that. They brought to my mind the wonderful, terrible eyes in that painting of the Devil-Vicar.

"I must tell you something."

I stepped back, away from the door and into the shadows again, oddly disturbed.

"Then tell me now. While there's still time."

"What made you say that?" he asked, still like a stranger, careful and polite.

"I—I don't know. I mean, before we go inside. . . . Tell me here." Then I believed I understood. I swallowed as hard as I could and made my voice sound level and dry. "You don't want to marry me. That's it. They are all going to congratulate us, but you wanted to tell me beforehand."

His laughter was genuine this time.

"You are silly, aren't you? Do you think I go about proposing to women I don't wish to marry? I've never proposed to another woman in my life—and expected to be believed."

I was not sure if this meant that I was more gullible than his other women, but to my enormous relief, he kissed me, and I thought that anything else in the whole world he had to tell me could not be so important as this.

Nevertheless, I was rudely jolted when a dry voice cut into our little moment from the open doorway, and the Owen maid said sourly, "Ye comin'? Do I wait the night now?"

"Let's let her wait," Marc whispered in my ear as he tried to kiss me again, but several people inside the house were now peering out and making low-voiced, amused comments, so I ducked away from his hands and stepped inside.

It was only then I realized we had gotten away from whatever it was he wanted to tell me. It did not matter. I would ask him at the end of the evening.

When we joined the rest of the party in the crowded front parlor, I saw that, thanks to the heavy maroon furniture and portieres with their fluttering ribbon trim, the room looked blood-red by the light of several elegant branches of candles. The parlor was small and over-furnished. Though I recognized everyone, they seemed like strangers in their best finery. Catherine, in particular, looked better than I had ever seen her. She had a high coloring in her prominent child's cheeks, and was wearing a shade of rich, golden brown that set off her hazel eyes charmingly. She was not in her wheelchair tonight, but "arranged" in a large chair not far from the fireplace, where the low-burning peat seemed in momentary danger of dying out. The folds of her gown, shimmering in the light of many candles, made her the center of attention, and I wondered with some easiness why Marc had never seen in her this charm and even this beauty. In spite of her sturdy frame, there was a fragile, helpless quality about her, and I had always supposed such things attracted men.

The Reverend MacDonnachie was holding Catherine's hand and flattering her in his great, elephantine way, so that Mrs. Fothergay tittered behind her fan, and inquired archly:

"Are you not jealous, ma'am? Miss Catherine seems to have made a conquest."

Mrs. MacDonnachie smiled her watery smile.

"Dear Cadmon. He does love the ladies." She was utterly unruffled.

Catherine turned away from her admirer to greet Marc and me, and to tell us how happy she was at the news that had come to her. Curiously enough, I had a notion that she was sincere in this, as she probably thought this left the way clear for her with her phantom lover, should he prove to be as real as she claimed. But then, Catherine was one of those complex creatures with honest eyes, of whom everyone says: "I read her character and her thoughts as I read a book. Clear as pure water." I was learning that if one studied a very deep stream, no matter how clear it might be on the surface, somewhere in the depths was obscurity.

Presently, the Vicar suggested that if Catherine would grace the evening with her inimitable playing of the pianoforte, he would volunteer to work the pedals, and otherwise oblige by turning pages, et cetera.

Marc was abstracted and, although he smiled and behaved in every way to indicate that when he saw me his thoughts were upon me, I wondered what troubled him during the moments when his mind was elsewhere. I think, almost without being aware of it, I had watched to see his reaction to the fireplace and its small, neat fire. He never went near it and, even more curious, never looked that way once during the evening.

A good deal of fun was made out of the moving of furniture, and the rolling of carpets into a corner that laid bare the clean, smooth sandstone floor—an odd dancing surface, but it served. There were any number of challenges and boasts of strength between Sir Gareth and the Vicar, both of whom claimed the title for Maidenmoor. However, I noted that while these two sturdy members of the stronger sex battled verbally, Marc and one or two other male guests managed to do most of the heavy work. I suspected Marc only wanted to get it done and out of the way. He seemed impatient with the whole business.

Nonetheless, when we danced the waltz together, Marc's mood improved perceptibly. We talked of the Continent and the places I had wanted to visit all my life from hearing my parents talk of them, and, most of all, we talked of ourselves.

I discovered during the course of our dances that Catherine could play very well in spite of her handicap. Her brother had lifted her to the pianoforte, and it was the Vicar who goodnaturedly turned pages and saw to the pedals. I could see why he did not dance. It would have been like a bear capering his tricks.

When refreshments were served, Catherine raised her hands to Marc and asked if he would carry her to her chair by the fire. He obliged without comment, and I noted a sudden silence from all parts of the room as everyone watched the two of them. He seated her carefully in her chair, and handed her the dainty little glass of mixed ices that the Vicar removed from a sparkling crystal tray which I took to be the remnant of more prosperous times in the Owen family.

A mill owner from Upshed and his wife made some to-do over the picture Catherine exhibited as Marc's shadow was removed from her, and she smiled.

"One would think you are in love," said the mill owner's wife brightly.

Before the rest of us could do more than look uncomfortable, Catherine smiled and agreed that, "perhaps I am."

Gareth cut in sharply, "Cathie! Gad's life, girl!"

But Catherine waved her hand at him teasingly.

"Oh, no Garrie. I must only make certain of whom I love. A small problem of identity." I saw then, as her fingers tightened over something in her lap, that she still held, wadded in a ball with her lace handkerchief, the note that Sir Gareth had handed her in church the other day. So she fancied herself in love with the oil painting! Whether he existed or not, it was unnerving to me and I wished the matter hadn't been mentioned at all.

There was a clatter of silver, and then a moment's silence as we removed our gloves and busied ourself with the ices. Catherine broke the silence.

"How provoking! Marc, would you mind putting more coals on the fire? You are nearest the tongs there."

Marc, who had been holding one of my hands, and yet seemed miles away in thought, stiffened, and I felt the fingers of his hand close on mine so fiercely that I nearly cried out. However, I was as near to the fire as he was, and I said quickly, while everyone in the room stared at us:

"There." I kicked several coals over into the faint glow of the fire with my slipper toe. "Now, Marc, you see what a good housewife I shall be! Always at hand—or should I say—at foot?"

The Vicar's laughter boomed out, and the others joined in. Marc, who had stared at Catherine without once looking at the fire, turned to me, and kissed me on the ear. I raised his hand and touched his fingers with my lips to show him that he could count upon me.

Catherine sat exactly as she had before, looking lovely, with a trace of brighter red in her cheeks, and a little puzzled frown marring the smooth broadness of her forehead. Beside her, the fire crackled as the coals caught on the pile of dried bracken that had been laid for the earlier fire and never burned. A spark flew upward to land on the hem of her gown, and I was much relieved to see Marc brush it off before I could reach it. When Catherine thanked him, he ignored her and asked me if I cared to leave, for the others were rising under cover of Mrs. Fothergay's noisy flirtation with Sir Gareth.

"Now, dear Garrie," she was saying, "you must not go out in the horrid cold just to see me home. I am quite sure the Vicar and Mrs. MacDonnachie will be pleased to oblige . . . . Well, if you insist. Really! I am quite overcome by such solicitude! Catherine, my dear, it will be a lucky woman who snatches your big, strong brother."

Catherine said civilly, "I am sure she will be, ma'am. Garrie is the most perfect of brothers." She put out her hand to me and said in a lower tone, "Please, Anne, stay a moment. Let them go."

Although I could see that Marc was in no mood to remain, I did not know what else to do. I watched the crackling fire as the little flames leaped up and then retreated into the cavernous recesses of the chimney. Marc went to the table and seemed very much interested in the crystal tray which took all the flashing light from the branch of candles nearby. Catherine watched him.

"Marc, dear, would you mind bringing me that branch of candles? I want to show Anne this lovely carving of the mantel here."

Without looking at the candles, he took up the base and handed it to her. I could see by his scowl that he was growing angry at her, or at something else which troubled him. I wondered at her attempt to upset him in this fashion.

When she had showed me the carving, I could see

nothing of importance about it. It was a most ordinary mantel, and I did not like the careless way she used that branch of candles, for the tallow dripped down upon the hem of her gown, and once upon the flying ribbons of the runner on the low table to her left. I felt sure she was doing this solely to bring Marc to some rash act, because of his well-known abhorrence of fire.

"We really must go," I said nervously. "It was a lovely party, and we had a delightful time." I dropped a curtsey to Catherine. All the time I was aware of the candles waving in her hand.

"The polite formalities, by all means," said Marc, turning to face us, as cuttingly sarcastic as possible. "Tell the lady how charming she looks, Anne. Tell her how she behaved with her customary good taste, and made them all adore her. Tell her that if she isn't careful she is going to burn the accursed house down just to drive me out of my mind! And she has succeeded, admirably, beyond her wildest dreams. I wouldn't care if she *did* burn the house down, and herself with it!"

He seized my hand and almost dragged me away from her.

Embarrassed at his shocking breach of manners, I went along with him, turning only, and against his tugging hand, to wish Catherine goodnight, and to say, "Please forgive us. I'm sure you understand."

She did not seem in the least surprised by this scene which was so horrid to me, for I had never seen a man display such manners to a lady, and it was doubly hurting that it should be a man I loved who did so.

In the doorway I looked back to see her sitting there in a frozen position, still puzzled, but also, I think, satisfied of some conclusion she had drawn.

From her look, which was certainly not love, I concluded she had given up the notion that Marc was the lover out of her favorite portrait. But still, she must be quite sure. Doubtless, she had hoped to prove it by these tricks with the fire. Marc was right. Her actions had been deliberate. As I looked at her, she reached over to set the branch of candles down on the little table. The candles, tilted by the imbalance of her position, threatened to slip off the table. Tallow dropped onto the hanging fringe on the table, and I pulled at Marc's sleeve.

"She shouldn't. It's so unsafe."

Shutting the parlor doors, he said impatiently, "Where the devil is that maid?"

Nettie finally brought us our wraps and Marc put mine around me.

The night was splendid, full of stars. Marc and I started to walk, arm in arm. I could see that, although he was shaken by his duel with Catherine, my own influence could not be negligible, for he was soon calm. He tightened his hold around my waist, and pulled me to him.

"What a long time I've needed you!" he murmured, and I could have cried in the happiness of hearing that. He added, still with half his mind on what we had left, "I wonder what she expected me to do? Run shrieking from the house at sight of her innumerable fires?"

"No," I said, thinking it over. "She expected to press you so hard with—with your dislike of fire that you would turn into the ghost of the Devil-Vicar before her eyes. And then you would be entirely her property."

"Grisly thought." He kissed my cheek and asked in a voice he tried to infuse with his familiar, teasing tone, "Do you know any young lady in market for property, slightly scarred and not precisely what the wrapping indicates, but still of the required species?"

I admitted in his own style that, if pressed, I might find a place for the property in question. For a few minutes it was the most beautiful night I had ever known. I almost forgot that in this village a murderer still walked free, although his savage canine weapon was silenced. I was rudely shocked by Nettie's screeching voice as she ran out onto the street after us.

Marc did not move. His face in the moonlight was the color of ashes. Then, as though ashamed of his own fear or whatever memory destroyed him, he covered his face with a hand that trembled.

"God! I knew it would happen. I've known it all along."

I started back.

"It must be those wretched candles. Or the bracken in the fireplace. They've caught. Come. . . . Marc?"

I had to call to him again, more urgently. This time, after a sickening pause, he returned with me the few steps to the Owen House. Nettie had pushed open the parlor doors and we saw Catherine across the room, trying to shift her chair out of reach of the little flame that had leaped to the runner of the table, and from the runner to the flimsy ribbons on the portieres. The candles lay burning themselves out against the sandstone floor, but a trail of fire scrambled up along the long window, the length of the portieres. Catherine saw us and cried out.

"It was an accident! Take me out of here. Marc!"

I was petrified. It seemed the natural thing to cross that room, to seize the burning materials and stamp them out; yet, with the ribbons of flame flaring out wider every moment, I could scarcely move.

But worse, I felt the deep, terrible reluctance of the man who had come in behind me. I could almost hear his heartbeat in the anguish of the struggle with his own morbid revulsion. Then Marc ran past me into the room, stopped at the pianoforte and leaned over the corner of the instrument, commanding her, just out of reach of her arms.

"Walk, Catherine! Walk! You haven't fooled me. Walk—or you will die."

She made a terrible effort, her face a deep, blood-dark color, the cords in her throat vibrating with the pressure she exerted. She leaped forward from her chair, the chair toppled over and she lay stretched on the floor, only inches from the smoldering flames. She screamed, holding out both arms to Marc, clawing at the air between them.

"Marc! I know you're not the Other One. You can help me. Please . . . Marc!"

I was as frightened of his reaction as I was of the fire so close to the invalid girl. His eyes glittered black and terrible. I did not know whether it was his fear of the fire, or his determination to prove once and for all that she could walk, which led him to say again:

"Come, Catherine! Walk to me!"

He held out his hands to her. I knew then, even if he did not, that she would have moved by this time if she could, and I ran toward her. As I did so, the portieres caught, and began to shower her body with shreds of burning materials. Even Marc was not blind to this. Whatever cowardice or cruelty had held him back was finally dispelled. He reached for her, seized her arms, and dragged her away. Then, as I beat the curls of flame off her skirts, he pulled the portieres away from her so that they hung half off their heavy rod. I helped him drag her away, conscious of the maid, Nettie, screaming out on the street, her every sound grating horribly on my nerves.

Marc was just lifting Catherine into his arms when the rod of the portieres snapped from its corner fixture, and its full length hurtled down across his neck and shoulders. Stunned, he went down on his knees under the impact, his body shielding Catherine. Though I trembled for his safety, I took Catherine from him, dragged her across the floor to the door, and only then could look back to see Marc getting to his feet with an effort. The rod and the burning portieres lay in a smoldering heap beside him.

Catherine was muttering, "I'm all right. See to him."

I rushed to Marc, helping him to the door and noting with sick apprehension for him that his clothing was seared in places, his hair disheveled, but his eyes were the most revealing. They were deeply shadowed with a pain and horror whose depths I could not begin to fathom. He leaned back against the door, and I put my arms around him. We hugged each other, to be quite sure we were both safe.

He buried his face against my hair.

"I never thought I could face it. I couldn't, if you hadn't been here."

"It's all right now, darling," I whispered. "It's all right."

"Is it—is it still burning?" He would not look.

I glanced around and saw that two men had come running from the street and were stamping out what little remained of the fire, which had burnt itself out upon the stone floor. A good deal of smoke filled the room, but the crisis was over, or so I thought.

Catherine sat on the staircase, with her maid hovering solicitously over her. She looked almost her usual calm self. She had not been burned, although she was picking at a burnt hole in the heavy material of her skirt, and sighing over the damage. She looked up at me.

"I'm so dreadfully sorry. I know now that Marc couldn't have gone back into that room if he had been the Other One."

"He is Marc Branshaw," I said coldly, "and you had best make up your mind to that."

Marc stared at me. He was shaken and dazed. His eyes had a fixed expression, as though he could not quite see me.

"Marc?" I shook him and he winced. I had almost forgotten the jolt he had received from the rod and the burning portieres.

"Darling," I said, when there was no response. "Let us go. It's late, and . . . I'm very tired."

He nodded, moved away from the parlor doors, and followed me. His quiet obedience itself was ominous. I said to Catherine at the last, "I'll have someone fetch the doctor to you—after he's been to Marc."

Marc scowled at this and seemed, momentarily, to recover his obstinate will.

"I'm perfectly fit. Send the doctor to Catherine. I'll see no doctor. Come, I'll take you home."

This was pure nonsense, but I did not make matters worse by arguing. I saw Sir Gareth hurrying up the street in a panic, having gotten word that his sister was trapped by a fire, and I went to him.

"She's safe. May we borrow your gig and the mare?"

"Yes, yes. Anything. In the stables behind the house. Good God. Branshaw! You in this too? What were you doing? Running away?"

"He saved your sister's life," I said sharply, as

Marc did not appear to notice him. When Gareth had hurried on, Marc murmured to himself in a puzzled way, "She cannot walk. She cannot—possibly—walk. It's all wrong. If not Catherine, who then?"

"Don't think of it now," I told him. He was in no condition to solve in one night the mystery that had terrorized the whole of Maidenmoor for months, perhaps years.

With the help of a husky millhand we managed to get the mare and the gig into harness. Before I could stop him, Marc lifted me into the gig, and then got in. He could not control the trembling of his fingers as he took the reins, and when I insisted on his driving to Branshaw Hall instead of the inn, he made no objection. The night was bitter cold, and I hoped it would revive him, but I was now aware that his hands were burned across the palms ,and that there were searing marks across his throat and the nape of his neck. I was concerned for him, for many reasons, but most of all because he seemed so distant, and did not say a word on the entire journey.

When we reached the Hall on the green brow of the hill, I jumped out of the gig without assistance, and called to the groom. Marc followed me, moving with a quick, easy step, and yet I could see that the effort at normal behavior took a heavy toll on his strength.

In the pleasant reception hall of the house Marc looked up the long flight of stairs. I read in his eyes his terrible weariness. In alarm, I reached out to him, but before I could touch him, he took one step, stumbled and collapsed at the foot of the stairs. Panic-stricken, I knelt by him and called for help. He opened his eyes, whispered something faintly.

"Don't—let them touch me."

Here again was his strange, abnormal fear of personal contact, and I tried to be matter-of-fact.

"Of course not, darling. Why ever should they?"

He seemed reassured.

When I called his name a moment later, he did not hear me. He had lapsed into unconsciousness. I turned down the collar of his coat and his shirt and gently examined the back of his head and his neck to see where he was hurt. The rod of the portieres had struck just above the nape of the neck and his hair was singed there. Probably it was this blow which had done the most damage, although I could see no abrasions. But as I slipped his collar away, I saw a sign that made me shudder:

Below the fresh, searing scorch on his neck made by the portieres, were the deeper scars of a terrible burning, long ago. I tore away the collar. The broad white tissue of scars branded his back in a dozen places. There could be no mistake. They were burns, some years old.

Hearing the voices of the Branshaw servants approaching, I hurriedly rearranged his clothing over the scars and studied his features. With his black hair free about his face, the light mockery gone, and haggard evidences of pain limning the features I recognized from the portrait in the church, I wonderer with a kind of horrid fascination, if I were looking at the Devil-Vicar who was dead these many years.

XVII

I STOOD IN the dark and gloomy upper hall of the Branshaw house, just outside Marc's bedchamber, awaiting Dr. Lowther's summons. I stood under the forbidding eyes of all the Branshaw portraits, whose puritanical faces looked as though they were aware that the one who was called the heir to the Branshaws was an interloper after all, and not one of them. I could almost feel their animosity, their tight-lipped resentment against the man who called himself "Marc Branshaw"—and who might be dying at this very moment.

I had been standing in this spot for some time and, as it took the doctor two hours to arrive, I could see that it would shortly be dawn. This was a relief, for the winter sun might thaw the abnormaly cold atmosphere of this house of illness and death.

I sent the housekeeper back to bed and Dilys was soothing the cook, who had gone into hysterics and had begun to see strange floating faces of dead Branshaws on the main staircase, plus other ghostly phenomena which she claimed would foretell the death of "Master Marc." She complained between sobs that "Master Marc would go the way of Miss Moyna." While Dilys explained carefully, and for the twentieth time, that the doctor was doing all he could (for we did not know in what condition Marc might be at this moment, or what his injuries were), I was sorely tempted to burst into hysterics myself.

I hinted to myself, during this long wait, that Marc might well be the man who had attacked me in the church and, almost as bad, the creature who had frightened me at Moyna's cottage. Could I really go on loving the man of the church darkness, the creature with those savage hands?

The thought of Marc's hands gave me pause. Surely, those fingers upon my throat, the terrible, powerful thumbs, could not belong to Marc. . . . Could they? I tried to recall his hands, but I could not. I could not visualize anything except his own suffering, for, whoever he was, it did not in any way diminish my feeling for him. The horror was there, but as something apart from him. I was bitter against the impulse which made him commit these acts—if he had committed them—and against a fate which gave him so many attractions and then pursued him relentlessly with attempts to burn him alive, and to give him an illness that plagued him, and who knows what other sufferings that I was not even aware of?

And I will confess that the idea of my Marc and that incredible, fairy-tale face in the portrait being of the same blood and loving me, was so overwhelming that I didn't care if he were the Devil himself.

Dilys looked through the open door of Moyna Branshaw's room and said idly, as she gazed across the room and out the window, "Someone is up and about, over at the Owens'. That Miss Catherine, with her fire tricks, she's a sly one. Always trying to make up to the master. Playing he's the Devil-Vicar. As if Master Marc wasn't just as nice as that Other One."

Poor Catherine. What would happen if she found out that the lover of her portrait was truly alive, so near her?

More important, however, was the attitude which would be taken by Dr. Lowther. It was his response that I awaited with such trepidation. When Marc still had not come to consciousness half an hour after the big Branshaw servant got him to his room, I knew I must send for the doctor in spite of Marc's plea for secrecy. I was determined, if the doctor made threats, to get Marc safely out of Maidenmoor before any action of a legal nature could be taken.

When Dilys mentioned the Devil-Vicar, I felt a strong compulsion to talk about him, and at the same time I was terrified for fear some tone in my voice, some casual glance or other little sign of awareness would give away Marc's secret.

"Did you know the Devil-Vicar?" I asked.

"Saw him once or twice, mum. But I remember him and Miss Moyna. They used to laugh—Miss Moyna did—and after a time, the Devil-Vicar would laugh too, at how they fooled the village. But he was much younger than Miss Moyna—twelve years, I'm told—and when he came, very serious. Sometimes he frightened the congregation when he preached of sin and the Devil and Gytrashes and all. It was terrible. After . . . the thing happened to him, we began to say he talked terrible and frightening because he was talking of his own sins. Do you think so, mum?"

"I'm sure I don't know," I said.

"It makes not matter, though. We felt dreadful to know he'd died in such a way. When Miss Moyna showed Miss Catherine and some of the others a miniature that her son had sent her—that would be just afore her death—we all was taken by surprise, and pleased, too. He looked so like the poor Devil-Vicar."

"And what did you think of Miss Moyna's husband, Dilys?"

"I tell you straight out, mum. Master Josiah, Miss Moyna's husband, was never one to make you take a fancy to him. Miser he was, and mean. Slapped Miss Moyna more than once, he did. Small wonder, a year after he died, Miss Moyna fell in love with the young Reverend when he come to Maidenmoor."

"Were there any others, before the Devil-Vicar?"

Dilys smiled. "None you might mention. She was very fond of young Master Marc and he come first with her. Such a sickly little boy he was! Miss Moyna did flirt a bit, that she did and no mistake. And then, even when she was in love with the Devil-Vicar there was others—the young curates that served the

Devil-Vicar, lanky, awkward things as they was, that she smiled at and perhaps kissed once or twice in fun. But she was that way, and freer to misbehave after she'd took her boy to France for him to get well. That was just before she returned and met the Reverend Morgan."

I burned with a bitter jealousy against the dead charmer, Moyna. It was she and not Catherine who was my real rival.

Dilys had left the door to Moyna's room open. Without interest, I studied the whitewashed crossbeams that made the high-ceilinged room seem so much lower. Then I glanced beyond the beams and out the window, to the green rolling flesh of the moorland. I hated the moors and resolved that whatever Dr. Lowther did, I, at least, would not let another disaster befall Marc like the one that cost him those terrible scars.

The bedchamber door made a scraping sound as it opened, and Dr. Lowther motioned me to come in. I did so, looking quickly at the bed and noting that Marc appeared asleep and comfortable. At least, the lines of pain in his face had been erased, which was my greatest relief.

"He will do nicely now, I think," said Dr. Lowther. "A bit of laudanum. Just the thing for such emergencies. As you will observe, I've stripped off his burned clothing and gotten him snug in his own night things."

I said, "Thank you." He had not mentioned the scars. Was it possible he would answer all my prayers and continue to play the innocent?

He rolled down his sleeves and I helped him into his heavy riding coat. The task took an interminable time, for I was in dreadful suspense. I asked finally:

"Will he recover?"

"From this injury? I see no reason to doubt it. The wounds from the fire are superficial. Nasty blow at the base of the skull, but that's all gone by. Only time will tell if there's damage within. Those . . . old scars are curious."

So it must come. I felt my knees weaken and leaned back against the little table beside Marc's bed, pretending a firmness I was far from feeling.

"I know. I saw the scars when he collapsed."

"Just so. The scars of a very serious burning. Ma'am, are you aware of the appalling episode in this village some fifteen or sixteen years ago? A mass hysteria directed against a foolish young man who had committed sacrilege in his holy office?"

I nodded, and to spare him further explanations, I said calmly, "Can he be Ewen Morgan? I don't know. But he isn't guilty of the things that are happening here, whatever you may think. I know him. He may be ill–I don't deny it– but he wouldn't do those things. He wouldn't kill . . ." I felt my throat automatically.

Dr. Lowther smiled, a little smile at human trust. "How easily we are convinced by love! Believe me, Miss Wicklow, I hope you're right. Several villagers during the past year have asked me if it was possible that this man could be the same as the one who died sixteen years ago–"

"But the bones that were discovered when the ashes of the parsonage were sifted," I put in, hoping to lead him off.

"My dear lady, the parsonage was built on a part of the old graveyard. What else but bones would be found if one looked? At any rate, when I was asked, I could not be sure, until now. But I should not think those scars he bears are sixteen years old, if that means anything. They seem scarcely more than a year old—at the most, two years."

He paused, considering.

"I believe it is, in part, the very fear that he *is* the same man, which has kept the villagers from laying hands to him and accusing him a second time. They didn't intend that murder sixteen years ago. When it was committed, they held themselves responsible. Now, in a sense, they are defending this man, hoping he will prove his innocence. Whether they regard him as the Devil-Vicar's ghost returned, or as that creature's natural son, they're giving him this chance, in order to sponge out that other, involuntary murder they thought they had committed. But the moment is at hand when there will be a reckoning."

"What action do you intend to take?"

He took up his valise, choosing his words carefully.

"None, for a day or so, until he's up and on his feet. I doubt if, in his present state, we need concern ourselves with such matters. Send for me if he shows any decisive change."

"What—sort of change?" I asked, thinking, with a sense of increasing darkness that this was what I had been afraid of all along.

His face lightened. He very nearly smiled.

"No. Not the kind you're apparently fearing. No sudden attempted violence. On the other hand, I join the village in suspecting that someone would like us to believe in his guilt."

"That thought never occurred to me," I said indignantly.

"I understand. But let me know immediately if you note any change in his manner, or any undue activity." He took my hand and I curtseyed to him. He turned away, hesitated.

"Miss Wicklow, I share your hope in the innocence of your friend, possibly because I can imagine his physical sufferings years ago, if, in truth, he is the late Devil-Vicar. But I must remind you again that he is a fraud, and that we still don't know what he's done with the real Marc Branshaw."

My face froze into a parody of politeness.

"It was quite unnecessary for you to remind me. Good day."

He smiled gently.

"There, there. Probably a very simple explanation. You had best get some sleep."

I sent Dilys to usher him out, while I pushed the table away and took up my place in a chair beside Marc's bed.

I sat there wondering how this would all end, and if we would ever discover the truth of the recent happenings. At least Dr. Lowther was withholding action.

What had become of the original Marc Branshaw?

The room was bitter cold. I wished I might light a fire in the fireplace, but I didn't dare because the noise would almost certainly disturb Marc. He was breathing quietly, as though his sleep were natural and not induced by the sleeping potion that the doctor had given him.

I don't know how much time had past when I was aroused from a half-doze to hear the frantic barking of the Branshaw dogs somewhere on the grounds, together with noisy shouts and screams of fury. I could not mistake the voice of the Branshaw groom, crying fiercely:

"Ay, my pretties! Worry him! The nasty outcomer! Set your teeth to him. That's my pretties!"

I looked over at Marc to see if the noise disturbed him, and got a severe shock to see him staring at me, his eyes luminous and wide, glazed by the drug.

I said softly, "It's just the dogs. Go to sleep."

A moment later I knew that he didn't understand. He was still under the influence of the laudanum. I closed my eyes so I should not be aware of that puzzled, confused stare. Then he whispered a name:

"Moyna?"

I felt sick at this blow, but said nothing.

Either the drug or some other calming influence overcame him, and to my intense relief, he closed his eyes and was still.

Outside, the quarrel over the dogs went on hotter than ever. I was to tense to remain quiet, and got up and went out into the hall and called to Dilys. She had brought a chair into the hall and was curled up in it, asleep, when I reached her.

"What on earth is that noise out on the moors, Dilys?"

She listened, yawning widely and smothering it with a mumbled apology.

"One of the villagers from Upshed, mum. They always take the crossing inside the Branshaw bounds. We don't stand for that, and set the dogs to them." She listened pleasurably. "Dogs caught this one, ay. Fair savaging him, they are."

"Well, tell the groom to stop the dogs, at once. They may do serious harm to the man."

The noise, the uproar and curses mingled to disturb us even here in the hall, but did not bother Dilys.

"I should hope they do hurt, mum. Everybody knows you can't cross another man's fields. Not in this Riding, you can't. That's what them stone bounds is for. Property's sacred, like church, it is."

"So is human life," I said.

"Now you sound like Mister Marc," she sighed.

"He always says we're savages." Reluctantly, she went to carry out my orders.

I returned to Marc's room, and resumed my vigil, wishing the dawn would hasten, bringing with it a little sunlight to this benighted country.

Before I knew it, it was morning, and I was being awakened by Marc's voice, speaking to me from his bed. As I opened my eyes, I saw his hand outstretched to me. I took it and smiled at him.

"How much better you look!" I said. "You have color again." I added jokingly, "I believe you will live."

"I intend to," he told me. His hand was healthily warm on mine. "How long have you been here?"

"During the night," I explained, hoping to keep from him the knowledge that the doctor had been to see him, against his explicit orders.

"You? Alone?"

I did not reply. I didn't like to lie to him.

He raised the covers, regarded his body under the coverlet, and observed that he was in night clothing. His eyes sought mine and, when I looked away elaborately, he laughed at me, and said in his sardonic humor:

"Dear little love, I hope you're not always going to be so shy of my person. How did you manage? With your eyes closed?'

It sounded strange and embarrassing to be called "little love," and the rest. It made me aware of him in a way that was unfamiliar but tantalizing, and I was ashamed to admit it. I made a motion to get up.

"Where are you going?"

"I thought you might want a glass of water. Or something."

"Please." He could be very persuasive when he set himself to it. "Come and sit down, there's a dear. If you are the only one who attended me, then I take it you have some questions."

I sat down again. This sounded hopeful. Perhaps there were answers ready. I would accept any. But in order to let him think they did not matter, I said offhandedly, "Later. When you're more yourself."

"Never felt more myself. Ask as many questions as you like. I don't promise to answer," he added, still in excellent humor. "But that need not prevent your asking."

"Well then"—I turned and faced him—"I have two questions. Number One: What does Moyna Branshaw mean to you now? And, Two: What became of the real Marc Branshaw?"

"One," he repeated precisely, mimicking me. "Moyna was the first woman I allowed to come into my life, and she came very shortly after my mother died. When I was hard upon ten years old."

"But—but—" I stuttered, more confused than ever. "Ten years old?"

He grinned. "You see, I met Moyna at a sanatorium in Southern France where my brother had placed me, at great expense to himself, hoping for a cure of what was called when I was a child—a "pthisis of the lungs." And it was to this sanitorium that Moyna Branshaw came, with her boy, Marc Branshaw, for the same purpose. I was luckier than Marc. The poor lad died, very shortly before Moyna was murdered by this accursed village."

"Your brother, the one who placed you in the sanitorium—"

"Was the one this village called 'The Devil-Vicar.' Though he was a kind of Dark Angel to this sickly brat whose life he saved. I owe everything to Ewen. I grew up obsessed with the idea of avenging his death when I was well, But Moyna would not have it so. She felt that her own son's sickness, the long, long death in life that poor Marc lived until his real death two years ago—all these were, to her, a sign that God was punishing her for what she called the 'seduction of his vicar'".

"When did you decide upon the vengeance after all?" I was beginning to see new and more murky terrors behind the old one. Was his vengeance the thing that had caused these crimes at Maidenmoor?

"When Moyna began to feel that Ewen's death had not been an accident caused by mob violence, but something planned, by a vicious intelligence still abroad in Maidenmoor. We discussed her suspicions by letter. This was at the time young Marc was dying. I had recovered some years before—six years ago, more or less—and gone to Paris, but I returned to be with Marc when he died. The end was sudden. Moyna had no time to make the journey. There was a fire at the sanatorium while I was visiting the lad. I got him out very nearly unscathed. But the exertion was too much for him and he was dead before I recovered from my burns. When they told me, I knew at last the full of Ewen's sufferings before his own death. And I swore an oath to Ewen, and to Moyna, that I should return and find the evil creature whose mind conceived his death. Then, Moyna died."

I put my hand over my mouth. Yet the words came out:

"She was murdered by this—what you call evil intelligence."

"Precisely. I never doubted it, once I heard of her death."

"Who is this monster?"

He paused, then said thoughtfully, "I was very close. So very close before this happened. I cannot be quite sure—yet."

I said nothing. He watched me.

"What are you staring at?"

"Your hand."

He looked at it. His understanding was quick. "You're wondering about the hand that attacked you in St. Anthony's, aren't you?"

I nodded.

He considered his hand, turning it over, then finally held it out for me to examine. "But I couldn't have done that thing for you."

"Of course not," I agreed quickly, and added after a pause, "Why?"

"Because, my darling, I too have wanted to murder you on occasion—such as the time you slammed the door on my hand, and the following day when you gave these poor knuckles such a wrench that I still feel the twinge. And once or twice during the last few days. For instance, your charming taunt that we should both marry the Owens and thus become brother and sister. Delicate thought, that."

I had to smile.

"But you see," he went on teasingly, doubtless to get off the subject of Moyna, "every time I murdered you in my daydreams, I found myself making love to you at the same time. It's a more difficult feat than an innocent like you might suspect. But I'm up to it."

I felt sure he was.

"Apparently such a double pleasure never occurred to your friend the other night. Perhaps he didn't hate you enough. Couldn't have been me, you see." His reasoning was perfectly logical, for him. "Unless, of course—our attacker was a female." He studied me. "Your brows are knit unbecomingly, darling. You will make wrinkles. What troubles you still?"

"Why did you come here as Moyna's son? Why not as yourself?"

"My dear child"—by his voice he plainly thought me idiotic—"Come spying about as Padric Morgan? Do you think the creature I search for would not know at once and destroy any evidence I might hope to find? It was Moyna's idea, in the beginning, when word came of here son's death. She had a notion that it would be safer, for what we had planned, if I came as her son. And then she . . . died. And I knew it was murder! I knew the monstrous intelligence that brought Ewen to his death had found Moyna out."

"Did she leave her estate to you or to Marc?"

He smiled. "No, my skeptical darling, I have not stolen Marc's estate. The whole of it shall go to her Glasgow relations when I've done with my work here. But it seemed simpler to come and assume charge of the Branshaw place while I had my work to do."

"Moyna!" I said, hard put to restrain my jealousy. "Even as a child, you must have loved her as your brother did."

He smiled, the dear smile that had so often won me in the past. "You are like Moyna in so many ways, Anne. Did you know that? Not in looks, but in ways that I love; and yet, you're so much warmer, closer. I understand you as neither I, nor I am sure, my brother, ever understood Moyna." He was running his forefingers absently along my palm as he spoke, but he was thinking back to a time I could not know. "Moyna never allowed anyone to share a deep emotion with her. Perhaps she had none, except for her son. It's different with you. You don't hide your deepest passions. Your quick likes and dislikes, your furious cutting angers, your jealousy—these are things I understand, for I too am like that."

His searching eyes read in me my doubts and fears and interpreted them correctly. He said in a quiet voice that made me suddenly aware how tired he must be after his ordeal, "Look at me, Anne. The rest are part of the background canvas; only you remain."

"How can that be? In so short a time."

He said in a tender, teasing way, pretending a gaiety that was a shadow of itself, "I know you better than you think. I've guessed your every emotion. I'm good at it, you know. I've played on those emotions shamelessly." He added, suddenly humble, "I kept hoping you would need me, as I need you. You will now know how much."

Watching me, he had become less certain. I wondered at it, but noticed the growing intensity in his face, his manner, and especially his voice as he studied me. He was beginning to show the extent of his illness, as though the tight rein of his determination had loosed and he could not pretend any longer. I should never have put him through the strain of this cross-questioning.

His voice wavered. "Or has my story changed all that? Its ugliness repulses you. Does it?" He shook my hand painfully in his insistence. "Well, tell me! Does it?"

I was thinking, "All this is very well. But doesn't it prove him guilty of the horrible crimes here? Who had a better motive? A motive he has confessed to me." Yet there it was. I suspected him of hideous things, and loved him still.

"How do you know Moyna Branshaw was murdered? How can you be sure?"

Against my quick gesture to stop him, he sat up in bed, leaning toward me in his intense conviction. The effort must have cost him considerable pain, but

I don't think he consciously noticed it.

"Someone removed the cover of stones and stout planks from the bog. Someone wanted Moyna dead. It was a dark, glowering day when the accident occurred. How easy to murder her so! And what murderer more convenient than Catherine? Or so I thought."

"But why Catherine?"

"Because she was one of Moyna's 'victims.' Moyna was always writing to me of her little amusements. She taunted Catherine about her absurd interest in the portrait in the Vicar's study. Moyna painted that portrait years ago, when she was teasing my brother about his dour, romantic look, as she called it. It was meant as a joke, she said, and she never finished it. Two or three years ago the MacDonnachies saw it in Moyna's house and asked for it, as a curiosity. A sinner to preach about, I fancy."

Tiredly, he rubbed the back of his neck and winced at the healing burns. I started to get up, but he reached out and held me.

"No. Don't leave me. Let me tell you the rest. I began my investigation with drunken old Will Grimlett, the creature who put the torch to Ewen's parsonage sixteen years ago. He was always prowling on the moors and might have seen something. He was so terrified of me when he first saw me last year that it took all the powers of persuasion in the village to convince him I wasn't my brother's ghost. . . . And then he was killed. Killed in such a way and at such a time that everything pointed to me; that is, to the Devil-Vicar. A ghostly killer, out for revenge, you see. With Abbie, it was the same. I very nearly had her ready to confess to me at one time. I used my resemblance to my brother deliberately. I hoped to start gossip, to frighten them all into thinking I was something unreal, ghostly. But every time I have nearly had the evidence in my hands, this monster—man or woman—has forestalled me. It's someone close, someone who knows, even before I do, what my steps will be."

"Yes, but which of them?"

"A mask," he murmured in a puzzled way. "Someone in the village is wearing a mask."

When I asked him nothing further, he said with a hesitation that was unlike him, "You keep putting it aside, Anne. Would it have made a difference if I had lied to you about my motives in coming here, about my masquerade as Moyna's dead son?" His voice broke as he demanded, in a way that twisted my heart, "*Why don't you answer me?*"

Dilys' voice came to us from the doorway, and I started, drawing away from "Marc," as I should always think of him.

"Mum, might I see you a minute?"

I got up, hearing Marc's desperate attempt at lightness. "Anne, this is a poor way to start our life together. You aren't very biddable."

But I wanted to ask myself what my emotions were, exactly. It is true that I was still suspicious, yet I knew that deep within me it did not sway my still holding doubts as to his innocence of the crimes; feelings as it should have done. I had a strong inclination to look back and give Marc a sign which would assure him that nothing between us had changed.

It was preposterous that I should have turned from him just when he needed me most, but there was a bit of Moyna in me, after all. I thought it would do him no harm to be in doubt for a few minutes.

"It seems I must get up and play the host or lose

you entirely, Anne," he began again. "Don't go. I've a feeling. Don't—"

I ignored him. It was a moment I would afterward have given my life to amend, and the opportunity was gone in the time it took to close the door behind me and step into the hall.

XVII

THE HALL WAS stale and damp after the long night. With the lamps turned out, I could scarcely make my way, except by the faint, death-gray light that comes with the dawn.

"I think he means it, mum," said Dilys. "He's getting up."

"Nonsense," I said. "He isn't as strong as he imagines he is. He'll soon change his mind. Well, Dilys, what is it?"

"It's Miss Catherine. Cook and me carried her up to Miss Moyna's room. Huggins—that's the groom, mum—he brought up that chair she moves about in."

I was bewildered. "But why Miss Moyna's room?"

"Fair puckers me. But she says it's that important, you wouldn't believe!"

I went into Moyna's white bedchamber, which was pervaded by early morning sunlight, and found Catherine sitting in her chair beside one of the large bedposts, doing a curious thing. She was trying to pry the head of the post out of its socket. She did not seem the least discomposed at sight of me.

"Anne, how is he?"

"Going on very well," I said stiffly.

She looked relieved. "I prayed so. I sent Nettie over several times in the night but there was no news. You know, of course, that the whole village is aware you spent the night here."

"Really?" The thought amused me in some perverse way. "Shall I then be burned as a Devil-Vicaress?"

She smiled but did not cease her odd occupation with the bedpost. "Dilys"—she turned to the girl—"you may go, dear."

Looking affronted, Dilys glanced at me and, upon my sign of agreement, she curtseyed and closed the door, leaving us alone in Moyna's room. Catherine waited significantly until this act was completed.

"He saved my life," she explain to me then. "And it was my fault. I was so stupid, trying to trap him." Her big hazel eyes grew rounder at the memory of last night's danger. "I wanted so desperately to prove he was Ewen Morgan. I only succeeded in proving he was not." Suddenly, the head of the bedpost came off in her fingers and she said with a flourish, "Behold, how simple! Look in this post. I'll swear it's hollow. It's going to prove Marc's innocence or guilt. I think it will be his innocence. Moyna herself may name our murderer."

I did as she bade me, and found, as I had begun to suspect, several tight rolls of paper, neatly bound in ribbons and slipped down the cylindrical hollow of the post. I drew them out.

"You see," said Catherine. "I believe it was I who gave the murderer the method of killing Will Grimlett and Abbie."

I looked at her, only half believing her. She appeared so calm to be confessing such a monstrous thing. Seeing my disbelief, she smiled, that sad little self-deprecating smile I was afraid of.

"I was so bitter when Marc would not love me. You must try to understand my feelings. It was then I began to write that awful novel. It gave me some outlet for my injured pride, and the trampling of my feelings. Someone read it, and even suggested ideas for Marc's guilt, as a joke—and later suggested those wretched fire tricks with which I tortured Marc. Someone I knew! As recently as last night, after the fire, we discussed it again. I asked questions. I was very careful, quite unsuspected. After that conversation I began to add up the little things—the attack on you, the dog, who was the weapon I suggested in my novel. I should have known before, but I couldn't bring myself to admit it.

"At dawn, I recalled something Moyna once said—that her bedposts could tell whole volumes to the gossips of Maidenmoor. I used to think she meant something indelicate. But this morning I thought at last I understood the allusion. Moyna's journals. Somewhere in those pages she might have recorded the reasons which made it necessary for her to be killed."

My fingers were shaking. I took the little rolls of paper and tossed them into her lap.

"Take some," she told me. "Glance over them. We may find the name I'm searching for. Read me anything that mentions a name—any name. I'll do the same with these."

"Whom do you suspect?" I asked, hardly daring to hear the answer.

She shrugged, getting quickly to the beribboned cylinders.

"If I'm right, you will see all too soon. Perhaps I shall make a novel of it." Her fingers went on unrolling the tight pages as she added words I found fully as ominous as she intended them. "Anne, the truth is so horrible, so unimaginable, that even I, knowing all the facts, could not believe it. If I told what I know, I should not be believed. I'm trusting to Moyna to give my word the weight it will need."

I shuddered, as much at her dreadful calm as at the horrors she drew for me. There was a feeling of unreality in this room that had belonged to the dead woman whose spirit refused to die. The bright winter sunlight was harsh. It did not belong here. It cast everything it touched into a sharp, ugly relief.

In my hands were many finely written sheets and it took some little time to separate them into dates and subjects. A number of items, which amounted to mere one-and-two lines of amusing comment about local citizens, culminated in several pertinent paragraphs which I read aloud to Catherine:

August, 1832—

Home now a fortnight. Must return to my poor little boy next week. Fortunately, the latest word of him is reassuring. Here in Maidenmoor there is some excitement.

The new vicar is that incredibly handsome young man I met at the French Sanatorium, when I was placing little Marc. I remember thinking what a curious thing, to see so presentable a male in the collar of that stuffy profession. But his devotion to that sick young brother of his was rather touching, and eminently suitable to one of the Cloth.

August 7, 1832—

The new vicar thunders about sin, not in the least aware of what sins his dark eyes and his other charms are planting in the minds of his parishioners. Absurd young man, and, somehow, endearing in his very ignorance of this effect. Was it pure coincidence he was assigned the perpetual curacy of this village? If it were not he who directed the assignment, can it be

Heaven who assigned him, or the Devil, perhaps? We shall see.

August 9, 1832—

There has never been a man in my life since Josiah died. My life is empty, and then I think of little Marc's illness. Is my loneliness and need of love a payment to me for producing a sick child? I am thinking of a man now, daily, hourly, as do many other stupid village women. But I cannot help myself. I am determined to have him. Whom do I mean but our dark-eyed friend, Ewen Morgan, at the chancel rail? I am even glad that my little Marc is away, with Ewen's young brother, for it gives us an added bond. Though in any case I shouldn't like my boy to see what I am about to do.

"Good heavens!" exclaimed Catherine. "She was frank, even then."

I would not admit it, for worlds that in her place, I too would have been hard put to resist the temptation of that new vicar.

"Pray go on," said Catherine eagerly. "If Josiah Branshaw were not dead, what a perfect suspect he would make!"

I read on:

September—

What delightful moments in the Wind-Rock! I wonder if he dreamed what I had in mind when I suggested that innocent lunch and stroll, to discuss "theological matters." I must return to France *next week to visit my little boy. Still, the infrequent letters say he is going on as well as can be expected. But, oh! One more week of love! That is all I ask to last me all the long years to come.*

. . . .

Ewen wants me to marry him. What nonsense! Where there is nine years between us!

At the cottage with him again. Tried to tell him to beware of certain cohorts, and the long, lank one, the dun-colored donkey, for example, and the people in the village. How that lank one tries to imitate him—walk like my love, stand like him, and what a farce! He has so little charm, so ungainly, so tall, lacking in every grace. He even makes an attempt to win me. I encourage him as a joke. It will possibly make Ewen jealous. He only laughs at him now. I have trained Ewen too well, I fear.

. . . .

How the village tingles with gossip! It may destroy Ewen's career but he was never meant for this. Meanwhile, the tales of Gytrashes, and of Ewen turning into a Devil on dark nights, serves to give us privacy. They think he can command savage dogs because he very wisely wore the coat belonging to the late Heaton Moresby yesterday, when Heaton's dog was savaging a trespasser. It was the scent of his dead master in the coat that soothed the dog. We said nothing. It was amusing to see the gullible faces of the villagers. They will accuse Ewen of having supernatural powers soon. What a joke!

. . . .

Tales are spreading absurdly. Ewen is truly a devil, they say. He casts a spell upon the animals and also upon the women hereabouts, they say. No one knows better than I that he has been true to me. Still, this is no part of the tale we have spread. Who wishes Ewen destroyed? There are one or two women in the village who seem so calm, so capable! Yet I have observed the looks they cast at Ewen, and him so unaware of them. I would not put the gossip beyond them, either of them.

I will go to France, to my little boy soon, but I have not definitely made my plans yet. Ewen would do well in France, as an artist, for example. But I cannot marry him. He does not realize, but I do.

. . . .

Who is our enemy? Someone who loves Ewen and is jealous of me? Someone who wants me and is jealous of him? Or a religious fanatic, caught over from those scenes of horror a quarter of a century ago. . . . I wonder.

. . . .

Our unknown enemy incited some of the fanatics to put a torch to the parsonage. Word was brought to me. I was sure Ewen would escape. But again our enemy forestalled us.

The creature came upon Ewen while he was at his desk, preparing the sermon for tomorrow, and struck him across the head. So it is gossiped in the village. And then, with the parsonage set afire and burnt to the ground— Oh, my love . . . my love . . . .

Catherine and I sat silent, considering what we had learned.

"Does it help at all?" I asked.

"I hate her," said Catherine. "It was her fault. If she hadn't done that to Ewen Morgan in the first place, there would have been no enemies, no envious admiring men who might turn dangerous, no gossiping, eager women. . . . I hate her!"

I told myself that I agreed with Catherine, but some part of Moyna's conduct seemed understandable. I found myself hating her less.

"What else?" asked Catherine.

"Very little that is pertinent in this roll. No. Stay! Here are two, some months later. In the winter."

Will God forgive me? Does it atone for Ewen's death if the Branshaw money cures Ewen Morgan's young brother? The boy shall stay in that sanatorium side by side with my little Marc, until both are cured. Does this atone, Oh Devilish God?

. . . .

Curious reversion to tragic days! Rumors abroad that young Abbie Hinchley saw the person who struck Ewen down, and that she is frightened and will not talk. She believes if she does a Gytrash will eat her up. Bitter irony, that a fright created by me should thwart me now in finding that monster who made my love suffer so—

Catherine took up the roll in her hands and spread it so that the edges would not curl so badly. A frown ruffled her smooth, broad forehead.

"No proof there, but something in one of these pages, I think, that fits her previous remarks. It was written the summer before she died. What do you think of it?"

I am troubled by suspicions of a familiar face—Something in the manner, the shifting eyes, a hint now and then, a ludicrous imitation of the Ewen Morgan who is gone so long ago. I do not trust that one, nor ever did in Ewen's day. I should, but I do not. . . . . Padric shall know of it. I must write him soon.

"But who is this 'Padric'?" asked Catherine, puzzled.

I did not answer, not knowing how much of his story my Marc wished her to know.

"Well, well, no matter," she said impatiently. "Read more."

I cleared my throat, tried to keep all emotion out, and so read the rest of the scribbled page:

Once more I shall play my little game. A choice collection of silly victims: a jealous woman or two, jealous or imitative men who were, perhaps, the butt of ridicule in the old days. One of them tried to murder Ewen long ago. One of them spread our silly lies about Gytrashes and made them worse until the fire came. If this one I now suspect is innocent, then why the mask? And such a mask! Preposterous. Ah! But if guilty! I shall intimate that I have guessed his ugly secret. Dangerous, intoxicating game! If I cannot have that which I surrendered long ago, then I shall make a few others suffer, too. . . .

Catherine tapped the paper on her chair. At the same time, Dilys opened the door and peered in to catch my eye. Catherine paid no attention to her. She was thinking over the lines she had heard, and said to me finally:

"I see the pattern. The how and the why. That stupid woman! She deserved her fate. But no matter. The guilty must be punished. . . . What is it, Dilys? You are interrupting, I think."

"Miss Anne, there's someone below to see you, asking after Mister Marc. Would you be so kind as to speak with her?"

"Who is it?" asked Catherine so quickly I was startled.

"Lady from London, mum. The one with all the frills. She says Reverend and Missus is picking herbs for Mister Marc's bedchamber and will be by presently. Miss Keegan too, and other villagers, maybe. That means tea for a large party, mum." This she addressed to me. "And Mister Marc will be that cross, you may well think!"

Catherine made a swift, harsh gesture that surprised both Dilys and me.

"Don't let anyone come up. You hear me! Not anyone!"

I said, "Naturally not," and went out with Dilys to take care of this new problem. This was one more distinction between the satisfying indifference of a large city like London, and the hospitable, neighborly nuisance of the countryside. I was ashamed of my resentment, but there it was. I was exceedingly anxious to participate in any of the discoveries Catherine would make in the voluminous pages which she was about to unravel.

In order to brace up Cook, who had doctored her concern or Marc by the application of large quantities of spirits, I went down to the kitchen first, and helped Dilys prepare a tea tray. By the time I reached the drawing room, I could see that I need not have hurried. Mrs. Fothergay was examining every item of decoration that she could lay hands to, judging the quality, the worth and, I daresay, what it would have meant to her if she had succeeded in capturing its owner as the next Mr. Fothergay.

"My dear Anne, how very odd to see you here, but so handy. I always say, we must sacrifice ourselves to busy tongues if we are to do the necessary work. How is the dear boy, by the way? Has he asked for me?"

She ran a gloved finger over the mantel, studied

the dust on the tip of the pink forefinger and sighed. I could not feel that I was responsible for the dust in a bachelor's house, but from her sidelong glance at me, it was evident she so regarded me.

"He is much better, I believe. Just badly shaken, and with some rather painful burns," I explained. "May I help you to tea?"

"Tea? At this hour? It is scarcely breakfast time. Still, I daresay the dear boy would want me to behave as though nothing had happened. Chin up, you know. The MacDonnachies will be along presently. Dear me. The tea is weak. I must say, this house certainly needs a mistress."

I was relieved to see the graying head of Mrs. MacDonnachie pop up under the drawing room windows, as she waved a streaming bonnet and a brave but pathetic little bundle of weeds at us, and then came around to the door to be let in.

"Do have them prepared, dear Miss Anne, in boiling water. Just on the boil, mind. Not a tisane. Dear, no. Ah, there, Cadmon. Have you had any success? Let me have yours too."

The Reverend MacDonnachie, puffing from his exertions, arrived from another quarter of the fields, rolling his eyes heavenward at the whole idea of herbs, and presented me with his handful. I thanked them both and took the dejected objects into the kitchen, where I consoled Dilys with the news that she might toss them out as soon as the guests were gone.

We were just entering the drawing room from the reception hall when a sound from upstairs, slight but nerveracking, caused us to pause and glance at each other uneasily.

"What a curious sound! Like a—a gasp!" whispered

Mrs. McDonnachie, looking up the stairs wonderingly.

Her husband, who was not in the best of moods, said, "If it were a gasp, especially a human one, you would not be likely to hear it this far away, m'love. More like an outcry of surprise, I should have said."

I was thinking of Marc, and the possibility that he had come out into the hall and perhaps been taken by one of those attacks the doctor had warned me of, so I was already on the stairs, hurrying up to find out what had happened. At the head of the stairs I stopped, shaken by the illusion I saw at the further end of the upper hall which was wreathed in mingled shadows and light from the open door of Moyna's room.

Standing in the doorway of that room, and facing me the length of the hall was the Devil-Vicar. The apparition was separated from me only by the weird, shifting pattern of the sunlight and shade which seemed to veer backward and forward in pendulum fashion as I stared at him. I saw the dark robes, the lustrous black hair, the same terrible, melancholy eyes looking enormous against the gray pallor of his face. A shaft of sunlight crossed his figure and the dreadful illusion was shattered, but not the panic that had been instilled by it.

The black habit that had misled me was nothing more than a dark dressing robe, whose hem just escaped the floor and blended into the shadows behind Marc, to produce that startling image. Wordless, he held out his arms to me. How far distant he was! I went to him, trembling with the foreknowledge that something was terribly wrong. The journey of a few seconds seemed forever, through twisting light and dark, elongated shade, piercing sunlit pools, and always ahead of me that one lengthening shadow swaying like a pendulum across Marc's face.

When I reached his outstretched arms, he drew me to him. He put his hands in my hair, taking handfuls and crushing the strands between his fingers as he began to kiss me. I was torn by stark, unreasoning terror, for I knew instinctively there was a purpose—perhaps mad, but logical—in this. His fingers were cold as marble but his pale lips had a peculiar, disturbing warmth. He kissed me on the lips and the cheek and the brow, and then I heard his almost incoherent voice at my ear, trying to lull my brain with his tender persuasiveness.

"I—came to look for you. That is all. And then I saw it. Let them think what they will. . . . It's a lie. . . . You know it's a lie, don't you, darling?"

"I know," I repeated obediently, trying to conceal the strain of fear for him that obsessed me. "What has happened?"

The pendulum shadow came between us when I stared up at his white face, and I became aware for the first time that the shadow had cut off part of the light from Moyna's bedchamber. Almost afraid to look, I gazed slowly into the room behind me. The shadow began with the length of rope fashioned in a noose, slung over a crossbeam, and from that noose a body hung, twisting slowly, the carefully coifed brown hair tangled and loose as a harridan's, the hands clawed, the feet helpless, dragging. One shoe had come off. The foot, in its white cotton stocking, barely touched the floor.

I could not bear to look at the face.

But I recognized Catherine Owen's sturdy, pitiful, slightly bundled body. The sight of it obliterated every thought in my mind except the all-pervasive one:

Marc must be gotten away before the others found

him here. I could not even ask him why he had done it. I must pretend to believe him.

But why poor Catherine?

Thinking this in despair, I made a slight movement in his arms, hoping to make him aware of his peril, but his grip tightened upon me, and I knew he thought I was about to desert him.

Our senses were assaulted by the chilling shriek of Mrs. Fothergay, who had come up behind me and stood staring, with her mouth open.

The Vicar, hard on her heels, took one look at the hanging figure, then had the presence of mind to rush past us into the room, saying, "I may not be too late. Help me, someone."

But it was too late. I looked for the first time at the head, twisted cruelly to one side by the knotted rope, and the face. . . .

It was too late.

XIX

MRS MACDONNACHIE and Bedelia Fothergay stood in the drawing room, drinking fresh-brewed tea and exchanging hushed and horrified whispers which were interrupted guiltily when I came into the room.

"Have they taken her away?" Mrs. Fothergay asked. "Dear me! What an appalling misfortune! And in his own house, too. I wonder where he found the rope so quickly. But I suppose murderers have such things secreted for . . . later use."

Mrs. MacDonnachie patted me furtively on the sleeve.

"Did you insist that he—lie down? Whatever happens, he must be himself, so that he may answer the charges. It will be hours before anyone reaches the Hall. The rest will do him good." She nodded complacently at Mrs. Fothergay. "He was not himself, you see. It is not a—what you call capital offense unless it can be proved that he knew what he was about."

"Small difference," put in Mrs. Fothergay in her irritatingly shrill voice. "He always hated the poor child. Never could see why, myself. Heavens! What a fate I escaped!"

At this, even Mrs. MacDonnachie's innocent features twisted a little and she gave me a side-glance. I did not care, either for the misplaced advice of the Vicar's wife, or the nasty and absurd comments of Bedelia Fothergay. For the past hour I had been desperately considering every alternative. Somehow, he must be gotten away, if the charge was to be murder. If, however, it could be proved that he was mad, then there would be some hope. I knew very little about these things, but I knew my Marc would come to himself one day, in the light and loving care, and that could only be accomplished if he were not tried as a sane man.

The Vicar had taken care of Catherine's body, a horror that haunted us women. I had only to see that Marc went back to his bedchamber, and then leave one of the servants on guard in the hall, to let us know if he stirred from his room.

About noon, Mrs. Fothergay remembered that she had not dined yet, and proceeded to walk back to the village in the company of the housekeeper, who promised to guide her clear of all bogs and unsafe moorland. As she left the Hall, she passed the Reverend MacDonnachie coming back. His huge figure burst into the drawing room like a wind from the moorland. All his red beard and his hair stood on end.

"What a business! Can't find her brother. He's over

in Teignford buying new boots, I understand. Poor creature. Well, she'll rest in St. Anthony's, of course. I've old Jonas Weir, the sexton, an excellent cabinet maker, busy at the coffin."

"Don't, my love," his wife murmured. "It makes it all seem so—real."

The Vicar glanced up at the ceiling and, by intimation, at the floor above.

"It is real, m'dear. And it poses a very pretty problem. Are we to surrender that young man as a common murderer?"

"But—what else is possible?" she murmured plaintively, eager to be persuaded.

I thought I caught an edge of hope in his voice.

"Have you some idea, sir?"

"Several, m'dear." He sat down, puffing, and opened his frock coat and waistcoat. He considered his boots for a few moments while we stared at him. I was aware that my heart had nearly stopped beating as I waited for that one small word of hope from him.

"Miss Anne, tell me exactly. What did Marc say to you when he agreed to go back to bed? He would say nothing to me beyond drinking that foul draught I poured him. The merest hind of laudanum. Great specific, you know. But he ignored me as though I were a spectre he could look through. Damned near dropped the glass between my hands."

I remembered Marc's silence as we left that hall upstairs and went into his room. He had said then, "I'm so tired, I can't think clearly. There is an answer. It's obvious, and yet I'm too tired to see it." Then, as I put his hands to my lips to indicate to him that he was not alone in this horror, he took me by the shoulders and studied my face. With a dear, gentle expression in his eyes, he gazed at me. "I trust you with my life, Anne. More than my life—my sanity."

When the drug finally overcame him and he lay down, I ran my fingers quickly over the robe he had flung across the foot of the bed, but I found no scraps of paper from Moyna's journals, nor had there been any remaining in Moyna's room. What could he have done with them in so short a time?

When he spoke to me of sanity, I was sure this indicated his knowledge of his own condition. It would make it easier to persuade him to any course I suggested. But I did not want the Vicar to know he had admitted anything.

"He said nothing, sir," I replied to the Vicar now. "Just that he was tired."

"I should rather think so," the Vicar muttered. "He'd had a strenuous half hour, I should say."

"Cadmon!" cried his wife, putting her handkerchief to her mouth.

He ignored his wife's interjection but after a glance at my face, rigid with sick horror, he apologized.

"Beg pardon, ma'am. Didn't mean any offense. But to get back to our problem . . . I have several theories. Number one. I do not believe, for a minute, that a young man named Marc Branshaw murdered that poor girl and those others, in cold blood, for the pure pleasure of it. Let us suppose he is, as I have often suspected, our old friend, the Devil-Vicar."

"My dear, you must be joking," his wife exclaimed. "Young Reverend Morgan died years and years ago."

"Hmph. That remains to be seen. How he escaped from the fire is no concern of mine. He was injured in that fire, I don't doubt. Let us say he received a brain injury. That makes easier what I have in mind. He returned last year when Moyna died. Last straw, don't you see? Final blow from these fiends in Maidenmoor. He has systematically murdered all those closely connected with the fire. Abbie, the girl who saw him lying in that house and did not call for help. Old Grimlett who started the fire . . ."

"But poor Catherine was not even in Maidenmoor in those days, love."

"True. But Catherine found out his identity. She came over this morning to taunt him with, let us say, something he betrayed in the fire last night. She had to die. Mad, utterly mad. And they don't hang mad men. They lock them up. He is saved."

It was so near the truth that it terrified me. If it would save Marc's life, I might consent that it should be known. But if it would not! The risk was too great.

"What do you say, Miss Anne? Shall we try for a confession from him that he is actually the Devil-Vicar? It may well save his life."

"How would you go about it?" I asked.

The Vicar shrugged his great shoulders. "I have one or two ideas. Been playing with them all morning."

"One might search him for scars from that other fire," Mrs. MacDonnachie murmured, and then turned pink with embarrassment. "That is, you might, dear."

"Crude. Very crude," snorted the Vicar. "We must make him admit his identity. A trick. I might reveal to him certain information that he would use as the Devil-Vicar, for example—information that would make him want to tear my throat out. He would reveal himself transparently."

"No, please," I put in quickly. "Nothing that will excite him. The doctor said no excitement."

"Just a few questions, nothing too alarming. I might pretend to have been one of his old enemies back in the days when he was Ewen Morgan and I was his curate. My love, think back. It must be someone with whom he was acquainted sixteen years ago, someone who might have wished him ill. I shall claim that man's complaints are mine. We'll see what sparks we draw."

Mrs. MacDonnachie wriggled in her chair and then leaned forward triumphantly.

"He had another curate before you—the one who held the office while I was still in Maidenmoor. Of course, you came just before I left for Scarborough that September. But there had been some nasty, jealous remarks involving the other curate."

"Yes, yes. But of what sort What type? It must be someone whose crime and omissions he might conceivably lay to me. We are not dealing with a fool, you know."

"There was the other curate, dear, a friendly little creature with a snub nose."

"Now, do I look like a little man with a snub nose?"

"No, dear. How careless of me! But dear Marc, I mean—if he truly is the Reverend Morgan, might be confused enough to put that curate's delinquencies at your door. I know, while I was in Scarborough with my family that autumn, Lottie Sandbower wrote that it was absurd to see some of the villagers trying to do things as the Reverend Morgan did them. One of them a pink-haired silly creature, she said, tried to kiss Moyna Branshaw, hoping to make her forget the young vicar. I suspect he was frightfully jealous of the Reverend Morgan. But Cadmon, I don't think . . . After all, Lottie told me so little about that pink-haired creature. Who was he?"

I thought of Moyna's journal. She had feared the same person Mrs. MacDonnachie described. Was that person still in the village, and had Moyna been killed because she guessed the identity?

Meanwhile, the Reverend MacDonnachie happily schemed to enact his part.

"Just the man! Yes. Kissing Moyna. Of course. Any other peculiarities about this fellow?"

"Well, there was an unpleasantness at Communion about someone, Lottie said. The poor fellow was so clumsy the Reverend Morgan called him an ass before the entire church. Some unkind folk laughed, I understand. But then, dear Reverend Morgan was very cross that day. Lottie says he was preaching on"—she lowered her gentle voice—"sacred and profane love."

Her husband smiled. "Remarkably apt theme. And as for the "ass," my name lends itself to "donkey" rather neatly. Let's see what we can make of that. But about the sacred and profane love—"

"It was a request from certain members of the congregation. You see, a movement was on foot to expel him, and they hoped to use this sermon as evidence, Miss Wicklow. But you remember, Cadmon."

"And did they use the sermon as evidence?" I asked.

"Dear me, no. He preached that to prevent adultery and profane love one must provide love, respect and understanding in a marriage. There was not a dry eye in the church that day—among the ladies present."

"I can vouch for that," said the Vicar.

The whole conversation was confusing to me. I hardly knew what he was talking about and even less what his object was, but it disturbed me that he should settle on that pink-haired man, whose jealousy and eager imitation of Ewen Morgan had been noted even by Moyna Branshaw in her journal. She had thought him dangerous.

"I don't think I follow your reasoning. I wish you wouldn't play tricks on Marc. He's far from well."

"You will admit, Miss Anne, it's better that we find a plausible insanity in him than find him well and healthy. As Marc Branshaw he is in far greater danger of the rope than as Ewen Morgan, badly injured and obviously unbalanced. What do you say?"

"I—I don't want to be present."

He raised his hands at my idiocy.

"But then, where are our witnesses? Of course, you must be present. Out of sight, if you will. We might—"

Dilys called to me from the staircase and hurried on into the drawing room.

"Mister Marc sent me, mum. Sir." She curtseyed to each of us in turn. "He says he's a right to be heard. He's that set upon coming down!" She looked indignantly at us. There was no doubt in her mind of Marc's innocence. I blessed her for her confidence in him.

"Quick!" The Reverend MacDonnachie pushed me to the archway separating the drawing room from the darkened and long unused dining parlor. "You can see from here, and I'll maneuver him so that he can't see you. You too, m'love. Must seem to be speaking to him alone." He rubbed his hands together and said with great self-satisfaction. "We'll save that boy yet."

I did not like it. I was pushed and pulled this way and that, tormented by my fears. I thought of Marc coming to this inquisition, this shoddy pretense which might throw him clear off his head so that even he might suppose he was the Devil-Vicar. Now

I wished I had been more vigorous in my refusal to permit this scene.

I heard Marc's light, swift footstep on the main staircase, and my heart thundered in my breast as I prayed for him. Then he came into the drawing room I was tremendously proud of him. He had dressed and looked almost his old self—a trifle pale, perhaps, but self-possessed and calm.

"Before you say anything," the Vicar began, "let me assure you that you are with a friend. An old friend, I might add." Nonetheless, in spite of his seeming confidence, I saw him raise one of the teacups to his lips, then put it down shakily.

Marc raised an eyebrow. "Old friend? I don't think I follow you. How long is it since I returned from France?"

"Well, my lad . . . Pardon. I persist in calling you that when, God knows, I have been aware of your true age for sixteen years."

Marc retained his cool indifference before this odd beginning. He remained standing in one place, however, almost as though turned to stone.

"You're being cryptic for some reason, I suppose."

"As between fellow delvers in the same soil—sacred soil, that is—don't you think you had better rely upon that identity and save your life?"

"I don't know what you're talking about."

The Vicar heaved a great sigh. I could not help thinking "bravo" to Marc for standing firm.

"My dear Reverend Morgan—"

"What did you call me? You must be mad. He died sixteen years ago."

The Vicar took a turn about the room, passing close to us, and giving us a faint nod of confidence as he did so.

"He'll manage, dear," whispered his wife to me.

"He's very clever, Cadmon is."

"No, my dear Ewen Morgan," the Vicar was saying, "he did not die sixteen years ago, though I thought so until the late Abbie Hinchley recognized me and asked me for money. Imagine! Asked a vicar for money! A good fright served her much better."

Mrs. MacDonnachie pinched me. "That was a clever remark. I told you Cadmon would do it."

Marc walked to the leaded windows and stared out over the green expanse of the moors. His back was to us and I wondered what he was thinking.

"Then it would be you who are the murderer, not this Ewen Morgan, even if I were he."

"Between ourselves," agreed the Vicar jovially, as one will agree to anything to humor a madman, "your deduction may be correct."

The Vicar, however, was a trifle upset by Marc's lack of response to his careful statements, and he ventured after a few moments of silence, "I'm afraid you must prepare yourself for the worst, my friend. Miss Anne had the doctor to see you. . . ."

It got its reaction from Marc, who swung about and faced him, blazing angry.

"That," he said deliberately, "is a stupid lie. Anne would be the last person to betray me to a prying doctor."

I winced at this dagger thrust, for I had betrayed him.

But it was too late, in any case. Perhaps the belief that he was the Devil-Vicar, insane and avenging, would save Marc. That was my only hope.

The Vicar shrugged.

"As you choose, sir, but I should think even your addled wits would tell you that you will do better in a court of law as yourself—since your identity is bound to come out—than as a creature who no longer exists. And he doesn't exist, you know. Marc Branshaw died two years ago, in a sanatorium in France."

The Vicar's wife and I gazed at each other in amazement—I at his discovery, she at the cleverness of her husband.

"Oh, yes," the Vicar went on. "I checked that, as soon as I saw the miniature of you that Moyna carried."

Marc stared at him, reaching absently for the back of a chair, to give him support as these facts came gradually and terribly to his consciousness.

"Who are you? Or rather—who were you, in the old days?" Marc's hand brushed against the teacup the Vicar had relinquished, and we heard the faint crack of his knuckles upon the china.

"Answer me!"

His command made the Vicar's wife shudder. She clutched me in her terror, but I was more concerned for Marc than for any possible danger to her husband.

"Dear boy, have you no recollection of that 'clumsy ass' your old curate, with the pink hair? Remember the Communion when you said poor oafish MacDonnachie should be called 'MacDonkey'? How that stung, dear boy! How that stung and festered, when I'd been prepared to like and admire and copy you, learn to be a gentleman, like you."

Marc slapped the back of the chair with his open palm. His eyes were burning.

"I knew you had been a curate but I never placed you. You must have been thin. And that beard of yours. You wore no beard then. . . . That is the mask Moyna was seeking."

Desperately, I saw that the Vicar was leading him to the very edge of insanity by confusing him so that what Moyna had confided to Marc of her suspicions now must surely make him believe he truly was Ewen Morgan.

The Vicar paused, no doubt to think up more frightening fables. "Precisely. Thought you'd guess. I've put on weight, physical and spiritual. I learned from you after all, even acceded to your dignities. But then, you were really too young for them, weren't you?"

I could not help wondering at the fabulous talent the vicar had for improvising.

He went on, obviously proud of his gift. "Used a few of your tricks with the ladies. . . . Always admired you frightfully, old chap. You should not have used me so contemptuously, for I could have been your veritable slave."

Marc made a face of revulsion and bowed his head, studying the grain of the table and thinking, I've no doubt, of those days of his brother's life which the Vicar brought back to him now in all their pain and culminating horror. He reached for the cold tea and drank it down absently, not looking at the vicar.

I prayed that this charade would end soon, so that I might be of some comfort to Marc. He raised his head finally and stared at the Vicar, who was scratching his red beard and apparently reflecting that he might have gone too far in his make-believe.

"If you are the one responsible for those lies and other horrors, then was it you who incited them to that talk of my—of my being a devil and my habitat fit only for burning?"

"Dear boy, you know that was begun by you and Moyna. Remember? I merely helped it along. Moyna would have none of me. . . . Exquisite creature she was. I've never forgotten her, you know. Even years later, when she began to be puzzled about me, to make foolish hints, I remembered the hold her beauty had upon me."

Mrs. MacDonnachie clutched my arm, but gave me a watery, sad smile, as she whispered, "He is so clever, Cadmon is. But I wish he couldn't talk about Moyna. There were so few men she could not have had for the taking."

Marc was beginning to add up these terrible disclosures now. I saw that all hope of his remaining calm was gone. I saw the mounting fury, the dark color coming into his face as he challenged the Vicar:

"And she recognized you, so you killed her. Then you had to kill Abbie because—because—"

"Tiresome girl, Abbie," said the Vicar, after too long a pause. He had plainly not expected to play a mass-murderer. He began to invent rapidly, almost, I suspected, as though he enjoyed his role. "She was no longer afraid of me. When you returned and she fell in love with you, she told me it was over. She was going to confess to you what she knew about the burning. Well, my dear boy, what could I do? It was Will Grimlett and Moyna all over."

"Three murders!" Marc exclaimed. "And all carefully planned to be put at my door. All that Devil-Vicar cape and robe nonsense, everything so that it would appear I had committed them."

More for our benefit than Marc's, the Vicar remarked smugly, "Deucedly clever, don't you think? Of course, I always wanted to be Ewen Morgan, anyway."

Marc leaned across the table. He was in a killing rage.

"But one more . . . You've forgotten to describe that. One more you must tell me about.

He had taken the Vicar unawares. His invention

flagged and he turned away from Marc, glancing in our direction, though he could not see us. I wondered if he were looking for help. Marc seemed about to spring at him.

"Ewen Morgan's murder! You haven't described how you crept up to him in the parsonage that day and struck him. . . ." Marc rubbed the back of his neck, where the fresh burns must still have been tormenting him. "You haven't described what it must have been like for you to know he was lying in that room—perhaps dead, perhaps not—!" He moved forward and the Vicar backed away almost involuntarily, his small, jovial eyes wide with fear at what he had unleashed.

"Don't be a fool, Morgan. . . . I was only play-acting for your sake! Don't—"

"Do you know what it is to die like that?" cried Marc.

This must have been how Marc looked, I thought, when he killed Catherine and the others—this terrible, dark-eyed fury, these passionate lips I remembered so well, twisted with pain and hate.

"Let me tell you, my dear, good Vicar—if that's what you are, and not a demon out of hell! I know what it is to be conscious and in a fire. I know what it is to find myself burning to death! I stank of the odor of burning flesh. My own flesh! I struggled. How long I struggled under that debris! I prayed for death to release me, but it would not come. Not even unconsciousness, for the agony was too unbearable. I was to endure it all, to be witness to the final consumption of my own body!"

It was done. I was sick with pain for him. He had begun to confuse his brother's death with his own sufferings in the sanatorium fire two years ago.

Marc's fingers curled into his palms uncontrollably

as he reached for the Vicar, who barely eluded him.

"You filthy, unnatural beast! I'll kill you! *This time I will kill you!*"

As I rushed into the room to stop him, he turned, hearing my footsteps. His face went suddenly white and he whispered:

"Anne—don't let . . ." He wavered. I saw that he was very near to collapse. As both the Vicar and I reached out to ease his fall, I saw his eyes close, and he dropped to the floor unconscious.

We knelt beside him, I frantically putting my hand to his face, pushing away a strand of black hair to find his forehead cold with icy sweat. The Vicar had put his hand inside Marc's jacket and upon his heart.

"Oh, Cadmon, what have we done?" his wife murmured tearfully, standing over us.

"Hush!" said her husband. "Get me some brandy. Good God! I didn't know he was so ill."

I was rubbing his cold hands frantically. "What is wrong with him?" I asked, not taking my eyes off Marc's chill white face.

"Must be a heart attack," said the Vicar. "My fault. I take responsibility for it. I'm to blame. But I didn't know there was any question of a bad heart. Where is that dratted woman with the brandy?"

Mrs. MacDonnachie returned almost at once with a decanter.

"Cadmon, dear," she ventured as her husband tried to force a few drops between Marc's colorless lips, "he nearly killed you."

I closed my eyes, thanking God that at least Marc had been spared that crime.

Mrs. MacDonnachie was standing over us, staring at Marc.

"My dear, are you sure he isn't—"

The Vicar said, "Be still, woman!" and felt Marc's

heart again. He waited too long to withdraw his hand. I raised my eyes to his across Marc's body.

"Well?"

The Vicar touched my hand—a gentle, brushing stroke for such a huge hand, and it spoke plainer than words.

"He's gone."

I was numbed. I didn't feel the least surprise. I went on rubbing Marc's hands absently, one at a time, between my own fingers.

After awhile, someone came behind me and lifted me up, and I went obediently where I was taken.

"She didn't sleep all night," said Dilys' voice.

I said, "Don't let them do anything to him until the doctor has been and gone. We must be sure."

"Later," said the Vicar's comforting voice. "First, drink this good, strong tea."

"There are so many things to do. To take care of."

"Drink, ma'am," said Dilys. "This will take care of all of them."

Dilys got me into bed and I looked around curiously. It was a lovely, happy room. I couldn't ever remember one that was more beautiful—all white, even the crossbeams. But the tea had made me dizzy, for I fancied the knob on one of the bedposts was set on crooked, and it bothered me.

There were things I had to do, but I wasn't sure what they were. It was all confused.

Presently I slept.

XX

DURING THE late afternoon I awoke to see the Vicar praying at the foot of my bed. He looked up at me as I moved. His odd pose confused me momentarily. I was not used to seeing him at his more Christian duties. He looked tense and strained as he attempted to soothe me.

"There, there. Don't be alarmed. You shall rest again after I've gone. But—we must work quickly."

"I don't understand. Quickly about what?" I asked, still vague.

"Sir Gareth has returned, my child."

This meant nothing to me beyond a certain shared sympathy with him in his grief at the loss of his sister.

"I am sorry for him," I said. "He loved her very much."

"Yes, my child. Unfortunately."

I began to sense the root of his tension.

"Why? What has he done?"

"Can you not guess?" asked the Reverend MacDonnachie sadly. "Whom has he always blamed for his sister's sufferings? And now, his passion for revenge can burn itself out only on the body of that poor devil who—"

I sat up in bed, trembling.

"You can't mean that! Sir Gareth is a civilized man. He cannot hate the dead."

"Dear Miss Anne, surely you know that men under strong passion of love or hate are not civilized. Already, he is stirring up the same violent feelings that caused the near-tragedy sixteen years ago. He will not allow Marc to be buried in consecrated ground. He talks madly of burning Marc's body. . . ."

"No, no," I cried. "Marc always hated fire!"

He nodded.

"It depends upon time, my dear, and upon you. If we act quickly, he is saved from—whatever they intend."

"Upon me? What must I do?"

He took a paper from under his coat and offered it to me.

"It was all I could think of. It will serve, providing the work is done quickly tonight."

I could not focus my eyes upon it for a moment. Then I understood:

It is by my wish and with my approval that my beloved affianced, known to me as Marc Branshaw, should be buried without ceremony and for the public good, at once, upon this night. I sign this, in my bitter despair, to attest that what is done and has been done by the Vicar and sexton of this church is done by the order of the unhappy, Anne Wicklow.

Why must he make it so unbearably hurting, to pour out my feelings in this way, upon a public document: "unhappy Anne," "bitter despair". . . almost the words of a suicidal mind. Perhaps they were true descriptions of my present state of unhappiness, but certainly I was not suicidal, nor ever had been. To read my unhappiness paraded in a legal document was almost more than could be borne.

"No!" I cried. "Not so soon." The pain struck me with sudden, poignant force. . . . I shall never see him again. Never."

"Dear child," the Reverend MacDonnachie murmured, "It is over. You must make up your mind to that, and look about you for a new life. Dr. Lowther has come and gone. It's upon his recommendation I am acting. He suggests that with all this tension building up in the village, by morning we may not be able to perform the burial."

The thought of the desecration of Marc's body, with the weapon which he had always dreaded, was enough to make me yield. The Vicar reached for his pen and offered it to me. Fumbling with it, trailing ink over the paper, I signed my name. I felt too weak to do more, and he took the pen and paper from me, placed his hand tenderly on my head, and I sank back upon the pillows, closing my eyes to this last horror, that Marc could not even be decently buried. He must go to his grave still as the murderous Devil-Vicar.

"God keep you safe," the Vicar said, and presently I heard the door close behind him and I was alone again.

I turned my face away from the door and began to weep.

Lengthening shadows of afternoon dissolved into the gray twilight of the North Country. Outside the windows I could see the long, endless march of the moors. They had won. By tomorrow their green tendrils would have captured Marc, just as I feared all along that they would.

Presently, small, twinkling lights appeared here and there in the distant farms, and I thought of those people I had come to know, yet whose secret hearts I had apparently not fathomed. At this moment they were planning the desecration of the body of a dead man. I lay in Moyna's bed and contemplated the village lights. I was beginning to react from the numbness of the afternoon, and the daze of what must have been a drug in the tea I drank. Now, the pain came and it made me want to scream at my loss, and at Marc's sufferings, which had all come to nothing but death.

I had known him such a sort time, I could not understand why his loss was like the loss of half my life. But so it was.

The room was quite dark when I heard the latch of the door move, and Dilys came in with a tray on which were the tea things as well as fresh-baked parkin and a pink china oil lamp.

"I've orders, mum. You're to eat and drink. You do look dreadful and no mistake. Please. Mum, don't be so unhappy. Reverend says he fears for your life. But you ain't that kind, to take your life, now are you, mum? You take that nasty laudanum indeed! What rubbishy nonsense he talked!"

She was talking rubbish herself and I didn't understand her in the least, especially about the laudanum. Why should I take laudanum? Pain is something that must be borne, not blotted out falsely by such methods. What would my mother and father have thought of me in such a state to join them?

"Is there any word from the village, about the violence, I mean?"

Dilys shivered. "Fair gives me the bumps to think of it the way the Reverend tells it. How could they touch poor dear Mister Marc? Like housekeeper and I says when the Reverend asks us for a shroud. Housekeeper made up one from Mister Marc's best sheets. But she couldn't bear to touch poor young sir. No more could I, so the Vicar alone put him into the shroud."

I cringed from hearing the details, but I could not protest. It seemed to me that if I spoke I should cry out, for the pain and anguish in my throat were suffocating me.

She sighed and went out again, leaving the tray.

The Branshaw dogs began to bark, first in the distance, then closer to the house, and I remembered the old superstition that they barked at a death. In my mind's eye I saw Marc lying in his makeshift coffin, with no one by him, no one to care for him. I had to be with him in that hour.

To take my mind off the terrors of the night, and to give me strength—for I intended to be present when Marc was buried—I reached for the tea and poured some into the cup. It was exceedingly bitter. I was about to take another sip when the door opened again, with so much caution my heart beat fast and I was half prepared for some new horror.

It was Mrs. Fothergay, wearing appropriate black, with some astonishing red frills. She came in and sat on the foot of Moyna's bed.

"Dear Anne, what a ghastly time you've had of it! But you mustn't think about it any more."

She made me so nervous, especially with her gloved hand patting my body under the coverlet, that I sat the teacup down with a clatter and tried to calm myself, to speak civilly.

"He wasn't the monster they thought he was," I said abruptly. "He'd been through so much, and he didn't know that he committed those crimes. I'm sure he didn't know. . . ."

She interrupted me by grating her shoe upon something at the foot of the bed and stooped to retrieve it.

"Dear me! A vial. Perfume?" She put the slim little bottle to her nose and sniffed. "No. Medicine of some kind, I should imagine. My late husband, the dear colonel, used to keep laudanum in a vial like this."

I had the notion that something terribly important had been said—yet my brain was so tired, and my eyes not focussing, so I could not concentrate. I took the vial and examined it. Why would laudanum be found in this room? Dilys had mentioned something about the Vicar's fear that I would take my life. Something about laudanum, but it had all been nonsense. Yet how came this vial to be just where I might have dropped it, if I had taken the poison?

My suspicion was confirmed by Bedelia Fothergay's dramatic exclamation of horror:

"Dear Anne, don't tell me you've taken the

wretched stuff! But you must not. Indeed, you must not. You have your whole life before you. What was that young man? A fraud. A murderer thrice over. And then, think of that poor Owen girl hanging—why—right there from that beam!" We both looked at the beam and then away quickly. "I tell you, I shall never forget it," she went on. "No, he is better dead, Anne. Believe me. Although," she added, "you are going to be stubborn about it. Just like Gareth. Now, tell me, dear, did you take it or not? We shall have to do something at once if—"

"No. I did not," I said quickly. "And I don't know why the Vicar has been going about telling such stories. But he was sitting just where you are now, and if anyone dropped that laudanum, he did!" Then I remembered the most important part of her ramblings. "But you've seen Gareth Owen! Surely, you can persuade him that this terrible business he's stirring up will only make the whole thing more monstrous. It will not bring back Catherine. You must stop him."

She looked at me with blank incomprehension. I felt inclined to slap her carefully powdered face.

"What are you saying, dear Anne? Why should Gareth stir up the people against Marc? He only arrived home from Teignford during the hour. Nettie told him of Catherine's death and gave him Catherine's last note. He's most anxious to talk to you. That's why I am here now—to speak to you on his behalf. But really! Stirring up mobs! That is not Gareth, I assure you."

I struggled to get out of bed, and whether it was that or her words, I was almost too dazed to comprehend these disclosures. Outside the window a dog howled mournfully, which set my teeth on edge, as I tried to banish everything but the essential fact.

"Am I to understand that Gareth Owen has not been in the village all afternoon stirring up people to—to burn Marc?"

Mrs. Fothergay looked as though I had said something utterly mad.

"Good heavens, Anne! Are you quite well?"

"Oh, God! The infamy of it! How wrong we've been, from the first! It was the Devil-Vicar, right enough. But we had the wrong vicar." I was reaching for my shoes when there was a rattle at the door and Sir Gareth came bolting in. He looked red and hot and kept putting his finger into the tight stock around his neck, to relieve the pressure, but he was a blessing to see.

"My dear Miss Anne, you must excuse this inexcusable intrusion. But ma'am, there is my poor little Cathy—foully done to death—over in St. Anthony's, and somewhere her murderer walks at large!" He took my hands and shook them both. "Dear Anne, we suffer our loss together. Can you help me, then, to find her murderer?"

"I think I can," I told him, while Mrs. Fothergay stared at us both. "You don't believe that it was Marc?"

"This note of Catherine's"—he waved a paper before me briskly—"puts that quite out of the question. Read it. And then tell me to whom she refers. I swear I'll have him done to death if it's the last thing I do!"

Hardly daring to believe this disclosure which, while saving Marc's reputation, was too late to save his life, I read the following:

Dearest Garrie:

I know that Marc Branshaw is not Ewen Morgan. If he had been, he could not have saved my life in that fire last night. But whether he is or is not has nothing to do with the horrors we have witnessed here recently.

Who advised me to use such dangerous methods, which could lead, as last night, to a real fire? Who desired that I should drive Marc out of his mind, even kill him? Let me say, it was my dearest and closest confidant. We were drawn together because he too, or so I thought, had an unrequited love. He had always liked the attentions of women, and whether he loved them or merely, as I suspect, had a passionate and ridiculous desire to be thought of as the Devil-Vicar's successor in every respect, I know Moyna accused him of some crime and was trying to prove it. I did not know that crime was the murder of Ewen Morgan. At the time, I thought Moyna heartless. All my sympathy went to my friend. "This dun-colored beast," she used to call him. When Marc repulsed me and behaved as though he suspected me of the murder of Moyna I was bitter, and wrote my absurd novel. I did not suspect that my reader, my critic and friend, would use the very methods I outlined to kill Will Grimlett and Abbie. He even suggested I let Marc read the book, as my revenge, he said. But I see it was to divide suspicion, for my friend must have followed my book exactly—keeping the dog savage by starvation and cruelty, and then turning it loose upon his victims who were, perhaps, already stunned.

His position, his faithful, if short-sighted wife, his good nature and popularity—everything about my dear friend—made it impossible to suspect him. Until tonight. Shock and near-death stimulate the mind. Moyna Branshaw's journals should give us some sort of proof, for she was the first to penetrate that jovial, warm-hearted mask of his. I believe I know where those journals are.

Well, Garrie, if you arrive home before I return from the Hall this morning, join me there. I think we owe Marc an apology, and the village the truth about the monster it is harboring.

Your loving Catherine.

"What does it all mean?" Sir Gareth demanded, as he stalked up and down the bedchamber, his heavy cloak swinging against the bedpost as he walked. "Who is this friend? She has so many. Obviously, he had committed the final atrocity. I must know his name!"

There were so many things that fitted now. The dun-colored creature Jamie had seen on the moor was Moyna's dun-colored beast. Of course, Moyna had to die. Not only had she suspected him long ago when she warned Ewen Morgan of the danger from "that creature who imitates and follows you in everything," but she made the mistake of hinting her suspicions, and of laughing and jeering at him as Ewen Morgan had. "The Reverend MacDonkey" was not a figment of Cadmon MacDonnachie's witty imagination. Ewen Morgan had called him that. And Moyna, that other jeering one, had to die, as Ewen Morgan had died. Our dun-colored beast was very proud in spite of his ridiculous exterior.

Poor Jamie told the truth when he said the dun-colored beast had turned into the Devil-Vicar. How easy to imagine, in the distant night, that a hunking, red-bearded man was a Gytrash, and what more natural than that this man should wear the vestments of the vicar he wished to be like, as well as the vestments of his own position! It served to throw suspicion on Ewen Morgan and, by inference, on the supposed Marc Branshaw.

Catherine's murder, besides being the most horrible, was the most ingenious. I remembered how, too late, that when Mrs. MacDonnachie arrived at the Branshaw door this morning she had looked around and called: "Ah! There you are," indicating that she and her husband had been separated on their search for those absurd herbs to help Marc. I never doubted now that the Vicar used his search for herbs to find and kill Catherine. Small wonder he was breathless and puffing, when he came to join his wife at the front door!

The supreme irony came when the good Cadmon MacDonnachie confessed the ghastly truth in the presence of two witnesses, and yet only Marc Branshaw, his victim, recognized it. The Vicar, knowing Marc's condition, had chosen one sure weapon and had driven Marc to his death deliberately. He had murdered Marc while we looked on.

Why not murder me next, since he must know that sooner or later I would wonder at the intimate knowledge he revealed in his confession to Marc?

I remembered the odd things that had transpired since this afternoon—the talk of my committing suicide, the laudanum vial where the Vicar could so easily have dropped it. Even the bitter tea which he could have dosed when Dilys was busy.

I rang for Dilys. Sir Gareth and Mrs. Fothergay watched me with great puzzlement, the lady interrupting my thoughts several times to inquire if I were quite well. But Sir Gareth's quickly outthrust arm, to silence her, showed that he at least trusted me.

When Dilys came, staring belligently at Sir Gareth, I explained to her quickly, "Sir Gareth is not an enemy. He is on our side. Now, do you have a particularly vicious dog on the premises?"

"Indeed, mum. There's Bruno. Took a big, nasty bite out of my ankle only last month, he did."

"Well then," I told her, "Take that tea out and tell groom to see that this Bruno drinks it. And—Dilys—!"

She turned with the tray in hand.

"Send someone to fetch Dr. Lowther."

"Dr. Lowther, mum?" Dilys stared at me. "But Dr. Lowther's been tight-bound to Upshed all day, so he has. Typhus real bad there, they do say."

I began to feel that we had not even begun to plumb the dreadful iniquity of the Reverend MacDonnachie.

"He was not here at all?"

"Not this day, mum—not since you sent for him last night and he came and went. Vicar said it weren't necessary, that he'd cared for the dead before this."

"My God, Miss Anne!" exclaimed Sir Gareth. "What are you suggesting?"

"Tell me what the Vicar said about my committing suicide, Dilys."

"He said he'd caught you with a laudanum vial and you'd tried to keep him from seeing it. Then he said he couldn't take it from you, but I was to beware."

I motioned her to go away with the tea tray. I turned to Sir Gareth. I felt the supreme bitterness of my own responsibility in all that had happened. Why should I have let the man's cloth stay my suspicions? I had allowed the Vicar to murder Marc and even abetted him.

"He wanted me to die as well as Marc. I heard his confession today."

"You can't mean it! Not that fat old friendly chap with the beard?" The baronet travelled back in his mind, remembering, I daresay, all the times he had seen his sister and the Vicar with their heads together, talking, planning. . . . There could be no question but that Catherine's "trusted friend and confidant" had been Cadmon MacDonnachie. No wonder she could not believe that the two killed on the moors had died at the hands of a dog deliberately driven savage by starvation and mistreatment. As in her novel, the dog had been but an instrument. To admit so much to herself, would have made Catherine, though without intention, an accessory to the murders.

"But I don't understand," Mrs. Fothergay put in plaintively. "If Marc is dead, why should the Reverend MacDonnachie act in secrecy and in such a hurry?"

I startled the poor woman by the frenzy which her comment aroused in me.

"Dear, dear Mrs. Fothergay—there can be only one of two reasons. Either Marc did not die of a heart attack, or—*he is not dead!*"

Sir Gareth started forward at my words, but then relaxed.

"That cannot be, Miss Anne. Think: MacDonnachie would be burying the fellow alive. Even the Vicar of Holy Church needs permission for such a burial as he contemplates—someone upon whom the onus of guilt will fall."

"He found one," I said bluntly, as I hastened to get out of bed. "I signed permission. It may not be legal, for I am not Marc's wife, but it could serve the Reverend MacDonnachie if any questions arose. And in that note I also confessed, almost in so many words, that I was unhappy enough to make an end of my own life. Oh, he thought of everything, did the good Vicar."

"But consider," Sir Gareth said. "So long a time has passed. If he were poisoned, then he's done for.

If it were a heart attack—"

"You don't understand. The only thing Marc drank, from the time I left him in his room to the time he died, was a small cup of cold tea in the drawing room. That may have contained laudanum. The Vicar placed the cup on the table in such a way, as I see now, where Marc could not miss it. I doubt if such a small dose, and in tea, would kill a man. So, if Marc is only drugged, then we may yet save him. Oh, do hurry, Sir Gareth!"

"Ma'am," he protested, stalking beside me as I ran out into the hall, "you don't even know that it was laudanum. It might have been the heart attack."

"Well then, we shall know. But if Marc is dead, why was the Vicar in so much of a hurry to tell those lies about you and about Marc's quick burial being the doctor's suggestion? He would have nothing to fear, even if Marc had died of laudanum poisoning; the Doctor prescribed that earlier. The Vicar had only to fear discovery that Marc was not *yet* dead."

I dared not believe it, and yet, inside me, I felt an almost frightening lift of spirits. To be so close to saving Marc, surely God would not let him die now. . . .

Mrs. Fothergay, who had taken Sir Gareth's arm, murmured softly, "One must bear in mind that so long a time has passed, we are certain to find him dead. The coffin will have been sealed, the grave covered over."

"Oh, I agree," said the baronet, puffing hard as he hurried after me down the broad main stairs. "It will be impossible to reach the poor devil in time. Buried alive! God, what a fate!"

I was remembering that a coffin had to be made for Catherine, and that country coffins were notoriously simple. A few pegs here and there and the thing was done. My greatest fear was that the coffin had already been overlaid with earth. There was no escape from that.

Sir Gareth's gig and the mare, pawing uneasily at the sound of the dogs howling, waited outside the gate. As we got into the gig, the Branshaw groom ran up to us.

"Mum, Dilys say ye want that dog to be put down. And down he is, mum."

"What?" cried Sir Gareth. "You mean the damned stuff was poisoned after all?"

The groom looked to me. "It was what ye wanted, no?"

"Yes," I said. "It was what I wanted to discover. Is the dog dead yet?"

"Not yet but as good as may be. Painless though. It will just go off into a sleep."

"We've not a minute to lose," shouted Sir Gareth. "Stand away from the mare's head, you there."

I had never thought I should say, "thank God" for that stolid, dependable Gareth Owen, but I said so now.

XXI

IN SPITE OF all that I had learned in the last hour, when we entered the village of Maidenmoor, at the top of the long steep curve of Main Street, I was prepared for disturbances among the villagers, and screams for the burning of the Devil-Vicar. I found instead solitude, and the deep, uneasy peace of night in a massive graveyard. All the shutters in town were bolted, as though against a common enemy. Occasionally a lone man—in the heavy black that was almost a uniform of the countryside—strode through the street, his face shadowed by the beak of his cap, the eyes staring downward at his feet.

The ancient stone church of St. Anthony's loomed up in the direct path of moonlight, and I got out of the gig without assistance and ran across the cobblestones to the entrance. The main portals were open. As soon as I entered, I made out one coffin behind the chancel at the far end of the nave, with candles at head and foot.

With Sir Gareth hard behind me, I went down the aisle, hoping against hope that I should see Marc's dear face when the coffin lid was removed. The lid itself had been left ajar. Sir Gareth moved it and we saw his sister's form, not yet in its shroud, but lying there in the candlelight as though she were alive. Only the telltale marks on her throat, and a certain forced set and rigidity about the mouth, told the true story.

Sir Gareth whispered softly:

"She was so when I saw her an hour ago. Almost as if she slept. My poor little Cathie."

I turned away, sick with disappointment and a presentiment of disaster. Could they have buried him so soon?

Sir Gareth saw my terrible dilemma.

"I'll look back of the altar. There's a storeroom. You go by the door in the south wall. They can't escape us both. Give me a hail if you see the gravediggers or the coffin."

I made my way through the family pews to the south door but it was locked as before. Then I saw the Vicar's office close by. A single candle burned and no one was in the room. Possibly there would be keys in his desk.

I fumbled at the desk, raised the lid and felt for anything I might use to prize open the south door. Suddenly, my glance wavered from the desk to something resting on the floor, beside the desk. It was the marvelous portrait of the Devil-Vicar that had raised such havoc in the village. Across its surface were long, ugly scratches and tears, as if done by a blunted knife. Only the eyes remained as they had been before, terrible in their poignant bitterness.

It was the face of Ewen Morgan but so very like my Marc as well. I touched the portrait gently with one finger, tracing the ugly cuts and rips in the canvas as my other hand sought through the litter of papers on the desk for the keys to the south door.

"What a pity!" said an unctuous voice behind me. "But I do think I have sought inspiration long enough from that portrait, don't you? And now I'm a little tired of it."

I had not been quick enough. I knew before I turned to meet him, that it was Reverend MacDonnachie. Even though Gareth was within shouting distance, I felt the fearful revulsion this monster aroused in me, but I managed to speak politely enough.

"Have you stopped trying to be like him, sir? Now that all those who loved him are gone, all those who could testify to his innocence?"

"Dear me, dear me," he said, stepping into the room. He moved very lightly and fast for a man of his bulk, suddenly rather like a horrid caricature of Marc's light tread. "I take it you did not drink the tea. What a shame. . . . You were ripe for suicide."

"Where is he?" I demanded, speaking loudly, aware that my voice carried in the great hollow confines of the church. "What have you done with him?"

He scratched his beard and shrugged.

"Too late. Just about . . . I should say . . . fifteen minutes too late."

I shuddered and reached behind me for a weapon, anything that might hurt this gross, dun-colored Gytrash.

"He wasn't dead. You knew that." If he would only agree with me, I should know there was, or had been, a little hope. He agreed smugly.

"But he will be by now, I think. There was so little time, my dear, in that drawing room, with you and my saintly Emily watching. Just enough laudanum in the tea cup to keep him quiet while the essentials were attended to. Once he was in the coffin it would make no difference if he came to consciousness. By that time it would just be a matter of . . . waiting. Yes. I think we may assume he is dead by now. I am sorry I had to destroy that portrait. I felt the urge come upon me quite suddenly. My dear"—he moved toward me slowly, putting his pudgy great hands out for my understanding. Upon me his touch had the same repulsive horror as an adder's fangs. I watched the moist little smile on his thick lips. "I am his match at last. I shall prove it—that is," he corrected himself, "I *have* proved it—tonight. That is all I have wanted for sixteen years—to be regarded as he was, to be what the young devil was when I was first assigned to this curacy. How I envied him everything! And how contemptuous he was of me—the clumsy, skinny curate with the pink hair! Well, that's all changed, my dear. It seems I laugh last. But you know about that don't you? I wondered if you guessed today during my catechism of the fascinating Reverend Morgan."

Waiting for Sir Gareth and expecting him momentarily, I watched the Vicar approach me. He had said something that gave me a flicker of hope, his words: "I shall prove that"—and then the curious change of tense: "I *have* proved that—tonight."

Did he mean the thing was not yet done?

"You do not congratulate me, my dear, yet I think I managed that tattling Owen girl rather neatly. I guessed, of course, last night, what she would be up to this morning, and followed her."

"And your wife?"

"Dear Emily, she is the perfect life partner—never asks questions. If I went around the back of the Branshaw house seeking herbs, what could be more natural? Admirable creature, Emily."

He raised his hands. At once I recognized the cruel, flat thumbs which had almost snuffed my life out a few nights ago in this same church. How could I ever have mistaken them for Marc's hands?

I taunted him with cold fury: "If you strangle me here and now, it would be rather hard to explain, don't you think?"

"Hardly, my child. You will be found to have taken laudanum, poor unhappy wretch that you are. And your body will be artistically arranged upon the grave of your monstrous lover. . . . It is not the first time we have met like this, you know. Remember the night at Moyna's cottage? I always tried to make sure Morgan was there alone before the Devil-Vicar made an appearance. But when you called out 'Who are you?' how relieved I was! I hated to kill you."

"You were not so relieved that night here in the church," I reminded him, imagining I heard Sir Gareth's booted steps out in the nave.

My back arched against the desk to avoid his hands, and my fingers groped for the nearest object. As he reached for me, I swung the object in my hand across his face. It was the candle.

He screamed and his fingers instinctively grabbed handfuls of his beard. I swung the burning candle once more and as the flame leaped at his face I cried,

"Where is he? What have you done with him?" He shrieked again, like an animal, and I felt nothing but a violent and savage joy. I was remembering Ewen Morgan and those terrible moments in the burning parsonage.

"Branshaw plot! But you're too late! Give me that candle, you little fiend!"

This time he was able to snatch the candle from me. It rolled on the floor and I eluded him just as Gareth Owen appeared in the doorway. I ran past Gareth, not looking back. I left the moaning, cursing MacDonnachie to the tender mercies of the baronet. The last thing I heard was the Vicar's indignant scream, "But I'm burned! The witch burned my face. Look at me! No!" And then more screams. I shut my ears to them and hurried to the north gate.

I pushed open the gate and saw the old, wizened sexton and Frederick Niles, with an audience of several silent villagers, all watching the work of the two grave-diggers.

They looked in dismay upon me, with my rumpled dress, my hair blown wild by the night air and by my struggle with the Vicar, and my very odd manner.

"Stop it! He may not be dead. You don't understand!" I cried to them. Even as I ordered them to stop, one of the grave-diggers let drop a heavy clod of earth and I heard it strike, not on the coffin as I had hoped, but on the earth that had gone before. The grave was very shallow, probably because they had been ordered to hurry.

"I told them so. I told them," sobbed a small voice from the darkness beneath Moyna Branshaw's great stone. It was Jamie. He had been huddled there, under the protective and gentle hand of the curate, and at my voice came out in a gingerly way. Recognizing me, he ran to me and buried his face against my bosom. "He ain't dead. Say he ain't dead. Not my Marc—truest friend I ever had."

The young curate said to me gently, "I know your feelings, ma'am, and I appreciate them. But do you think it right to encourage the boy? Dr. Lowther pronounced Mr. Branshaw dead."

I ignored this. "Don't cry, Jamie," I whispered. "They will raise the coffin. They must. I order them to."

The sexton frowned at me, while the grave-diggers halted in their work and rubbed their hands. I could smell the wet, rich earth around us. I shall never smell that odor again without thinking of death.

"Is it Miss Wicklow, ma'am?" asked the sexton. "He's dead, believe me. Dr. Lowther says so."

"How do you know?" I demanded, beginning to lose control of myself in this dreadful moment. As the moonlight appeared suddenly from under a cloud, the great gray statue that hovered near the Branshaw plot began to cast its slanting shade over us. It seemed to me, in my overwrought state, like the shadow of death waiting to snatch Marc from me. "Did the Vicar tell you Marc was dead? He lied!"

"Reverend said Mr. Marc was dead. Said Mister Marc was to be buried quick-like, so there'd be no trouble. Said you'd ordered it, what's more."

"Stay!" the Reverend Niles put in, startling us all, as he stared at me intently. "What do you mean, Miss Wicklow? I protested the indecent haste of this whole business. Do you mean that Dr. Lowther did not examine Mr. Branshaw? That the permission from him was forged?"

God be thanked for this man, I thought. He took the matter out of my hands.

"Open the coffin," he ordered the grave-diggers. "Do as the lady says."

The varied shadows of the tombstones gathered slowly, marching inexorably upon us, lengthening under the brightness of the moon. Every second added to Marc's peril—if, indeed, it were not too late already.

"Best oblige the Reverend Niles," muttered a rough man in the gathering crowd. Others took up the demand. The grave-diggers thrust me aside and shuffled behind the great Branshaw statue. I stared in stupefaction.

"What is it? I thought the coffin was in the ground."

"No, no," said the Reverend Niles hastily. "Not yet. But even so, we cannot do more than hope. Inside the coffin so long—"

"I know. Open the coffin!"

The grave-diggers dragged a rough hewn coffin into the moonlight. I noticed frantically that the box was not airtight, but revealed space here and there, where the boards joined imperfectly, or between the pegs that had been driven in around the top. I tore at them with my bare fingers, breaking nails, feeling none of the pain, nothing but my desperate hope. Vaguely, I heard the old sexton crying, almost dropping the lamp he carried: "Don't listen to her. She's mad. Vicar says she's mad."

"Nonsense," the Reverend Niles cut in at once. "She's as sane as you and I. Proceed."

By this time several passersby had gathered, among them Mrs. Fothergay, and lamps were being lighted in the Yorkish Lion Inn. Mrs. Fothergay's tongue was not idle. There was a whispering among the watchers that Marc was innocent as they suspected, and I heard the Reverend MacDonnachie's name repeated.

Miss Rose hurried through the graveyard.

"So here you are, Jamie-boy. Do you know I have been near frantic about you, love?"

Jamie looked up at her, his face tear-stained and older than I recalled.

"I had to be with Marc, up to when they put him away."

"Open the coffin!" the curate ordered the grave-diggers a second time.

This time they drew back and finally the Reverend Niles himself took the spade from one of the men and, as I continued to tear at the slivered boards, he began to pry off the lid while Mrs. Fothergay uttered a shocked gasp. Seeing that the curate and I were in earnest, several men in the crowd came forward and, with their bare hands like myself, did the screeching, tearing job of removing the coffin lid. Everyone moved forward to look into the coffin. We saw the shrouded figure, and a superstitious moan went up through the group as they backed off, slowly, step by step.

I ripped the threads of the shroud, and revealed at last Marc's face and then his body, just as I had seen him during his furious encounter with the Reverend MacDonnachie in the drawing room of Branshaw Hall. The Vicar must have been in a great hurry when he arranged Marc, for the black hair was dishevelled and the collar of his jacket twisted. These small items made him seem doubly dear to me. Gently, fearfully, I brushed back his hair and rearranged his collar.

Someone screamed. Under the bright moonlight his face looked unbearably white and fixed as marble. The curate studied him in what I saw to be growing discouragement.

A woman murmured with the dreadful finality of

a requiem: "How peaceful he looks!"

I told myself that he had looked peaceful last night under the influence of the laudanum. Perhaps this might still be the case. I touched Marc's cheek and knew that if he were truly dead it had only been in the past hour, for in spite of his marble look he had none of the rigidity of a corpse. From the tortured sleep of the drug, his close confinement must have produced this coma. The easing of the lines of suffering in his face relieved me of one of my many horrors—that he had awakened in his coffin, and realized his fate. There was still hope. I began to rub one of his hands frantically as I saw the curate doing on his other side. All the while I was staring at his form for any slight sign of life. He was so cold, so very cold! But Marc had grown accustomed to colder temperatures than the rest of us. It would not be the first time his flesh seemed chilly to me.

The Reverend Niles looked up at Rose Keegan. "If you please, fetch a mirror to apply to his lips. We must try every test. And fetch hot cloths, steaming. They may be of some help in restoring the action of the blood."

She went away at once.

Jamie knelt at the other side of his friend and called softly, as if he expected to entice Marc back. There was a terrible, aching hope in the child's face that kept me at this vain work, for I began to feel the lifeless chill of Marc's fingers creeping into mine.

I had come to the end of my shallow residue of hope. I bent over his hands and wept. The Reverend Niles put one hand upon my shoulder to give me comfort, and others came up, offering their wordless sympathy, but I did not know one touch from another.

Suddenly, there was a stir in the silent group of

onlookers, and Jamie, raising his head, caught his breath. At the same instant I became aware of a slight, almost infinitesimal contraction of the muscles in the cold fingers under my hands.

My mind only half registered this movement and I remember thinking with despair that it was the last muscular spasm before the fingers stiffened in death. Then Jamie whispered in religious awe:

"His eyes, ma'am! His eyes!"

The Reverend Niles' voice murmured joyously, "God be praised."

My own eyes travelled slowly, unbelieving, over Marc's still form to his face. His eyes, luminous in the full moonlight, were open wide, and gazing at me. His pallid lips moved as he tried to speak. In the absolute silence of the northern night, we all waited for that word, and what he whispered was, "Anne. . . ."

I leaned over and kissed him and rested my warm cheek against his cold one. I was too overcome even to thank God for this miracle, but the people of Maidenmoor, and especially the good curate Niles, did so for me. They had proven their devotion and friendship in these last few minutes, and were saying all that was in my heart. I looked up at the curate, just for an instant. The Church was in good hands at last. The people of Maidenmoor could thank God for that as well. When my gaze returned quickly to the coffin, Marc had managed a faint semblance of a grin.

"Help me, darling. . . . I was never one for narrow beds."

His words were repeated through the crowd and presently they were all laughing their relief that Marc Branshaw had come back from the dead as flippant as ever.

Rose Keegan made her way through the crowd with steaming cloths but had to set them down to keep her eager, happy nephew from climbing all over his resurrected friend.

Marc's hand sought mine as he said, "I dreamed you came to me."

Yet I had nearly failed him. I blessed his dear confidence in me. I should never fail him again, as long as he lived.

He could not see the crowd around him which was beyond his range of vision, but he sensed their presence and flashed me one of those warm but willful smiles by which he always got his way.

"Anne?"

"Yes, darling."

"I want to be alone with you. Can't we go home?"

"Where is home?" I asked, not caring, so long as he was with me.

With an effort he raised his fingers and touched my lips as he answered softly:

"Wherever you are, love."

"How very odd!" exclaimed Jamie as his aunt finally lifted him off Marc by the scruff of his neck. "He called her *love*, like she be a Yorkshire lad."